T0285407

# PRAISE FOR *CODE CRISIS*

"An exquisitely developed and propulsive novel that delivers high tension, humor, and magnetic characters in equal measure. *Code Crisis* is not only an addictive read, it shines with the authenticity of the author's insights into medicine, criminality, and the emotions that make us human."

**–T.C. BOYLE,** author of *I Walk Between the Raindrops* (2022) and PEN/ Faulkner Award for Fiction winner *World's End* (1987)

"Joe Purpura's stunning debut features Vince DeLuca, a doctor battling loss and burnout who stumbles onto a sinister plot, revealed when his patient mumbles details under anesthesia. Purpura, an MD by training, weaves action and gritty tradecraft but never loses sight of DeLuca's humanity, and the result is a novel that's impossible to put down."

**–JAMIE FREVELETTI,** award-winning author of the Emma Caldridge series and Robert Ludlum's The Janus Reprisal

# CODE
# CRISIS

# CODE CRISIS

A NOVEL

# JOE PURPURA

GREENLEAF
BOOK GROUP PRESS

Published by Greenleaf Book Group Press
Austin, Texas
www.gbgpress.com

Distributed by Greenleaf Book Group

For ordering information or special discounts for bulk purchases, please contact Greenleaf Book Group at PO Box 91869, Austin, TX  78709, 512.891.6100.

Design and composition by Greenleaf Book Group
Cover design by Greenleaf Book Group
©Shutterstock.com/KK Stock; ©Shutterstock.com/Images_By_Kenny

Publisher's Cataloging-in-Publication data is available.

Print ISBN: 979-8-88645-013-2

eBook ISBN: 979-8-88645-014-9

To offset the number of trees consumed in the printing of our books, Greenleaf donates a portion of the proceeds from each printing to the Arbor Day Foundation. Greenleaf Book Group has replaced over 50,000 trees since 2007.

Printed in the United States of America on acid-free paper

23 24 25 26 27 28 29   10 9 8 7 6 5 4 3 2 1

First Edition

To my family, for their love and encouragement.

And to the women and men of our country's intelligence services,

for being the patriots who see it all and keep it all inside.

Before you embark on a journey of revenge, dig two graves.

—CONFUCIUS

To love is to recognize yourself in another.

—ECKHART TOLLE

**SANTA BARBARA, CALIF.**– Federal Homeland Security investigators are looking into the mysterious discovery of a possible smuggler's panga boat found abandoned and going in circles in the open waters off the Santa Barbara County coast. A fisherman, who spotted the thirty-five-foot-long boat about three miles off the coast of Gaviota yesterday morning, observed that there appeared to be no one on board, and that the wheel had been tied. The Coast Guard was called and a cutter dispatched to the scene to investigate. Two guardsmen subsequently managed to board the abandoned vessel and bring it under control, whereupon it was towed to Santa Barbara harbor. Except for several military-style bungee straps, there was no sign of cargo. A Coast Guard spokesman stated that this type of boat is commonly used for smuggling drugs and weapons from Mexico into the United States.

# ONE

ONE THING WE LEARN IN medicine is how to bury things. And just like that, another night is laid to rest. Orange flecks dance the walls of my tiny, on-call bedroom as I sit up to face the sunrise through the open window.

A mild ocean breeze pushes night-blooming jasmine scents over me thick enough to stick to my clothes. The bed creaks when I turn to my iPhone, sitting silent on the cherry nightstand, reminding me of my last call of the night—one of the gyne residents, covering his butt, was getting buy-in on some post-op orders. After that, I dodged all the bullets.

I rub my eyes, grateful for a quiet Friday overnight at an insanely busy place called Santa Barbara Community Hospital. Colleagues tell me I'm good at saving lives, but I'm at a point where a patient in trouble is not fun anymore. Besides, I have enough trouble trying to resuscitate my own life.

Don't get me wrong. Sometimes I sleep, run between the ICU and ER between catnaps, or stay up all night doing surgery. I don't care. It's fun running around putting out fires, being needed, teaching residents how to do the lifesaving. I love taking call—and not just because I'll likely die alone in a house full of dogs and empty wine bottles.

The hospital's also a nice break from being out in the community. It's shelter from nosy jerks with their little side hugs that last too long, punctuated with pats on the back. "How are you? What's going on in your life now?" Some don't even try hiding the schadenfreude behind their "concerned" knitted brows and pinched-up ugly faces—faces I want to punch out.

"Are you okay?" *No. I'm not okay.*

The amber splash glowing on the horizon is hypnotizing, then my cell phone clangs and lights up with a text like a goddamn Christmas tree.

> Dr DeLuca, please call me in the ER re a patient who needs surgery stat.

So much for dodged bullets.

I'm praying to God that the patient is not some train wreck about to consume my entire day—a day that I need to recharge my badly rundown emotional and physical batteries.

"Hi. It's Vince DeLuca." I don't sound like me, one of the faculty nice guys. I'm sure senior gyne resident Jane Clark picks up a smidge of my being pissed at the prospect of a problem to deal with thirty minutes before I go off call. Okay, Vince, find Mister Softie mode. I'd kill for a double espresso.

"Hey, Doctor DeLuca. Jane here." She ends on a downward inflection. "Do you have time for a quick question?"

So far, no quavering voice, no hint of an unstable, dying patient. I take the bait. "Of course, Jane, and thanks for the quiet night." I lighten it up, yet know a patient is now an obstacle between me and home, food, sleep. Sex. Life.

Jane becomes a human radio, recounting her entire night. I don't hint that I want her to get to the point except for a few rude interruptions—which the first-generation Italian Americans in my family simply cannot control. Nothing personal. We do it to everyone.

She presents the patient: name's Jacquelyn Carter—goes by Jackie—forty-two years old, sexually active, missed two periods, has pelvic pain and spotting. Fuck. A goddamn ectopic pregnancy. Surgery time. Bad Doctor Vince is about to ask if it can wait until the day shift arrives, but Jane intervenes.

"Ectopic for sure, Vince, and it's ruptured or close to it."

Those who lack the skill or conviction to act—analysis paralysis—have their days numbered in medicine. *Sometimes right, sometimes wrong, never in doubt*—the surgeon's creed. Jane gets an A-plus today.

"Vince, I explained everything to her and Brent, her husband. But when I said you were in-house, she recognized your name and asked—begged, actually—if you could come talk to her before the day shift takes her to the OR."

"Okay, great," I lie, picturing the hemorrhagic, gelatinous mess deep in Jackie Carter's pelvis. "I'll be right down."

I predict I'm going to get nailed into doing this case, but that's our other creed: *Get in, get out, go home.*

# TWO

**I PUT ON FRESH SCRUBS** rather than meet the patient in ones I'd slept in. Scrubs, by the way, are the most comfortable sleeping garments on earth. I hope bouncing down three floors will wake me up. If that doesn't do it, my backup is the jazzed-up vibe of the emergency room. With multidimensional noise and a perimeter of curtained cubicles around the control desk at center court, it's a "room" like an NBA arena is a "room." Simply setting foot in the place is an emotional face slap as sensory isobars soar, driven by screams, rib-snapping CPR, hot lights, the scent of fresh blood. It's a sexy burnout zone.

Today, however, there's only the occasional hiss and grate of a police scanner radio. Odd, since the sleek vinyl flooring and tile walls can reverberate a hallway whisper all around the place. I'm guessing everyone's stable and those in pain have been given a few milligrams of intravenous shut-the-hell-up.

I hug the wall, letting a crew rush past—a near-critical patient with a type of heart attack we call a STEMI on her way to the cardiac cath lab. She'll survive, and, sizing up the whiteboard, I'd say no one's leaving in a box today. This includes the drunk with a head laceration who, judging by smell, suffered a Code Brown at some point during the night.

I get to the desk and the staff glance up, never missing a keystroke of data entry—they do it picturing how their charting will look to a jury.

I beat the cops and paramedics to the last Krispy Kreme, snatch it up, and stand behind one of the residents. He asks, too loudly, "Ladies, do we have Mrs. Carter's stuff for Vince?"

Today's nursing supervisor, Stutz—known as Nutzie Stutzie—shoots me a menacing look with those seen-it-all eyes. She's annoyed at the resident, either for treating the staff like acolytes or me like someone special.

"No problem, don't bother. I'll find it," I say, defusing the hierarchical crap.

Stutz is an insufferable battle-axe who holds grudges and loves to inflict nurse-on-nurse violence. With her demeanor, she'd own the alpha slot of any Rottweiler pack. She feeds on med students and interns.

I'm told Jackie's in 21, the "gyne room." Special, since it has a real door, not the usual curtain that mystifyingly invites everyone to stick their fucking heads in, no matter what's going on with the poor, shivering patient on the other side. Twenty-one was designed for privacy—to do pelvic exams, discuss gyne problems like miscarriages, rape, STIs, infidelity.

"Vince," yells Stutz, a hint of glee in her voice, "she really wants to talk to you alone before I give her pre-op sedation, so let me know when you're done."

Never a good sign. I stare at the ceiling outside 21. I knew this night was too good to be true.

////////

I knock, pause a second, then enter. Twenty-one's immense exam light is on and swiveled so its white-hot beam blasts into the corner, shimmering off ugly green tiles, stainless steel counters, and the rock-hard bed. Someone's attempt to cozy things up, I guess.

One peek at Jacquelyn Carter and I know I'm not going home anytime soon. She's deadpan, in fetal position, shivering under two of those ten-pound hospital blankets. I assume the skinny grandpa seated at the foot of the bed, head down in a three-year-old magazine, is her husband. He doesn't look up.

I remember her from around town—Coffee Bean, a restaurant, a party—back when she appeared to be among the living. I'm also sure I saw her in the past as a patient. Abnormal pap smear, maybe? Memories of grandpa now come back to me as well.

She's slight, with sculptured features surgically unmodified that are somewhat exotic. Italian or Greek, Persian perhaps. Piercing light brown eyes looking like they're lined with kohl, framed by straight dark hair that California sun—no, probably a stylist—highlighted with luxuriant chestnut tones. This morning it's dry lips, greenish-gray skin, and a paucity of movement despite my walking in. Not good for someone jacked up on ER adrenaline.

"Hi, I'm Vince DeLuca." I follow the IV line under the blankets and hold Jackie's hand, a dead fish. "Do you remember me?"

I nod toward Brent Carter, silvery and chiseled, as he drops the magazine, sits bolt upright, and, folding his arms chest high, appears to be sizing me up. But Mister Sensitivity can't hold eye contact for half a second.

Jackie turns slightly, eyes barely open. "I remember you, Doc. You were there when I needed you." She sighs. "And here you are again." Brent shifts in the chair.

"Doctor Clark told me what brought you in, but tell me how you feel right now."

"Can you tell Vince how you feel, love?" asks Brent, staring at the floor. I lock onto his flaky, sunburned forehead capped with that perfectly dressed casket hair.

She forces a feeble smile. "I feel like shit. Like I'm gonna die or something."

Well, at least we're both thinking the same thing. I watch the rainbow of graphs dance across the monitor—good blood pressure, heart rate a little high but normal rhythm. Not dead yet.

She rises on an elbow and tells me about her past hour of increasing pain. When she tilts her head back, I see beyond this illness, remembering Jackie's natural beauty. Nothing like Carter's previous wife—number two, three?—the requisite five-foot-ten, arm-candy blonde. An idiot, as I recall.

Brent rubs sunken eyes, shrugging. "I've been out of town, Vince. Tonight's the first I've heard of it."

And that's another thing: Where does he get off calling me Vince? He exaggerates this military straight-backed posture thing with tucked chin, both feet rigidly flat on the floor. It makes him more like a pelican than it does a Camp Pendleton marine. I recall him being in defense—a CEO or some other kind of muckety-muck—and generally acting like a dick, holding court in the usual high-end spots in this little town. He drives vintage Porsches or 'Vettes, often with unfamiliar women riding shotgun. Yeah. Good ol' Brent Carter.

When I turn back, I know Jackie's reading my thoughts. I lay a hand on her shoulder and she tells me her story.

"Tonight, this . . . it's different," she says. "It's major pain. Ahh, crap!" She falls back onto the mattress with a thud. "Ohhh, it hurts, especially when I move . . . I have to throw up."

I dive for her emesis basin, which has a few bubbly spits in it, hold it under her chin, and lean away. No. Just more dry heaves. I pull some tissues, wipe her mouth, and move out of projectile vomiting range.

"Okay, okay, just slowly lie back," I say, helping her. "You don't have to sit up. Relax for a few minutes."

Jackie stares into the chrome reflector of the exam light, eyes darting, then stopping on me, asking for an opening. I give it.

"I'd like to gently check your abdomen, then we're done. Is that okay with—?"

She springs to life. "Brent, why don't you wait in the hall?" Before her second word is out, he dives for the door.

*Alone at last. I'm sorry, the guy creeps me out.*

# THREE

NO DOC LEARNS ANYTHING FROM examining a patient who lies there instinctively guarding a painful abdomen so taut you could tap dance on it. And I'm not going to torture Jackie just to do the cover-your-ass bullshit. I want her to talk.

I cycle the BP cuff, buying time for Jackie to get her shit together. Pressure's still good, but her pulse is pushing the century mark, consistent with what I thought when I first walked into the room. She's bleeding internally and we need to get to the OR.

"Jackie, I don't need to examine you." I move closer. "Are you okay?"

She sniffs, eyes closed, head bobbing. "I'm okay."

I watch her hands fidget, hoping she doesn't yank out the big-ass IV Jane started in case we need to dump blood into her. Which will be soon, if I don't get this show on the road.

"We have to get you to the OR, but the nurse said you had some questions before we roll." I adjust her blankets.

"Vince," hands wringing now, "what do you think?"

What I think is her shock-clock is ticking down to zero, so I rush her through my reasoning, my findings on exam, labs, ultra-sound. Class dismissed.

"It all makes sense, Doc."

Her frozen, watchful face doesn't convince. I linger a moment, then ease away.

"Listen, Vince." She looks skyward. "I mean, do people ever die from this? Could I not wake up or something? Does that ever happen?"

*Yeah, Jackie, if I fuck up, if the damaged tissue in your pelvis looks like taco meat and won't hold sutures, if you suffer an anesthetic catastrophe—any of the above—you're either dead or gorked for life. Why do you ask?*

"Jackie, you know things can always happen, but major complications are extremely rare. You're healthy going into this, and that's ninety-nine percent of it. I understand this is a frightening thing to happen to you. One minute you're pregnant, the next, strangers are talking major surgery. I get it." I grab another tissue, this time to blot some tears while I hold a hand that's regained some life.

"Well"—her chin hits her chest—"I remember you were easy to talk to. And this isn't medical stuff."

"Jackie, anything we talk about is confidential. Totally."

"Okay, okay." She chuckles. "Ahh . . . oh shit, it hurts when I laugh." She gazes into the light pooling in the corner. "This may not be my husband's baby. I mean, the tubal pregnancy—whatever—is probably not Brent's. He's been traveling. It could be his, but it isn't likely."

"All right, just lie flat. Take it easy." Jesus, I'm an idiot—like posture is going to help. As many times as I've heard this story, it still dumbs me up. I stumble on. "Well, is there any chance, I mean, how sure—"

"It's not his." She waves a dismissive hand, staring up with piercing eyes that convert me. "I know for sure when it happened. I could make Brent think it was his. I mean, I have to make him think that, but . . ."

"Okay, all right. You're still going to be fine."

She turns away. I'm powerless watching her pain—worse now, coming from the heart. I have to be a trusted friend, who just happens to be a guy, who just happens to be her physician. I look at the closed door.

"Jackie, is the other guy around? I mean, is there a relationship? Do you need to talk to him?" Assuming, of course, you don't fucking code in the next minute. Pulse 140 now.

"There's a . . . we're friends—all of us, I mean—but I couldn't call him now. I couldn't explain it to Brent."

"I could arrange that when we get upstairs. I can—"

Her hand launches. "Thanks anyway, Doc."

"I understand."

"Vince, if something happens, could you talk to him, and uh . . . tell him that I was thinking about him . . . missing him? I mean, I could ask a nurse or . . ." Her eyes move to my chest and pause long enough that she knows we've crossed a line. We have. But we're still inside the gyne doctor-patient zone.

"Jackie." I put a hand on her shoulder. "Jackie, look at me. You can trust me. It's okay. I can be discreet. I'll do whatever you want. I can call him for you now—"

She cuts in, "No. Just if something horrible happens, okay?"

"Okay, Jackie. Whatever you want."

She flattens herself into the cart, holding out a hand. "I need to write something, Vince."

I grab a notepad and pen from the counter.

She scribbles, hands it all back. "Call this number if anything happens—no one else would ever answer that phone—and, uh . . . just tell him who you are and whatever . . . whatever happened to me. And that I love him."

"You got it, Jackie." I turn and she sits up with a thousand-yard stare that freezes my heart.

"Tell him this hospital's treated me so well. It's perfect," she says. "Be sure to tell him that. I mean . . . if he ever needs one."

"Well, thank you for the confidence in our hospital." She's getting weird, not enough blood to the brain. I help her lie back. "So, we should talk after you recover, Jackie. We can all use someone to talk to, you know what I mean? I know some good professionals."

"Okay, we'll do it. I promise. And, Vince." She puts her hand on mine and looks deep into me. I swallow hard. "Vince, I can tell you understand how I feel about him. You'll let him know that . . . tell him how I feel, right?"

I nod. She's right. Terminal heartbreak—I've got that down pat.

Once I'm in the hall, the jumpy OR nurse who's waiting behind the desk pops up, hand outstretched. "Are we ready to roll, Doc, or what?"

I glance at Jackie's note. Her dude's name is Sal-something, has an out-of-town number.

"Yeah, we're ready." Ready for a fucking soap opera.

# FOUR

**I HUNT DOWN BRENT, GIVE** him the diagnosis and the proposition—his wife needs surgery stat, and he sees why.

"Thanks, Vince. I trust you'll do a good job."

His snarky comment, parsed with a pause after "trust," would make a politician proud. Cell phone back to his ear and too smug to ask questions, he leaves looking rather calm, all things considered. I guess CEOs are composed under pressure. Just like surgeons.

By the time I'm scrubbed in, Jackie's asleep on the table and Jane's assembling the laparoscope that will show everything through an incision half an inch wide. Despite being hauled out of bed, everyone gives me a cheerful greeting. They know I do my damnedest to not waste their time, keep it light but professional. A tense OR breeds stupid mistakes. It happens to any team that has a lurking bully or an asshole in the mix.

"You do the case. I'll assist. You cool with that, Jane?" I want her to start taking command. The scrub and circulating nurses nod a vote of confidence.

"Sure, Vince. I'll need you to hold the scope for me while I put the other trocars in." A trocar, deadly in the hands of the inept, is a seventeenth-century, sharp-as-hell spike for penetrating a body cavity. A nurse dims the overheads, and warm light from the monitors shadow us like we're figures on a Caravaggio canvas.

Anesthesia gets to pick the music, and the scrub nurse and I jab Pratik that the sixties Motown he selected makes us feel old.

Jane jumps in, eyes smiling. "Oh, I love this music, Vince. Your generation is timeless."

"She has good taste, something you don't always see in a surgeon," says Pratik. "And we have some Four Tops coming up."

"Holy fuck!" A cry from Jane, someone rarely as vulgar as the rest of us. And it's not about the Four Tops. The monitors show pale tan loops of intestines breaching a maroon ocean.

"We're all right, okay? That's old blood. You didn't cause it, and she's stable, right?" I turn to Pratik and get two thumbs-up. I race through the what-ifs: What if the diagnosis was wrong; what if this was big upper abdominal bleeding—a leaking aortic aneurysm, say; what if we missed a perforated ulcer or some weird traumatic liver hemorrhage or a ruptured spleen; or, what if—the ultimate embarrassing way to screw the pooch—Jane did ram that trocar into her vena cava? What if I have to go out there and tell Brent A-Hole Carter his wife is dead? I try my best to sound calm and move on.

"Just get the next trocar in and get going with some suction. We're gonna need a lot of irrigation, ladies."

The first time a surgeon sees seriously big intra-abdominal bleeding, it's both disturbing and unforgettable. For a doctor in training—a time when trouble is still fun—it's Dickensian. The best you hope for is to be catapulted face-first into a confidence-instilling opportunity to rescue someone from the precipice. It's *The Movie* that one replays over cocktails for themselves, colleagues, friends. Yet, the worst moment of a nascent career is coming to realize there's no place to run in dangerous moments, and forevermore patients will be putting themselves in harm's way because they're counting on you to not fuck things up.

"Okay, what do you want to do, Jane?" I ask, just to gut-check her composure and get myself together.

Jane takes a breath and asks for all the right instruments to unload a liter of Jackie's blood. It races across the floor through the suction tubing, a red serpent that climbs the wall and splatters into a two-liter canister, nearly filling it in seconds.

Jane finds the right fallopian tube, pink and bloated to the size of a cocktail wiener, bleeding where placental tissue has torn through. She methodically uses a fine water jet to detach the ectopic, at times pausing to stop the bleeding with electrocautery. Jane is definitely in the zone, doing a great job of communicating and keeping the entire team working as one. Surgeons get high on this shit.

The worst over, we check for any other pathology in the abdomen and pelvis—all is well—and close. Time for some cheerleading.

"Beautiful dissection, Jane. Really nice dexterity, keeping away from big bleeders, not wasting time sweating the small stuff," I say, and the room agrees. "She reminds me a lot of myself." Everyone's heard it before, but it draws a laugh.

A half hour after we started, Jane Clark and I are out of the OR.

"Wow," she says, shaking her head.

"Yeah, wow. You did a great job, Doc."

"Oh, man. Thank God you were there, Vince."

"And what if I wasn't? You would have done the same damn thing, right?"

"Jesus, I don't know. That was scary."

She looks down, kicks at the floor. I know she's walking through the director's cut of *The Movie*.

"Seriously, Jane, you did a great job, and don't forget that."

She holds a big breath, then sighs. "Thanks for letting me handle this, Vince."

"See you in recovery, Doc."

We take a few steps, then freeze when the OR fills with the Four Tops's anthem, "Reach Out, I'll Be There."

"Remember," and here I point, "*this* OR when you're the attending physician, Clark. Nothing builds confidence like success." I turn and walk. "Along the way, let other people feel success."

# FIVE

I'M MOTIONLESS, SITTING IN RECOVERY, letting the surgery buzz wear off. Jackie's the only patient here in the row of beds, and the room is creepy quiet and almost dark but for light scattering from her monitor.

My buzz eases, but then come thoughts of another Saturday of nothing. Or, should I say, nobody? Five years ago, okay, maybe ten, it was a shower, some food—or no food, just a few glasses of Pinot at noon—then a quick snooze and I'd scream off into the Santa Barbara night. Now, food then sleep. All day. Maybe until Sunday morning.

Jackie's groans are more frenetic as the fentanyl wears off. They're odd sounding, almost foreign, with a different cadence or inflection, if that's possible for a primal sound. Her numbers are good, though. Camilla, her nurse, wipes her forehead with a moist washcloth. Thank God for nurses.

"Saaa . . . ssss . . . saa," Jackie sighs, lips barely open.

Camilla glances from the monitor screen and begins her hammer-and-anvil instructions. "It is okay. You are in recovery now. Your surgery is over. You must lie still." Her perfectly articulated syllables are startlingly loud, echoing off the hard tile surfaces of the room.

"Everything go okay, Doctor Vince?" she asks.

I nod while rewinding the case, my mind in a weird-ass, sleep-deprived rumination. I have to finish up here, ditch these scrubs, shower, and get home where Jackie and her secret note, the surgery, the hospital smells—the goddamn Four Tops song stuck in my head—the whole fucking night can fade like a strange dream.

"Doctor Vince, what do you want for pain medication?"

"Demerol pump."

"Okay, Doctor Vince. I'll call Pratik."

"Ssaa . . . ssal," louder now. "Sal, Sal, where are you?" Jackie lifts her head three painful inches. I go to the bedside, motioning for Camilla to stay on the phone.

"Jackie, it's Vince DeLuca. We're all done. You're in the recovery room. You're okay. The surgery went fine."

Jackie's head hits the mattress as she shouts, "Sal . . . Sal, you and me . . . we don't need him . . . Sal, love, love." Her misted face shows no pain but contorts from giddy joy to sadness, then back.

Here we go. Damn Pratik and his beloved propofol—Milk of Amnesia—a creamy-white fluid he gives IV-push in the OR, then in three seconds it's lights out. Some patients awake mellow with a nice retrograde amnesia. Others are jazzed up, goofy with ramblings like they're hypnotized. Jackie is not treading the mellow path.

"Jackie, listen, you're in the hospital, in the recovery room, remember? Just rest. You don't have to talk." I glance at Camilla, who shakes her head—no contact with anesthesia. I hold Jackie's hand, protecting her IV site. "It's all right, just rest."

Her head lifts again, eyes focusing acres behind my face. "Ahhhh . . . listen to me, Sal," she says, louder now. "I love you, and we'll get . . ." She lowers her head and rolls toward me, panting.

"Jackie, you're going to hurt yourself. Just stay—"

"Grails . . . we'll get grails, if not . . . sting, stingers . . . good stingers and . . ."

"Where is the good sting? Where does it hurt, Jackie?" I ask, checking her leads for snags. "Jesus, what is she talking about?"

Jackie's head rolls to me, giggling. Eyes closed, she whispers, "I'm talking about . . . about a bad revenge." She giggles again, now like a slurring drunk. "Sal, honey. Hon, you know . . . was here a . . . was here . . . Waziristan . . . heavily. What I'm . . . talking is . . . about a bad . . . Sal, what are you talking about? Babe, it's our revenge time."

Camilla looks over my shoulder as I lower Jackie to the bed. "The IV might be giving her arm a good sting, and she must be praying. Holy Grail, Doctor Vince. You know, the cup at Christ's Last Supper."

"Yeah, I know the Holy Grail." But I'm thinking Sal is a thirty-something greaseball Italian without the brains to keep a goddamn condom on him. And whose phone number I've got in my pocket. Part of me wants to call and find out why they want revenge on Brent—they should just fucking do the Splitsville thing, then it's happily ever after.

"How about Demerol 25 IV-push now?" I ask.

Camilla winks, opening her hand to show me a syringe of exactly that.

I finish charting and return to the bedside. Jackie's peaceful but with a twisted smile, almost wry. No more pain, no more Sal. No more Holy Grail. Nothing like a little Demerol to bring out the best in people.

# SIX

**THE AUTOMATIC DOOR SWINGS AND** I see Brent Carter pacing the hall, on his cell phone as usual, but now with a blue blazer over his yellow polo shirt and pressed khakis. He waves and ends the call.

I show him to a sedate room we use to meet with family. Despite a table and leather club chairs, he leans against the wall, head tilted, eyebrows arched. It's a look I last saw when my mother awaited an explanation to some adolescent fuck-up I'd engineered.

"She's fine, in the recovery room and stable. It was a ruptured ectopic on the right, as suspected. We stopped the bleeding without having to remove the tube and didn't need to transfuse her, but we'll watch her blood count."

"Hmm, transfusion. That can be dangerous."

"Yeah, there can be reactions and infections, so it's a risk-benefit decision that we make. Unless a patient is in a life-threatening situation—and Jackie is nowhere near that point—we rarely give blood. As I said, there's no active bleeding, so aside—"

"You didn't say that," he interrupts, forming a thin smile of satisfaction.

"Didn't say what?"

"That there is no active bleeding."

I pause, trying to recall if he's some kind of lawyer or just a conventional asshole. I also have to decide whether to accept his invitation to this penis-measuring contest. I choose the high road but crank up the jargon in my explanation just to mess with him. I leave off the "Any questions, dickhead?" ending.

Brent twitches, like someone wearing itchy, too-tight clothing. He purses his lips, nodding like he was assessing the accuracy of my logic, as if he had any fucking clue as to what I just told him, and says, "Very well, Vince. It sounds like things are well in hand. I think I'll head out for some breakfast and a Bloody Mary."

His cell phone buzzes as he races away on clipped footsteps.

"Okay," I call after him. "We have your cell number in case we need you, right?"

He stops without turning and says, "Yes. She'll figure this out. Thanks for everything," then keeps walking.

From here on out I'm with Jackie—if I was married to him, I'd have no problem cheating on his sorry ass.

And with him gone, I want to make sure Jackie doesn't wake up alone. I see Jane in recovery dictating the op note. She swivels her chair toward me, looking pissed.

"Hey, what's up, Jane?"

"I just got a call from a patient that I swear is stalking me. Typical summertime stuff. You know, everyone says, 'Hey, I should feel great' and when they don't, it's like, you know, time to go to the gynecologist and tell her you're sure you have a hormone problem."

"You sound like me, but it's fuckin' twenty years too early."

She pouts, leans back. "Do you miss it, Vince? I mean, OB?"

"Well, I do miss my OB patients. They were friends, not customers. We'd share family stories, photos, I'd see their kids grow up—and some became patients of mine. Great for the ego, but I thought I'd end up with a wife and kids. And being married to my job, I couldn't stand the thought of missing out on a family. So, I gave up OB. Then 9/11 happened." I wait for questions, but Jane shifts gears.

"Jackie's stable, doing great. I talked to her before they sedated her again. Did you talk to Mr. Carter?"

I space out for a moment. "Wait, did I talk to Carter? Yeah, I guess you could call it that. He's a weird bird. On the spectrum or something, surprisingly hard to communicate with for someone who's the public face of his company. He might just be nervous. Took off to get food, didn't ask to see Jackie."

"What's he do?"

"He's CEO of a defense contractor, one of the big ones, makes missiles or some spooky shit like that."

"Well, he's had a long night—just like you and me—and he's probably stressed."

I get the hint. "Yeah, I guess you're right." I pause, drifting to Jackie's plight with her lover. Jane tilts her head, but I leave it unsaid.

"Well, Jane, I'll be home chillin', so call me if she goes south. If I'm not drunk, I'll come in and help you."

"God, that sounds great." She laughs with that smile that can make its way through a surgical mask. "No, uh . . . hormone problems in your life at the moment, huh?"

"Problems maybe, just no solutions," I say, hoping a pithy comeback will kill this. She knits her brow, so I go on. "The last date I went on felt like a job interview. I mean, midway through dinner I was expecting her to ask for a fucking net-worth statement—lot of gold digging in this town, Jane."

Her laughing stops with a stare. "Thanks, Vince. Seriously, thanks for everything. This was a great case and you made me feel so, so comfortable, I guess, handling it. I'm happy it was you on call with me tonight."

Before she chokes on thank-yous, I smile and retreat as fast as I can without being rude. In the locker room I pull Jackie's note from my pocket. In shaky script it reads,

Salaam  R  412  555  0883

I crumple it into my paper scrub hat and mask and bank-shoot the whole mess into the recycling bin as I grab some towels and head for the shower, dreaming of a double espresso.

# SEVEN

**FOR ME A "QUICK SHOWER"** is maybe twenty minutes. I put on the jeans, white T-shirt, and light jacket that I wore to the hospital last night. Even with sunshine, the slap of offshore wind makes me glad I have the jacket. I pick up a doppio and bag of almonds at Coffee Bean, and five minutes later I'm sitting on some rocks at the beach enjoying—sharing's the better word—breakfast with the gulls. Yeah, California gulls are big and they know it. They eat plump almonds whole; they might even eat you if you don't bring them an offering.

A cloud line slices the sun as it balances on the horizon, painting the coastline pink and sparking up the indigo-colored Pacific. I shiver, not from cold but from wonder about what the first beings intelligent enough to be captivated must have thought of this. Did they celebrate? Did they run to embrace one another?

When I'm post-call, drained of serotonin, oxytocin, and other juices of the brain that make us human, make us seek others, make us fun to be around, it's NPR on the mobile that I count on for no-strings companionship.

I missed *Weekend Edition*, but I'm in time to enjoy the stilted and quirky BBC news. The first story comes from Afghanistan where surveillance footage at Karzai International caught an orange-vested airport employee passing an explosive device to a complicit passenger who was to become an airborne martyr. Fortunately, the idiot detonated it before the Airbus was high enough to fully pressurize, resulting in him ejecting himself through a five-foot gash. Still flyable, the plane landed safely. Interesting, but all too common these days, and I drift from my headphones back to the view.

Just as I start to walk the beach, something on BBC jolts me: for the second time today, I hear the word "grail." My skin ripples and I turn my back to the wind.

In the queen's finest, the announcer goes on that a rogue squad of militants carried out a deadly attack on India's Pathankot airbase near the Pakistan border to derail peace talks. The report goes on to say the militants were caught with an arsenal of assault weapons and a stash of highly effective, Soviet-made antiaircraft weapons—NATO code–named *Grails*. They're portable and give a foot soldier a reasonable chance against a helo or low-flying aircraft, including fighter jets like those at the Indian base.

My surgeon sangfroid falters. I check my surroundings to see no one, aside from a few Montecito couples walking dogs on the beach. Sunrise goose bumps yield to a cold sweat as I try to deny what I'm piecing together. Brent, the defense industry kahuna. Jackie, the unfaithful spouse banging her honey, Sal, or whatever his name is, and her fucking ramblings about Grails.

Okay, I'm fast-talking myself. Jane Clark and I just saved a life two hours ago, I'm sleep-deprived, this is just an eerie coincidence, and I'm looking for a little excitement today, right?

Except Jackie's bizarre post-anesthesia moans and slurs—Sal, Grails, heavily, a bad revenge—fill my head. They make me feel my insignificance, my aloneness on this sedate beach as clouds wander inland, dimming the sunrise. I'm unstrung, but I connect with those first primates who recognized the sun's movement as more than lighting the way to more food, more things to kill.

As I climb the steps from the beach and reach the sidewalk, a gray sedan near the curb that I thought was empty starts and makes a slow U-turn away from me. Unsettling, but probably a napping surfer. I walk to the aging eucalyptus clinging to the ridge above the beach where I often go to decompress. I relax against it, then flinch at a sound over my right shoulder. I see, unsteady on a straining branch, one very gutsy blackbird, facing me down with a cocked-head stare.

I want to visit Helen's grave, but I need to go home. I need a nap.

*/////////////*

Well, my take-a-nap idea turned into a session of marathon watching the Science Channel followed by pizza from Tre Lune, savored with the better part of a bottle of Nebbiolo. That turned into marathon sleeping until Sunday morning, waking up in time to make it to mass at the Mission before checking on Jackie. I'm giving the Catholic Church a second chance. After all, J.C. has always been my man, despite organized religion's stupidity.

Mass is also my opiate of choice for the relapses of emotional mono that shadow Helen's visits in dreams, like the one from last night. The fallout requires monumental distraction—a friend's crisis, a patient in need—to lift me. The calculus is simple: no crusade, no happiness. And my heart stays in the shop. Out of service. Yet, I don't want her to stop visiting me. Ever.

Beneath the choir's lilt, I'm auditioning Jackie's voice and the story of her dude, her douche bag husband, her Grails—whatever that means. Church isn't helping me sort this shit like it usually does.

////////////

I park in the doctors' lot, which is the one sandwiched between the ER and a fermenting dumpster. I'm certain administrators planned it this way as a reminder they'll always be nipping at our heels. I walk fast and poker-faced, a warning to anyone that I'm all out of nice today. I don't give a fuck about you, so please don't bother me.

The automatic doors slide and I dodge a pair of young nurses, sucking my thirty-six-inch gut into my thirty-four-inch waistband. I pledge to hike Hot Springs Trail this afternoon. Right after my social call to Mrs. Carter.

# EIGHT

**THE HOSPITAL'S SECOND LEVEL IS** a maze of glistening floors, depressing artwork, and lukewarm lighting. RNs and care techs crisscross each other as they pass meds, take temps and BPs. The glass-enclosed nurses' station is empty except for the unit secretary, middle-aged, large, and focused dead ahead, laying emery board to nails. I log on to the EMR, the digital version of the patient's paper chart, to check Jackie's numbers—all good. I linger, checking out her address—East Mountain Road, nice; occupation—housewife; guarantor—Brent Carter, BC AeroSystems.

Why? Why would a sophisticated, upper-class woman—a housewife—come out of anesthesia talking shop about ground-to-air missiles? No, procuring ground-to-air missiles. I want the screen to tell me she's employed by an engineering firm or by Brent, The Nepotist. No luck. She's a housewife in Santa Barbara, a town where the only procuring is for the next tennis game with the neighbors or a good Bordeaux—no, I doubt wives procure ground-to-air weapons. But then, how many are bangin' a guy named Salaam?

I enter her room but it's empty, except for flowers everywhere. I lift the cover on her lunch and see she's eaten a healthy half of the broiled salmon and broccoli. I hope it's not all over the floor somewhere.

I hear footsteps and turn to the door. A swarthy guy in medium-blue sharkskin glances in, then scurries on, a shuffling limp in his step. I move to the door and head toward the patio, jumping as I hear a gasp.

"Oh! Hey! Vince, it's me!" Jackie goes back to the wall to avoid being flattened by my clumsiness, moving her hands over her pink silk robe in the vicinity of her incisions. A red rose she was carrying falls at my feet.

"Hey, Jackie! Wow, how are you?" The near miss has me babbling. "What are you doing out here?" I pick up and hand her the rose, then turn to see the limping guy has vanished.

She leads me by my arm into her room. "Why are you here on a Sunday? Are you worried about me? I'm doing well, right?"

"Yeah, yeah, you're doing fantastic! I'm just running errands and I thought I'd just swing by on my way home. Do you feel as good as you look?"

She lifts her arms, modeling her robe in a slow turn. "Vince, I feel like, like send me home today! I mean, I'm walking and eating well. How 'bout tomorrow morning for sure?" Jackie sounds high on meds, rambling.

"Well, it's really too soon. I mean, with all the bleeding you had, and . . . where's Brent? Tuesday morning is what I was thinking."

Her head drops. "Brent's in DC, flying back tonight. So he can take me home first thing in the morning. I wanted him here today, if things were good for me to leave, but then he got this call, saying, 'We got a little problem.' One of his divisions almost lost a 350-million-dollar deal when they only had 200 to lose."

Her candor surprises me—maybe she really is involved in his business details, missiles, Grails. Either way, 350 million on the line is worth a red-eye trip.

"You'll be ready the day after tomorrow, Jackie. I'll come by early, make sure your blood count's stable, give you all the instructions, and then I can discharge you. I promise. Brent can come whenever he wants, okay?"

"That's fine, Vince. I really feel good, and I'll be able to take it easy at home. God knows I'll get more sleep. That room across the hall—there's a senile man in there, poor thing, who yells out for Audrey all night long."

"I'll see what I can do about that. Try to have a good night, okay?"

"All right." She sits on the bed, smiles, and offers a hand. "Vince, thanks for understanding the other day in the ER. You know, about my friend?"

"I remember, Jackie. And I understand. Like I said, if you want to talk sometime, just give me a call."

"Thanks, Doc!" Her head tilts back with a smile that isn't all there.

"And thanks for complimenting our hospital that morning."

She squints, shaking her head.

I move closer. "Remember? You said to tell your friend this hospital was perfect."

"I said that?" she asks, turning away. "Oh, yeah, I remember. And I meant it."

I know she hasn't a clue. As I hit the hallway, she shouts, "Hey, let's all get together for dinner at the club sometime, okay?"

*No, Jackie, remember? It was in the papers. I'm solo. No dinner foursome here.*

"Deal! Get well, then we'll do it!"

My choked-up stridor echoes down the hall. A nurse pushing an empty wheelchair turns and smiles. I wave and we meet halfway, my hand on her shoulder as I whisper, "Please tell Audrey on nights to be sure that guy in 2911 gets his sleeper, okay?"

"I'll take care of it, Vince," she says. "Enjoy your day off."

Ugh. Serious "Sunday night feeling" after that comment, but hell, it's early. The doors open on a crisp view of the mountains hanging up there in sage and brown, unruly and full of ambition.

When I get in my car, I notice a couple watching from the second-floor patio. It's the man in the medium-blue suit. With Jackie. I can't explain it, but their gaze crushes my mood more than any Sunday night feeling could.

I run stop signs to get home. After a quick change, I'm at Hot Springs trailhead where my only heebie-jeebies come from tucked-away rattlesnakes.

# NINE

**I MAKE IT TO THE** three-mile mark and then back down, no venomous reptiles, no slobbering dogs, no human interruptions—a perfect hike. Well, okay, I'm jealous and love dogs, but living alone, the exigencies of my job just don't align with "doggy logistics."

When I get to my car, some cirrus clouds have turned salmon pink and refuse to be blown away. Stunning, but it reminds me of Jackie's lunch wreckage. I hear a gust racing through the arroyo, and dead leaves coil up beside me. The chill brings me right back to my Grail dilemma—obsession is now the word—making me want to get home, shower, and google the living fuck out of Jackie.

I'm out of the shower, into jeans, button-down, cashmere sweater, and planted in front of my laptop. It seems Jacquelyn Carter doesn't exist or maybe her husband's company pays a security firm to expunge her from cyberspace. Brent does exist, but I find nothing that I don't already know. I expect to see at least a few charity-event photos of him with Jackie and other well-to-do couples reveling in the suburban dance-of-death scene, but no dice.

Grails are another story. NPR was right in reporting they're shoulder-fired surface-to-air missiles that one combatant can operate.

Russia handed them out like candy during wars in Afghanistan, Africa, Southeast Asia, everywhere. They also suck because their small warhead often lets planes get away with minor damage.

I search "Sal," "Salam," and "Salaam" and get a zillion hits. Adding "missiles" to the names gets me one story of an Immigration and Customs Enforcement trap that pinched two guys in 2004. ICE agents posed as buyers of a shoulder-fired missile and stung two men with al-Qaeda ties as conspirators. The story comes up only because their mosque had the word "Salam" in its name.

But the story's sting angle reminds me of Jackie complaining of stings, or being stung, or something, so I add it. It circles back to the 2004 operation. There are also pages describing Stingers—same concept as Grails, but premium, American-made versions that work. A page-three hit is about black-market Stinger missiles, and I click. It leads to about a dozen five-year-old news stories, three of which mentioned Salaam (no last name), who was some on-the-run rain-maker in the South American arms market. Then it hits me: that was the spelling on Jackie's long-gone note.

"Salaam" by itself gets over fifty-million hits, the first six pages mostly Middle Eastern restaurants. Then I'm hit again: I'm getting hungry and this is a fatigue-triggered waste of my fucking time.

# TEN

LUCKY'S. NOT SOME VARIANT OF owner Jimmy Catalano's name.
Although "Cat's" would fit, owing to cougars' love of the place with
its ample supply of flat-bellied Montecito dandies and überwealthy
greyhounds. Pity I'm not in either sweet spot. Instead I go for good
food and spectacular people watching. My favorites are the guys
born on third base acting like they hit triples. They're eaten alive by
predatory females who, with little effort, penetrate their empty souls.
Unless the females' souls are empty as well—then it's an even better
spectator sport.

It's a neighborhood Italian steakhouse that never changes, to the
point where the wood floor and trim around the bar could use a little
aesthetic surgery, but Jimmy wisely leaves it, showing plenty of char-
acter. The year-round white Christmas lights along the beams and
rafters don't hurt either. He left out—or maybe has patched up—any
obvious bullet holes.

"Hey, Vince!" Always upbeat, Micah begins his barkeep shift
as usual by rolling up his sleeves. He's a little round, plays a little
too hard, keeps his mouth shut over witnessed indiscretions, and
makes the best damn cocktails on the central coast. He starts mine

before I even sit down. Tito's vodka, up, three regular olives—a guzzle that blunts pain and polishes the night no matter what I've been through.

"Micah, how are you, my friend?"

An unfamiliar couple to my right scoots over to let me squeeze in. To my left, a group of young women behind a line of cosmos and lemon drops are discussing something that allows simultaneous, earsplitting speech while staring blankly into luminous cell phone screens. I lay my phone on the bar as if expecting something indicative of having a life. Micah's pours are generous, so if you lack the steadiness of a neurosurgeon, picking one up for that first sip can be a sloppy humiliation. Best to slide his cocktails close, then bow in defeat.

"I've been thinking about this all day."

He laughs, his pour dead center. "You joinin' us for dinner tonight, Doc?"

"Yeah, I need to treat myself."

"Okay." He motions to a barback. "Can you get Vince set up, Silvio?"

The woman of the couple next to me leans in. "It seems like you're a regular here?"

"Yeah, unfortunately I am, but I'm fortunate to have this place in the neighborhood." They're amused, sympathetic maybe. I field the usual interrogatories about the menu, the town. They're nice people, but enough chitchat. I fake an incoming text, though one of their raisin-rye dinner rolls is more likely to get one before I do.

The screen's Google app nags me. So does Jackie, the Grail thing, and whatever revenge she and Sal are up to. I look to the televisions hanging at both ends of the rectangular bar that's now starting to fill up. Preseason baseball—bottom of the fourth, no score. Boring. I'm back into the phone.

The newsfeeds offer distraction, but I lurch into the same headlines as this morning, including the India-Pakistan border skirmish. I
surrender and type: Salaam, Stinger, missiles.

Rereading the hits in the midst of half-martini calmness, I get the
bigger picture. This Salaam, along with other arms dealers, provides
legit help to South American bad guys. Small arms, ammo, artillery,
Grails—a Weapons Walmart for insurgents and drug cartels. I guess
embracing the legit part depends on whose side you're on, but he
doesn't read like an especially violent supercriminal. It seems Salaam
worked a hustle on a former partner, then went dark. End of story.

The big picture also tells me Salaam is a common name—definitely for restaurants—and any connection with Jackie has to be
coincidental. Even if the South American arms dealer is Jackie's Sal,
there's nothing to it. Yeah, I'm sure it's nothing—I can feel it.

"What are you feeling tonight, Vince?"

My jaw drops as I look up at Micah, who's ready to scribble my
order on the back of a coaster. Over his shoulder I catch a pale, drawn
face in the mirror behind rows of bottles. It's mine, unfortunately, and
it better be my startle response and not my general state of health.
There's also the reflection of the pack to my left and one woman
staring at me—smiling now—not with friendliness but with, say, the
confident, greedy intentions of a wildcat.

"I . . . uh." I pause, weighing desire for my usual bleu-cheese
wedge and New York strip against not appearing piggish in front of
the possibility to my left. "I'll do the usual." Fuck it. Life is short.

"Great, Doc. Any wine?"

"I'll do a Margerum M5 after I drain this Tito's."

"You got it."

He turns away; Miss Twenty-Something doesn't. It's flattering
to have pried a woman off her phone, but anyone her age interested
in a guy my age is either running the checklist of a bachelorette

party or, well, ain't right in the head. Okay. To be fair, I've met amazing women that age with a better handle on life than me, or any other guy I know, except maybe Shakespeare. Not sure why. Maybe they don't have the ghosts, the blunders, the voices rattling in their heads. She's very attractive, but I'll pass on the "man and his niece" scene tonight.

Right now, my rattling voices have been at it since Jackie and medium-blue-Armani-suit guy stared me down from the hospital patio. No smile, no wave. Just pure creepiness.

My Tito's has me in that early-stage, rising blood ethanol–level magic, pushing the room's cheerful din into the background. I can audition three or four distant conversations at once. Jimmy's soundtrack, heavy on Rat Pack stuff, cues up Sinatra's "Come Fly with Me." I see my dad sitting by the stereo, lighting up a Benson & Hedges, captivated by a dog-eared album cover of Ol' Blue Eyes boarding a plane, suit coat draped over the shoulder, the fedora rakishly tilted. But tonight, it makes me squirm and swirl the last of my drink, envisioning a surface-to-air missile bringing down a planeload of terrified screaming Americans.

The televisions also evoke the recent Homeland Security public service pokes, "See Something, Say Something." I hear it continuously and soon it's Helen doing the voiceover, "If you see something, say something, Vince!"

Goddamnit! This won't end until I grow a pair and talk to someone about it—and I don't mean Micah or some twenty-five-year-old accident waiting to happen.

My barstool screeches, getting Micah's attention. "I gotta do a quick call and be right back, okay?"

"No problem, Vince. I'll time things right for you."

Too bad he didn't time Jackie Carter's trip to the ER right.

Just steps away from the front door there's a driveway to the

adjacent hotel, about as private a spot I could hope for in the neighborhood. I scan the cars and sidewalks for Jackie's friend or similar
goons. My heart's bucking—I'd go back into Lucky's for a roadie if I
thought I could do so and stay coherent.

Instead I tap Google, type F-B-I, and let her fly.

It comes up with a crowdsourced customer review section off to
the right, like it's a dry cleaners. Only this says "FBI Los Angeles
Division" with an address on Wilshire and a phone number. Closed
today, Sunday. As any good dry cleaners or elite law enforcement
agency would be. I click the homepage.

There are sidebar vignettes of busted minor thugs. Shouldn't the
FBI be 99 percent antiterror and leave the bit players for sheriffs to
perp walk before the news cameras as a publicity pinch?

I rock side to side. I'm making a big mistake.

No! The fucking Western world has been at stake since 9/11.

The Contact Us section offers an e-form option to send a tip
on crime/terrorism. Really? Like fucking United Airlines lost my
luggage?

My heart settles some, and I stand outside the glass door as a
hand-in-hand couple enters. I watch baseball until there's a lull with
news updates. The sight of any "Breaking News" banner—even
the one that just pops up now, announcing a sanitation workers'
strike—paralyzes me since I lost Helen on 9/11. They send me back
to that day and scenes of melting, fractured metal and endless flurries
of paper. And falling bodies.

I touch the phone and a white rectangle pops. *Cancel* or *call*? I do
what I don't want to do.

# ELEVEN

ONE RING, THEN A NEUTRAL female voice. "FBI." Way too brief for me to get my shit together. I consider saying, "Sorry, wrong number," but I'm sure they've IDed me by now. *Fuck, hang up. Now!* I can explain, I'm drunk. She continues in emotionless, civil servant style, "FBI. Hello? FBI." They're used to agitated idiots calling, right?

"Hello, yes. I'm here." My throat is tightening down to the diameter of a thirteen-year-old's. "Ah, I'd like to ask a question . . . Are you open? I mean, should I call back tomorrow? It's not an emergency or anything. Maybe I should send it in on the website or . . ."

"Sir, please slow down. Are you in any danger?" she asks, now with a hint of humanity.

"No, no. I'm not. I guess . . . I think I'm cool." Except I need to do some Lamaze breathing.

"Would you like to report something? Do you need to talk to an FBI agent?"

My heart pounds up through my carotids as sweat driblets tickle my flanks. I tug, fluffing some air into my sweater, almost launching my phone. "Hello . . . I'm sorry, I lost my phone for a second."

"Sir, hold a moment so I can get an agent for you," she says. An older, motherly tone now, and I exhale slowly. "I'm putting you on hold now, so don't go away."

Jesus, what the fuck am I doing—I should hang up now and get back to my booze and food and the young flirt.

"Okay, no hurry. Thanks." I give Micah the thumb-and-pinky phone signal through the window and he returns a thumbs-up. Ten seconds. Silence, no hold music, and I'm sure they're coming to get me. A stern male voice crackles in.

"Agent Gillette. Can I help you?"

"Yes, I don't know if this is anything, but it made me a little nervous, but I think"—a hard swallow, then I go full throttle—"I'm a physician and one of my patients said some things to me that seem weird. She was asleep, I mean coming out of anesthesia. I . . . I don't even know what I can legally say that wouldn't be a HIPAA violation. I'm her doctor and . . . I don't know."

I picture Gillette's stubby pencil scratching single words like "doctor" and "bonkers" on a skinny notepad. Then he says, "I get it, so let's keep it anonymous as far as the patient goes. What was the nature of what she said? What's it about?" He's now speaking slowly, recognizing he's got a basket case. I'm sure all their nut jobs come out on weekends. Just like at our ER.

"Yeah, well, that's what I'm not sure of." Another Lamaze breath. "I mean, she talked about another person, not her husband . . . And her husband, by the way, is a defense contractor big shot, Northrop Grumman or one of those serious ones in Santa Barbara. And, uh, in the same rambling about this guy, Saleem, or, no, sorry, his name was Salaam—two a's—she started talking about revenge and Grails and then—"

"About what?" Gillette interrupts, Big Brother in his voice.

"Grails. You know, like Grail missiles. I think they're Russian missiles. I heard a story on NPR about them, but—"

Gillette cuts in, "I understand. Grail is the NATO term for them."

"With her husband's job and, I mean, I still don't know what she meant by revenge, by Grails."

"Who am I speaking to?"

Wow, he's not laughing. I go professional. "This is Vince DeLuca, a gynecologist at Santa Barbara Community Hospital, faculty at UCLA Geffen." Never hurts to drop a little credential chrome when you're about to shatter your life.

"Doctor, you're on your cell in an outdoor location, correct?"

How does he know? I see only empty parked cars on the street, no limping man. I check the sky. No drones, no drama. Just Orion and ten thousand more stars that make me want to be on the beach rather than on this call.

"Yes, there's no one around, but I can move inside if you want. Whatever you say." I mean, what the fuck? By now the FBI probably has my genome. "Just so you know, she's still in the hospital, so it's not like she can do anything."

"Doctor . . . DeLuca, is it?"

"Yeah, Vince DeLuca."

"Doctor DeLuca, why don't we stop talking about this now? Do you think that there's any immediate danger to yourself or to anyone else?"

"No, sir, I don't. You can call me Vince."

"Okay." He pauses a moment. "Vince, I'd like you to meet with someone in person."

In an instant, I'm fully sober. "Okay, I could come down to LA tomorrow. I'm only in the office in the morning until ten or so and, uh . . . or, do you mean tonight? Because if you do, I—"

"Doctor, I think we should come to you. Just give me a number where we can reach you tomorrow morning."

"You can use this number. It's my cell, or call my office number."

"All right, Vince. If we miss somehow, please don't call us back. We'll get in touch with you on this cell phone, understand?"

I want to say, "Roger that," but don't. "Sure, that's okay with me. Thanks for your time." Gillette vanishes with an eerie click.

After another furtive glance around the street, I'm back inside the safety of Lucky's, navigating chock-a-block patrons three deep at the throbbing bar.

"Here you go, Vince," Micah says on a double take. "Hey, you okay, Doc?"

I peer down at a glass of ruby liquid. "Yeah, I'm okay."

Micah tilts toward the flirt and says, "By the way, it's on her."

I guess that means I'm not that bad looking. For a ghost, that is.

# TWELVE

FORTUNATELY, NOTHING HAPPENED AFTER THE gracious gift of a delicious M5. Just a thank you and some flirtatious banter, most of which centered on my profession after the predictable *What do you do?* inquiry. One minute you're flirting, then suddenly you're giving off-the-record professional advice. I'm even regularly asked to feel, then opine on, breast lumps. In public. I refuse, of course, but leave satisfied knowing that, if Guinness had it, I'd own the record for Fastest Time to Second Base with a Total Stranger.

Anyway, when one longs for a truly great relationship, it's early to bed without so much as a memorable dream. It pays off when I get to work today, focusing on patients, not reliving the guilt of some weekend misadventure. Before long it's lunchtime, which means vending machine peanut M&Ms and a Coke *al desko*. I wonder when, or if, I'll hear from my new friends at the FBI.

I bring a patient's insurance form to the front office—something not taught in med school—waving it in the direction of our receptionists. Peggy, speaking into her headset, reaches back for it. She's pushing retirement age, has had it tough, and is determined to get even for her lot in life. I whisper, "Thanks," and turn, but stop when I hear something ominous.

"He's with patients. May I have his nurse help you?" She relishes gatekeeping.

I wait for a wave-off signaling it is a prescription refill request or another routine matter. Peggy slowly turns her chair, giving me a once-over. I return her creased-brow expression, dreading that it's last night's wine-gifting young woman.

Peggy grabs a pen but stops short of writing. "Okay, let me put you on a very brief hold." She herds me to the break room out of earshot of patients.

"What's up?" I ask. Why in God's name didn't I accept the drink with a smile, then walk away?

"Someone named Ann Baker. Says it's an urgent business matter." Her smoker's cough interrupts. "Says that you called last night around nine and that you'd know what it's about."

I fumble for my cell phone and gasp, seeing two calls from a blocked number. My phone has been on silent! How could I have screwed up Cell Phone 101, today of all days?

"She says she'd like to hold."

"Goddamnit," I hiss. Peggy's face tells me I look like someone to be wary of. "I'm sorry, Peggy. I'm mad at myself. I missed their calls."

"It's okay, Vince. She doesn't sound angry, but she ain't takin' no for an answer. Transfer it to your office?"

"Yeah, give me ten seconds, okay?"

"Sure thing, Vince." She winks. "Take a deep breath before you talk to her." God, she suspects this is one of my few-and-far-between assignations of which the office rarely gets wind. Let the tittle-tattle begin.

I open the bottle of water I brought from the break room, take a sip, then lift the receiver.

"This is Vince DeLuca." Stern. Confident. I'm pleased with myself, except for my right leg's uncontrollable bouncing.

"Hi, Doctor, this is Ann Baker. You spoke to my associate last night about nine." Her voice is professional, reassuring, and smoother than Skippy. None of that false up-talking I hear from someone trying to sell me some crap.

"Yeah, I . . . I called last night and spoke with a Mr. Gillette, I believe."

"I'd like to meet with you today, Doctor DeLuca. Will that be possible?"

"Okay, sure. I'm finished with patients, so anytime is good for me. You want to come here, right? That's what he said last night."

"Yes, I'll meet you at your Santa Barbara office at eleven thirty, so please let your staff know to expect me, if you don't mind. I assume that you've kept the issue and your call to us last night confidential, correct?"

"Absolutely. It's you, me, and Mr. Gillette. That's it." Immediate regret. I'm too chummy.

"Excellent, I'll see you at eleven thirty then." There's a smile in her voice, thank God.

I take a breath and the bouncing leg slows. Suddenly the time on my phone makes me sit up straight. It's eleven. My heart flips. She couldn't have called from Los Angeles hoping to make an eleven thirty visit to my office, so she, they, whoever, must be here already. Watching me. All right, I'm getting wound up over nothing—this is not that important. Besides, I'm sure after last night I'm on some fucking list of nutty do-gooders to be mostly ignored. Or possibly watched quite closely.

# THIRTEEN

**I SURRENDER TO THE NOTION** of being a kook. So why not stand at my office window scanning for blacked-out Suburbans? So far, just random cars of staff and patients.

The intercom chimes; I jump three feet. "Hi."

Peggy's sing-song voice. "Miss Baker is here, Vince. I asked her to take a seat."

"Is she alone?"

"I didn't see her walk in, but it looks like it." She laughs. "Should we be worried?"

"No, no. I'm a bad businessman and don't want to be double-teamed on a prospective deal." There's a pause. She's not buying it.

"Okay, let me know if you need anything." Another pause. "A Xanax maybe?" They know when I'm stressed and go overboard with the nurturing-mother shtick. But she's right, I need to calm the fuck down.

"Ha, no thanks. I'll be right there," I say, then scurry to the waiting room.

The area's got soft lighting, comfy couches, a fireplace—everything to thaw frost. There are five or six women sitting there. Some relaxed, some not, but none I'd guess to be my visitor. I rule out any-one engrossed in magazines or keeping children off the coffee tables or out of potted plants.

"Ann Baker?" I call.

One head turns, and it's a surprise. I had reflexively filtered her out since she is the only woman in conservative business garb with a briefcase. I'm sorry, but a tall, well-groomed, attractive blonde—male or female—in a physician's waiting room carrying anything but an infant is a pharmaceutical sales rep until proven otherwise.

She steps across the room and hits me with some seriously con-fident eye contact. She has a great stride. Her hair is pulled back in a French twist deal like naval aviator patients of mine wear. Ex-military. Crap, this is going to be bad.

Our eye contact dissolves into smiles. Then muffled laughs. Weird, but it feels natural. Feels great, actually. She extends a determined but surprisingly damp hand.

"It's very nice to meet you, Doctor."

"Likewise, very nice to meet you, Ms. Baker."

She focuses on my ID badge and says, her voice down a notch, "Can we go someplace to talk? Perhaps your office or an empty con-ference room?" She smiles again, this time with a little head jog that goes flirtatious for a few milliseconds. On second thought, she might be thinking I'm an amusing idiot because I'm completely frozen. Finally, she leans in, "Someplace private?"

Eyebrows raised, I blurt, "Oh! Yes, of course! We can use my office." I can feel my staff suppressing giggles.

Her hand on my shoulder encourages me into the hallway before I can yak out something daft. After a last scan of the waiting room, she leads the way, like she knows the place.

She's taller than me. And smells great—faint light citrus—Acqua di Giò? It relaxes me, makes me want to move closer. I know it's just my jazzed-up sensorium because I'm stressed, but I can't stop looking at her legs. Just a guess, but maybe a 100-inch inseam? My numbers might be off a little.

She stops at the door with my name and motions to me. I nod, focused on her outstretched hand, wondering if she's ever killed anyone. Or maybe she's just someone with a desk job, like our office gatekeepers screening calls from crazies like me. Yeah, I'll go with desk job.

She picks one of the chairs in front of my Queen Anne desk and sits, briefcase on her lap, legs parallel and crossed at the ankles. This is my territory, yet I'm the one immobilized by this professional, this powerful woman in my office. My office that yesterday was a comforting retreat is now alien, violated by unfamiliar, intimidating people. There's a soft click as I close the door on the demons that Jackie Carter's surgical adventure has unleashed on me.

# FOURTEEN

ENTRANCED BY HER SMILE, I manage to speak. "Uh, can I get you some coffee or a soft drink? Miss Baker, is it?" I stammer, hands gesticulating. "Look, okay, I'm really nervous about all of this, and you, you probably think that I'm unstable or impaired or, I don't know."

She springs up, extending a less clammy hand while flashing a brown leather folder holding an FBI badge and photo ID.

"It's Special Agent Carolyn Talbot. Nice to meet you officially, Doctor DeLuca."

I look at our clasped hands, then longer at her. There's that god-damn smile again.

"Apologies, Doctor, for the damp handshakes. It must be a reaction to being in a gyno's office, so nothing personal."

She's trying hard to get me to chill, and I appreciate that. I think it's too early, but what I want to say is, "I'd love to have your sweat on me." Yeah. Too early.

"I'm sorry. Agent Talbot, I thought . . ." I fixate on the ID photo. Carolyn tips her head down, grabbing more eye contact. I'm sure I'm going scarlet.

"It's okay. I used the other name just to be safe for both you and me. Call me Carolyn. And I'll have a regular Coke, if you have it."

"Yeah, me too. And you can call me Vince."

"Let me review some background, then we'll go over what happened to you, all right?"

"Sure, I'm free the rest of the day. By the way, they're Mexican Cokes. Is that okay?"

Her eyes widen. "Love them. Thanks."

I settle down some, shaken by her little name game, and study her profile, her pouty-lipped smile, some sadness in her eyes. It reminds me of portraits of English nobility. A few tiny facial scars, but that's okay. Just perfect enough. She looks at me, imperturbable, and then back to her work with a wily grin that says, "It's okay. I know I'm fucking beautiful-gorgeous. Go ahead and stare. Get it out of your system."

I gotta admit, I'm giddy and, Jesus, feeling joy I haven't felt in years—not since Helen. I come within a breath of tearful laughing but turn away with a shudder and call for two Coca-Colas.

I drop into the chair next to Carolyn. She leans back, takes in my skittishness, and shuffles folders in her briefcase. I'm still curious how she called from her office and then showed up here less than an hour later.

"Did you fly up here from LA?"

"No." Terse, eyes on iPad.

Well, that's settled.

The knock is gentle, and I accept a cork-covered tray with ice-filled glasses and two bottles of Coke. I lay the goodies on the desk in front of us and fill the glasses.

Here I take an opportunity to stare at her hands, starting on the left. No mate retention devices—in fact, no rings at all. Artist's hands, elegant movements, nails natural with pearly overhangs just long enough to belong to a woman, well-kept. Wrists and arms well defined, alive with tiny golden hairs. I follow the tailored jacket up to small, muscular shoulders that I want to touch. A ballet dancer's neck. Everything says feminine and class, but something else says hard as a fucking diamond. I turn just as she looks up.

She straightens, head slides back, gazing at me with crystalline blue eyes. All I offer is an embarrassing stare needing no explanation. She blushes—good to know she responds when I mess with *her* sympathetic nervous system.

Bottles clank as I almost dump the tray. She reaches to help.

"Are you okay?" she asks, laughter going from soprano to baritone.

My turn to blush, eyes meeting and stopping time. No, I'm not okay. Because, Special Agent Carolyn Talbot, you and I are not together, and I see old age coming for me. Then again, I see our unborn children chasing, pushing into our world. And I never give up.

# FIFTEEN

CAROLYN. SHE SURE AS HELL isn't a pharma rep, but I'd sure as hell prescribe anything she was selling. And lots of it.

She sits a yard away from me—tailored navy blue suit, crisp white shirt open one button shy of Too Far, and a skirt hemmed high enough over the knee to make up for it. I consider saying something flirty but see a tilt of her head, her honey-blonde hair, and a hypnotizing gaze. She studies me, penetrates me, makes me feel naked. Is it her, or do they teach this shit at Quantico?

She holds the ends of her Cross pen in front of her, rolling it, assessing it, feeling its heft, like it's the baton of an all-knowing conductor about to downstroke a symphony's first note. I feel like I'm heading into a ferocious deposition or a job interview at Google for a position I'm not qualified for. After what feels like an hour, she speaks.

"I want to carefully go over everything that you reported to Agent Gillette last night, starting with your patient and then what transpired. I need you to be as open and accurate as possible. I'll cover HIPAA for you." She holds her gaze long enough to make sure I understand this is serious shit. I nod, regain my sanity, banish my fantasies, and silently pledge to have an intelligent conversation. "After we cover last night, I'll need to know a little about your background—just general things for our investigation; you're not in any trouble."

Not yet, that is.

"Okay, I'll tell you everything I heard. I know this may all be a misunderstanding—I mean, I don't want to get anyone in a bind, but I also don't need any guilt over not speaking up."

"I totally understand, Doctor, and we appreciate you calling us."

She wants details on my past medical dealings and everything else I can remember about Jackie and Brent Carter. Aside from the few prior visits regarding an abnormal Pap—likely HPV-related via Sal or her philandering douche bag husband—there wasn't much there. The fun started Friday night, so I unwind my weekend, from Jackie showing up in the ER to the limping creep standing with her as I walked to my car.

I focus on Jackie coming out of anesthesia, and Carolyn prompts me to pry loose details of the gibberish Jackie spewed about "a bad revenge," the word "heavily" over and over again. She turns to her iPad, shaking her head, appearing to be as bewildered as I feel at this moment, then asks, "Was she—"

"'Waziristan!' I forgot, she said 'Waziristan' a couple of times. And it freaked me out the way she said it, in a weird cadence or accent."

"Just that word by itself?" Carolyn narrows her eyebrows and moves closer.

"Yes. No context, but then she went into the revenge stuff again, as if she was talking to Sal. It was spooky."

I save the best for last—the part when Jackie gives me the name and number of her paramour—yeah, the note that I tossed into recycling forty-eight hours ago. Carolyn listens, then breathes a special sigh, one that fills my sails with judgment. She leans back from the iPad, raising one of those perfect eyebrows, her lips pursed off to one side. More slow pen rolling.

I have to say, it's the most professional, nonverbal, "You fucking idiot! You did what?" that I've ever been slammed with.

Crap! Plan B. I try unsuccessfully to keep from laughing as I mollify and point out that, on weekends, housekeeping doesn't do the OR lockers unless they are specifically asked, like when there's been a contaminated case or it's been super busy. She politely suggests that I calmly, but immediately, get my sweet ass over there to see if that's the case. As I leave, she's calling to let people know there may be some high-priority dumpster diving in their future.

I picture fishing through a recycling bin that's dressed with gloppy goo from half-full milk cartons and coffee cups. I should never have tossed it—I mean, I made a promise to Jackie. She could still die from a post-op complication or at the hands of her A-hole husband, if he's on to her. As I close my office door, Carolyn laughs and gives a thumbs-up.

I sprint to the OR, get into scrubs, and enter the clean side of the unit's locker room. My heart plummets when I see an empty plastic bag in the hamper. I have to convince myself by peering into the bag, hoping housekeeping took the easy route, reusing the bag and just dumping its contents into one of their trash hoppers. No luck. No note clinging to the side of the bag. No face-saving.

t"Can I help ya, Doc?"

I turn and see someone from environmental services pushing a gray hopper. "Hey! Jim, right?" He nods. "I, uh. I was looking for the trash from the surgeons' locker room. I think I accidentally tossed a . . . a patient's callback number that I need."

"Okay, well, that ain't out yet. Cart's still in the hall. Let's go take a gander."

There *is* a God—and it was a quiet weekend. In the last of three bags Jim pulls, my scrub hat, mask, and the note are at the bottom with only a folded Sunday *New York Times* on top of them.

I stay in scrubs and race back to my office with the note.

# SIXTEEN

**CAROLYN'S HEAD SNAPS TO THE** door when I enter. She's leaning her butt against the edge of my desk, arms folded, but I get the feeling she just stopped pacing. She's my sixth-grade teacher awaiting my bullshit excuse for missing homework. I hold out the crumpled note, triumphant yet sheepish, but instead of taking it, her eyes give me two interminable up-and-down scans. I'm blushed as hell, for sure. Did I ferry dumpster aroma back to her?

"You're clean. Did you do the Santa Barbara thing and pay someone to jump in the dumpster for you?" The snipe answers any aroma doubts. "By the way, those scrubs look extremely comfy, Doc."

"Well, I can get you a pair. I mean, if you want."

Another coy smile. Sweet Jesus, God in heaven, this woman is fuckin' killing me. She sits and studies the note. Now I lean, chest heaving, against the desk, trying to get my heart rate below 200.

"Does this guy, Salaam, mean anything to you?" I ask.

She turns to me with a damn good Mona Lisa smile. "Not yet."

She takes photos of the note with her iPad, then puts it in a plastic zip bag.

"I'm sorry. I should have hung on to it."

She pushes a palm at me. "Say no more. No one can withstand retrospective scrutiny."

I get the feeling that she's no stranger to screw-ups. Her eyes dampen after the little pep talk, and so do mine. At least we've got soul.

"We need to cover some other things, Vince."

I watch her rummaging in her purse, sensing some inner fatigue. She reapplies some lip goop from a tube.

"Do you have any more Coke? If not, water is good."

"I'll be right back."

I return with a couple of bottles, refill our glasses, and sit. Carolyn swipes her iPad, a crossed leg slowly dangling a shoe in front of me. Nice shoes, nicer ankles, but before I can go insane, she breathes deep and turns to me.

"I'm not sure we have anything here, Vince. But in the meantime, I need to see if you have been, or can be, compromised in any way."

I sit up straight. "Compromised?"

"Sorry. I know you have no criminal record, a clean medical license. But I have to know your off-the-record personal background to make sure that if anything becomes of this with Jackie, her husband, her Salaam—whomever—none of the bad actors can hold anything to blackmail you."

"Oh, background. Yeah, you said that before."

"This is routine, so just relax." She raises her glass. "Cheers."

"*Salute.*" Vodka would be so much better at this point.

First, she wants to know all about me. Grew up in Pittsburgh. First-generation Italian, only child, hence perfectionism. Catholic education, hence wild streak tempered by eternally ingrained guilt. Northwestern medical training. Why'd I leave Chicago? Chicago weather is great—if you're a fucking rock or a pine tree. A wise person once told me that to survive a Chicago winter you only need two things: a fireplace and to be in love. I never managed to have both at the same time, but I did go through lots of firewood. My age—forties—but who's counting?

Past relationships and why they ended—some serious, others not. Ended because I'm a workaholic. Current relationships—none. I tend to kill them when they escalate beyond recreational sex because, well, I'm a workaholic. The whole psychological enchilada just like sitting with my therapist day one.

Carolyn sits there handwriting notes onto the iPad. Then stops, cocks her head back, and judges me with an eyes-only smile. I feel something way beyond the awkward silence. Quantum entanglement, perhaps? I bite my lip and start with leg bouncing worthy of a three-day welt from Sister Mary Satan's yardstick.

Back to business. She gives me forty-eight hours to get through a to-do list of things. She wants electronic copies of Jackie's hospital records; all the meds Jackie took before, during, and after surgery; any hospital records of her husband's I can find. She says she doesn't want to move her crew in there, tipping everyone off that something is up, so I'm being asked to cooperate—only if I want to. It makes sense and I'm okay with it. After all, I started this whole thing by calling the feds.

Also, I'm to get on the EHR system—the hospital's Electronic Health Records archive—and search for a "Salaam." I'm hesitant—hospitals watch for snooping and stalking shit—but she assures me that she'll cover any blowback, as she calls it, from me nosing around.

Carolyn gives backstory on her visit. She's recruiting me as a principal investigator in a clinical trial for a new nonnarcotic post-op analgesic. She hands me an impressive investigator brochure with her bogus business card attached.

"Don't ask." She laughs, proud of it.

"Don't worry, I won't." I shake my head. "But it's very cool that you have this."

"Well, you just stay cool. Don't do anything rash. If anybody asks, we're prepping for a clinical trial. I'm going to do some homework and be in touch soon. Here's my mobile just in case you need it, okay? And, seriously, thank you, Doctor."

We stand, but I hesitate, running a finger on the card. She tilts her head, knowing there's more.

"So, Miss Talbot—Carolyn," I say as I slump, "just one more thing." Christ, I'm goddamn Columbo.

"Sure, Doctor—Vince, what's up?" she asks, jabbing my "Miss Talbot."

"Well, relationships. Just to be complete, I mean, I should have told you, but it's hard for me." I hold a breath, then, "Wow, this is hard!" I say with a laugh, then blurt, "I was engaged once. Back in the late nineties."

"Ohhh," she says, slouching, going eye to eye. "Okay, well, what happened? How did that end? I mean, sorry to ask, but any scandals that could erupt?"

"It ended in 2001."

"Okay, so a while ago. Are you two still acquaintances, still friends?"

Those words usually stack like bricks between me and whoever utters them. But not today. I look to the floor, shuffling, then back into her eyes. She reaches for my arm and squeezes, saying nothing. Her hand moves to my shoulder, and it takes all of me not to melt on her.

"It ended in New York on 9/11."

"Oh! Vince, I am so, so sorry." She embraces me—a professional, government-issue hug, but one that's all comfort—and no "you poor thing," tap-tap-tap.

I'm sure she's been there, felt this. I compose; she graciously says she'll find her way out. When her voice fades, I go to the window facing the parking lot and watch her vanish.

# SEVENTEEN

**THE FRONT OFFICE STAFF ARE** finishing the day as I sit at my desk with Charlie Parker on Sonos. I can't focus, and it's not Charlie's fault.

My locked-away photo album that I unfold transports me to times, to feelings with Helen. Pictures of Helen, her ever-present earbuds cranking tunes from her iPod so loud she'd turn heads on a subway.

But inevitably come comparisons with the coup de foudre I've just experienced. Genuine, or just my pituitary sending me my latest fix of oxytocin? No. This ain't just another hit of the cuddle hormone. Please, there's nothing I'd rather do than run my hands with slow deliberation over every inch of Carolyn. But so much more, I want to watch her think, hear her sarcasm, her innuendos, her confidence—I want all of her. Next to me. Woven inside me.

Her eyes told me she's open to hear more about Helen but only if I want to spill. Funny, but this is the first time after mentioning Helen to someone I feel hope and peace, not hell and panic triggering my usual routine to frenetically hit the streets eyeing women, seeking ones who resemble her, or shuffling Starbucks change for coins struck in her birth year—saving those from the tip jar. It might just be dreams of a "next time" for Carolyn and me.

This is the usual stupid-ass thinking I produce with a wine buzz. But I'm sober—it's midafternoon for God's sake!

Then, the reality of why Carolyn and I ever connected slithers back as I sit, nonplussed by the weight of possibly holding the key to preventing another 9/11. Since it began with Jackie, I carried this weight alone until now. Until now, until Carolyn—her card, her fake name, her bogus brochure, her scent hanging on my shoulder since the hug. Her glass. I hold it up to the window slowly turning it, watching sunlight transform her lip prints into three-dimensional etchings. Pale pink prints that I study, then lightly roll onto my finger.

And this time, for once, I'm not trying to catch dreams at the bottom of a bottle.

# EIGHTEEN

I NEED A FRIEND'S HELP to recalibrate. That means either home alone with Kenny Chesney and Glenlivet 21 or out with my college pal, Henry Datillo. I must have drained the scotch a few days ago so I choose Henry. I pitch his downtown after-work hangout.

Tracey, behind the bar, lays three fat olives in the Y of a shimmering long-stemmed glass, rattling a shaker in her other hand. The mixture spills over them like a perfectly aimed icicle.

"I've been needing these a lot lately," I say.

Tracey smiles and says, "Oh? And to think I was more worried about Henry here," with a nod to my longtime friend.

The busy bar is well stocked with liquor and mementos, mostly black-and-whites of old Hollywood types who'd periodically escape to Santa Barbara for secluded recuperation or a romp with a paramour. Behind us the downtown after-work crowd settles at red-and-white checker-covered tables bristling with breadsticks and wine glasses.

"Yeah, Tracey was worried about me when I was in here an hour ago drinkin' by myself," says Henry, fumbling in his suit jacket for cigarettes. "Now, here's Doc ordering straight-ups at six o'clock and she doesn't seem so worried. Hey, how about loaning me a cigarette, Tracey. I just ran out. Got any Marlboro reds?"

Datillo is big, loud, prone to interrupting himself, and everyone's lovable friend. He has the perfect job for a locked-in-the-eighties big guy who likes big drinks, big steaks, big tits: entertainment law. Oh, and there's occasional side work for the teamsters, which we don't talk about. He's carved out his niche and is likely set for life. I respect him for getting there.

"Let her do her job!" I say.

"Okay, okay. Sounds like he really needs a drink, Tracey."

She glides my drink over and chuckles. "Hey, give the good doctor a break, Henry." She rolls two cigarettes out to him as we dip into our drinks. Two sips later, Henry excuses himself, taking the precious Marlboros out to the sidewalk. He's back in five minutes.

"So what's up? You call me, 'Let's meet. Joe's Cafe, tonight. Not tomorrow!' That kind of call from you, Vince, usually means trouble. Am I right?"

"No, I just needed to get out." I finger the stem of my glass, sneak a glance, confirming my friend sees right through me. "Plus, I have this problem with the FBI."

"You're shittin' me, right? What did you do, kill some patient—or wait!—sex with a patient? I knew it was just a matter of time, pal." Datillo thigh-slaps himself.

"No, dickhead. You are so—I hope you fuckin' choke on that drink." Too harsh. Okay, he can be an asshole, but he's never failed me. When Helen died, he was there, really there for me in a way that no one else could manage. "Okay, Henry, we trust each other, right?"

"Vinnie, of course. Vince, what the hell? You're scaring me now."

"So, I had this thing that a patient told me. I thought it might mean something weird."

Henry slides his stool closer and leans in, his royal blue foulard a pendulum between pinstriped lapels. "You're serious, right?"

"Yeah. I met an agent yesterday. At my office."

"What stuff are you talking about—drugs, right? You bust someone dealing opiates in Montecito? We're gonna get clipped tonight, right?"

I shake my head at the mirror behind the bar.

"Stockbroker, then . . . white-collar greed in suburbia? Something new for a change, huh?" Datillo wants headlines.

"No!" I cringe to let him know I'm for real on this.

Datillo speaks to his drink, "Fuck you, then. Don't tell me."

"This agent, she said I should shut up about this, but—"

"Whoa, whoa, whoa. 'This agent, she.' For starters, bad grammar, pal. She? Wait a minute." He pushes his glass out for refueling and cocks his head. "What the fuck are you doing?" A pause. "Vince! I know that look in your eye, buddy."

I can't hold my gaze any longer without a grin. I turn away, but Henry presses on.

"Back up. What did this patient do? Tell me that story first, then we'll get back to *this agent, she.*"

"The patient didn't do anything. Apparently, she had an affair, then—"

"Madoń, I'm glad you're not my doctor! Have a little bounce, you call in the feds." Henry cracks up, laughing at his own joke the way he does. I follow because, well, because you just can't help it when you're with Henry.

"If you want to hear this, jackass, shut the fuck up! She comes in to the ER with an ectopic—tubal pregnancy, not in the uterus, right?" Datillo's bobbing head doesn't care to understand. "So, she tells me about her lover who she wants me to call if she dies"—I wave to dismiss—"then in the recovery room she starts babbling all this junk."

I take a breath; he interrupts. "What junk?"

I snap away, buzzed and slightly irritated, then continue. "She made a reference to getting some Russian antiaircraft missiles. They're called Grails. One dude can hold it and shoot down a helicopter, jets. An airliner, if you wanted."

"What . . . the . . . fuck?" Henry drops his volume. There's a pause followed by an almost compassionate smile, like he thought I was crazy. "How do you? I mean, Vinnie, why? What did . . . ?"

I bark, "I don't know shit, I mean, for sure. I just have this 'feeling.'" Air quotes. "And her husband works for BC AeroSystems. They make missiles, crap like that."

Henry's rocking nod hints he's buying in, then the tedium of friendship returns.

"You're losing it, right? You're bored." He laughs, then stares, stone cold.

I shrug, nothing more to say.

"Okay, so forget about all that. What about 'this agent, she?' Maybe that will make more sense to me." Datillo can raise an eyebrow with millimeter precision.

"Go to hell," I say, feeling my blush. "She was nice. What? What are you staring at?"

Datillo's grin breaks into a highball laugh. I have to join.

"She's nice, huh? Is she a tough-broad cop? Did she teach you some karate or cuff you for a twenty-minute frisk?"

"Are you finished? Are you done?"

"Well, tell me! What's up?"

Tracey wanders back. "Another Tito's, Doc?"

"Ahhh, why not, Tracey. Thanks." I torture Datillo and take my time on each olive in the glass. "Well, I told you, she came to my office to hear about this patient, and . . . well, she was . . . gorgeous. Well, not really gorgeous, just something about her. No words spoken—her eyes held it all—and whatever it was went right to my soul. Made me crazy." My brain's numb, nothing coming after my soliloquy. And I've come to know Henry's vacant stare over my head means I've sent him to another world. Longing for what I felt today.

I continue. "She's not . . . I mean, I expected, you know, a fucking FBI agent. But she was, I don't know. Normal. And she's not married. Well, I mean, I never asked her, but no ring."

"You're nuts, pal," Henry says, grinning at the floor.

I ignore his diagnosis. "She's gonna meet me again somewhere, maybe my office, after I get some info for her on—"

"Look to your right"—he raises a finger—"in three . . . two . . . one, turn now."

I turn as two cookie-cutter beauties glide behind us.

"Jesus, God, Henry. Listen to me! Stop with the women. You follow the news, right? ISIS, al-Qaeda, everyone's been talking about this since 9/11, especially after we got bin Laden. Then there's the mess we left in Afghanistan with a drone strike on an ISIS-K car bomb that turns out to be an aide worker and seven kids. Border patrol's picking up bad dudes crossing the southern border every day."

I see he understands, then talk into my drink. "The *agent, she* is very professional. Sharp. Intelligent. No attitude." I turn for approval, but all I get is his first serious face since I sat down.

"Here's all I know, Vince. First, if you believe this airliner shootdown shit is real, you have to take it on one hundred percent and kick fuckin' ass. Like you always do. Remember, I'm here for you."

"I will, and I appreciate that, Henry." I wait out one of his dramatic pauses.

"Second, I haven't seen you mentally screwed up like this over any woman since Helen, rest her soul."

He's on the money. I look over my drink and sip, waiting for the usual crush of guilt amid the vacuum of Helen's loss to ambush me. It doesn't. "She's un-fucking-believable, Henry."

The ambush of a different sort is a hostess with menus and a cheery, "Your table's ready." We rise and follow, then Henry stops and turns. "I'd say you were right, Vincey. Sounds like you got a problem with the FBI."

# NINETEEN

COOKING FOR ONE IS THE gateway to suicide. I mean, let's face it, cooking is something that you do *for* someone. You go out, buy fifty dollars' worth of groceries and a forty-dollar bottle of Pinot Noir, then your place smells great as you juggle the pots and pans, and you have great fun putting it all together, talking to yourself while listening to Miles Davis, Diana Krall. But in the end, you sit there alone. With a mess to clean up.

It makes you think about all the mawkishly happy couples you see, publicly fawning over and kissing each other until you want to go out to your car, get your Louisville Slugger, and do them some serious harm. But you don't, because you see yourself there in that picture, in the not too distant future, feeling it all, inhaling her into you until your fingers electrify with her heartbeat, her breath, her existence, her presence, and as you look into her eyes, you can feel her rearranging your DNA, making you understand how the two of you will weave yourselves into this cruel and capricious universe.

That's why I eat out most nights.

But after a day weirding around in medical records, searching for all the stuff Carolyn needs, tonight feels like an order-in night. I dither through favorites on my phone while sipping a nice Grenache when my landline—a holdover from an era when cellular was way too iffy for doctors—rings.

"Damn." Unknown number. I'm not on call and ignore it until med school guilt kicks in. A crew in the OR might need help.

"Hello."

"Hi." Then a nothing pause, but I know this smiling voice. Carolyn's?

She asks, "I was in the area and wondered if you got any of the info that we need?"

*We* need. That feels good.

Before I answer, she continues, "It's all right, your phones are okay. At least for now."

"Oh, hi, Agent Talbot. Yeah. I'm sorry, I wasn't sure, uh . . ." *Why does this woman reduce me to a chopped-phrased jackass?*

"Listen, can we meet somewhere?"

I run inventory: decent jeans, gray T-shirt, and quarter-zip sweater. "Well, I look like a slob, but I know a couple of casual places."

"I look like a slob too, so relax," she says.

"Well, I doubt you look like a slob, but . . ." My words fall like stones into a bottomless abyss of silence. Strike two. "How about San Ysidro Ranch?" *Shut it now, Vince.*

"Okay," she laughs. "I'm just down the street, so I'll pick you up."

Jesus, my place is a mess, but I feign excitement. "Perfect."

"Be right there."

I pause at the hall mirror—acceptable, but too late, regardless. I can always play the "up all night saving lives" card. A knock. I pull the door and get a blast of spring's blossoms or Carolyn. Or both.

She's got that goddamn model-pose down, leaning with one leg forward, a long arm down its side, opposite hand on hip. She lowers her head, lifts an eyebrow, and gives me a smile that's impossibly coy.

"Hi!" I say, backing up, only to crack my elbow on the door's edge. A brilliant pain shoots down to my fingers. "Come on in." I extend a numb hand.

The entryway light reveals a little roughness in her face that I want to stroke and perfect teeth I want to kiss. Is there mandatory slammer-time for that, or would she just shoot me on the spot? Her hair, unlike our first meeting in my office, is down and tickles her shoulders. She's wearing jeans and an oxblood leather motorcycle jacket over a cable-knit sweater, obviously cashmere, in a lavender that plays off her eyes.

I'm guessing about eight, maybe nine hundred a layer, and I still haven't checked out her shoes. She's so well turned out—studied casual, let's call it—I wonder what the hell they pay FBI agents. She floats in, a gracious slouch bringing her down to my altitude again.

"Hey. I'm glad I caught you tonight," she says.

I step out of the way, feeling a nice frisson as I follow her into my living room. Same perfume, a headier dose of it. Purple suede tassel loafers, by the way. Add another eight hundred. Wait. Prada logo, so let's make that eleven-fifty.

"Do you have company? I hope I didn't interrupt anything."

"Not at all. I was just thinking about maybe ordering in. I mean, how about you, are you hungry, Agent Tal—?"

"It's Carolyn," she cuts in. "And no, I'm all right."

I lean back, hands on the counter. "That didn't sound very convincing. Are you sure you're all right?"

There's no small talk on its way, giving our eyes time to lock, something we've avoided since her arrival at my door. Finally, her blue eyes tell me in silence, *Yes, you're sensitive. You feel it. I am not all right.*

"I could make—"

"No," she says, an edge on her now, after our little eye tango. "I mean, maybe some other time. Let's go to . . . the Ranch, was it?"

"Great, you'll love it. I'll drive." Did she just say *some other time*?

"I mean, as long as you don't have plans."

*Like I wouldn't frickin' cancel an audience with the frickin' Pope to be standing here with you right now.*

# TWENTY

TUCKED INTO THE TWISTS AND ridges of the Santa Ynez foothills is a precious little drop of heaven called Plow and Angel. It's small, intimate, a little dark, and a stone and timber refuge of mine. Candles on linen paper–covered tables and a generous fireplace make it a perfect retreat for someone who spends time under soul-draining operating room lights and needs to relax with a glass of wine and some comfort food. And who has, well, not an antisocial side, but an anti-idiot side, let's say.

The valet takes my car, and I lead Carolyn along the rosemary-bordered walk through a bougainvillea pergola to the hostess inside the glowing archway. Tonight it's relatively empty except for a foursome of elderly regulars and a few families scattered about the room.

We gravitate to the fireplace and I help her out of her jacket, slipping it onto the back of the chair she chooses—not facing the door, as I would have guessed from my vast knowledge of spy movies—but facing the bar and most of the tables. That leaves me the Sicilian spot—my back to the wall and a full view of the comers and goers. The server brings menus, a plate of olives and radishes, then takes our drink order, a chilled Sancerre and my usual Tito's.

We small-talk the menu, the ambiance, then, aside from Carolyn's laughter tinkling among the glasses, there's only Stan Getz's "Desafinado." I offer a toast.

"*Saluti a te.*"

"Cheers." She sips with more of that lowered-head eye contact.

We order cheeseburgers—hers gorgonzola, mine cheddar.

"Instead of fries, may I get the mac and cheese?" I ask, then pre-empt Carolyn. "We can split it, if you want."

"That sounds perfect."

*Goddamn right it's perfect.* "So what's it like?" I ask, almost a whisper.

She squints across the top of her wine glass. "What's what like?"

I lean toward her, palm extended. "You know, being an FBI agent. Like carryin' a gun and stuff. Where is your gun, by the way? I mean, are you all wired up right now, like with guys listening out in that van I thought I saw in the parking lot? Have you ever shot anybody?"

*Holy hell, did I just say all that out loud?* Well, being an impatient man, I go for broke, wide-eyed and laughing at my own jokes. God, I suddenly realize I'm more like Henry than I thought. But she encourages me with crossed arms, eyebrows snapped together, and silent giggles.

Then Ms. Serious glances around and gets close, chin on inter-locked fingers. "My purse," she whispers.

"Your purse? Did you leave it in the car?"

"The Beretta's in my purse, and if you don't settle the hell down, I'm going to pull it." Punctuation, a *do you understand* head tilt.

"Oh, okay." A moment passes, then our laughter turns heads. I raise my glass for another toast, and as I put it down I feel her gaze on me. Remnants of a smile are there, but more in the eyes, like she's about to weep. Or, she realizes she turns me into a full-blown, unmedicated, ADHD basket case.

Vodka on an empty stomach. Bad idea. I sit here wondering if Carolyn's another species of human. She's not knockout gorgeous, but close, and her deportment sends the message that she knows cool things, things of significance. And that's so goddamn sexy I want to take a bite out of her.

"Do you come here a lot? It's not where you called from the other night," she says.

Another sly smile, but I drill right back—*as if you don't know, Agent Talbot*. "No, I was at Lucky's the other night. I come here once a month or so. You gotta be in the mood. It can feel a little creepy with the stained-glass Saint Isidore portraits staring at you. Brings me back to choir boy days. Just needs Sister Mary Satan swinging that sword of a yardstick."

She throws her head back, laughing so hard I expect part of her drink to exit her nose. Finally, the I'm-in-control cockiness is gone. I want to stroke her cheek, breathe her in.

"They have great ribs here, and I see you're a fan of their pro- sciutto mac and cheese," she says.

"You've been here?" Vodka-fueled voices tell me she's cavorted here with Hollywood dudes or dumbshit bad boys. Yep, I see her writhing beneath some sweat-sopped drummer, his trucker hat on backward.

"I live in the area," she says, with the same *forgive my deceit, it's part of the job* feeble-ass smile, like when she came clean on her name. She's probably jivin' me on that, too.

"I wondered how you got to my office so quickly." I pause, no response. "I haven't seen you around Montecito."

"I travel a lot for work."

*I bet you do.* I gnaw the side of my thumb. "I hope this isn't wasting anyone's time, but I've got a bad feeling. Jackie convinced me something weird is going on."

"So, talk to me, Vince," she says, eyes softer now.

Cheek on a hand, I drift. "I really do feel that I know you."

"I'm just easy to talk to. An old soul, maybe." Her hands, flat on the table, slide toward mine, then pull back, inches from disaster. She checks for reaction, stiffens with a flip of her hair, then speaks to the wall. "So, go on. Talk to me." She tries for all the tea in China to go nonchalant.

"I copied the charts on Jackie and Brent but got kicked out of medical records by some IT maintenance guys before I could run a search on any Salaam R's. I'm going there tomorrow at lunchtime and—"

"Those were our guys, by the way."

I scowl, but she continues.

"They were there to flash-copy all the med records before any bad guys sent in a cleaner or you lost access."

I translate that as in case they find my desiccated body at the bottom of Cold Spring Canyon next month. I gulp some Tito's.

"Okay, you're the cop—excuse me, FBI, whatever—what do we have?" I'm a little ticked at Carolyn and her "IT guys."

"Listen, Doctor," she says.

My head tips, wild eyes exaggerating attention. (I need to give up drinking.)

"Okay, Vince, cut the shit. We're very concerned about what you're telling us. Your patient's husband works for a major defense contractor. Bad actors in agencies of terror often gain what they need through loved ones of well-placed employees within sensitive and strategic industries. You are not wasting my time."

Understood. Carolyn caresses her wine glass, slowly running her thumb and fingers up and down its stem and along curves of the bowl. After what seems like ten minutes watching her hands move, she looks at me.

"Do you know what Stingers are?"

I nod and say, "Small surface-to-air missiles that one guy can fire, right? I'm kind of a nerd for stuff like that, plus it came up when I googled Salaam." When one has no life outside of medicine, marathon-watching the Military Channel or *American Pickers* fits the bill.

"Four hundred Stingers that we gave to anti-Qaddafi insurgents in 2011—who later turned out to be al-Qaeda—are missing in Libya. CIA's spending eighty million, up from thirty million last year, to try to buy back the Stingers we gave to anti-Soviet guerrillas in Afghanistan. We don't know where they are, and we're sincerely worried about being outbid. Why? Terrorists. The Islamic State knows that in places like Afghanistan today there is no law and order. Heroin and weapons are the commodities. The Stinger is the best weapon of its kind, highly accurate up to seven miles. Soviet Grails are the '57 Chevy version of these—and I don't mean restored hot rods—I mean shit-box Havana taxicabs. Imagine a Stinger in a conveniently remote long-term parking lot at an airport in New York or Chicago."

"Or LA," I add, as if I know what I'm talking about. Saying it stuns me.

"How about a couple on nearby rooftops of every major airport in the Western world? There's a crap-load of these out there, Vince."

I try for stolid. Goose bumps betray me.

She's on a roll. "Have you ever looked at the arrival side of LAX? It's an all-day rush hour."

Carolyn plucks one of the crayons from the glass next to our candle and shoves the olives out of the way. She draws on table paper like a crazy person, laying down a horizontal red line. At one end of it she writes "LAX," and at the other "FUELR" with "7000" six inches above it.

She sees my blank face. "Check out runway Two-Five Left from the approach waypoint near Fullerton, named FUELR for short."

She draws another line sloping down from the "7000," forming the long side of a triangle where it apexes at LAX. "Think of this as a twenty-six-mile downhill highway in the sky starting seven thousand feet above Fullerton and ending on Two-Five Left at LAX. The spacing of slow and dirty jets gives you about ten in-range targets from seven thousand on down. That's just one runway, one airport. Factor in Two-Four Right and you're up to twenty simultaneous events at LAX."

"How could . . ." I shake my head, tapping fingers on the paper.

"Exactly, Vince. So this piece is not a waste of anyone's time."

I'm suddenly unnerved. "Should we be talking about all this here, in public?" I ask.

She laughs, a hint of sarcasm in her amusement. "Everything I've just told you is pretty much out there; it's common knowledge in law enforcement and the press, some of the press anyway. I haven't told you anything that's classified, the *really* scary stuff."

I can hardly wait.

Our waiter interrupts my stupor with food, and Carolyn scratches zigzags over her artwork. I let her begin, whereupon she cuts her burger in half and tears into it like it's her first meal of the day. And it probably is.

# TWENTY-ONE

**THE MAC AND CHEESE HERE** arrives not at a temperature for food, but one you'd find, say, in a steel mill or under the hood of a car. Her fork fractures its brown mantle, and through a wall of steam she motions for me to join her. I guess the FBI knows that I'm disease-free.

"How do you know all this LAX stuff? You're a pilot?"

She swallows hard, with a *shut the fuck up and let me eat* glare, then says, "Way back." Another truncated *don't go there* answer. Fair enough. Still, I'm curious after letting this siren's song put my career on a direct course for the rocks.

"Can't you guys just approach Jackie and her husband to get to the bottom of this?" I ask. She steels up, focusing on steam rising from the stoneware between us.

I push. "Look, I get it. I'm Mediterranean—Sicilian, for Chrissake—and you, you look Nordic. My approach is to sit down with adversaries, share some wine, some food, settle our issues. You probably feel better just lopping off their heads with a poleaxe."

She turns away, bouncing with stifled laughter.

"Oh my God. Vince, the last I checked, you Sicilians do the wine and dinner thing just to postpone the inevitable, right?" She's struggling to control her laugh, and it's infectious.

"Yes. We invented revenge," I joke, but my heart won't let it last. "Seriously, should we be worried? I mean, the two of us, tonight, right now? Could someone be after us?" I ask, my heart prancing in my chest.

Carolyn's eyes drop to her food as she reassures, "No," then looks up. "At least not yet."

"Jesus! You're serious. Should I buy a gun?" I collapse into the chair. "How will I know?"

"Relax. You won't, but I will. And the fact is we need you and your relationship with the Carters to get us as deep into this as we can go before we move on them or before they move on us."

"You mean move on me?" I ask.

"No fucking way—excuse my language; not gonna happen. You're nothing to them except for having been given contact information on a possible accomplice, and I'm going to get your ass out of that as soon as possible."

"How? They know I have the info, so I'm toast."

She moves closer, shifting up on her elbows, and I fixate on her gold necklace, a diamond horseshoe, swinging inches from me. The closer she gets, the deeper I inhale.

"Look at me," she scolds.

"I was admiring your excellent neckwear."

"I know."

"Nice horseshoe."

An eye-roll, then three resolute taps to the table. "Pay attention."

I end the game; this is getting real.

"Jackie Carter may have told lover boy you have his phone number, but it would be a stretch if she, her guy, or anyone with them would think that you connected the dots on this so soon, let alone called FBI on it. Normal people don't think that fast. They aren't obsessed with worst-case scenarios like you are, evidently. Like we are." She beams, places a gentle hand on my arm, and whispers, "Must be a doctor thing."

The "we" resonates once again. So does the armlock. I nod, looking dead into her soul, feeling we could stay like this all night, neither of us wanting to break off this chemical whammo.

"Thank you," I finally say, "but I need your help. I have no clue how to proceed since this happened, and . . ." I drop the *since I met you* part. "Medical shit? Bring it on, I can handle anything, but this sort of thing, well . . ."

The waiter rolls in, clears the table, and drops a dessert menu, suggests the chocolate soufflé, says it's like chocolate cashmere. We offer a half-hearted cringe before a simultaneous, "Sure, why not."

After a pause she continues, sotto voce, "Okay, so the rule is to be yourself. Period. You're a smart, seasoned professional. Do your doctor gig like you always do, and let me and my crew worry about keeping you safe and developing assets."

"Assets?"

"People. People to use. People that we need to identify, meet, then turn or burn. Or both."

"Jesus fucking Christ." My stomach pole vaults—this is starting to sound like fun, but my naive glee must be showing.

"I'm serious, Vince." She pauses, stroking the wine glass again. "We need you. I hate to lay it on with a trowel, but, dude, your country needs you."

I stroke my chin.

"What if I say no?"

She looks at the ceiling; ten fingers run through hair. "Then you go back to work. And we go on without you, possibly missing out on an incredible fucking piece of good luck that sashayed her ass right into your ER Friday night. We also lose an inside shot to run the hell out of some assets for HUMINT—"

I cock my head.

"Human intelligence," she says. "Intel on something we all know is coming our way. The next 9/11."

I close my eyes and I'm driving Helen to the airport when she left for New York. Then, a day later, she's missing somewhere in the incomprehensible crush of it. I replay haunting vignettes of the planes, the firemen and cops, the jumpers—the couple holding hands before stepping off into the September air. I see it all again, then unclench my fists and release the grip my teeth have on my lips.

"What if I say yes?"

Carolyn droops, emotion taking up both of us. She reaches for her purse—I expect Kleenex—but instead out comes the ziplock bag with Jackie's note. She lays it between us. I look at her, my palms up, my head shaking. In return all I get is a sympathetic smile and then both of her warm hands firmly clasping mine.

"Go see Jackie tomorrow. Go be the amazing doctor I know you are."

I sit, entwined in her grasp, encouraged by a zillion stars in the indigo sky I see through the doorway beyond her shoulders. Yet, the all-is-lost scenarios play out in front of me. There's no future in my "Carolyn and Vince" fantasy; maybe I'm just an asset she's working. I could get my ass seriously hurt or killed. Or I could screw up, blowing what may be an opportunity to prevent lives lost from something more hideous than 9/11, if something more hideous is even conceivable.

But what if this was 2001 and I had a handle on something that could have saved Helen and others? Helen. If she were somehow here today, would she be telling me to save the Helens that other people love?

Carolyn reads my drifting mind, giving three quick squeezes of my hands. All doubt vanishes when I look up and focus on the reality sitting before me, a stunning heroine in an Old Norse saga. And she's wearing a horseshoe. Heels pointing up for good luck.

I pause, then say, "Hell yes."

# TWENTY-TWO

AS THE VALET STOPS MY car, I open the door for Carolyn.

"Getting the door for me? Nice."

"What? You've been dating Neanderthals?" She and the valet like that one. Behind the wheel, I let out a breathy sigh and shake my head. Carolyn places her hand on top of mine on the gear shift, and in an instant we're winding down the mountain.

"Vince, this is investigative work, just like a physician trying to solve a patient's problem. That's all it is. You just have to play along. And the beauty of this is you'll gain invaluable intel." She pauses. "Information, I mean, just by doing normal doctor stuff."

"I'm not a very good liar, you know."

She laughs. "Are you kidding? How about the 'this won't hurt a bit' fucking bullshit you dish out to us?"

I'm loving her foul mouth. "You're right. What do you want me to do?" I ask, checking the rearview.

"Take Olive Mill down to Butterfly Beach," she says. "We'll go for a walk."

I should silently high-five myself, then pop an Altoid. But she's still a little scary.

Seconds after I get out of the car, the dank, flag-snapping wind off the sea has me cold soaked. Before I can protest, Carolyn makes it to the concrete railing above the sea wall. She swings over the wide slabs like a gymnast and sits facing the Pacific. I struggle doing what her long legs made appear effortless.

We stare in silence at barely visible islands and sparkling ships on the horizon, then she turns to me. "This is my favorite time of year, end of spring. Everyone expects sunny days, warm nights, and we get June gloom and chilly nights—kind of like punishment for perfect weather the other months."

"Yeah, but don't forget spring sunsets throwing out sparks. We're blessed to live here."

Head down, she nods, tapping her shoes together.

"So, Vince, you're good?"

"Yeah, I'm good. I just don't want to get you or me or anyone killed."

"You won't screw up if you just play it as if the Grails didn't happen. Tomorrow, she's just another post-op patient you have to make rounds on. And then, what? Send her home? Is she ready to check out?"

"Discharge." I chuckle. "'Check out' is death. She could have gone home yesterday if she hadn't lost so much blood. So, yeah, I'll send her home tomorrow."

"If you change her bandage, can you get us some tape from it?"

I'm perplexed, but then, of course: DNA. "Sure, but I can get you a ton of DNA without you having to scrounge for it on gauze."

"Actually, I want skin cells, and tape is perfect for that. What do you usually do with an old bandage?"

"There's a gauze two-by-two that I remove and red-bag in the dirty utility room. I'd tell a patient I'm leaving for a sec to toss it."

"Great, Vince, but if it doesn't seem right, just forget it. All I need is some tape that was in contact with her skin."

"I'll do my best."

"Okay, how would you normally handle the note, the lover, all of that?" she asks, waving.

"I'd tell a patient that I'm available if they want to talk, or I'd give them names of good psychologists or couples therapists. Some patients seem more willing to talk to me later on, like when they come in for their two-week post-op visit. It depends. She seemed more concerned about dying and never seeing her lover again, rather than fixing her marriage."

The onshore wind dies momentarily, the sixty-one degrees linger, and we shiver less.

She offers her palm and a question. "Let's say we don't have two weeks to wait. Is there a plausible way that you can try to force this conversation? Somehow try to—"

"I can tell she'll unload," I interrupt. "I mean, if she wasn't at death's door, she and I would probably still be sitting in that goddamn ER talking about this. It's something a doc feels."

"Can you make time to see her for an extended period tomorrow? I mean, not making it seem unusual, right?"

"Yeah, I have one case at seven thirty, a minor surgery that should be over by about eight."

"Holy moley, who the fuck is up working—cutting people open—at seven thirty in the morning?"

"Did you just say 'holy moley'?" We giggle and shiver. "That's when I do my best work," I say with a smug nod. The moon burns through a ring of mist, amplifying her eyes.

"Ha, I bet you do," she says, inching closer. "Well, tomorrow just go see her and tell her whatever you always say. Then give her the note. Tell her you kept it in your locker until you knew she was safe, and see how she handles that."

"I never write down details of what a patient tells me on shit like this. It makes them nervous, and then they tend to clam up. Do you want notes?"

A train horn blares behind us as the Pacific cranks up the wind. She sees me fidget.

"Come on, let's go back to the car," she says, holding on to my shoulder for balance as she spins around and hops off the railing, a perfect dismount.

Back in the car, I shiver, dial up the seat heaters, and say, "Thanks. I was getting cold. So I may not remember everything Jackie says."

"I'm going to give you something that will help us with that." She pulls out her iPhone and a short FireWire connector. "You have an iPhone, right? The one you called us with on Sunday night?" She holds out a hand.

"Yeah." I produce it, no longer suspicious about her knowing everything about me. She connects the two, dials a number, then sets them down and turns to me. I clasp my hands, biting my thumbs.

"Chill, Doc. This is all reversible. Your phone will continuously transmit to me and some analysts without you having to do anything. It can be anywhere on your person. Do you usually carry your phone on rounds?"

"Yeah, I'll have it in the back pocket of my scrubs. Or I can change into street clothes."

"Not necessary. Remember, stick to your routine. Just have it on you somewhere—even in a briefcase or backpack is okay."

"Really? How the hell is that possible?" I ask.

Mona Lisa smiles again. The connected phones simultaneously beep; she separates them. "Just so you and your other patients have privacy, we won't activate this until after you're at the hospital and done with that surgery, I'm assuming around eight, right?" She waits for my nod. "You'll know that it's activated because we'll send you a text message from a CVS pharmacy telling you to call them regarding a prescription refill request, patient name Ann Baker—the name I used when we met. If you don't see that text between seven and eight, call me. But you'll see it. Anytime after that text, go visit Jackie. Make sense?"

"Jesus, I guess so," I say, then hear her huff.

"Look, Vince, you'll be great. All you have to do is go in there and be her doctor, let her do all the talking, and let's see where she takes us. Remember, this is just the beginning, so we may get nothing from her tomorrow—and that's okay. I don't want you to pry or interrogate or do anything that might appear suspicious and sabotage your relationship with her."

I shudder, my talkative self nowhere to be found.

"Your phone also lets us know where you are at all times. So, let's say they're on to us. If we hear anything sketchy, I'll have people there that can move in immediately."

"All right," I murmur.

"I'll be in touch with you tomorrow evening when you get home, so keep your phone charged and with you. We'll talk next steps then," she says with the smile you'd expect to see from someone you just bought a house from—a fixer-upper, say.

Driving back to my house, my mind churns, certain she's using me as bait. I pull my car next to her BMW and shut it off.

I expect her to eject, but she sits, eyes ahead. I want to put a hand on her thigh. I don't. But it's the thought that counts.

"Nice car," I say.

She chuckles with some restraint. "Same to you," she says, her eyes landing on me a few seconds too long. She breathes deep, looks through the sunroof before letting it out with a breathy, "Okay."

I take it as my cue to open the door for her, but as soon as I move, her hand tightens on my arm. I turn to her, holding my gaze as long as I dare.

"This is going to work out, Vince. We'll be okay. I can feel it."

I'm not so sure what "this" refers to. "Yeah, we will. I feel it too."

I stand alongside her car, intent on watching her leave. The ignition starts, but before dropping into gear, the driver side window rolls down silently. I approach her frisky grin through the opening.

"Remember, we're just going to play doctor tomorrow."

I respond with a head-shaking laugh, then she's gone. And, frankly, this is huge fun, except I keep picturing myself kneeling in some abandoned warehouse with a black hood draped over my head, about to be decapitated while Jackie Carter and Salaam watch.

# TWENTY-THREE

**WELL, AFTER A NIGHT OF** thrashing I was due for some good luck. My patient showed up on time, had nothing to eat or drink after midnight, and anesthesia was on time—the trifecta of outpatient surgery. At five to eight I hear Carolyn's bullshit text from "CVS Pharmacy," and I'm on my way to see Jackie.

She's at her room's door in street clothes—if that's what you'd call designer jeans and a form-fitting T-shirt under a Hermes bomber jacket. She raises a welcoming arm and beams, as if ushering me in to a dinner party.

"Hey, Doc, how are ya? I'm glad you're here early. I showered and wore the tee so you could check me out without me getting back into one of those dreadful gowns. Does it still look like I can get out of here today?"

I wonder how much caffeine she's had already. "Hi, Jackie. Yeah, everything's great. How do you feel?"

"I feel amazing! You did well, Doc."

"Hey, just did our job. You get the credit for being healthy to begin with." My agenda hounds me and I rush. "How about lying down so I can check things out?"

She maneuvers herself onto the bed and hikes up the T-shirt.

"I'm going to just gently check the incisions and put a new bandage on the big one by your belly button, okay?"

She nods. I hit the hand sanitizer and don gloves. Her abdomen's flat, only mild bruising around the wounds. I carefully remove the larger gauze dressing over her umbilicus but hold it in my palm as I strip the glove off so that it ends up inside it.

"How do they look, Doc?"

"They're really great, healing well. I'm going to replace one bandage to protect them on your trip home. Tomorrow after you shower you can take it off, but call me if any area gets red or tender, okay?"

She nods and I continue with the post-op do-and-don't stuff as I scoop up all of her old bandages.

"Think of any more questions you may have while I get rid of this stuff. I'll be right back."

I run to the door, expecting her to ask me where I'm going with her DNA. Not a word.

In the hallway I maneuver around a visitor leaning on a linen cart near her door. I expect it to be Brent, but it's not, and I don't think it's the limping creep either, although he doesn't move. I catch a glimpse of his jet black eyes as they dart from mine to the soiled bandages in my hands, the turned-out gloves, including the one with the skin cell–laden surgical tape inside it. Is it my paranoia, or does his gaze linger there longer than necessary?

I fumble, saying, "Oh, excuse me, sir!" He raises both hands in silent apology, backing away from the linen cart like a surrendering gangster. His movements shout the rancid odor of cigarettes. Cigars maybe?

In the dirty utility room, I open the biohazard bin and dump all but the glove containing her large dressing, which I compress gently and slide into the back pocket of my scrubs. I knock on Jackie's door again, expecting to see the hallway guy in her room, but she's alone. Tobacco again.

"Any other questions, Jackie?"

"Nope, I'm good, Vince."

I reach into the shirt pocket of my scrubs and hand the note to her with a grin. "Here. I think you've survived."

She crumples it, throws it into the trash, and stares after it, as if making sure it doesn't jump back out of the can. "Oh, Vince, what a year this has been."

I slide a chair to the bedside. "Hey, we all have up and down years, right?"

Finally she looks up at me with moist eyes. "After the kids were grown, I felt so alone. Brent was alone too, I think. We had nothing left between us. Then he"—she glances back to the trash can—"my . . . friend, just showed up and became . . . well, he became everything. I couldn't stop it—we needed each other more and more as time went on."

So true. I nod.

She smiles a crooked smile, head cocked to one side. "There's no future in it, though. He knows I'd never leave Brent."

"Well, I guess it's hard to start over, even with your kids grown and all. Then there's all the legal messiness."

"Oh, that would be the easy part." Again, a nod to the trash. "He could buy and sell ten Brents if he wanted to. It would be easy for Brent, too. He could have everything here to play with, including all his girlfriends. But I don't want to hurt our kids."

She wells up and I reach for tissues. Déjà vu of the ER.

"Did you meet him in town?" I try to help Carolyn, but I'm also curious.

"He did some business with Brent, then we socialized when he would come to the States with one of his gals. He was never married, although he did have a bride-to-be or whatever they call them in Saudi. She was on the plane the navy accidentally shot down over the Strait of Hormuz in '88." She looks at the floor, shaking her head.

"Oh my God, that's awful, Jackie." I remember the day, an American embarrassment right before the Fourth of July.

She stares at me, emotionless. "That took awhile for him to get over. But I helped him."

*Tell me about it,* my brain silently urges. I reach for her hand. "I bet it did. I'm sorry to hear that, Jackie."

"Oh, he's over it now. He's at the point where we can talk about it. That's the best gift we've given each other, being open and honest without having to weigh every thought before speaking."

I nod but dearly don't want her to ask about my life, pry open my emptiness—not with Carolyn and team listening.

"But, you know," I falter, trying to move the topic along with no clue where to take it. I slide my chair back and we sit in silence. "Jackie, I can get you some names of people to talk to if you want. I mean, you can always talk to me, but I'm not a counselor, and I think a professional—"

"Vince, I don't need a counselor. I have something in this relationship that most people never experience." She breaks into a broad grin. "I'll need counseling if Salaam ever leaves me."

There's nervous laughter. "Jackie, I'm here if you ever want to chat about this. How about if we do your post-op visit in about a week, but call if anything—medical or otherwise—becomes a problem, okay?"

As I suggest this, I picture Carolyn and crew cussing and gritting their teeth that I just put off any further probing of Jackie's motives for a week or more when they want information now. But hey, Agent Talbot told me to do exactly as I would normally do. So this is me.

"Okay, Vince. You've always been great to talk to, and I appreciate that—your patients all love you and this is why. Don't ever lose that."

I give her a hug. "Thanks for saying that, Jackie. It means a lot to hear something like that."

"Well, I mean it, Doc. You don't just go through the motions; you're the real thing."

I leave her room genuinely elated by her words and glad that Carolyn heard it. It's an only child thing—constant need of praise, adoration. I'm also fearful that I may have heard this praise just after committing career suicide. I walk to the locker room loaded down with remorse, a surveillance device, and a pocket full of Jackie's DNA.

# TWENTY-FOUR

**AS I LEAVE THE DOCTORS'** parking lot, a gray Camry full of swarthy dudes in sunglasses slows to let me exit. It reminds me of the car that came to life when I left Butterfly Beach after the NPR Grails story. They follow me to the hospital's main entrance, then to the 101 on-ramp. The rearview reveals all four laughing, passing around a cell phone. I can't make out the license number, but it's a Nevada plate. For some reason I can't put my finger on, I think they're facilities management guys—probably nothing. No need to panic. But once on the 101 I nail it, hitting ninety, go two exits past mine, then take back roads. Just to be safe.

At home, that oh-so-potent mixture of Catholic guilt kicks in and has me reaching for a bottle of Vermentino. I top off a clear plastic glass with the straw-colored liquid. Then another. I'm thinking a good marksman could grease me through the kitchen window, so it's out to the patio. As I settle into a lounge chair, I get a call from Unknown. Against better judgment, I answer.

"Hey. Are you alone?" It's Carolyn.

"Hi. Yeah, just sitting outside. Uh, hate to admit it, but having an adult beverage, actually." How long until she realizes I'm always alone? And always drinking? "I guess it's never too early, right?"

"Listen, can we get together to talk about our clinical trial?" Interesting. She doesn't trust me yet or knows my house is bugged.

"Absolutely. Just say when."

"How about now? I'll pick you up in a half hour, and bring that stuff we talked about with you, okay?"

"Sure. I'll be ready."

It was light, chippy Carolyn, her voice smiling, but I wonder if I screwed something up. I throw on some jeans, T-shirt, and V-neck and pace until I see sun glinting off of her black BMW.

I buckle in and ask, "What's up? What the hell's going on?"

"A lot. I'll tell you when we get there." She holds out a ziplock bag for Jackie's stolen bandage, still inside the rubber glove, then drops it in her purse.

"Where?"

"My house."

So this is Big Trouble or, remotely, she's my Dream Come True Woman about to tell me I'm free to make a move on her. I see her pursed-lip smile as I run the calculus between those possibilities.

"Vince, you may have stumbled on to a very big enchilada."

I wish I hadn't given my brain the afternoon off. Food will help, so I throw out a test question. "Speaking of, have you eaten lunch?"

"We'll order in. I need you to focus on some critical stuff."

"Sounds good." I stare at her navy suit jacket, pencil skirt, and heels. This might be the wine talkin', but I want to reach under the steering wheel and run a hand from one of her ankles up to her crotch. Yeah, wine. I better not.

"Then I'll update you," she says, catching me glued to her legs. I watch the road spin by as we turn sharply into a hand-hewn stone entry with a wrought iron gate protecting a long driveway. She touches the nav display and the gate moves.

"Where are we?" I ask.

"My house."

"What the . . . you're kidding, right?" I'm stunned.

"I don't lie, Vince." She laughs. "At least not to you anymore."

"Jesus. Who the hell are you? I mean, really. This is your place?"

The curving path drops down between lavender and bougainvillea that's been there since the Chumash pruned it. Her laugh is infectious, and I giggle as we level out onto a circular courtyard in front of a two-story stucco Monterey Colonial with a terra-cotta roof. Calling this a house belittles the four or so acres that this dwelling consumes with room for eight or so bedrooms. I get out, able to see the shimmering chrome-blue Pacific and verdant mountains without turning my head—it's breathtaking. I look over the roof of the car to Carolyn, who seems not a bit smug, just happy to be home.

"Wow," is all I can muster.

"I grew up here," she says, swinging in a circle to take it all in.

"Does your whole family live here?"

"No." She kicks at the pea gravel of the driveway.

"Siblings, parents?"

She raises her head, proud, and says, "No, just me. I'm an only child."

"Oh my God, me too!" I want to ask about parents.

"What do you feel like ordering in?"

She gestures to the front door and I follow. She puts her thumb on one of those biometric thingies, and I hear a soft click. An entryway, big as my entire first floor, has a staircase winding around a central oriental with wildflowers on a pedestal. She cues up some Charlie Parker. I follow her over thick planks of a massive dining room that's got a bay window and fireplace, slowing to notice Central Coast oil paintings and maybe a Georgia O'Keefe or two mixed in. In the kitchen is a faded Persian runner that could cover a lane at a bowling alley. She's got a sixty-inch commercial Thermador with pot hangers, all the trappings. It's flanked by an island with four ladder-backs shoved up to stoneware place settings on its perimeter.

"I guess you like to cook, huh?"

"Ha, yeah. Love it." She laughs, hands behind her on the countertop between the range and one of several sinks. "But I never do. It's a bitch to cook for one, you know?"

"Totally."

She leads me over to a distressed-wood table and simultaneously opens a drawer in a mahogany sideboard. "Sit. Here are some menus."

"Well, whatever. I'm good, so—"

"Zip it, Vince, and tell me what you want. You've been boozing up and I need you to eat something so you're able to think with me." She tries to get serious, but I stare until she blushes and holds back a laugh. Then she surrenders.

"Okay, *Italiano*. Let's get pizza and a salad from Via Vai."

"Pick one out—I can eat anything. I'll be right down. I have to get out of these shoes."

"*Gratzi*," I say as she floats out of the kitchen on those goddamn long legs. Why change? The shoes are perfect.

A shout from the stairs, "Get the squash blossom pizza with burrata and cherry tomatoes. Little Gems salad. I mean, if that's okay."

"Got it." Well, she knows what she likes, just like me. I call the order in, and the person asks me if this is for Carolyn on Picacho Lane. A creature of habit. Just like me.

I venture from the kitchen to a clubby, paneled library and media area with inviting puffy couches and a few leather chairs. In the corner is a leather-topped cherrywood desk with a closed MacBook on it. The rooms are tasteful—nothing overdone. Just like her.

She reappears in Madras flats, white jeans, and a navy crewneck, combing through damp hair. I can't turn away.

"What?" she asks.

"Nothing."

"Okay, take this out to the patio." She pulls a bottle of Acqua Panna from the wine cooler and hands it to me along with two glass tumblers. "I'll bring lunch out as soon as it comes, but I want to print some notes for us."

Flummoxed, I set the bottle down, giving in.

"So, where are your parents?" I cringe, expecting a story of, say, assassination or salacious divorce, perhaps both.

She studies me, but before I can retract the question, she melts into a long sigh. "My dad was killed working in the Middle East—civilian contractor—long story."

"Oh, Jesus, I'm sorry." I put a hand on her shoulder.

"Yeah." A wave, another sigh, and it's dismissed. "Then a year later my mother—totally healthy"—a hand arcs toward the tennis court—"my athletic mom, just . . . fucking . . . dies," she says with a soft laugh. "In her sleep. Her doctors said she died from a broken heart, I guess."

There's an unhurried look into each other's eyes. I don't go clinical, talking takotsubo syndrome.

"Does that ever really happen, Vince?"

"Yes."

"Honestly?"

"I'm certain it does." I tighten my grip on her. "It happened to me."

# TWENTY-FIVE

**OKAY, CAROLYN WANTS CLINICAL. SO** I do a crash course in broken heart cardiomyopathy, explaining how toxic levels of my own epinephrine and norepi messed with my left ventricle, led to bouts of chest pain, shortness of breath, dizziness, and finally a fervent desire to check the fuck out. All this after 9/11, after Helen died. There, I said it.

Before she can launch into anything, I escape from my feelings—and her sympathy—by stepping out to the patio, a sunlit entertaining area with fireplace, grill, wood-burning oven, full bar, seating for a million. In front of me are terraced gardens on sloping lawns, a pool and tennis court—all of it upstage of the Pacific. I sit at an umbrellaed mosaic table facing the ocean and a warm, heady breeze.

When I turn, through the bay window I see that Carolyn sits at the desk with her MacBook.

Since I lost Helen, loneliness prods me into impossibly dark places. Places where drumbeats hammer away, making me dread never again feeling all that one feels in a truly great love. Is my reaction to Carolyn—something I've not allowed myself to feel since Helen—what I felt back then? The Real Thing that ignites at first sight? More weird-ass quantum entanglement?

I hear the French doors, then Carolyn walks onto the patio balancing the pizza box, a couple of ceramic plates, the salad in a clear plastic box.

"Thanks for paying," she says, sitting down next to me.

"Hey, the non-Neanderthal thing to do, right?" I wink.

"Okay, my turn."

"Absolutely, you first," I say, pouring her water.

"Q and A."

Christ, now what?

"Why'd you quit?"

"You mean obstetrics?"

She nods, her mouth a grim line.

"I guess I thought I'd end up with a wife, kids, going to dinner parties, country club—the whole suburban dance of death—and couldn't stand the thought of being married to my job, too. So, I gave it up. Then . . . you know the ending."

"That makes sense. Go ahead and eat." She's merciful to shift gears, but I'm in a mood, and I just want to finish the logic, such as it was, behind my career decision—*our* career decisions.

"She . . . Helen left for New York two days after we celebrated our decision that I'd just do gyne. I wanted to be present, you know, totally with her. Not recovering from all-nighters like some goddamn zombie husband."

Her eyes dampen. "Help yourself while I give you the down-low on what we have so far."

I take a slice of pizza and some salad as she leafs through papers she's printed. She hands me a knife and fork, watching as I use them to cut the salad, then as I use my hand to fold and eat the pizza.

"Good. I just wanted to make sure you weren't going to cut the pizza and eat it with a fork like some chooch."

"Hey, remember?" I gesture with a thumb aimed at my sternum. "Italian."

She folds her arms and leans back with that brilliant smile.

"By the way, you know where chooch comes from, right?" I ask.

"No clue. I learned it in college."

"*Ciuccio*. Italian slang. Means jackass, idiot, moron."

"Well, I've met my share. Thank you for the etymology lesson, Doctor."

"You're welcome, Agent Talbot. Are you going to just watch me eat or what?"

She digs in, giving me a sheet to read. It's a time-stamped transcript of my visit with Jackie. She wants me to see if anything was heard incorrectly. As far as I can tell it's an exact record of what happened. "This is just the relevant convo between you and Jackie with all the background voices removed. We left one in. It sounded like you met someone in the hall about two and a half feet outside her door."

"Yeah, when I came out with the biohazard stuff there was a guy standing by a linen cart right outside her room. I was keeping an eye on the bandages and apologized for almost slamming in to him."

"Did he say anything?"

"Uh, I don't think so. He just raised his hands as if to say, 'No problem.' Then when I came back he wasn't there and I thought he'd be in her room, but he wasn't. Kinda weird since he was right by her door. But maybe he was waiting for someone else. He smelled like he just had a cig."

She nods. I get the deposition feeling again; my heart races.

I read to the point when I was dumping Jackie's bandages and pocketing her DNA, and see an entry highlighted in red:

SOUND TO BE IDENTIFIED

# TWENTY-SIX

"WHAT'S THIS MEAN?" I POINT to "SOUND TO BE IDENTIFIED."

"I have something I want you to listen to inside, something my audio techs couldn't identify as a typical hospital sound."

"There wasn't any cleaning or repair stuff being used near her room. It might have been respiratory therapy, maybe a ventilator in a nearby room since—"

"No, we would have IDed any health care device or HVAC. This is odd. Just finish and we can listen."

"We" again. I flounder out of my element, but it's fun stepping onto the thin ice with her.

After lunch, a more real Carolyn, one with sorrow in her few wrinkles, speaks of cousins coming here to swim, play tennis, spending summer days at the beach or on the hiking trails. She tells me the place has been in her family since it was built in the thirties. I don't ask the obvious. She doesn't say who in her family holds the patent on beach sand to make all this affordable.

She turns from the view, very content, and says, "Come on, help me with this stuff and we can listen."

I shovel everything up.

"Thank you, sir. I'll get the door."

Her head-high walk, the confident walk I saw when I watched from the window as she left my office. A walk I'll never forget.

I follow to the study where I'm sucked into one of the plump couches. She sets her laptop on the coffee table in front of us. After a few clicks, the flat screen next to the fireplace blinks to her computer's desktop of a Santa Barbara sunset. She holds up a memory stick.

"Listen to this. Tell me what you think. By your location and the timing of the known sounds, you were most likely in the garbage room disposing of her bandage material."

"Dirty utility room."

"Oh my God. Whatever. Just listen, Doc."

"Is it a critical sound or something? I mean, who cares?"

"We do—we don't like not knowing things." She smugs up and clicks the WAV file.

The volume jolts me. She hits pause.

"Sorry, it starts really loud, but in a few seconds we've filtered out everything but the critical sound, then the level comes down. Just bear with me, okay?"

"No problem. My mother bought me an electric guitar when I was twelve, so I'm essentially deaf."

Eye-roll with head shake. "Spoiled brat. You have to tell me all about that sometime. Okay, here we go."

I brace, then hear the sound of a crackling bonfire—crumpling bandage wrapper—then Carolyn points to the screen showing a linear magenta graph superimposed over the waves of scrunching paper. It's much lower in pitch than the crackling, and eerie, like a recorded voice that's been slowed, played backward, or digitally altered. It's otherworldly to say the least, and I crinkle my face turning to Carolyn. It's "Revolution 9" on *The White Album*. Backward. Sideways. Who knows?

Another pause. "I know. Kinda weird, isn't it? Listen to it some more. You'll hear footsteps come in, then fade. They're in that lower frequency register close to this one, so don't get confused."

I nod and she hits play again. It's very regular, almost like a piece of machinery, say a washing machine beating out a one . . . and a two . . . three . . . and a four. A song in a four-four rhythm with some tied eighth notes thrown in. Strange. Then it fades with a Doppler shift like a passing train.

"Well, what do you think?"

She's eager, but I bite my lip and squint, unable to deliver. "I'm sorry. I can't define it, Carolyn. It's somehow familiar, but not in a way like it's something I've heard in the hospital. Could it be interference?"

"No," she snaps, palms up sharply. "We've cleaned the fuck out of this, the HVAC, the chatter in the halls, the flushing toilets, the sixty-cycle AC hum from your crappy fluorescent lighting. Everything."

"I know, hospital lighting is the worst, right?"

"Seriously, Vince. What do you think?"

I close my eyes. "Play it again."

After about ten seconds I hear something new and do the cut gesture across my neck.

"What's that midfrequency up-and-down droning, about once a second?"

"It's fifty-eight beats per minute, actually. It's your blood in that big artery going into the leg closest to whichever butt pocket you had your phone in."

"Femoral."

"Yeah, that one."

"Jesus fucking Christ, what'd you do to my phone?"

"Fear not, it's back to being your phone again."

"Yeah, right," I say and get the sideways smirk.

"Seriously, Vince, you have no clue on this?"

"Carolyn, I would love to figure this out for us. And I hope this isn't wishful thinking, but it does stir something in me. I just can't put a make on it."

She swaps our Acqua Panna for Sancerre. "Okay, get it out of your mind, but promise me that as soon as you wake up tomorrow, you'll listen to it." She brightens up. "An old navy trick my dad taught me to help zero in on something elusive."

"Okay, you gonna give me a flash drive with it?"

"You already have it. Check your iTunes 'recently added' folder for 'Carolyn's Song.'"

"What the hell are you guys doing to me?"

She blushes. And I know there's a little bit more.

# TWENTY-SEVEN

**"YOUR NEW PASSWORD IS BURRATA469,** all caps."

"You're kidding, right?" I flush with anger and she's on it.

"Listen, Vince, things may start moving fast, so you just have to trust me. There are things that I can't explain to you." She pauses, turns away, then back. "Even though I want to, I just can't."

Her face kills my pique. "No, I understand."

"Vince, this could be serious—incredibly serious, frankly—so I need you to stay cool and just work with me and my team, okay?"

My Sancerre's nearly gone. "Of course I will. I told you that at dinner." I study my glass, then her, and she tilts closer. I breathe in the ethanol on her breath.

"How serious?" I press for more. "Are you allowed to tell me that?"

The corners of her mouth droop; a hand lands on my arm.

"We worked the number Jackie gave you—Salaam's number— and it turns out he's been on a watch list as the first of many Libyan and Syrian top-leadership bad guys that crossed the US southern border. But he cleaned up his credentials, then went dark, and we lost all trace. And no Jackie connection. Until you showed up, Doc." Her eyebrows rise.

Hurrah. I sink back in the couch. Waiting for a Milk-Bone.

"We'd hoped some of his friends would get sloppy once in the States and lead us to him and others who are planning the next big thing—not the one-off, call-to-arms, chicken-shit stuff these clowns have been pulling over the past couple of years. But it seems like Jackie made Salaam trip on his dick at some point—the most reliable tradecraft, by the way. Even better in the wild like this, when we just sit back and watch." She sips wine; my coronaries dilate, relax.

I ask, "You mean like all these mass shootings, trucks into crowds we've been seeing?"

"Chicken shit," she says. She's looking over her glass at me, again with that damn eyes-half-closed smile. But this time it's Marilyn Monroe, not Mona Lisa.

I'm picturing her somewhere exotic. Performing tradecraft.

Over protests, my glass is refilled. "It's okay. Remember, I'm driving?" She kicks off her shoes, hugs her knees to her chest, and starts slowly, rhythmically rocking. "Salaam just made contact with people on the East Coast who know how to pull off a coordinated Stinger attack. If they had them."

I move to the window seat and park it. The ocean is no help but gives me time to let this big enchilada simmer. Her expression says she'd let me sit forever.

"Okay, what do we do now?" I ask.

"My team and I are going to stay close to you, like I said before, just in case." Another eyebrow lifts and her rocking tempo picks up. "Just give me a little runway on this, Vince. If Salaam's close to the top and Jackie told him she gave him up to you, even in doctor-patient confidence, then you may be perceived as a threat to them."

"Them?" No answer needed.

"Vince, I don't like that you're in this any more than you do, but you are."

"Fuck!" I shout. "Why did I call the FBI?"

"Do you think that's what got you into this?"

"I don't know. I don't know anything anymore."

"Excuse me!" she shouts. I jump. "But you got into this, like it or not, when Jackie gave you the name and number of the guy she's banging." Pointing at me now, louder, "That dumb bitch got you into this. And there you were—in it all by yourself. Then your good judgment, your sense of duty made you call FBI. And it was absolutely the goddamn fucking right thing to do."

I'm feeling Carolyn's stare penetrate me.

"Vince, you also got pushed into this by Helen." She comes over, taking my hands as she kneels. "And you're still in it, but you're not alone anymore. You're in it with me. And I'm not going to let anything happen to you. And we've got a fucking army of professionals to keep us safe and get us to the truth."

I watch her slender fingers weave into mine. I move to her brilliant eyes. Game over. "I know you're right. We have to stop them. How do we do that?" I ask, wanting a compass.

Carolyn sits back on her heels, cheeks puffing as she exhales. "You're our link to Jackie, Jackie's our window on the cell—we keep workin' the hell out of that. Meanwhile, my team will see what her DNA and proteomics tell us about the who, where, and when of her."

I nod, no longer questioning the bag of tricks at her disposal, especially after the legerdemain she pulled off with my phone.

She goes on, "You tell me what your routine is for the next few days, and I'll put together a scenario where I or one of my crew can protect you without being noticed. Trust me, we won't be noticed."

I tell her Thursdays I see new patients and post-ops in the office from nine to usually around four. I go home, grab something to eat, then go to Dargan's, a divine Irish bar with a great house blues band.

Their last set usually ends around eleven and I'm home in bed by midnight at the latest. The blues are worth a little lost sleep.

///////////

Carolyn drops me off at home but stops as she's leaving. I walk back, as she's framed in the car window, streamers of hair wafting over the best smile I've seen yet.

"This is my space, Vince. I work here. This is my OR. And you're in it with me and a bunch of other professionals who know what we're doing. Don't forget that." She adds with a chuckle, "Trust me, I'm a doctor."

I hope to hell she runs as tight a ship in her OR as I do in mine.

# TWENTY-EIGHT

**NOT MORE THAN FIVE MINUTES** after Carolyn left, headlights reflect off my kitchen wall. Unfortunately not her, but a white delivery van. I turn on the outside lights and watch from the door. It's a kid in a hoodie maybe in his twenties carrying a tall, stapled-up yellow and white flower bag like I've seen in patients' rooms.

"Doctor DeLuca?"

"That's me," I say, stepping outside.

"Delivery from Hogue Flowers from Jackie Carter," he says in uneasy English, inflections in all the wrong places. I'd guess maybe Eastern European.

"Thanks very much," I say. "And here." I reach into my wallet for a ten-dollar bill. "Thanks for working late."

He sticks out an arm on fire with a demonic, multicolored skull-and-sword tattoo, mumbling something while pushing money into his shirt pocket. I watch him back out, glued to his cell phone as the van curls recklessly back onto the street, then zoom off. Demonic tattoo plus weird accent—xenophobia, yes, but I stare at the bag and very gently set it down on the lawn, then run back to the house.

I take a big pour of Templeton's with me on my way to the backyard where I begin to text Carolyn. A text from her beats me to it.

> Just flowers. No bomb. So enjoy in silence until my crew can do a full bug sweep. ☺

> WTF! How do you know all of this?

> I have ways. I promised you we're going to keep you safe—go to bed!!

Then, another beep.

> If you're going to lose sleep, google portable neutron scanner. ☺

Well, I guess nothing says love like stalking.

I tear into the bag. There's a blast, but of color from a half-dozen dahlias in crimson, pink, and white, some variegated, in a pewter vase.

I howl and chortle, but they remind me of the trapdoor that opened in my perfectly safe, predictable life the morning Jackie Carter showed up in the ER. I turn to more whiskey, an ill-advised attempt to relax, and end up even more jazzed.

I replay the day, trying to make sense of her. Of Carolyn alone in that house, her mystery family, her decorous well-bred class interposed with foul-mouthed eruptions. By ten o'clock the bottle of rye is half gone, and so am I.

///////////

I make it to the six fifteen alarm, waking up feeling surprisingly refreshed. I'm eager to keep my word to review the sound first thing in the morning. I keep the lights off and reach for my iPhone.

Headphones on in case my flowers hide a bug, I enter the password that Carolyn gave me, tap "Carolyn's Song," and let it play as I lie in bed. With my eyes closed, I see myself in the utility room with the dressing from Jackie's wound. I try to picture the hallway scene, the usual morning routine of the nursing staff, food service, housekeeping, phlebotomists with their tubes of drawn blood—everything. None of it connects in any way to this damn sound. I play it over and over to the point that my hands are tapping out its rhythm on my bed. Nothing surfaces and I'm pissed. It has to be artifactual! Something this mutant iPhone picked up from outer space, the electrical grid or something. Worse, I'm sure that "Carolyn's Song" will stick in my head all day like some boy band's song. So far, the best part of the morning is Jackie's dahlias sitting on my kitchen table.

After a shower and a stop at Coffee Bean, I'm on my way to work, continually scanning all clock points, looking for someone with a car bomb or a Kalashnikov. Just after I park, my phone dings with a text. Carolyn.

> Good morning ☺

It makes me suspect she knew the instant I turned my car off. I'm good with that. As I begin to answer, another ding.

> Any luck?

Rest assured it will be in my head all day and
will keep working on it.

K. thx esp since just found out that no SCAM
covered that area. ☹

I ponder "SCAM."

???

surveillance-cam

I fumble to type.

Too bad!! But this is my big challenge.
I'll keep at it!!!

Her wordless reply another smiley face, but this one winks at me. Oh, the wonderful idiocy of modern digital communication.

I feel like a teenager and wish to hell this could be something purely social with her and not just my new second job. I'm too fucking old for a second job. And maybe too old for a Carolyn.

# TWENTY-NINE

**WHEN THE BAND TAKES THE** stage for its third set, the room is crowded and hot enough for Dargan's to give off its signature smell of bleach and bad decisions. I'm planted for the night in my usual spot—the section of the bar closest to the stage, reserved for deaf people or the insane. After the week I've just had, tonight I'll identify with the latter. Barkeep Patrick keeps me comfortably numb with Templeton's.

The room is filled with all the usual mistakes, the flirty UCSB twenty-somethings, a few cougar packs. There's one ageless woman who piques my interest—a fire of confidence and intelligence in her eyes—but she's a tad on the wrong side of skanky. Don't get me wrong, some skank is mandatory. But let's call it, say, "skank in moderation."

The guys are mostly variations on your basic thick-necked drunks—beards close-cropped, jeans, T-shirts. Most sport flat-brimmed trucker hats down to the ears in a way that would make a valedictorian look monumentally stupid.

The house lights dim and, against the sparkle of the stage, I catch a glimpse of blonde hair coming through the door from the patio. Plenty of women in Santa Barbara are faux blonde—light ash being the tincture of choice—and pumped so full of gels and silicone, if you fucked them they'd bounce. Any Pavlovian response of mine to a blonde was extinguished long ago, but she's different. Maybe it's the challenging lighting or my third Templeton's. She's on the tall side, thirtyish, fit but not in that insane Southern Cali way. And the hair—you could tell it took time and a boatload of money to land in the golden sweet spot straddling the fence between boardroom and escort service. More Paltrow than porn star. Then I see the walk of this perfect woman. The last person I'd ever expect to step into a bar like this—Agent Carolyn Talbot.

Even at a distance her smile says, "I can be a great friend. You will have an intelligent conversation with me." She skirts around the edge of the dance floor and I see more. A gray poncho draping like cashmere with wide diagonal black stripes, white cropped jeans, and black pumps. She scans the room, sweet, sure, and relaxed. Why the hell not? Everything's working.

She starts moving in my direction, and, of course, I assume I've been followed by someone or she's checking up on my sanity. Or maybe she's just a blues fan. Without a wave or other greeting, I assume this means I'm to relax and remain a stranger. I straighten up, suck in, and stare at the stage but can't avoid furtive glances her way every three seconds. I see her apologetic smile which, along with the fact that there are no nonregulars in the bar, I take to mean I'm not in danger.

She floats right by—no eye contact—to the corner of the room next to the front-of-house sound man. I catch the clean smell of something they spray on you if you make it to heaven. She stands at an empty table a few feet in front of me fussing with some of her accessories—a black clutch, Cartier Pantera (or a really good fake), some gold bangles. And, just my luck, the ultimate accessory, a ten-foot-tall jabroni who looks like a fucking Navy Seal emerges from the shadows.

But I say, who cares? I'm allowed to look, and women like this happen only a few times in your life. The truth of it is I couldn't avert my gaze if my life depended on it.

# THIRTY

**THE DANCE FLOOR ILLUMINATES, AND** there she is again. She's ditched the poncho as she was pulling Mr. Gorilla out of his seat. Not that I'm a great dancer, but he dances, well, like a gorilla. And he's totally disinterested in Venus undulating within arm's reach. She hovers, every part of her in rhythm as only sensuous souls are able to pull off—you can't teach that. She surveys the place and catches me gawking, watching her become one with the music in the midst of the heat and the crowd.

The next song ends and she rejoins Gorilla Man, who's retreated to their table. She sips amber liquid from a rocks glass that a server brought along with the guy's beer. They talk without her taking her eyes off the room, and our eyes meet again. This time she stops cold and walks directly to me. I freeze.

I inhale slowly—think Lamaze breathing—having been called out. When she breaks the five-foot perimeter, we giggle. I'm hoping to stave off a reprimand for not being discreet. Before she speaks, I raise my palms and plead, "Listen, I apologize. I know I've been staring at you all night, but I've been drinking and I must say you are—"

"Why didn't you dance with me?" she interrupts, moving right up, bumping my barstool and standing between my legs. I'm burning a thousand calories a minute with leg bouncing.

"Because you scare the hell out of me."

A hair-flying head shake, then another scan of the room.

"Is everything okay?" I ask.

She nods and whispers, "Yes. Just making sure no one's here who shouldn't be."

My legs slow, our eyes bond briefly. A head tilt, and I want to kiss her neck. I realize she's gripping my arm.

"So, is your boyfriend going to announce himself or am I just going to hear the gun going off?"

"Ahhhh, not my boyfriend. He's a friend of mine. From work."

"So then . . . we could hang out?" I go full throttle into life-is-short mode.

"Yeah." Then a calculation. "We could." She tips her head, again offering her neck but studying me. "I want a cigarette."

"You smoke?" Crap, blew it. "I used to." Okay, Vince, shut up.

"Well, just when I'm a little drunk," she says, leading me by the hand off the barstool and out the side door to the patio.

We get one of the small wooden tables, and I sit as Carolyn scans the scene. I wonder if something's up, but she walks over to a table of young women smokers. Looks back at me and mouths, "You want one?" I concede, she hands one of them a five-dollar bill, then returns, laying two American Spirits down between us. I reach for matches I stole from Lucky's, lighting hers, then mine.

It takes one puff to reawaken all my habituated flourishes, flips, and twitches, to turn me into a chain-smoking steelworker sitting at Dee's Cafe in Pittsburgh. It also immediately jazzes my cortex, sending a "big mistake" message to my pounding heart. Great drug, nicotine, but a wicked delivery system.

The side door opens and your typical plasticized, Botoxed, platinum blonde walks past our table to her friends.

I feel a light kick under the table. "What are you looking at, Doc?"

"Nothing. I thought she was a patient of mine, but I'm wrong."

Carolyn smirks, blowing a smoke ring at me.

"Actually, I think she's an actress. I saw her in a movie."

"Really?" She leans back, drawing out the question sarcastically.

"I'm sure of it," I say with a confident nod. "It was called *Student Nurses in Heat.*"

"Oh my God," she cracks up, "you're sick, but very funny."

"'I'm funny how? Funny like I'm a clown? I amuse you, I make you laugh, I'm here to fuckin' amuse you?'"

I have her going now, wiping tears, then holding up a hand. "Stop!" She catches her breath, then slowly shakes her head while giving me a long look of . . . something. "That's probably your favorite movie, right?"

The laughs taper, then comfortable silence.

"So how come you don't have fifty boyfriends?"

She draws long on the cigarette, eyes closed. "Thirty's enough." Her eyes lock on for a second, then quickly downward. "No," another puff, "I just haven't found the right person."

"Yeah, I uh . . ." I stop, not wanting this to turn from *Goodfellas* to a Donna Reed movie. "So maybe we could hang out. I mean, just friends, you know?"

She gives me that sideways glance of hers, lips snapped up into a sly smile. "Yeah, right, friends." Veiled in filmy blue smoke, she's tough, scary. The nicotine-induced dizziness kicks me hard.

"I'm serious."

"I'm seriously saying, '*yeah, right, friends.*'" She stubs out her cigarette after a few puffs. "Filthy habit." She grimaces. "I'm good, so put yours out if you want."

"I agree but love it sometimes."

"I love it too, sometimes," she says while fumbling in her purse, pulling out a small orange spray bottle of organic breath mint. I've seen those at Whole Foods and wondered who buys that crap. She stands, extending a hand. "C'mon, let's go back in."

I look her up and down a little too long before taking her hand. As soon as I stand, dizziness nearly drops me and I reach for the table. Carolyn turns and immediately saves me in an embrace.

After a moment, I say, "I really do feel like I know you from somewhere. Are you sure we haven't met?"

"No, we've never met," her head now on my shoulder, "but like I said, I'm an old soul." There's nothing better than the smell of alcohol on a woman's breath, especially on top of her scent that's already got you intoxicated.

"Now I remember where I know you from."

"Yeah, where?" she breathes.

"I was having this dream where I was hugging the most beautiful woman in the world. And you were in it." I feel her silent laugh and a tighter embrace. The booze keeps me digging. "Or, I know—in a previous life. I was Claude Monet and you were an endlessly fascinating haystack?"

She blurts long and loud, still holding me at arm's length now. We have the locked-gaze moment when people feel *The Feeling*. I think, God, she's got any guy she wants. She's taller than me and I've got about ten years on her and a hundred other reasons to retreat. But I can't. And don't want to.

Carolyn loosens her hold after making sure I'm stable, but a kind of intense, irresistible radiation continues to emanate from her eyes.

"You are extremely beautiful, Agent Carolyn Talbot."

She moves closer, insinuating a knee between my legs. Then a whispered order, "Close your eyes and open your mouth."

Hypnotized, I comply, and out of nowhere comes the sweet sting of organic spearmint.

# THIRTY-ONE

**THE BAND IS DOWN TO** its last few songs of the night when
Carolyn and I tread back onto Dargan's beloved, perfectly sticky
mess of a floor.

"Do you want to leave soon?" she asks.

Booze and nicotine transport me to my pre-Carolyn life, where
a comment like that needed no analytics, no calculus. But I wonder
about her reason for coming here tonight.

"Sure," I say, "but we can't leave during a song. It's rude to the
band."

And here she shoots me a look. "Makes sense." She puckers to
one side, thumbs on her phone. "Can you drive me home?"

"Of course. What about your friend?"

"He's leaving. We're sure this place is safe for us."

Again, us. "No prob. I've had a few drinks spread out over the
night, but I'm okay to drive. My car's in the city garage next door."
The band breaks into "Sweet Home Chicago" and I shout, "Let's
leave after this one!"

She nods, then sways, getting into the pocket.

I ask, "Are you a musician?"

"Can't play a thing, but I love all types of music. My father played sax in a few jazz bands, so I think that's where I caught it. He always had something playing in the house."

I remember the Charlie Parker she had on. The song ends and she screams and claps, and I ask, "Are you sure you want to leave now? They probably have a few more in this set."

"You know, I'm not sure. They're really good, but maybe let's go or we'll be here all night."

I take her by the arm and lead us past the pool tables into refreshing night air. She takes a few steps, then stops.

"What's up?" I ask.

"Nothing. Let's make sure no one follows us out." I notice her hand inside her clutch, as if looking for something, except it's motionless. A bouncer asks if we need a cab, and I jump.

"Stay cool," she whispers, then to the doorman, "No, thanks anyway."

"Jesus, what's going on?" I ask, my heart a kick drum.

"Absolutely nothing. If we're being followed, I want to know now and not when we're wide open in the fucking parking lot or sitting ducks trapped in your car."

"I thought you said it was safe, I mean your guy—"

"Vince, that was ten minutes ago. A lot can happen in one minute even with clean surveillance." A pack of college guys stagger out, too drunk to notice me or the babe I'm with, followed by two couples who for some reason smile and wave at us. "Okay, let's go." She grabs my arm and we're off on quick strides.

I fumble. "What? Was that some kind of signal?"

"They're with us."

*No shit, Sherlock.* She won't elaborate.

"Okay," I say and help her into my car.

"Just drive, Vince," she commands, checking all quadrants. I get to the street as fast as I can without burning rubber.

"Should I run red lights? What's up?"

"Nothing, we're good. We were in a perfect little kill box, a choke point, a place—"

I interrupt the sugarcoating. "I get it. All the photos show dead mobsters just outside the door of their favorite Italian restaurants." I try my best to laugh. Then I see it.

"That car making a U-turn behind us. The gray Camry. I know it's a small town, but I've seen those guys like a thousand times since Jackie's surgery."

"Slow down. Let this light go red so they get closer, but if I tell you to go, run the fucker." She leans my way, checking the view in her side mirror, a hefty automatic pistol now on her lap. "Nevada plates, right?" she asks, edgy, while sending a text.

"Yeah, that's the same one that—"

"We're working it," she chimes after the chime of a text hits her phone.

"What the fuck?"

"It's a rental. One of my partners slapped a GPS on it after we saw it pick up your bogus flower deliveryman—long story, but we're okay."

Easy for her to say. I check the rearview. "Whoa! A pickup truck just cut them off, forced them onto Anacapa!"

"Really? How rude, and what a coincidence." She laughs, edginess gone now, gliding the Beretta back into the side of her clutch. "Circle the block. Let's check on them."

# THIRTY-TWO

I GET MY SHIT TOGETHER, make three right turns. The Camry is in the middle of the block, parked—or should I say, pinned—between the pickup and a Chevy Tahoe that has angry blue and red lights flaring from the depths of its grille. The people that waved to us when we left Dargan's are there; two more in the street hug the pickup, others stand shielded by the Tahoe's open doors. All wear badges, as far as I can see, and they all have guns trained on the Camry, which is impossible *not* to see.

Carolyn raises a hand. "Can you do a J-turn?"

"A what-turn?"

"Never mind, I'll teach you another time. Let me out, then turn around and be ready to nail it, if I say so." She exits, keeping the door open, her pistol now out of the purse, held close. Two new figures in black emerge from the Tahoe and converge with her on the Camry that's now bedazzled with red and green laser sights.

I drive ahead a little, pull a U-ey, then swivel in the seat to keep watch, ready to join in if this goes badly, needing medical cleanup. There's shouting now from the area around the Tahoe.

"Out! Hands where we can see them. Everybody out! Now!"

The two young men who emerge from the front seats are immediately face-slammed to the hood, disarmed, and cuffed. The back door facing Carolyn cracks open slightly. Then nothing. She approaches, arms outstretched, holding the Beretta with both hands.

"No!" I plead to myself, everything slow motion. Hands—empty hands—creep up over the top of the Camry's door. One of the Tahoe team yanks the door wide open; another hunches down and trains a red dot on the forehead of some person coming into view. In an instant, the person—older than the first two and with an unexpected smile stapled to his face—is yanked out of the Camry, searched and cuffed, his back held to the doorframe by two supermen.

Carolyn moves to him, shouting, "You need to be a better listener. Do you understand English?"

Defiant, he snaps away from her, spits on the ground. His handlers give a shake, bounce him against the car a couple of times.

She stays squarely in his view. "Can you talk? Open your mouth!"

Finally, eye contact, then a leering glance at his buddies, a grin that says, "Watch me handle this bitch." Carolyn's team shuffles, seeming suddenly skittish.

Her left hand launches onto his nose, clamping it, forcing a reflexive gasp of air through his mouth, into which she shoves a goodly portion of pistol barrel.

I open my door, ready to run to the wounded but picturing his head Jackson Pollocked all over the Camry.

"We're not your friends, *haji*. So don't ever, *ever* confuse kindness with weakness or stupidity. Unless you want me to make you an organ donor. Do you understand, you dickless motherfucker?"

Bloodied saliva drizzles from a corner of his mouth. With wheeze and gibber and bulged eyes, he nods.

"What's that, mookie? I can't hear you."

There's a gargled sound, maybe a "yes." Hopefully a yes.

"You know, I take it back," she says, and here she turns to his stupefied compatriots. "I wouldn't put your fuckin' organs in my dog." She extracts the gun from his mouth, followed by a sibilant, "*Salaam Alaikum*," shout to his face. She strolls back to my car, pistol held out to the side.

"Wait. You have a dog?" It's all I can muster.

She's high as an adrenaline-powered kite, leering. "I was just messin' with him."

"Jesus, Carolyn, you have to teach me that . . . gutsy."

"Or lunacy? I wanted to soften him up. Hopefully now we'll get some good leads out of them . . ." she says, trailing off, looking at her weapon. "Agh, do you have any tissues?"

I open the console as she holds the damp pistol like it's something that washed onto the beach. She squeezes hand sanitizer on a Starbucks napkin, then wipes down blood from the gun's business end.

"What's that?" I ask. It's so fitting, she probably got its elegant dark mahogany grips at J.Crew or Bergdorf's.

"An 8040. A 40 cal Beretta Cougar."

"Forty's big, right?" Dogs, calibers—let's get all the dipshit questions out of the way.

She looks right through me. "A couple hollow-point forties will get you out of whatever you're in." She extracts one from the magazine and displays it proudly. "One hundred and eighty grains of diplomacy. I don't like wasting ammo on human garbage."

WTF. I wait until she's closer to earth. "So, I guess we're in the big leagues now, huh?"

"Yeah, Doc, and you're on the all-star team," she says, pumped as hell.

I take Cabrillo, keeping nothing but the beach to our right, hotels to our left. If any car seems suspicious, I'll see it. At a stoplight, I hear her sigh and feel her hand covering mine on the gearshift.

"You're handling this well, Vince. I mean that. And my crew will be there as backup like they were tonight."

"Thanks. One thing I'm used to is pressure. It focuses me." And I'll make damn sure I'm not one loud noise, one odd smell, one stranger's weird-ass glance from becoming a clumsy liability for Carolyn's crew.

"Let's go down to Butterfly," she says.

We drive in silence. The beach is deserted and moonless as we stand by the sea wall, a stiff onshore breeze keeping us close. I speak to the sea.

"Listen, Carolyn, I'd kill myself if you got hurt because I fucked up, so I won't let you down. I'm just used to being in control of everything in my life—in patients' lives, for God's sake—and now this new gig is like nothing before. Plus, I'm dealing with the FBI."

Silence. Then it's her turn to talk to the ocean. "I'm not FBI."

# THIRTY-THREE

**I SHIVER AND GLARE, SWIVEL** a glance over both shoulders, then get in her face. "What the hell are you talking about? What do you mean? Who the fuck are you, then?"

Carolyn can't look at me. And what am I doing here on a dark, empty beach?

"I'm an officer with a company working with FBI. They brought me in after you called because—"

"You mean the Central Intelligence Ag—"

"Yes. '*The Company.*'" She schools me with air quotes.

I need to brush up on spook lingo.

"Seriously, Vince, you've given us the only credible lead on something we've known was coming since 9/11."

Waves crash, carotids slam in my neck. *Who is this woman?*

"So, everything's the same," I say. "Just who you work for is different, right?"

She curls around, facing me. "Yes, that's all, Vince. We had to go slow until we checked into you, your story. Then Jackie and her story. Since you called FBI, that had to be my cover for action. I wasn't going to tell you, but now things are moving fast and you'll need to know more. And meet some of my team. That's all. Get it?"

"I guess." I should feel honored to be trusted by our clandestine services. "Wow, you're really a great liar."

"They teach a lot of crap at Langley."

She takes my hand. I unknot the notion that I'm about to be clipped. "So, are you quitting the CIA or something? You guys never talk unless it's over, right?"

"Come on, let's go," she says, the wind getting vicious. We lock arms and slow-jog to the car.

Another silent ride up the foothills, then we're through the gate and standing at her door, every window radiating warmth. The scent of the spring garden flowers fills the space between us. I don't want to say goodbye, and she knows it.

"Come warm up," she says, "and if you're ever with me when I'm wasted, the code is my birthday: ten-four, space, then another ten-four."

Inside's as comfortable as the windows hinted. She fiddles with her phone, puts on Miles and Trane this time, and we move to the kitchen where she pulls down two tumblers.

"We need this," she says. "Templeton's was it?"

I nod, then follow her into the library. She crouches to light the hearth, which sparks into a satisfying fire. She rises over me, and I love it. The fire snaps and intensifies, revealing things in her face, mortal things I've never noticed. Sorrowful fine lines, forgiving eyes, and a few small scars that will tell another story another day. The world dissolves around us.

"So," I falter, but her eyes encourage, "look, I feel like something may be happening . . ." I gesticulate, vibrate in every direction.

"Yeah, I feel it too."

"You do?"

In a child's voice, she draws out a whispered, "Yes," then takes a step closer, welding a leg to mine. She's got one arm on the mantel, one on her hip.

"Please don't stand like that," I say.

"Why the hell not?"

"Because you're giving me fuckin' chest pain." A deep breath. "By the way, just so you know, if I die here tonight, I forgive you."

Smirking, she holds the pose. Just when I expect her to tell me to rein this shit in, she speaks.

"You. Are. Adorable. Doc."

My hands find her hips, and they're home, calm. She inches nearer, my fingers massaging their way up her back. I comb a hand into her hair, bringing her open mouth to me for our lips to meet in a perfect fit. After the kiss, I bury my face in her neck, breathing her in, my hand lightly gliding under her shirt and up between her breasts to her neck.

"Ohhh," she moans, spinning us onto the couch, collapsing, her on top of me as she runs her knee up to the bulge that's been there since she walked in my office. I hear a guttural, evil laugh and it excites the hell out of me. I move a hand under her poncho and slip it into her jeans, unfastening every button of her fly all the way down to a velvet pussy.

"Nicely done, Doctor," she growls.

I bring my moist hand up, placing it between both of our lips. Another moan, this one punctuated with a full-body shudder. Her eyes flash as she pulls away from me, throwing off the poncho, inviting me to keep going and lift off her blouse.

I sit up, then she stands, drops her white jeans and thong in one move, and slams me back onto the cushions, straddling me, writhing her way upward while unbuttoning my shirt. She stops, looking at me with tilted head—like I'm not going to give her the green light!—and

I yank her up to my face where I think her scent will remain forever. Then, still pressed into me, she does a one-eighty swivel to give herself access to my jeans, and in five seconds I'm naked.

Her breathing gets rapid, and I feel a fine mist of perspiration all over her back and thighs, and she flips herself off me and sits back on the couch, wiping her brow with the back of an arm, like she just finished ninety push-ups.

"Are you okay?" I ask.

"Oh, yeah. I'm fabulous. I just want to stretch this evening out a little. Are you okay?"

I kneel on the couch and lean toward her, lifting her chin, kissing her, moving gently, undulating, massaging my body against hers. "Hell, yes."

She stands, fetches our drinks from the coffee table, and returns, swaying to the jazz in the background. She takes her time, dancing for me, with an evil smile. She's backlit, scintillating with every flare of the fireplace, and I struggle to believe I'm here with her.

She moves toward me, teasing with her narrow hips surging to the music. She knocks back some whiskey, runs a finger over my upper arm, and says, "I like this ink. What does it say?" She reads, "*La vita è bella.*"

"I wish I could say it was a moment of youthful indiscretion, but I got it five years ago in Italy. I'm using the Campari Negroni defense. It's Italian, so it squeezes a lot of meaning into few words. It means 'life is beautiful,' and it means you are extremely beautiful and my whole life I've dreamt about colliding with a woman like you and what took you so long, and I don't want this night to ever end and—"

She quiets me, a finger over my lips, and rides me again, face-to-face—another perfect fit—running the back of her hand across my lips and chin, kissing my forehead. She gives me the "I'm disease-free" whisper and I give her the "me too," not letting on that I would be honored to catch something from her.

"You like to fuck, don't you?" I ask, grasping two handfuls of her hair and draping it across her face. She lets it stay.

She whispers another drawn out, "Yesss."

Immediately she has me inside her and I can't stop. I roll on top of her, stroking every part of her, lifting one of her long legs over my shoulder, kissing her ankle, seeing her perfect hair, now wild all over her face, watching her body rise, her abdomen undulate with every breath, keeping me hard. It's longer than I thought possible before we collapse together, catching our breath in a slippery, steaming heap.

I get up on elbows. We share smiles. I say, clutching her hips, "You have magnificent anterior superior iliac spines. And you really fire my neurons such that my emotional state exceeds my ability to self-regulate. Am I being too clinical?"

Her eyes laugh, but there are tears before she crushes me in an embrace. Our cheeks go damp with her all-out crying.

"Hey, what's wrong?" I ask.

"Nothing, I'm fine," she says as she pulls back with a sealed-lip smile.

"You don't look fine. Really, what's up?"

"Nothing," heavily sobbing now, burying her face in my chest. "I really like you, Vince. I'm just really, really happy."

I cradle her against my chest and gently we rock, my tears flowing now, knowing for the first time in years I, too, am really, really happy.

# THIRTY-FOUR

**AT SOME POINT IN THE** night I find a luxuriant fleece next to Carolyn's couch and cocoon us into a marvelous deep sleep. My internal alarm clock (a sorry curse of my profession) wakes me at five thirty, but I'm rejuvenated in many ways. I carefully untangle without her stirring and find all my clothes. On a knee, I whisper that I'll be right back.

She sighs, barely audible, "Tall Red Eye."

My tires hiss on the damp pavement as I drive through my sleepy village's long sunrise shadows, a spicy balm of eucalyptus permeating my car. I want to sing with the songbirds. I want to tell the barista about Carolyn. If there was rain, I'd be singing in it.

As I walk out with breakfast, a gray Corolla with tinted windows parks across the street, chilling my blood until two college women exit. Like the tide, the realities that brought Carolyn into my life return, but this time it lifts me somehow.

I return to a quiet house smelling of sex and Carolyn. She's still sleeping, but awakens when I place our coffees on the table. She sits up, bringing the blanket with her, and fluffs her hair, smiling like a kid on Christmas morning. I hand her the Red Eye. She pats the couch, and I sit.

"What happened last night?" I ask.

"Something I think we both wanted since day one."

"Why?"

"Hormones, pheromones, I don't know." She shrugs. "You're the doctor. Figure it out."

"Wait, I'm impressed with your neuroendocrine knowledge."

She drops her head to one shoulder and looks up at me.

"Were you drunk?" I ask.

"Not on booze."

I lunge, crushing her with an embrace.

"What's in the bag, Doc?" she asks with a yawn and stretch.

"Oh, this?" I joke. "Why, it's Satan's breakfast selection—a blueberry scone, a cheese Danish, and a chocolate croissant. I didn't know what you like, so I did a junk-carb sampler."

"Ahhh, did I just hear the word chocolate?" she asks, sheepishly pulling the blanket up around her neck.

"Yeah, you did." I stroke her cheek with the back of a finger.

She breathes deep, thinking, then flips the blanket off, planting a foot on my crotch. "I want you to fuck me again, but this time come on my face."

I shudder, lips stretching into a thin grin. Another trifecta: intelligent, beautiful, loves sex. Whatever happens, I'm forever connected to this deliciously insane woman.

# THIRTY-FIVE

**A THIRTY-MINUTE SHOWER DOES LITTLE** to help me recover from last night's white-water ride with this confident, playful woman I never dreamed existed. But after the Camry caper, what else comes with her?

Now that I know she's with the CIA, I don't see her in a white blouse and conservative suit, toeing the line with FBI nerds. I see her unfettered and wild, sexually buccaneering across all places exotic. All the gonzo characters, *Bourne*'s Matt Damon, *Homeland*'s Claire Danes, *Taken*'s Liam Neeson. Flashbacks in scenes where compatriots are expendables, deftly eliminated at the pleasure of explosive Washington puppet masters.

My go-to sanctum for clear thinking is Figueroa Mountain, and I blast my iTunes blues playlist on the way. At a traffic light near the beach, I watch a homeless guy cross the street pushing a shopping cart piled ten feet high with heartbreak. He turns, hearing the deafening tune—it's the reprise of last night's "Sweet Home Chicago"—coming from my car as he tries to arrange a crinkled, nearly toothless smile. I wave him over and hand him one of the Starbucks ten-dollar gift cards I keep for these moments. It helps assuage guilt from living here among so many homeless.

"God bless, brother," he shouts. "Hey, that's Lonnie Brooks pla-yin', ain't it?" And before I can say yes, he adds, "Hell, yes, it is. I used to see him play on Lincoln Avenue in Chicago, mm-hmm. I sure did. That's Lonnie."

I nod and watch him dance—shuffle, really—across the street tapping out the beat on the handle of his shopping cart. I catch his enthusiasm and begin the same beat on my steering wheel, frozen there at a green light until a horn taps. I drive on, but then it all hits clear to me. I turn into a beach volleyball parking lot, scattering a dozen gulls.

I rewind to the beginning of the song, tapping out a basic Chicago shuffle. I fumble through the songs and find "Carolyn's Song" and play it. Then Lonnie Brooks, then back again. The rhythms meld into one.

I jump out of the car with my cell phone and frantically text Carolyn.

> All is well but please call ASAP.

Immediately it rings. "Are you all right?" she asks.

"Yes, I'm great, really great, and I think I know where I heard 'Carolyn's Song' before," I shout, talking a mile a minute, elated to be telling her this.

"Really." She drags the word out, reminding me of last night's sultry growls. She's not taking me seriously?

"Really, Carolyn, I think this is it. Long story, but I was listen-ing to 'Sweet Home Chicago' again this morning in my car, and a homeless dude heard it and started jiving to it and that got me jiving—"

"Wait. Why were you with a homeless guy this morning?"

"No, he was just on the street and he heard it coming from my car and started dancing a shuffle, then I tapped it out and it's the sound. You know, 'Carolyn's Song' on my phone."

"Vince, if it was music in the hospital, we would have easily IDed the signature of it. We can tell you song, artist, format, bit rate—"

"No! No, Carolyn, please. Listen for a second. It's foot drop." I take a deep breath and slow down. "The homeless guy's walk—his dance—was a shuffle, just like what happens if a patient has foot drop. It's a condition where the common peroneal nerve, a nerve behind your knee, gets damaged, and you can't pick up your foot when you take a step, so it kinda slaps down in a shuffle rhythm. Make sense?"

"Yeah, okay," she says. Zero enthusiasm. "So you and I can check the admission diagnoses of patients on Jackie's floor and see if anyone had this—what is it, leg drop?—then mystery over and we move on, right?"

"*Foot drop*, but there's more. I remember the day after her surgery on Sunday, I visited her and there was a guy near her room that had a weird gait when I heard him walk away. And I have a feeling it was him standing in the hall outside her room the day that I got the DNA for you. It would explain the foot drop sound that you guys picked up that day."

"Interesting." She pauses. "Let me do some work on this. What are you doing later today?"

"Anything you want, Carolyn."

# THIRTY-SIX

FIG MOUNTAIN, IN ITS SPRING bloom of California poppies and blue dicks, can't take me any higher than I am after nailing the mystery sound thanks to my homeless friend, my *talismano*. After an hour's hike, a circling hawk reminds me I'm alone up here. Time to return to civilization.

When I get close to the village, my phone rings. Carolyn.

"Hey, how are you?" I ask.

"I'm good." The pause and tone set me up for bad news. "I'm on Pacific Coast Highway coming back from LA. Can we meet?" She gives it a beat, then adds, "Somewhere in public?"

I assume "in public" means no sex. In case I'm getting ideas.

Traffic's light on PCH and she'll be in Santa Barbara in twenty minutes and wants to grab a late lunch. I suggest one of Tre Lune's outside tables—as public as one can get in Montecito without being in an Oprah paparazzi shot. Two sips of my water, and her BMW pulls in. Business garb again, sand-colored suit, three-inch heels. Heads turn.

"That fuckin' drive never gets easy, does it?" she mutters, draining half her water glass. Her breasts strain a white silk T-shirt as she removes her jacket.

"Yeah, it sucks." Then I test the water. "So, is that why you wanted a public place, because you look so marvelous?"

"Thank you, Doctor. That's very nice to hear."

We order salads, Carolyn deferring the wine list to me. I feel the weight of her eyes as I order a bottle of Vermentino. As soon as the server walks away I see that little cat's grin of hers.

"So, tell me something," she asks, a glint playing in her eyes.

"Well, for starters, I see that you've brought those goddamn legs with you again."

"Down, boy. Be serious."

"Okay. What the hell are you doing here, sitting with me?" I ask, playing some self-effacement for a laugh. "I mean, you are an extremely beautiful, intelligent woman, and I'm . . . I don't know, a medical geek. At least I'm not old. I'm just approaching forty."

Her eyebrows rise.

"Unfortunately, I'm approaching it from the wrong direction."

Finally a laugh, then a squint. "I'm just using you because I can tell you're a loser. Is that what you want to hear, Doc?"

Busted. I weigh confessing that I've been lost since Helen's death up until Carolyn walked toward me that day in my office and the entire universe dissolved. That I've thought of nothing but her ever since. But I don't. "I thoroughly enjoyed hanging with you last night."

"Me too." She looks to the street. "I like blues bands."

I throw my head back. "I meant—"

"I know what you meant," cutting me off. There's little breeze to contend with, but she flips her hair and ties it with a band.

"Carolyn, what new information do you have?"

She lets the server pour our wine, then toasts. "Cheers." She gazes at me, amused, silent long enough for ocean air to put dew on our glasses.

"FBI wants to focus on Jackie's husband. He's got dirt with some arms dealers."

"What kind of dirt?"

"There's a shipment of Javelin anti-tank missiles that was stolen from a freight expediter, then showed up in South America when a cartel used a couple of them on local police."

I'm puzzled. "That happens all the time, no? How is that Brent Carter's doing?"

"He was the only one who knew all the shipping handoffs. The army doesn't use UPS for shit like this."

"Why isn't he relaxing at a Club Fed?"

"We set some canary traps—documents that all have unique changes to find leakers—but no hits, so it's watchful waiting."

Just like docs who haven't a clue as to a diagnosis.

She continues, "As far as your theory on the sound, we've narrowed our list to three, maybe four bad guys who are challenged walking and may be in-country. Not definite foot drop, or whatever you call it, but injuries that could impede gait."

"Are they seriously bad? Threats, I mean. Dangerous?"

"Two of them, possibly. One for sure, but he's likely not in the US. The thing is, all of them have reasons to try to get something from Brent. We'll know more in the next few days."

"Can't you check the security cameras of the hospital, the entrances especially, to see who came in?"

"We've been watching them since you called FBI. Nothing. Just patients, visitors, staff with normal gaits except for those on crutches or in casts. We're trying to do facials on them, but your cameras suck. There're gaps, bad angles, grainy crap, outdated big time. You can't read a fucking license plate without ten minutes of algorithmic rework. I don't know how your security people can use them."

"What about the Camry guys?"

"That's the best news. Low-level scum, but they're turning."

"Where are they? I mean, if you can tell me." I'm picturing dog collars, waterboarding.

"At a secure site. That's all I can say."

Here she settles into a new state, cheek on a fist and a wicked giggle. It's Carolyn from last night. A shoeless foot sneaks under my pant leg. I place it in my lap and massage. She goes limp.

"Hey," I say, my voice grating. She goes wide-eyed until realizing that I'm joking. "I'm talking to you."

"Shush," she snaps, eyes closed.

"Okay, then." I move closer, whispering, "Little Miss CIA, what's up with us?"

"Oh my God!" She laughs. "Don't ever, ever stop the foot rub and I'll tell you."

The server interrupts with our food and we begin in silence. Carolyn picks up a thin breadstick and taps it on the edge of my plate, then uses it to flip over a piece of radicchio.

"Vince, I really like hanging with you too. You're smart and funny, and I can tell you're kind."

She stops. I wait for the "but," which doesn't come.

"All that's going on with what you found doesn't mean that you and I can't be more than friends. Or whatever we are after last night. We just have to stay focused."

I nod. "Could you get in trouble by hanging out with me?"

She looks around, then leans in. "Being in public with you is exactly the thing to do now. If someone sees us, we're a couple, right? And unless my cover's blown, it puts you under my watch for your protection and for my intel work."

I gaze at my wine, slowly swirling it. I'm pensive and she knows it, cocking her head and giving me an adroit, blue-eyed stare.

I ask, "So what's real? I mean, real between us, and what's spy bullshit?"

She caresses the contours of her wine glass, like at the Ranch, staring at it, seeing things in it, speaking to it. "Everything, Vince. I don't do this unless it's real. I've never done this, felt this, with any-one before."

With that, she's up from her chair—I'm thinking ladies' room—but she moves behind me, leans down, wrapping her arms around me. I hold her head against my cheek, hearing only a sniffle, a sigh, then a lifetime of emotion is over in seconds.

She goes back to her seat. I smile, more contented than I ever thought possible, and reach for the other ankle and slip off her shoe. "That's just what I wanted to hear from you, Slim."

"Slim?" She blushes big time. "I like it."

I nod and continue giving stress-reduction therapy.

"By the way, Doc, you're hired."

//////////

We finish lunch and agree the proper next step is for me to keep Jacquelyn Carter in a normal doctor-patient relationship. After my call-in about Grails, I'm labeled a casual informant. I guess, due to my professional relationship with Jackie, I have information of inter-est. My take on it, I have no obligation to continue cooperating and can accept or reject any amount of control from Carolyn I choose. But I'm okay with it, and I make sure Agent Talbot knows that I will accept any control that she sees fit. She doesn't say, but I assume there's an element of protection baked into the control part.

Her team at CIA—she instructs, "Only a chooch calls it 'the CIA'"—will keep supporting FBI (no "the" here either), and she'll let me know what she can, as she can.

The bad news is that she's out of town on business for three days but gives me the cell numbers of an FBI specialist and a backup. One's Rachael, who, it turns out, was in the group waving at us when we left Dargan's and also joined the after-party with the Camry dudes. Carolyn wants me to check in with Rachael at least twice a day by text or anytime things don't seem right, especially if Jackie, her husband, or Salaam contact me. The first two, fine, but it comes as something of an eye-blinking shock to even imagine that Salaam would actually contact *me*. I guess because I must still be processing just how deep I really am in this thing.

She tells me to change my routine a little this week. No pressure there, Carolyn. There's also an offer of a baby Glock that she rescinds after I tell her I've not touched a handgun since high school. I was clowning around on my uncle's farm with a .22 revolver and accidentally drilled a water tank. She'll instruct me on how to use a semi-auto without shooting myself when she gets back.

As far as Carolyn and I, well, we agree it's a free country. So far at least.

////////////

Saturday I do as I'm told, get up early, and rather than walk my customary walk to Butterfly Beach in Montecito, I drive fifteen minutes to the café in Summerland. The beach is deserted except for a lone dog walker, and I'm entranced by the gauzy canopy of sky giving way to sunrise over Rincon Point. The coffee's perfect, and under different circumstances it would be a glorious morning. I text Rachael a thumbs-up and immediately receive a smiley face. Comforting, and it reminds me of Carolyn except without . . . oh, never mind.

When I get to my car, a sparge of windblown leaves drops from the bluff and covers the pavement like a Pittsburgh snow squall. I pick up a perfect leaf, turning it over and over in my hand. I see in its veins the image of the tree that shed it. I miss her madly.

# THIRTY-SEVEN

**NOW THE CHIME OF A** text. It's Rachael.

R u ok?

All is well.

Does she know something I don't?

C wants u to hve something BRT black Chevy
p/u truck

Her texting style puts her in her midtwenties, max. I want a drink but settle for aromatherapy from my espresso machine. I make two.

As soon as I walk to the window, a Silverado crew cab drives up, a slight brunette behind the wheel. I open my door, motioning for her to come in, but she waves me to her. She leans to open the passenger door, and I see tousled hair with six inches of blowzy ponytail.

"Hey, hi. I'm Vince. I think we waved the other night."

"Rachael. Rachael Woods." She's smaller than her voice but offers a crushing handshake, then flips an FBI badge like Carolyn's, fake.

"Do you have any free time today?" she asks, studying me with sincere green eyes.

"Yeah, I'm free all day. What's up?" I try like fuck, unconvincingly I suspect, to sound in charge, like FBI stops by regularly. She's wearing a grape-colored Patagonia, black running tights, and Nikes, everywhere muscles trying to rip through. I hope to God she's not going to ask me to go for a run. And I smell bacon.

"Everything's okay. Let's go up on the mountain." She pokes a finger into my T-shirt and says, "Maybe grab a light jacket."

I throw on a quarter-zip and jog back to her truck.

Rachael sizes me up again. "Did you eat breakfast? I have sandwiches from Coffee Bean."

"Thanks," I say, still in a whirl over her surprise visit.

"Grew up on a farm in Indiana. We eat breakfast."

*Well, the bacon smell makes sense now.*

"You're good with that stick shift. Is this your truck or—"

"Agency's, but it's just like what I drove raising Tennessee Walkers back in Indiana. I can't give up the feel of a good truck."

*Horses?* I'm absorbed with her squared-off jaw that lays down this softened "don't fuck with me" look when she's not smiling. She's fit and determined as hell.

"Yeah, there's more to driving than just sittin' there, right?"

"Yeah, something like that," she says.

We take San Marcos Pass up into Los Padres forest. The haze is gone and the windings along the cliffs yield a breathtaking vista of Santa Barbara and the Channel Islands. I love this view, but it's grim now. I picture plumes of ground-to-air weapons snaking up from my town.

"Okay, what's going on?"

"Honestly, Doctor, nothing. Carolyn asked me to keep watch over you and texted saying you're probably going stir-crazy and I should get you out of your house."

"Did I screw up going to Summerland? Carolyn said to change it up."

"Not at all. She thinks today would be a good time to give you basic handgun training."

I hesitate, calculating. "I never thought I'd need a gun." The thought excites me, though, in a James Bond sort of way. Okay, I'll cut the shit—it's sexy.

Rachael turns with a thin-lipped smile. "Well, it's a skill that can come in handy."

She's hot-footed, and I picture her in a pickup screaming down an Indiana farm road, leaving a roiling dust plume in her wake. Soon we're dancing along the mountain crest into the gun club. Rachael gets out to check in with the range master who eyes me for a moment, then hands her two targets in wood frames. She throws them into the back of the pickup and we drive to the range.

She drops the tailgate, throws her duffel in, and sits on the gate, elbows on thighs, hands steepled. "Oh, yeah, rattlesnakes are back, so be careful where you sit, step, or reach. I haven't seen any, but be careful." She has dimples close to the corners of her lips that give her a perpetual smile. Wisps of hair have escaped the ponytail and dance over her face in the breeze. It softens her, but I still see her taking me down and zip-cuffing me in three seconds.

"Good to know, thanks." Snakes. One more layer of creepiness.

She goes over pistol basics with military cadence and verve, making me teach them back. Treat every gun like it's loaded. Never point your weapon at anything you're not willing to destroy. Never put your finger on the trigger until you've committed to shoot. Always have situational awareness of your target and surroundings. I sense she's getting high with training a dunce.

"Okay, Vince." No more Doctor.

She's pleased, and we move under the rusting sheet-metal roof of the firing line. We're the only ones here. Rachael takes two black plastic cases out of the duffel, one with a strip of white tape labeled "Vince D. Glock 42." She hands me glasses, noise-suppressing headphones, and a carton of ammo.

She turns to me. "I'm going to set the targets. Just stand behind this line and don't touch anything, understand?"

"Yes, ma'am."

After targets are set, she calls, "Range is hot" to the empty area. Safety is well taught at Quantico, I guess, and there's no straying from the protocol whatsoever. We spend the next hour on range rules, how the gun works, loading mags—not clips—holding, aiming, and firing a pistol. We then go through the "pick it up, grip with two hands, hold it close, left foot forward, knees bent, aim, and fire" at a dark target with an orange bull's-eye twenty feet away.

"Wait, where's the safety on this?" I'm gleeful that I asked an intelligent question.

"There's no conventional safety. This is a combat weapon. It's designed for you to pull out and shoot someone."

I do an open-mouthed nod, hoping I don't shoot myself with Carolyn's little gift.

"Okay, let's go hot," she says. "Watch what I do, then you're up." I wonder where law enforcement agencies get a coterie of women that include the likes of Rachael and Carolyn. The government must have some hidden kick-ass woman factory near Quantico and Langley.

Before my next breath, there are three quick cracks, a slight pause, then a fourth. I feel the shots more than hear them, and see a two-inch line of three overlapping white circles on the black edge of the bull's-eye, a sole yellow blob nearly dead center. The smell of nitro lingers as the valleys echo.

"Jesus, how—" I turn to her.

"Practice, Doc, practice. Same way you learn surgery." She beams— not boastful—beams like a kid admiring her handiwork. "Make sure you tell my hero, Talbot, I'm still layin' down a tight pattern."

"I will. Amazing job, Rachael."

It takes awhile, but by the time I'm down to the last five rounds in the box, I'm within one circle from a bull's-eye and only a little low left. We pack up and head to her truck, a spring in my step now that I know how not to kill myself with a semi-auto.

Rachael hands me my target and some paperwork to sign and put a thumbprint on. I'm told she did a background check. Somehow I passed, even though in my mind I'm *boombots*. They must've missed the time we got pinched bringing three-two beer—3.2 percent alcohol and legal in some states for sixteen-year-olds in small quantities—in a five-car caravan back to Pennsylvania from a West Virginia road trip. Then there was that party in Cleveland . . . Oh, never mind.

"Congratulations, Doc. I now pronounce you man and personal defense weapon." My uncertain smile is well received.

The drive down the mountain is filled with stories of idiots who were trained yet did stupid things with guns. I tell the same stories about trained idiot doctors with lasers. I also hear about her years training with Carolyn, then bonding on ops.

In my driveway I ask, "So, how bad can this get?"

"Vince, we've been waiting for this, this other shoe drop. We know streams of Afghani zealots, al-Qaeda are coming in from Mexico—and who the hell knows about Canada."

"Jesus, God, Rachael."

"We'll be okay. We're ahead of it."

I see her first dead serious face of the day.

"I appreciate the private lesson and your patience."

"You know she likes you, Vince. A lot."

"She's a very interesting woman. And I do sense—"

"Oh, cut the BS! She's like a sister, and she's never been this bat-shit over a guy." She glances from my shirt to my shoes, huffs, and shakes her head. "A doctor, no less."

Usually this is the part where I'm sucked beneath waves of Helen memories, fantasies, then back out again for quick breaths. But I'm afloat on a smile shared with Carolyn's best friend.

# THIRTY-EIGHT

**AFTER THIS WEEKEND'S TRIP UP** the mountain as a women's health care doc and coming down two hours later a jittery guy with a palm-sized piece of deadly force, I welcome a day of familiar office routine. My schedule this morning mercifully shows no potential disasters, no difficult patients with fabricated, insoluble problems just to get face time with someone who has to listen and whose advice they ignore. The patients who've called the overnight answering service for prescription refills or the restless insomniacs with nonurgent questions are all routine, except for one.

Jackie Carter called the answering service at the ungodly hour of two thirty a.m. Not an emergency, but she wants to see me today. Even if it wasn't Jackie, post-op patients own surgeons for as long as they want. It comes with the territory, as they say. As soon as I arrive at the front desk, I ask my nurse to return the call and tell Jackie I'll see her over lunch. I text Rachael immediately.

The reply arrives, and surprisingly it's Carolyn.

Just be a doctor and call A-SAP after.

No emoticons, no "how are you," no "I miss you." Nothing.

Just before noon, I pass the door to the waiting area and see Jackie head down, thumbs to phone. No Brent. My nurse says she's doing fine, just wants to talk in my office. Soap Opera, Act Two. Unless she's here to murder me. That would make it Act Three, Final Curtain.

When I enter my office, she jumps up and greets me with a hug. But Jackie's sullen, with no makeup on a face shouting several sleepless nights.

"Vince, thanks for fitting me in today. I'm doing fine. I just need to talk to you."

"Of course, what's up?" I ask as I settle into the chair next to her. When I suspect drama, I toss the chart onto my desk, allaying fears of a paper trail crammed with tidbits of cuckoldry.

"Vince, well, you remember my friend—the one whose name and number I gave to you?"

I shrug as to say, *yeah, kinda, what's the big?* If she knew me better, I'd be out of Oscar contention.

"Well, Sal—Salaam is his name—hasn't returned a call or a text or an email since I called him after I woke up from surgery last Saturday. And that's something he's never done, so . . ."

She pauses. I instantly feel the flush and rush and galloping heart of impending bad shit. I know what's next and wait for the question.

"I just have to ask you—I mean, this is really wrong of me to ask. I know I never should have put this on your shoulders. I mean, giving you his name and number and all that, but I was sure something was going to happen to me. To punish me. I wanted you to—"

"Jackie, remember, I gave that note back to you when I discharged you, and I knew that you were going to be just fine, so—"

"Oh, thank God. I thought that maybe you spoke to Brent or that Brent had an attorney call you or something. You know, I'm sure he knows there's someone else. I mean, he'd have to be a fool not to suspect that. Oh, Vince, I'm so relieved."

"Nowhere, Jackie. It went nowhere." I strain to melt into my compassion face while thinking, hoping, this cannot be the result of my doing. Can it?

"Okay, great. Vince, I was worried as hell. Salaam's in a very dangerous line of work, you know. He deals with very powerful businessmen who are at war. Literally." She stares too long. "I mean, it's all legal, but, you know, he sells Brent's stuff all over the world. Some of his customers have deadlines and don't put up with failure."

No tears yet, but I lean over, hugging her to avoid more contact with my lying eyes. I hear simpers.

What I've done with FBI—CIA now, for God's sake!—and the immense breach of doctor-patient trust, kills me. I pull myself together, remembering Carolyn's text to just be a doctor. My doctor brain makes me wonder what kind of a jerk stops responding to his lonely, married lover when she's in need.

Offering a half box of Kleenex and every excuse my guy brain can conjure doesn't explain Sal's dick-like actions. I'm sure Jackie's still carrying most of the grim weight she came in with, yet when I walk her out, somehow she's back to the Jackie I remember. I know her heart needs to hear from Salaam. And Carolyn needs to hear this soap opera from me.

# THIRTY-NINE

I TEXT CAROLYN TO LET her know I saw Jackie, and Salaam is MIA. She sends a thumbs-up icon and a promise that she'll call as soon as possible. I'm out of the office by midafternoon, then to the doctors' lounge to pick up mail and hang out as long as I can tolerate pissed-off docs whining about managed care and lawyers.

Outside, disappearing chunks of gloom have unmuted the jacarandas' captivating purple and the mountains' green dapples. Since the night Carolyn and I commingled tears, views like this make me check for signs of her. Nothing. This must be what Jackie Carter feels.

I stop for apples, mixed nuts, and booze to bridge my restaurant visits. When I get home, I have two texts: a check-in from Rachael, another from Carolyn.

I dispatch a quick reply to Rachael before opening Carolyn's, which sits unread another five minutes while I unload groceries, then make my way to the patio. I lie on a lounge chair, then tap the phone.

> Hey sweet man!! Need to see you—and lots
> to talk about.

> Let's get together today??

Like I won't make time?

> BTW, R said you did a great job on the range. ☺

What the hell, was Carolyn kidnapped by Martians, or is this off-duty Carolyn texting? Not sure who I like better, but I'll take both.

> Of course!! Let me know when and where—free the rest of the day. R was a great teacher!!

> Come to my house. Just landed at SBA so give me an hour. Let's say threeish.

> K.

Before Carolyn, I'd come home, play out the afternoon chilling—well, drinking actually—put some Charlie Parker on, then maybe an old movie. Repeat steps one through three until dead. It's not even funny. I need this woman on so many goddamn levels.

Time is glacial until "threeish." I press her gate's intercom at 2:46.

"Jesus. Let yourself in, ya chooch." Her laugh scratches from the intercom.

Smart ass. How the fuck does she even know it's me?

At least she locked the front door. She's in the kitchen, head back, leaning against the Sub-Zero chugging Acqua Panna like she just finished work in a silver mine. Except in silver mines, they wear more than a white Oxford shirt and lank, dripping-wet hair.

"Slim! How the hell are ya, and how did you know I wasn't someone coming to kill you?"

"Don't be silly. You know I'd kill you first." Her eyes sparkle, then she shouts, "I missed you. Get over here. Now! Then we'll talk about Salaam."

Three strides and we stretch into a kiss that I've missed all weekend—all my post-Helen life, maybe. We run the back stairs and land, a writhing tangle on her bed.

I'm entwined in an arms-and-legs embrace as I cradle her head.

She nuzzles her face in my chest, shivering, and says, "Oh, yes. Yes, this is where I want to be in my life. This is my life."

Minutes pass before I ask, "Are you okay?"

I feel her nodding. "You're a good snuggler, Doc," she breathes.

I inhale her, damp shampooed hair and all. "So, where were you? Can you tell me?"

"Langley. My boss expects me to kneel and kiss his ring every so often."

I squint. "Anything else he wants while you're on your knees?"

"Ughh. Hell, no."

"Does he ever touch you?"

Her eyes roll, laughing. "Never. Why, Doctor? Are you jealous?"

"No, not really. But if he does, let me know so I can arrange to have his hands crushed in a vice, okay?"

"Oh, God, I've missed you." She lunges for another long hug, then we watch my finger trace figure eights up and down her leg.

I whisper, "I've missed you too. Waited forever for you, Slim."

She's silent forever, then stirs, murmuring, "Oh, Vince. Can this happen?"

"What?"

"Can you . . . move beyond Helen?"

"I can now."

Eyes meet and stay put. "Vince, I can't begin to know what you've gone through after losing her, and I, I don't think I can—"

"You already have."

"Vince, how?"

"You can't replace her. Helen's with me forever."

Point made, she inches closer with tilted head. "So, then . . ."

Okay, smart guy, what do you say now? You're not on the set of *The Bachelor*, so fucking tell the truth. "You, Carolyn, have allowed me to feel something, to go to a place I never knew existed. And it's nothing about Helen. She and I had something, but the moment I saw you . . ."

A merciful finger to my lips silences me, followed by a soft kiss floating me off to more places I've never been.

# FORTY

WE DOZE FOR A WHILE, then I awaken to her up, leaning against pillows, swiping an iPad. I sit up and take a swig from a now room-temperature Acqua Panna.

"So, what do you think, Slim?" My thumb oscillates between us. "Can this happen?"

She turns a long, deep stare on me. "I've been waiting too, Vince. Never even got close."

"Really? I mean you're—"

"Exactly. I attract guys who love the look but never get to the woman. Once they see I have a career, ninety-nine percent of them bolt."

"Of course they do. You're smart, you scare them. But that's the turn-on. Shakespeare said it best, it's the brain you're fucking."

"Get it right, Vince. 'Love looks not with the eyes but with the mind.' God, you're such a cad," she adds with feigned disgust.

I reach for an ankle. "Come. Let me clutch thee."

She shakes her iPad. "Later, wild man."

"Do you think some are after your money?" I ask.

"Hell, yeah, but one can tell, right? I'm sure you get that. How do you tell when it's *not* about the money?"

"When it's fate," I answer. "Like, say, some idiot calls FBI with a crackpot story and then an angel shows up at his door."

Her smile precipitates moist eyes, and she moves a skosh closer.

"The other one percent?" I ask.

"Big-money guys, thinking just because they're rich, they're the big-cock geniuses of the world. And they'll change me, make me give up what I love, just so I can fly in their Gulf Streams, do the club thing with other wives."

"Dance of Death."

"Right again." She laughs.

"But when they see I've already got my own G-450 so I don't need theirs, and then, next they feel the burn of my hatred for pretentiousness, it's bye-bye." She shakes her head at the floor, then shows me that devil's smile. "The orgies were the only thing that crowd had going for it. I've got great stories to tell you sometime."

"Jesus, Slim."

"Yeah, they were just new-money guys. Use people and toss 'em. Vince, my father, his dad, and the family busted their asses to get what they have. And they did it without lawbreaking or swindles. Their employees were family to them."

"What did they do?"

"Engineers, inventors, mostly anti-collision systems for aircraft. Tons of patents, companies to manufacture the stuff, government contracts. It adds up."

I nod, "Like TCAS and shit?"

She bounces. "I love that you can challenge me, Vince. What guy knows about Traffic Collision and Avoidance Systems other than a sexy nerd like you?" There's longing in her eyes while she stares at my hands, stroking them. "You know what else is cool? You fucking do surgery."

I hate compliments. Plus, I'm thinking, *You probably have a license to kill people, so we're even. Let's move on.* "Speaking of surgery," I ask, "did it come up, the stuff I called about?"

That noble stare resets the mood. "It's all we talked about," she says, a pinched smile portending bad news.

"What can you tell me?" I gulp water.

"Well, we think we found Salaam, thanks to his Pittsburgh phone number you gave me. And a cadaver dog that sniffed out a corpse."

My eyes widen, thoughts rushing back to the line of bullshit I shoveled at Jackie.

Carolyn ignores my emotion. "How did Jackie seem to you?"

"Sleep deprived, scared. By the time she left, she seemed like she'd handle it."

"Interesting." Carolyn tilts her head back, pondering, then goes on. "The body was on the Allegheny's south bank near the tracks at Twenty-First Street. Minus a head. So, it might be him unless DNA says otherwise. His real name's not Salaam, by the way, it's Azim bin something or other. Salaam's the name he uses when doing arms business in South America. That's where he started collecting enemies. But we think he's just a fall guy insulating the boss. Anyway, like most of them, he was loaded with thumb drives, SIM cards, three burner phones, all the usual shit. They're always ready to go on the run, so it's a jackpot when you snag one before they're able to smoke their trails."

I want more about the boss. She drains the water bottle, her swallows audible, somehow comforting.

"What the fuck, Slim?" I'm rocking now, pulling the throw around me. "Jackie's post-op visit is tomorrow."

"We think the man with the foot drop—great call, by the way—fits a bad guy known as Reza. Arms dealer, Persian, more money than God. And, since the Vincennes goofed and downed an airliner with his cousin onboard back in '88, full of righteous rage and vengeance. He played all his cards during the Gulf War, so we thought. It's a surprise to see him out again, especially with his notoriety within intel and DHS. We have a hunch he came in over the southern border during all the chaos down there."

"So what's Reza doing in Santa Barbara if he's some big shit? Was he chasing Jackie's boyfriend? I mean, that's dangerous for a higher-up, isn't it?"

"Excellent question. Makes no sense to us, either. We want to see if he's been hounding Brent Carter, looking for Stingers or, more likely, getting proportional navigation upgrades for them. The platform's changed a lot since we handed them out in the Middle East. There's plug-and-play software that tightens up their lethality big time."

"But wouldn't he send an emissary to deal with Brent rather than risk discovery?"

"This is black market. Maybe that was Salaam's job. Then he caught pussy fever hangin' with Jackie. Got distracted, got slow, lost 'the cause.'" She does air quotes, then continues, "The more we learn about Salaam—any background—would be helpful. But be careful or Jackie will know you're fishing. Think about it—"

"Wait," I interrupt. "How'd you get Salaam's DNA? From Jackie's bandage? But it was just Jackie's, and it wouldn't have had any of Salaam's DNA, am I right?" I lock in a puzzled face.

She taps her thumb on her chest. "Molecular genetics at Yale when the agency pulled me in for physiological intel work. Skin cells have DNA and proteins, and that means intel. Identity, state of health, a person's recent life. Chemical exposure, explosives, toxins, weaponized pathogens, pollen from travel. It's all there." She pauses, letting me process. "I can't give details, but those data also track human contact. I was in Afghanistan using DNA and proteomics to close in on bin Laden." Her lips pout into a satisfied grin, then infectious laughing for us. "Yep, we knew his ass was in Abbottabad for sure when—"

"Where?"

"Abbottabad. The Pakistani town where he was holed up. You've heard that, right?"

"Yeah, of course," I reply, yet I'm thinking, *why do I seem to have heard about that more recently?* A weird chord resonates, but I smile and move on. "Jesus, that's, that's extremely cool, Carolyn. Hangin' with you, it's like, better than Disneyland! Except with real guns and dead bad guys."

"Thanks." She waves at a pile of journals next to her bed. "At least that's what I did before I got dragged into this little Stinger clusterfuck of yours."

# FORTY-ONE

CAROLYN GIVES ME A REFRESHER on my magic iPhone and reminds me to just be a good doctor. But news of Sal's grizzly demise turns this intriguing parlor game into back-alley Russian roulette. I can't wait.

Jackie's my last patient of the day, and aside from needing a limo to make the four-mile trip to my office, her exam's normal and she looks great. Physically, at least.

"Jackie, you've done a marvelous job of recovering from a life-threatening event." I pause. "But how do you feel?"

She looks away, pulls her head back, and studies the ceiling. "God, Vince, I'm sad." She shakes her head, laughing. "I just don't know what happened to him. He was such a big part of my life, and then just like that he wasn't. Just disappeared. At first, I thought he panicked and got worried about Brent finding out. But he and I had talked about just letting things happen. You know, Brent and I have been finished for a long time. I mean, who cares at this point, right?"

I nod, wondering if my knowing he's possibly dead shows in my eyes, tells in my shuffling feet.

She runs fingers through her hair, staring nowhere. "I really thought this was my last chance, my one shot for a real relationship. Maybe it was too good to be true."

"Jackie, you didn't do anything wrong. The ectopic was plain bad luck and—"

"Yeah, and maybe God showed me he really was too good to be true, just using me, and he wouldn't be there when I needed him. I don't know."

"How did you guys meet?" I picture Carolyn and crew checking one off their list.

"Sal was an assistant to one of Brent's customers from way the hell back. I first met him at a conference in Geneva. It was funny. I initially thought him to be sort of a sleaze, nothing like all the polished Middle Eastern GQ-types that Brent did business with. But I don't know. There was something about him. Maybe some bad boy thing I couldn't get out of my mind. And he always seemed to be there when Brent and I traveled together to meetings—like he was looking for me. Then one time I stayed in London while Brent flew on to Tehran, and Sal called me to see if I was free for dinner. And . . . that's all it took."

"Well, it happens."

She turns to me, coy and smiling.

"You know, he turned out to be one of the most sensitive men I've ever met and . . . well, here I am without him."

She holds the smile and sighs.

"Jackie, can you ask Brent about him? Diplomatically? I mean, if they're business partners or whatever, maybe you can bring it up casually or something. That would at least give you some answers, right?" I can't believe Carolyn's turned me into a lying sleaze, but I'm proud of myself.

"I could if Brent brings it up. It would make no sense for me to start that conversation. Weird thing is, Sal told me that he'd be in town all this month to work out a deal with Brent." She sits straight and proper, composed, in control.

I do a wooden nod and pray for her to elaborate. Nothing, so I ask, "Wow, a month. Must be a huge deal."

"Vince, this will work itself out—I'm a big girl. And, sincerely, thanks for letting me talk about this."

The ball dies in her court. Game over.

"Never a problem, Jackie." I give her a hug and ask, "Would you like something to help you sleep? A few good nights' rest can really make a difference."

"Yeah, Vince, good idea. I need some clear thinking. Thanks for being a great doctor and a great friend."

"Okay, I'll see in you in two weeks, sooner if you need anything."

We hug and walk to her driver who's strutting the waiting room like he owns the joint. I smile, but the stone-faced jerk turns for the door.

I get the feeling she's going to make it—or she's a better actor than I am. Maybe Salaam was just a plaything, a fling in its death throes.

I call in an Rx for my favorite brain-eraser, Ativan, but a sub-lethal dose in case she pops all of them after learning Salaam's in Pittsburgh. In two pieces. One of them as yet unaccounted for.

# FORTY-TWO

**AS SOON AS I'M OFF** the phone with Jackie's pharmacy, Carolyn calls.

"Oh, that's right. You're in control of my iPhone and you know my exact whereabouts and everything I'm doing."

She laughs in a way that confirms my suspicions.

"What can I say? You're valuable to us, Doc. That's all."

"I didn't get much today, did I?"

"Oh, quite the contrary. We knew that Reza had quasi-official dealings with BC AeroSystems way back, but not as recent to fit her timeline with Salaam. That was huge."

"But she didn't mention Reza by name, did she?"

"No, but Salaam's phone traffic has Reza all over it."

"Interesting," I say, waiting for a hint as to next steps.

"We think this is just the beginning. Your relationship with Jackie can be of much more value." There's a pause. "I mean, if you're still cool with it."

"Of course I am." I pause for the hitch. Silence. "But I won't see her for two weeks unless I invent some bullshit issue. I mean, she was moving normally today, and the limo was probably—"

"The what?"

"She took a limo to the office, but she probably could have driven."

"Was it Brent's limo? Who was with her?"

"I didn't see the car. Just some asshole driver. What's—"

"Stay in the office and wait for my call. I'm coming to get you. Five minutes, max."

One thing about Carolyn is she's always early. Four minutes after we hang up, she calls, telling me to act natural and come out to her car.

I scan for weirdos, then walk to her car and get in. There's the electric smell of tension.

"What the fuck, Slim? What's wrong?"

"The limo. Doesn't make sense. We've tracked her driving for the last week. I just didn't like the sound of it. Plus, we missed it—never saw her getting picked up."

"Well, thanks. Thanks for looking out for me."

"Are you carrying?"

Here we go. I frown.

"Your Glock?" she asks.

"Christ, it's a fucking doctor's office. Why would I need—"

"Because you need it. Trust me."

"Okay, okay! I'll . . . I'll carry from now on."

"Let's do a random drive."

I know what she's saying. *In case there's something else we missed.*

We're silent, fingers entwined. She gets off the 101 as soon as possible and makes for Pacific Coast Highway like a bat-out-of-hell crazy woman. As we fly by migrant farm workers hunched over verdurous fields, she tightens her grip on my hand. In an instant we're on two-lane PCH, cutting through Mugu Rock into shafts of sun and redolent ocean air. Two hands on the wheel now, she sees me touch my seat belt and turns to me, dead serious.

"I can't do this anymore." She sees the corners of my lips sag as I gaze at my lap.

Here we go. Typical woman. You fall in love with them; they disappear. This time it's a little later than expected, but I'm prepared to be—forgive me here, F. Scott—borne back ceaselessly into the past, into the cozy arms of my ugly old friend, Ms. Heartbreak.

"No. Oh, Vince, no. Not us. My job."

I'm relieved—for now. But why end what is, by all appearances, a successful career at CIA? I struggle for something to say, and it's lame.

"I'm fighting burnout too. Medicine's full of negative people pissed off at the world and taking it out on patients. I can't stand being around them. But we're both doing valuable work, and . . ." Her face says she's way past pep talks. "I'm sorry. I should have let you go on."

She continues. "Meeting you was . . . miraculous. And I don't want to lose you. I don't want to lose a chance at something great."

I choke but have nothing to say.

"Vince, I really meant it the night after Dargan's when I said that I feel it too. And it feels so right."

"Carolyn, I know and I support whatever you have to do with the agency. I mean, what I know comes from TV and movies, but I get what you go through, I get it—"

A hand chops in my direction. I stiffen.

"But do you, Vince? Do you? I mean do you really get my life? You know, I spent a lot of time over in the sandbox and Afghanistan. I don't mean downrange all the time. Mostly I was inside the wire with detainees."

Her eyes moisten, knuckles whiten on wheel and stick.

"Vince, I know the Taliban—the guys who love torture—said no reprisal killings, we're going to work with the infidels, blah, blah. How do you think the T-men are treating our allies, our terps, and the Afghan security forces now that we're gone? How do you think the policewomen are doing? The professional women? Christ, how do you think *any* of the women are doing there?"

The ocean, mountains, and dizzying curves speed toward us. I see in my side mirror a tornado of tan sand. She downshifts, then unloads.

"I mean, media shows you the big event scenarios that everyone knows about or tries to guess anyway, but never the cleanup of bombs, of killings. It can't show you up close the evil shit that happens every day. It can't show you when two twenty-somethings, that you've been working with, get knelt down so some motherfucker can put a twelve-gauge to them, blowing their heads up like basketballs, eyes popped out, like dangling plums. The sick assholes chanting and celebrating. Vince, little kids were there—I mean five-, six-year-olds—like it's a goddamn soccer match. And I have to stand there acting, with my face like a mask. For the next three weeks every time you inhale . . . it's that sulfurous stench of gun smoke and brains and blood, and it's so bad you can't wait to get to the stink of a foul latrine just to kill the smell—to break the image. But it stays. It never breaks."

My hand strokes her shoulder. She doesn't shrug it off, but keeps venting.

"The other great part TV hasn't gotten around to showing is a guy or a woman or a child thrown off a four- or five-story building. They make a nice popping sound when they hit. Did you know that? Even in sand they pop. What else they don't show you is that this shit is happening all the time—not once every six months. It's all the time because no one—not one goddamn motherfucker, Vince, can be trusted. And that means everybody's on the take, expendable, that they can be rationalized, moved out of the way. And you never know when it's your turn to kneel in the sand or be on a rooftop or walk up to be crucified. Eventually you start dreaming of strapping on Semtex and walking into a camp of your so-called allies, squeezing it off, and taking out as many of the sick fucks as you can. They're goddamn animals, Vince."

I brush her hair back from her face and she starts a laugh that turns into a full-blown cry.

"Do you want me to drive?"

"No!" she barks. "If I can wipe friends' brains off my boots, I can fucking drive PCH while having a fucking goddamned good cry."

Her hand motions to the glovebox. Napkins. I help her blow her nose, fighting against a glance at the speedometer. Says eighty-eight, if you really want to know.

"Okay, just asking." The back of my hand strokes her cheek and she tilts into it.

She sighs, unloading some grief. "Remember the physiologic intelligence stuff? It's measurement and signature of the human body—we call it MASINT. Everything has to have some goofy acronym." She sits up in the seat, slows down, her eyes lighting up at the bending highway. "Vince, it's incredibly cool stuff and it has such possibilities about who people are and where they've been, just about everything they've touched, for Chrissake. I mean, it's huge, and we won't need hundreds of operatives poking around in harm's way. That's the valuable work I could be doing."

"Why Yale?" I'm just curious, is all.

"I knew I'd be bored as hell living all the clichés and equestrian rigmarole at one of the Seven Sisters. I mean just 'cause a girl's smart doesn't mean she has to do dumb-fuck things, right? Okay, I'm preppy, but can you see me in dirndl skirts and scarab bracelets?"

"I knew there was something I loved about you, Slim."

She pulls into a beach parking lot and reaches for my hand. "So you're okay with all this?"

"Of course I am. I just don't want this"—I lift our hands—"to end when our . . . whatever it is, investigation is over."

"Vince, I would never use you like that."

I trace her lips with a finger. "I know."

"This is a beginning." Her eyes make me a believer, followed up with a crushing hug. "So, how about I drive you to your car, then you pick me up for dinner—my treat—say, about eight thirty?"

"Perfect. Our place, Plow and Angel, right? I'll call and get us a reso."

"I already did," she says.

# FORTY-THREE

THE WEATHER REPORT CALLS FOR the pitiless furnace of north-east wind we call a "sundowner," but at eight twenty this evening all I feel is the brutal weight of still air. The heady smell of eucalyptus concentrates into an arid, woody blend that burns eyes. Carolyn's property is far enough up Picacho Lane to catch some of the rising onshore coolness, but no luck tonight.

I take five at the entrance, making sure I wasn't followed by any more creepy gray sedans, then key in the code. The gate swings, and immediately something's off. I've been up here without moonlight, yet tonight it's a deep black cavern, almost a new shade of blue. Normally she's got every light on so the place looks on fire, but I barely see the outline of her house against the last of the twilight.

Farther down the brick drive, I see a reflection of light from the house on the garage windows. I relax and picture her shoes off, flopped on the couch, something good on the Sonos. When I get to the circle by the front door, there's no light, no life, just the bulk of her big-ass house looming even larger in the dark. The reflection wasn't from house lights, but from a dim yellow fixture over the garage doors.

I wait, hoping she ran to the garage for something, and I'll soon see that wide smile and dreamy eyes Carolyn deploys only after six. I stand by her front door, listening. Nothing. After entering the code, I put my shoulder on the carved beast of a door, lean in, and feel the hit of her cologne, her candles, fresh flowers, and lavender sprigs. Carolyn's world.

"Hey, Slim! Where are you?" Silence, save for the whoosh of ceiling fans—good, no power failure.

I walk to the glowing light switches in the kitchen and flick everything. There's Vermentino, cold and unopened, puddling condensation. Next to that, the distinctive cork from Templeton Rye, no bottle in sight.

My steps echo on tile as I walk to the fireplace in the kitchen's eating area. Her midnight blue Rag and Bone clutch sits eager on the table. Good again, no burglary. There's a shoebox, open and empty, spewing tissue paper. The sight makes me ill.

My heart bangs away, but I'm grateful for taking her up on carrying my Glock. I pull it and shout again, with no answer other than reverb off floors and empty hallways. I check upstairs and it's empty. That leaves only the garage, detached and a long fifty-yard walk in the dark.

My cell phone light helps for two or three feet in front of me, yet it's hard to remember my way. Left of the front door, then curving along the library's windows, then slowing down for the change from gravel to flagstone pavers set into the grass leading up to the garage. But I misjudge and almost face-plant. *Who the fuck builds a stone and grass "play area" for their goddamn car?*

As I get close, I see through the side door's window a flicker of light. Okay, now I'm in doctor mode. I'm sure she's unconscious after a trip-and-fall, fixed and dilated from an intracranial bleed. No, maybe murdered fits better. I swear I hear rock music. I reach for the door handle but suddenly freeze and jump backward, cowering at the window.

Carolyn's in the garage. And she's got company.

# FORTY-FOUR

**I DRAW BACK FROM THE** door, stumbling into the shadows by one of the garage's windows. With its wood-beamed ceiling, herringbone stonework, and flickering candles, I could be peering into a Tuscan country church—except for Carolyn, slinking around some sweat-soaked guy fastened to a chair with cable ties. She's in lacy black panties, matching bra, and leopard stilettos, so not really dressed for church. I pull my phone, set for 911. Just in case.

Wild strands of hair cling to her damp face. She blows some away and flips the rest with the back of her hand while pacing in a slow, deliberate circle. I want to run to her, but she'd probably cap my ass as soon as I touched the door.

Her pacing stops and she crouches close in front of him, one high-heeled leg out to the side. I sense a hint of madness in her eyes. She twists a strand of hair, the other hand tapping her leg, keeping time to an AC/DC tune blasting. AC/DC, for God's sake—did I interrupt some sexual adventure?

"Where's the Shâhin?" Louder now, closer. "Where the fuck is Reza, and what does he want?"

He looks straight through her, saying nothing, head back defiantly.

She reaches behind her and grasps something, sliding it under her waistband. He clenches his teeth in a grimace, then shivers for a few seconds and goes limp, chin to chest.

"I don't know Reza!" he shouts.

"Wow, you don't know shit today, do you?" She fists the side of his head. "You lyin' fuck face!"

Dazed, he raises his head, eyes closed and with a ghost of a smile. Carolyn inches in, expecting answers.

"I know," he says, eyes all over her, "I know, where I come from, girl with blonde hair . . . is girl who to pay money for the sex."

I recoil, awaiting the volcano. But no, she rises, strides the length of the room a few times, returns, and takes her time doing a seductive straddle on him. I sure as hell want to turn away, but who could? Her finger under his chin gradually lifts his head until eyes connect. Her other hand retrieves the cell phone from inside the front of her panties and moves it back and forth under his nose. She tilts his head up and to the side and moves in even closer, rubbing herself on him. I want to scream, present myself, but there's a blinding flash, then two more in quick succession.

"Oh shit, these are good," she says, showing three selfies. "Don't ya think? Where should we post them? Besides Al Jazeera, I mean." He frowns. "Don't worry, I'll write great captions. To let all your jihadist friends know you're not weak. Yeah, I know, you let a half-naked blonde chick deck-slam your ass and hog tie you, but you're not weak. You're just a dumb fuck."

As she leans away, I see him regain some awareness, seeming lucid. He turns to my window and I drop into rosemary bushes, then move to the other window. From here I have a better view of Carolyn's face. Any sign of derangement I imagined is gone.

"Where," she whispers, pauses, then continues, each word climbing a crescendo of rage. "The. Fuck. Is. Reza?"

He looks up, mouth open to speak, then wilts. She tilts her head with raised eyebrows, prompting him. She lifts each leg off of him and walks back to a red tool cart. Her Templeton's. She fills a third of the glass, then swirls it, blowing liberated esters and ethers at his face. He shudders and blinks.

Carolyn emits an abrupt, sick laugh, scaring the hell out of me, and shouts, "Hey, scumbag! You don't drink I guess, huh? Well, I do. And it makes me goddamn, fuckin' crazy."

I see his eyes go wide, fearful, looking her up and down as she sips booze. She pauses, then splashes what's left in his greasy face. He doesn't react. He's got to be on something.

"You know what that means? That means I'm done asking questions." She looks down, shaking her head, four fingers inside her panties. "Yep, I'm done."

She faces him, walking backward. I'm ready to jump in if she falls, but she makes it to the cart, feels for the stun gun's grip, then lunges at him, shouting, "I'm fucking done with you, asshole!"

"No!" he cries. "No! No more."

I'm cheering inside—he's cracking—but she looks increasingly unsteady, a hand on the cart as if she's trying to calm down.

"Okay, dickhead, no more shocks. Knives maybe? You guys like knives, right? Taliban says no schools for girls, so I say no balls for guys. Fair enough? Or, how about this? I know you like cutting heads off. I've seen it—looks like fun, but I wonder what that feels like . . . if it's done really, really slowly. Maybe from back to front, just you and me all the way till the final cut through your carotids? Yeah, I'm gonna do those one at a time." She's back at the cart, speaking to herself, rattling tools. "So you get to be with me as long as possible. How's that sound? I know—messy. But I need this floor painted anyway. Okay, let's see what I've got here."

His eyes widen. I want to intervene if she goes nuts—more nuts—

on him, but I'm thinking if I startle her, I'm probably dead meat. Then again, I'm likely dead meat being in love with a crazy person.

She moves closer to him. "Right, motherfucker? Knives are cool, aren't they? Hey, wait. They told you that if you get schwacked by a chick, the seventy-two virgins deal is off, right? Hey, dickhead, jihadi jackass, I'm talking to you!" she shouts, spit spraying, leaning over with her hands behind her, now inches from his face. She cocks her head and inches a hand up, showing him locking pliers.

"Ha, fooled ya!" She's got an open-mouthed smile one would give a toddler after pulling a teddy bear from behind one's back. His head falls backward, she seizes his jet black hair, shakes him, and continues the adult-to-child tone. "Oh, you wanted a knife. I'm sorry. Well, how about I get a knife," she says, motioning to the tools, "while you hold on to this." She locks the pliers on his left index finger. I hear a crunch and a shriek.

"Say, you're right-handed, correct? I mean I saw your cheap-ass Swatch on your left wrist," she says, moving back to the cart. "I wouldn't want to ruin the finger that you point with when you're pontificating your fucking death-to-America bullshit or fingering your bitch. They gave you a wife, right? Or did they lock a vest on her before you got your slimy mitts on her?"

He stares at the clamp, then at her quizzically.

"Let's see, where were we?" She puts a finger to her chin while revealing a large, black-handled chef's knife with her other hand.

"Oh, yeah, that's right. Reza. Where is he and what's he want from me?" She approaches, the knife held low. I hear clicks, then see the knife tapping time to AC/DC on the pliers and dusky wad of flesh. Her other hand circles, deep inside her waistband. What the hell?

She steps back, satisfied. "Do you want to give me some answers now or do we keep going? Pliers. Then knife. Pliers. Then knife. That's no fun. Boring, right?"

I watch his gaze move between the knife and the shifting hand inside her panties. Finally, his eyebrows droop and his face goes blank.

Carolyn broadens a grin. Victory.

I see his chest rise. "He doesn't want you," he says, in feeble sigh. "He wants your doctor friend."

As his words trail off, I hear something guttural, then the clatter of steel pliers hitting the damp garage floor.

# FORTY-FIVE

CAROLYN SEES ME AS SHE scans the windows, then moves out of my line of sight. The door slams open.

I rattle off a run of shouts, shielding my head. "No. Oh my God. It's me! Oh, fuck. You fucking scared me to death! What the—"

"Vince, you need to get out of here." Carolyn's voice is calm, directive as she walks to where I dropped back into the rosemary. "You cannot be part of this."

"The hell I can't! I already am! I heard it. He came for me, for God's sake. I'm being tracked, and you guys . . ." She's chagrined. "And I sincerely appreciate that you, you saved me, but I ain't going anywhere. What were you doing? Why are you dressed like . . . ?"

I adjust to the new glare through the open door. She's sweaty—I mean, post-marathon sweaty—skin sparkling as clumped, ropey strands of hair cling to her shoulders. "Carolyn, what's with the outfit?" I start at the shoes, shaking my head all the way up. "What the hell happened? Was he waiting for you, for me, when you got home?"

"No, he showed up about two hours later. I was getting dressed for you—"

"So did he jump you, or what?"

"The security system let me know . . . my dad was nuts. I knew it wasn't you since the gate code wasn't used. It told me the house and garage were secure, no movement, no forced entry, so he had to be in the weeds. I went down and opened the front door a crack, like I would do for you, and waited."

*Guts or stupidity?* I think.

"The system said only one intruder, so when he showed his face I tased his ass, cleared his AK."

*Okay, guts.*

"Then sedated him and waited, making sure he didn't have staged backup. Then I dragged him to the garage."

I look from house to garage, visualizing it. "Obviously something is going on. Did we screw up?"

"Someone screwed up, but not us."

"Slim, you're not in trouble, right? I mean, you . . . you're fucking killing someone in there, but . . . you can do that shit, right?" I turn away. Wondering what I'm doing here.

I hear a laugh. She goes hand to mouth, stifling her chuckle, but keeps smug eyes, full of sexual aggression I've seen on her before. She moves close and throws her head back, holding back glee.

"Love, you're safe. And I'm just doing a little rapport-based elic-itation." Her knuckle lifts my chin. "Wasn't I great? And damn, I feel"—she drops a hand below her knee and slowly runs it up to her waist, whispering—"I feel long today." "Long" is dragged out and punctuated with those goddamn half-closed Marilyn eyes again.

I'm confused. And getting hard. "Are you drunk? Shit, you are, aren't you?"

"Well I'm entertaining someone, but he's not having any tonight, so all the more for me. But no, I'm not drunk when I work an asset. Justice. Drunk on justice maybe." She's sane for two seconds, then throws her leg for me to catch. "By the way, like the shoes?

Louboutin faux leopard. Got 'em just for you, for our date." She raises a palm, a child explaining, "Don't worry, I was careful. No blood on them."

PTSD has my deepest respect and wide dispensation for screwball behavior, but this is stunning. The Carolyn I know is very sexual, but who's the other woman dressed like an escort, acting like a violent demon, getting off on sadism?

I look over her shoulder at the person lashed in the chair. He's wearing black high-top Nikes and skinny jeans. I slowly move around her and see his slicked hair, faded black shirt, his waist tied, slumped over. He appears fit, thirtyish. And possibly dead. I turn back. Carolyn responds with a *What do you expect?* shrug.

"Jesus." I'm unable to look away. "Should I rescue this bastard?"

"I told you to get out of here. I'm working," she says in sing-song, stroking my arm.

"What are you going to do?"

"I'm going to take off a few more extremities, get more intel, then top him off with this little cocktail of mine I like to call perma-sleep. Then I'll call cleanup, who'll take him, freeze him, and toss him into a wood chipper on a barge out by Santa Cruz Island." Her head bobs. Case closed.

Shocked, I see she's not drunk but working. She's in the pocket.

"Why do you ask, Vince? This's my job. Remember what we talked about in the car today? Tonight was perfect timing, a gift from God, when this piece of shit shows up to jump me tonight. Then kidnap you, by the way. He's my precious little gift. Personal, luscious revenge." She tilts, plants a kiss. "Get it, Doc?"

My shock becomes curiosity. I turn away from the garage scene and lock onto Carolyn. "Who the hell is that?"

"Keep it down! You'll wake Scumbag, and I need a break."

I turn an ear and ask, "Is that AC/DC?"

Carolyn blurts a twisted laugh. "Yeah, they hate rock. I've got this track looping. What the fuck is it? I think it's—"

"'Rock and Roll Ain't Noise Pollution.'"

"Yes!" she purrs, with a rub against me. "Very hot. We need this on the next time you fuck me."

That makes it now official: nothing this woman says or does will ever surprise me. I expect her to block me as I move toward the doorway, but she doesn't.

His breathing is labored, and he's oblivious to my presence. I'd check his pulse, but don't for fear of electrocution for all I know. His chair is tied to a metal support pillar between the empty car bays. On top of the Craftsman cart are several sizes of locking pliers, a foot-long screwdriver, propane torch, stainless steel mixing bowl, and one of her Wüsthof-Trident chef knives—the ten-inch with a rust-colored smear of oxidizing blood. There's a slow drip from his right hand, no pumpers. An empty ten-cc syringe, needle capped, startles me more than anything. I snap to Carolyn.

"It's not mine," she protests. "It's his. I mean, I gave it to him. Used it on him. Whatever."

"Never recap a needle unless you want to stick yourself."

"Excuse me, Doctor. I had a few other things on my mind."

I move closer and check the bowl. It's empty except for a crumpled paper towel and two lavender nitrile gloves, partially inside out. It's an eerie sight ripped from an ER exam room. We love purple gloves and Craftsman carts. Somehow, it relaxes me . . .

"It's under the trash in the bowl," she says from the doorway.

I frown at her. She leans on the doorframe, arms crossed, a bent leg resting on the toe of its stiletto—it could be a famously hot, Clio-worthy Victoria's Secret ad. Minus the half-dead dude.

"The finger. In the bowl. If you're dying to see it."

I lift the gloves and recoil. I want to be a physician, yet, more,

I want to run. To run from Carolyn, the woman I thought I knew, to run from whoever she is or has become, run from whatever was happening tonight. Is this sex-crazed nut job someone she's hidden from me? Is this the real Carolyn, different from who I convinced myself—invented for myself—I'm in love with? Is this how she wants to destroy "us" tonight?

She drops her head, embarrassed and uneasy, as I turn and walk to her.

"Oh, sweetie, don't leave me," she says, her voice breathy, relaxed, as if to say, *Things are not what they appear.* As if to say, *This is Hollywood, this is fake.* I gaze around at the Hitchcock movie I landed in tonight.

She, too, looks the scene over, as if awakened, wondering where she is, how she got here. Her proud, beautiful face crumples. I clutch her as tightly as I can; her body wilts.

"Help me. Help me now, Vince. Stay with me. Please help me."

"I will. I will, I will," I say, pressing my face against hers. "We'll get through this. We're gonna get through this." I push back, looking for her eyes, but she won't show them. "We're connected, right, Slim?"

She nods, and I keep a secure grip on her as we rock in silence. It's terrifying seeing firsthand these blurred lines between her sex drive and need for payback. I know every word came deep from my soul. Yet I'm riven by how much longer I can survive in Carolyn's world. Or outside of it.

# FORTY-SIX

"YOU'RE IN THE BIG LEAGUES now, Vince," Carolyn says, eyeing 9-1-1 cued up on my phone. "Call Rachael and her crew." From what I know about cops versus FBI on TV, she nailed it.

Rachael keeps us on the phone in case whoever's in the garage has goons waiting. Soon, there are headlights in the driveway and Rachael running, gun drawn.

"You guys okay?" she asks, then double-takes Carolyn's getup, then me. I give a "not my fault" shrug. She steps into the garage, shaking her head as she returns to hug Carolyn.

Seconds later, two black Suburbans with unearthly glows from blacked-out windows park near us, angled to block the driveway but leaving themselves a straight shot to the road. Men, women, all with combat gear and maybe a paramedic or two, rush out. I see night vision goggles on helmets as they beeline to the house, some scattering across the grounds, three to the garage, Rachael following.

"Okay, can we get some lights in the garage? But leave 'em off outside," Rachael snaps, more apprehension than irritation in her big-breath command. Rachael signals the others to enter as someone tosses me a blanket for Carolyn. Someone with hypervigilant eyes darting tells us the house is secure. We move inside.

I would have put money on being up all night, holding hair back while she puked, but I was wrong. Tonight is all Carolyn; zero booze and a shower is all it takes. When we get to the kitchen, Rachael and two guys in camo Kevlar are at the table. They stand.

"Wow, someone smells good," says Rachael.

Carolyn throws her head my way. "It's him. He's been rolling in my rosemary all night."

"You dudes okay?" Rachael asks.

"Yeah, we're fine. How's the Delta Bravo?" she asks one of the guys, then provides a translational aside to me, "'Douche Bag.'"

"He'll do well, ma'am. We're going to take him in to wait for the meds to burn off a little before going back to break him. Did you put that tourniquet on his finger?"

Carolyn looks confused.

"I did," I confess. "I tore it from the cleanest shop towel I found. He still had active bleeding when I got there."

"He's a doctor," says Rachael. They all look at Carolyn, who responds with a smile. Some pride, too.

"Great job, Doc; not too tight, not too loose."

I nod, then he moves to Carolyn. "We're taking ID shots of him in the truck, and I'll be back with hard copies for you. Also, if it's all right, ma'am, we'll keep electronic positions outside tonight, have men in the area and wait for further instructions."

"I don't think it's necessary, but I won't argue. Thanks, guys, and by the way, his AK is cleared and safe. I threw it in the bushes just outside the front door," Carolyn says and shakes hands. She turns, assuming we want whiskey. She assumed right.

Silent and sipping, the three of us stare at the lights on the ocean oil rigs. Carolyn looks shell-shocked; I am shell-shocked.

Rachael speaks. "So, let's talk about what happened. I'll scribe."

Carolyn, elbows on the table, looks at her glass and then at us one by one.

"Vince and I took a drive down PCH. I'm positive no one followed us."

Rachael swivels to me.

"Well, if they did they were in a Formula-1 car," I say.

Laughing, then Carolyn continues, "Drove home, nothing behind us. Dropped Vince at his car, then came back here to get ready for our dinner date."

"Vince?" asks Rachael.

"Yeah, that's it. I showered, read a little, then drove here. No visitors or calls, no weird cars. I'm sure no one tailed me."

Carolyn says, "I was upstairs getting ready when I got a hit on the security system. Usually a mule deer or a mountain cat jumps the fence. But when I go infrared, it is human. The trail heat came over the front fence just off the road. No cars.

"So, I knew someone was there, and it wasn't Vince since he'd use the gate code. It showed the house and garage were secure, so the IR sig moving to the house meant he or she was solo. I went down and opened the front door a little, like I would do for Vince, and waited. Then when the system showed him just outside the door, I held until I had a shot, then hit him with the Taser, disarmed him, cleared his AK. Then I juiced him, made sure he was alone, and dragged him to the garage."

"Don't you have an audible alarm?" Rachael asks.

"Yeah, but I silenced it during the seven-second delay."

"Makes sense," Rachael smirks, and goes on, "so you didn't have time to finish getting dressed?"

"Hell, no." She pauses, winks at me. "Plus, it fucks them up more the way I did it. You should try it sometime, Rach. Just summon your inner slut."

Rachael giggles, checks my reaction. I look at both of them like they're insane, but, hey, somehow it's making sense to me now. This is their life. They can act, they can lie, they can pretext. *They can fucking kill you and get away with it, for God's sake.* No wonder Carolyn wants out. I'm thinking I want in.

"Where was I?" Carolyn resumes.

"Dragged him to the garage," says Rachael.

"Yeah, strapped him in, loosened him up, and worked him. It only took ten cc's."

I lift my chin, wanting the recipe.

"Can't tell you, Doc, but it's magical. So, he's not giving whereabouts on Reza, but when I ask using his *nom de guerre*, Abu Shâhin—Father of the Hawk—he knows I'm for real." She pauses, glances at me. "Then says Reza wants my friend."

They turn for my reaction and see maybe the whiter shade Procol Harum had in mind? Nobody speaks, then two brisk, double knocks hit the front door.

Carolyn reaches for my hand. "Relax, it's our crew," she says, pointing to the security screen. Rachael answers, hand on gun, and returns with color glossies of Mister Delta Bravo. In his birthday suit.

"Jesus fucking Christ!" I see the tattoo. "This clown delivered my flowers the other night."

# FORTY-SEVEN

"**SO RACH, THIS FUCKS UP** everything, right?" Carolyn bangs her empty glass on the table.

"Hell, yeah, it does. I'll set up a call with JTTF tomorrow, for what it's worth."

"Thanks," says Carolyn. "That's 'Joint Terrorism Task Force,' in case you're wondering, Vince. I'll see what's come in over the last twenty-four while we wait for flower boy to break hard. I suspect he was on a one-way and doesn't know jack."

They feel me thinking and give an opening. "I thought jihadists didn't defile their bodies with tattoos. Was he an outside hit man, maybe here for something else?"

The two of them hesitate, locked on each other. Carolyn stiffens up like when she's going CIA on my ass, saying, "Vince, he was sent here looking for you. Period."

Rachael adds, "Some follow the call after getting inked up. They tagged al-Zarqawi, the Green Man, with his crude prison tattoos."

I glare at Rachael, reading her poker face. "Bring him back. I should have helped the fucker bleed out."

Carolyn continues, "You and I are welded together for the

immediate future. No John Wayne stunts, nothing happens to you. Do you understand?"

"Yeah, I understand. Should we get out of town? I mean, I don't have any surgeries coming up. I could get coverage, disappear for a while. Maybe we could go to—"

"Vince, please. Think this through with me." Carolyn takes my hand and looks at Rachael, welcoming any support. "You are safe with me. And this house is a fucking fortress with state-of-the-art security and safe rooms. So we don't have to go on the run. You do need to get out of work until we get more information—"

Rachael interrupts, "Information on the intruder, who he works for, that kind of stuff. He may be working for Brent Carter, just spying on his wife." She chokes on that one and knows it.

Still I nod, trusting this angel, Carolyn. I go to the library to leave voice mails for my partners and office manager, letting them know that I need to use at least a week of vacation time. They'll be good with it, and I see thumbs-up from the two whisperers in the kitchen.

When I return, Rachael reassures, "This is all going to work out, Vince."

"He knows that, Rachael," says the woman who two hours ago was an unhinged fiend. Yet, I'm glad she's on my side.

"So what's the plan for the next few days?" I ask. No answer. "Why aren't the cops here?"

"We're better than cops," Rachael blurts out. "Right, partner?"

Carolyn picks at the label of her water bottle. "Fuckin' A." Then to me, "Okay, write down a list of the clothes you need for maybe a week or two, and I'll send Rachael to your house to get them tomorrow."

I agree.

"Then tomorrow I'll call in to the JTTF meeting, and we'll know a lot more about Mister Douche Bag and company. That should give us ops for the next few days."

I shrug.

"How we operate, where we go, where we don't go, when you go back to a normal life," Rachael explains.

Carolyn pours us a whiskey refill with an eyebrow flash. "Except normal doesn't exist as long as he's hangin' out with me."

I laugh, but she's right. I also know I'll be going to bed full of rye whiskey and a craving for some sweet, old-fashioned Sicilian revenge.

# FORTY-EIGHT

**I'M SNUGGLED INTO CAROLYN'S CREAMY** sheets enjoying one of the better dreams of a fitful night—she's holding a gun while pushing a cart down the produce aisle at Whole Foods. Half naked, of course.

"Hey, you," with a whisper, her hand gently roving across my back.

Through a seaward window, I see a yellow stain on the horizon turning a few clouds red below an early blue sky. There's the scent of coffee. Strong coffee. I feel her collapse on the bed's edge.

"How do you feel?" she asks.

"Not bad, considering I probably had zero REM sleep. How about you?"

"I'm fine, considering I haven't gotten jazzed like that in a long time."

"Well, we all need it once in a while, Slim. Thanks for saving my life."

She leans over and strokes my forehead, her damp hair cool on my cheek. "I see you beat me to the shower," I say. "I guess I should get up."

"No, relax. It's not even seven yet. I have a conference call I have to do in private. Here's an espresso I made for you, and the paper."

I roll and shake myself awake. I reach for her from under the quilt and hold on for dear life.

She falls onto me and says, "Take your time and I'll come up as soon as I'm off the phone. Rachael's coming over, then you and I can sneak out for a while. Maybe get some breakfast." She tosses me the remote as she closes the door.

I savor espresso while searching local TV news for stories of intruders with missing digits. None, so off it goes, letting me focus on last evening, my new reality. Instantly, I've got palpitations—probably caffeine, not terrorists—so for the next half hour I seek the solace of Carolyn's waterfall steam shower. Its droning hypnotizes me back to the Pittsburgh of my youth, sharing sticky summer Market Square sidewalks with pigeons, the air a mélange of roasting coffee beans, peanuts, and Italian sausage hawked by street vendors. The stand-up bar at Oyster House—fish sandwich, two Rolling Rock ponies, no proof of age needed as long as you could lean in like a millworker and order with conviction. The latch of the bathroom door clicks me back into life.

"Vince, you okay?" Carolyn stands in the archway, expressionless, holding a mint green towel.

"Sorry, just wandering off in here. How 'bout you?"

"Yeah, all is well," she says, laying the towel on the counter between the sinks. "Just come down when you're done." I take the towel and tone to mean, *Get your ass downstairs—all is not well.*

She's pacing in the library, phone to ear. I hesitate but get waved in and taken by the hand through the French doors to the patio. When she scrapes a chair away from the table, thrushes burst from olive trees lining the walkway to the pool. I sit. She's away to finish her call, all the time staring at me. When the call ends, she looks at her phone, sighing and bearing the expression I have when I'm about to tell a patient she has cancer.

"What's up, Slim?" I kick out a chair for her.

"That was Rachael. They're moving fast, and that's why they're hot to get you out of the way."

I've heard those words spoken only in movies—well, maybe a few hospital boardrooms, now that I think about it.

"There was a deep hack by Russia, ISIS-K, or both maybe, into NCP." Before I can open my mouth, she adds, "National Continuity Policy. It's a linkage of Homeland Security, Defense, CDC, Energy, FCC—essential agencies who have to talk to one another during a crisis. A shadow government to survive anything catastrophic. Theoretically." She drops her head. "It looks like all the comm links were hacked—code names, people, FEMA plans, maybe even mission-essential functions . . . all that shit may have been compromised." She laughs, shaking her head at the ocean.

"Jesus, how could this happen?"

"Vince, that rig was so fucking loosey-goosey, a kid could have hacked it. Probably was a kid." Her lips move over her teeth. I come closer, expecting tears. They're right on time. "That's the news from Rachael. The JTTF call was worse. So bad we're meeting again at one o'clock." I use my cashmere sweater to dry her eyes.

"Just don't blow your nose in it, Slim."

She stands, cackling. "Come on, I gotta get the hell out of here before the call. Let's take a ride."

# FORTY-NINE

**WE DRIVE TO A DESERTED** Loon Point, hunching into the breeze on our walk to the beach. It's low tide, so the wind has a lot of sand to play with. We find a few flat rocks against the seawall and sit. With the cupped hands of a pro, Carolyn lights a cigarette for us.

"So how does this hack fit with last night?" I ask, blowing smoke over my shoulder as I hand the cigarette back to her.

"Hacking NCP means they want us helpless after an attack. No NCP, no quick response and recovery. Last night means they think Jackie may have blown this op by giving you Salaam, so you're a big problem." She hands back the smoke, then doodles a finger in the sand. "The mission last night could have played out two ways. If they succeed in getting you, they've got more time to plan the attack. If they missed you, they have to attack as soon as possible, even if all the pieces aren't in place."

"So, they missed last night and . . ." I wave a hand.

"They'll figure out Douche Bag is burned, not just AWOL, and you're still a problem. If I was running it for them, I'd pounce. A-SAP." She turns and barks, "Make sure that's out when you're done. Some crow's gonna pick it up and set the frickin' mountain on fire with it."

I glare and stand.

She lunges for my arms. "Oh, Vince," she sighs. "I'm sorry for snapping."

I tug her close. "Forget it. You're stressed."

I feel sniffs muffled by my sweater and crashing waves. She surfaces after a third or fourth wave and holds my face in her hands, looking deep into me.

"Listen, Vince, please. I've never felt this before." The squeeze tightens. "Vince, I love you. I love you very, very much. Please don't ever forget that." She pauses, head down. "I know you think I'm crazy—this job has made me crazy. But I can be normal again, I will be normal again. For you, with you . . . I can do that. I just need time and—"

Here, clinical Vince wishes he was a shrink, but, no, I know what I'm feeling. Time to fess up.

"Carolyn, this is nothing about Helen. She and I had something real, but the moment I saw you, the universe flipped on me, and I knew I've never, ever really loved anyone before like this. You, Carolyn, have allowed me to know love again. A truly great love that I never knew could exist."

A smile breaks through her tears, and I know I'll put up with anything to be with this woman.

"Slim, I'm your companion through whatever it takes. A companion who loves you."

She's suddenly frail, her head against mine, murmuring, "I know . . . I know that."

A breaker folds with a pop and pushes suds to within a yard of our shoes. "Let's walk before we get trapped, Slim." She turns to me, staring a little too long, then we take off to where the beach widens. I squeeze her hand three times in quick succession. She expects me to say something, but I'm silent, staring at the rocky ribs of an orange-tan bluff ahead.

We face the Pacific. "Vince, someone on Rachael's team from Homeland found a panga boat running in circles up past Refugio."

"Drugs, right? What's the big?"

"Negative drug hits. But a bomb dog wanted to marry the fuckin' thing."

"So maybe it was gunrunners, ammo and shit. They hatchet holes and leave 'em circling so they scuttle."

"Pangas don't sink. The spectroscopy and neutron swabs came back Ultra HE. Military grade."

"You mean high explosives, warheads? Like—"

"They found olive drab color . . . scrapes on the inside hull that matched the plastic used on battle cases of MANPADS." She beats me to my question and says, "Man-portable air-defense systems. Like Jackie's Grails. But this was residue from US Marine cases— Stinger cases. And the wheel was tied with bungees like the ones used to bundle up Stinger rounds."

"Jesus fucking Christ. Why here in Santa Barbara?"

"Why not here? South American drugs have been coming through here since before I was born, and what? They catch maybe one every five years? The central coast is quiet, and you can go everywhere from here untouched. All the high-level security's up at Vandenberg for launch threats, not the weekly milk runs of reefer and coke."

I stare at the dazzling water.

"We're broke, Vince. Not just defense money, but the will to protect our borders, defend ourselves, fight our enemies. Our will has been broken."

"So Jackie and Grails might be real, huh?"

"Ha," she laughs. "Understatement. We've got dots from Afghanistan floating around out there to connect, and the call today is all about that. Let's just say there's been a lot of spikes in some unusual activities over the past two months. More so in the last week."

I tap her thigh. "See, we need to boogie out ahead of this." It falls flat as I entwine my fingers. She subdues them with silken hands, hands that nearly murdered someone last night.

"I'm not leaving you out of my sight, so—"

"I get it," I interrupt, scanning the empty strand. "So let's go back for your call."

We climb to the seawall, then she stops a step above me, taking me by the shoulders. "Vince, we'll be okay. But we gotta be smart."

I look into eyes that smile but seem to ask if I understand how serious this is, that ask if I get it—the fact that the dude could have clipped both of us last night. "Carolyn, I know."

"Holy moley."

"What?"

"Calling me 'Carolyn.'" Air quotes. "Now you're Doctor Serious all of a sudden."

"No, Slim. Just seriously trusting you, *Carolyn*, to get us the fuck out of this mess."

# FIFTY

IF ANYONE'S WATCHING OVER CAROLYN'S place, it sure ain't with boots on the ground. It's deserted except for Rachael's truck in the driveway and her waving from the front door.

"Hey, guys. Are you good?"

"Rach, you bad-ass bitch! Yeah, we're okay." Carolyn hugs Rachael and lifts her with a yelp and a twirl. She's loosened up from the intruder.

"Great. Fed my dogs so I can do the call from here."

Plural. I picture large and agile dogs enjoying life from the bed of her pickup. We move to the kitchen. I give space with a start for the back door.

Carolyn wags a finger. "Stay, Vince. Grab a Coke and sit your butt on the patio in case we need you."

I flop into a lounge chair, curious as hell but wishing this was just about the babe of a lifetime minus the Stinger part.

They tap and swipe iPads in silence, Rachael getting up every few minutes for pacing and watch gazing. My phone says it's five minutes to one when I hear Carolyn joining the call. They stare at one another for a moment, then Carolyn speaks, Rachael types like a court reporter.

After forty minutes or so, Carolyn raps on the window, snapping me from ocean gazing. When I enter, I hear a guy winding up with thank-yous, vague next steps, formalities. It's the delicate dance of egos I'd imagined, only it sounds like they actually accomplished something, unlike medical meetings. She mutes the phone to tell me it's her boss, Bruce Potter.

Rachael whispers that he's nervous. (She's sure a past lover dumped him for a doctor.)

"Lucky her," I whisper.

Carolyn asks, "Sir, Doctor DeLuca is with us, if you have any questions for him."

After a curious pause, Potter speaks. "Hello, Doctor. Again, just to clarify, the gentleman you saw being detained at Carolyn's residence last night"—and here, Rachael and Carolyn grin while mouthing "detained"—"you have a recollection of seeing him before, correct?"

"That's correct, sir. He delivered flowers to my home. Supposedly they were sent by Jackie Carter." Rachael slides a bottle of water in my direction; Carolyn unwinds me with bouncing palms down.

"Okay, then I think we can end this call and proceed with our action items, continue watchful waiting, and, umm, regroup tomorrow morning. If something changes, be sure to contact me first," he says. They all reply with robotic, anonymous "okays."

My companions look to each other, and I want an update.

"Let's move in here," Carolyn says and begins a deflated walk to the library. She opens a skinny door in the paneling beside the fireplace and pulls out a painter's easel and throws on a flip chart. She takes in its blankness, then us, all the while tapping a leg with a red marker.

"Okay, Woods, what do we know for sure? Let's start with the known facts."

Rachael, next to me on the couch, tilts my way.

"He's fine, Rach, go with it all."

"Well, rewinding, you and Doc here almost got capped last night by a guy who has a DNA tag link to Jackie but no ID hits, no nothing except for that skull thingy tattoo—"

"Skull and sword," I interrupt, and they both turn to me with wide *say again* eyes. "I got flowers allegedly from Jackie the other day, and he was the delivery guy. For sure. Same face, same tattoo, inner forearm."

Rachael nods. "We can confirm him with pollen traces. Do you still have the flowers?"

"Yeah, they're still beautiful in a vase on my kitchen table." My thoughts wander. That could have been the night of my last breath, but he chose not to kill me. I want to get in my car and drive fast. Mexico. Canada, maybe.

Carolyn feels me peering into the abyss again. "Vince, he was just gathering intel on you, where you live, who else lives there, and so on."

Bullshit. It was a near miss.

Rachael opens her iPad. "Santa Barbara PD found an abandoned delivery van in Goleta last night," she reads. "White, no markings. Reported stolen from a Ventura bakery seventy-two hours ago."

Carolyn scribbles on the flip chart. "The guy who was banging Jackie, pending DNA results, may be dead and she didn't know anything about it, right, Vince?"

I nod as Rach speaks up.

"Doc remembers a guy with foot drop, or whatever—"

"Exactly right, Rachael," I interrupt.

"—visiting Jackie in the hospital."

Carolyn writes "Reza" on the flip chart just as her cell phone rings. "Talbot," she answers. After ten seconds of listening, she's shaking her head at us as she says into the phone, "I'm sure it's Russian script kiddies again." More head shaking, but exaggerated. "You're joking, right? No fuckin' way. Thanks." She turns back to the chart.

"What's up, Carolyn?" asks Rachael.

"There was a distributed DOS this morning . . . big-ass," she turns to me, "denial of service. It nearly brought Chicago, Washington, the entire East Coast internet to its knees. Amazon, PayPal, AT&T, parts of Google . . . all of them were down for a time."

"How can that happen?" I ask.

"There are centers that take human-language internet addresses like Google.com and help routers find them. What the punks do, though, is add something to the front end of the address so the centers logjam trying to find them. If they hijack all the things that are enslaved to the internet like your car, phone, thermostat, doorbell—whatever—the centers clog and no one gets anywhere. Including government and security agencies."

"Has this ever happened before?" I ask. "It has, right?"

Carolyn shrugs. "Not this big."

"So why was it just the East Coast?" I ask.

She turns to us. "I have no idea. Maybe it's our defensive weak spot?" Back to the chart, she writes "DB" next to Reza's name and links them with a line. "They also found texts on Douche Bag's phone to Salaam, Reza, and Jackie. Her bandage DNA links all of them with recent contact." She adds Salaam's name, forming a triangle.

Rachael, pacing, locks eyes with Carolyn again. I wonder where they're going, then Carolyn scrawls "Jackie" under the triumvirate of Reza, Salaam, and DB.

We fixate while she keeps circling the marker, forming a fat, red bull's-eye. The silence breaks when Rachael's phone chimes.

# FIFTY-ONE

**"WOODS," SHE SAYS, TURNING AWAY.**

After a minute or so, Carolyn wanders to the window, staring at silver-white sunlight on the trees and a few clouds over the Pacific.

"Understood. Standing by."

Rachael's as white as the clouds.

"What's up, kiddo?" Carolyn asks as she turns from the window.

"LA District Office. They're sending DNA readouts from Jackie's bandage and Mister Delta Bravo. There's also phone data from him with pictures of hands that might give up fingerprints."

"Okay, good news. So why do you look dead?"

"DB was positive for ANFO and screaming hot with gamma."

Carolyn backs up, one hand fisted on her hip. "What the . . ."

I lean forward on the couch. "What are you guys saying? Gamma, as in ionizing radiation? What's going on?" *They stare like I'm—hey, fuck them.* "And, wait, you can get fingerprints from an iPhone picture of someone's hand?" No answer. Makes sense. Most bad guys are always waving in selfies.

"Let's go outside," says Carolyn as she grabs her iPad.

She pulls chairs around the fire pit and lights it. I see a few crumpled, lipsticked American Spirits that weren't there yesterday.

"What's with ANFO?" I ask.

Carolyn begins, "Ammonium nitrate fertilizer in soybean-sized prills, then coated with fuel oil—diesel usually. Farmers figured it out way back when their barns were blowing up from a leaking John Deere. They used the stuff to blast out stumps. Cheap, always had it lying around—"

"And safe," Rachael interrupts. "You can throw it, run over it, hit it with a hammer. It needs an initiator to function."

"Right, like blasting caps, det cord."

"So," I ask the Chemistry Club Girls, "what can they do with it?"

"Uh, for starters, a fifty-pound bag of it can level your house and your neighbor's," says Carolyn. "A Ryder truck with four barrels of it brought down the federal building in Oklahoma City."

"Christ, why do they even make the shit?" I blurt.

"It feeds the world, Vince," says Rachael. "We think we control its distribution, but for DB to have contacted it, handled it . . ."

"But I still don't get the Jackie connection, the Stinger missiles," I ask. "What does that have to do with fertilizer?" Silence. "What else did we learn, Rachael? I mean if you can tell me, or I can leave."

Carolyn pats my leg. "No, stay, Vince. I did some work on Jackie's gibberish you heard in the recovery room."

Rachael and I scooch forward.

"Vince is positive he heard 'Grails,' 'Stingers,' 'revenge,' and 'Waziristan.' Less sure of 'heavily.' Then there's her strange construction of 'a bad revenge.' Nonsense, but look at it phonetically."

We nod but have no clue where this is going.

Carolyn turns her iPad. "Check out words we're certain of against the phonetics of the weird shit. Start with Waziristan. What do we know about it?"

I shrug.

Rachael answers, "Pashtun tribal area in the mountains between Afghanistan and Pakistan. Size of Connecticut."

"Correct. Mean anything else, kiddo?"

"Not really. It's the wild west of the area?"

"Osama bin Laden's hideout, built by a Waziristan big shot, was opulently out of place. The locals called it the Waziristan Palace. In Urdu, it's Waziristan Haveli." She lets it percolate.

"In Abbottabad!" I straighten up and shout. "'About a bad revenge' is Abbottabad revenge. 'Heavily' is Haveli, no? It's what Jackie was saying?"

Rachael jumps in, "Revenge for the raid on Waziristan Haveli."

Goose bumps draw all to the fire pit. An inch closer, we'd be in it.

# FIFTY-TWO

CAROLYN SCANS US, AS IF probing for more intel. "So what do you think, Rachael?"

"Great work, Carolyn," she says.

"Thanks, but no. I mean what else came today?"

Rachael taps her iPad. "DB's phone shows contact with Salaam, Jackie, Reza—we could have guessed that. They seem to be the nucleus of something."

Carolyn sags with the analogy, then Rachael goes on.

"Still seeing the same spikes of assault rifle and ammo sales whenever there's a threat of a ban." She swipes her screen. "No off-the-books ANFO anywhere except a few minor audit deficiencies at small farm supply stores—twenty-five- to fifty-pound range that fit into the background loss, spillage. There was a small jump in truck thefts nationally. Appears random, in both metro areas and the suburbs."

"Rental van skip outs or—" asks Carolyn, then shoots up a hand when we hear a rustle and snap from the swale between the patio and the gardens. She looks at her phone. "Squirrels. Man, I'm getting a lot of monitoring interference lately. Keep going, Rach."

"Yeah, I'm getting false hits at my place too. Okay, where was I? Vans," Rachael reads, "all over the place, delivery services, grocers, auto parts . . . yeah, one U-Haul mover, landscaping trucks with trailers, that kind of shit."

"Send that to me, will ya?" Carolyn asks.

Rachael nods, then moves on.

"Jackie's bandage DNA—thank you, Doctor Vince—shows close contact with all of the above plus some unknown males, three in number, that we're running profiles on. Two of them showed the DNA changes that we would expect to see from an opioid addict, say, OxyContin. Ever give Jackie any of that?"

I recoil at this question from a fed. "I have never prescribed that. It's for chronic pain, but my patients have short-term pain. Maybe it's three days of Norco post-op, then they're on NSAIDS."

Their smiles say I protest too much. Carolyn says, "Okay, cool it, Vince. She ain't DEA."

Rachael goes on, "So DB was hot with gamma, and they're trying to get the counts and spectroscopy done on it as soon as possible. It could mean he'd been transformed into a human dirty bomb by being fed plutonium or strontium-90."

"Like literally fed isotopes?" I ask. "How long can a person live?"

"Long enough," says Carolyn. "Five days, a week maybe."

"Sorry," I query again. "So when he blows, he'll cover the area with deadly slime?"

Rachael nods, then goes on. "They confirmed Russia was the source of the distributed denial-of-service attacks during our continuity of government exercises," she scrolls, "and, as usual, they can't exclude Iran, China, or North Korea as complicit."

"Well, DB seemed well to me last night," says Carolyn. "Not like someone with radiation sickness. He still had a full head of filthy black hair. That's usually the first to go. Right, Vince?"

I nod, staring down at the patio stone.

"Whoa!" Rachael gets a text and snaps back in her chair, shouting, "We got an exact DNA hit on the headless dude in Pittsburgh."

Carolyn and I stare, counting heartbeats.

"It's not Salaam. Nabil al-whatever—many aliases—arms dealer, in town with one of his pleasure wives." She eyes me, then fixes on Carolyn.

"You don't look finished, Rach," Carolyn says.

"Now the LA team thinks they matched a voiceprint on a call to Jackie. It was Salaam, but they were afraid to tell us before the DNA was confirmed." She offers the iPad to Carolyn, who reads to us.

"Jackie and dickhead small-talk, like lovers . . . talk about a wedding." Carolyn pauses, slow breathes. "Then he asks, 'Did you get the wedding presents?' She says no. He says, 'Well, the wedding might be moved up.' She says, 'Okay, get me the guest list, and I'll work on getting the presents ready.' Dickhead says, '*Enta habibi*' and ends the call." She looks up. "That means, 'You are my love.'"

A tentative Rachael holds out a hand for the iPad.

Carolyn huffs, "Goddamn, mother fuck. *They sat on this?*" handing the tablet back, but not before both hands lift it, Moses-style, as to smash it against the stone fire pit. "Wedding. They use that all the time in the sandbox—a wedding is an attack. They like it, it works."

It simmers, then I ask, "So, do you guys think we've got this under control? Like should you guys move on Jackie?"

Rachael defers to Carolyn, whose upward gaze is endless.

"No," says Carolyn to the sky. "We need to step up surveillance on her until this plot gels so we can kill it all. Otherwise, we bust Jackie, Brent, whomever, and the snakes go back underground and wait for another time to strike." She pivots to us, glaring. "I know it feels like we need to do something, but this is an art, not a science. And the art is knowing the best time to move on an enemy."

*Rachael's impressed. Me? I say never let the sun set on a hot appendix, but that's a whole other life-and-death thing.*

Carolyn lets it simmer, then continues. "Yeah, I think we're good. Doc, here, busted this open just at the right time. Jackie's phones, email"—she rolls a hand—"have been stone cold, so I'm guessing Salaam will show up here soon, unless he's ghosting her. We keep watching data, stay on our toes—eyes and ears on everything—then move on to our next crisis. Hopefully, the photos on the phone will give us actionable prints."

Rachael, unconvinced, looks to see if I'm buying it. No sale. She springs for the house and says, "I'm starving, so I'll get us lunch. Okay, Carolyn?"

"Yeah. I need some time to think this through, maybe stroll the property, call my boss and the team," she says, eyes on the mountains. "Take Vince, stop at his place on the way home to get clothes."

I get a bad feeling about Carolyn . . . safety and sanity. I ask, "Shouldn't we stay with you and just order in?"

I get Carolyn's *Are you fucking serious?* head tilt with a simultaneous shoulder tug from Rachael saying, "Let's leave her alone, Vince."

She heads for her gardens, I see tears starting to well, then she paces like a starved panther.

# FIFTY-THREE

RACHAEL BEATS ME TO THE car. "I'll drive—just in case there's anything funky." She gives me the over-the-shoulder glance I saw when she clustered the bull's-eye at the range.

"Wait. Can't you teach me to do that high-speed evasion stuff?"

She fixes me in a squinty stare.

"Sorry, dumb joke," I say. "And funny ain't fun anymore."

"At least you guys really hit it off, huh?"

"Yeah, and I'm not sure why. It just happened. Two souls, paths crossing at the right time. I think neither of us had control over it. A cliché, but it happened."

"Well, like I said at the range, Carolyn and I go way back and I've never seen this before, Doctor." After a deep sigh and slumping her head, she taps my leg. "Just don't fuck it up, okay?"

I see a friend's happiness—no jealousy. "So . . ." My words tail off as we stop at an intersection.

"What?"

"So it's not a Boyfriend-of-the-Month Club thing, right?"

A horn taps from behind.

"Screw you, dickhead!" she shouts.

I jump and she lays a hand on my arm.

"Not you. This asshole behind us in the Tesla." She stays put and glares into the rearview with eyes that, were they lasers, would melt down the Tesla. I squirm, waiting for the horn blast that doesn't come.

Finally moseying on, she says, "I told you I grew up on a farm in Indiana, right?"

I guess no one's in a hurry in the heartland.

She continues, "So, yeah, Boyfriend-of-the-Month. No way. I mean, let's face it. The girl's hot, and she's had guys—probably any guy she's wanted—but she never looked real in those gigs, you know what I'm sayin'? Our gang would just sit back, let it play out, then crash and burn. Always did," she says, nodding. "You've been a very positive addition to her life."

Excellent info. The lunch crowd has moved on, letting us park close to Janelle's, a small bistro in the heart of town. We climb the wooden steps between the outside tables and bougainvillea, then walk a narrow aisle to the takeout station. The place is empty except for staff, a few people in line, and a young couple with two kids avoiding the sun, sitting at a back table. We order and I foozle on my phone. Rachael takes a chair by the wall so she can eye all comings and goings.

Just as I walk to her, there's the sound of a revving car engine outside. With the amount of drinking, and lovely elderly in this town, I wouldn't be surprised to see one of those gas-pedal-versus-brake mix-ups take out a few sidewalk tables. This could be the day.

The car revs again, louder, as Tim, an old friend, comes through the door. He raises his seventy-something hand in a big wave to me and Rachael, adding an infectious Irish smile.

"Rachael, allow me to introduce to you Tim Yeats. Smartest man in Santa Barbara. Knows about everything from law to baseball to Shakespeare to women to . . ." I realize I'm straining to be heard over yelling added to the hideously loud revving car that sounds as if it's inside the restaurant. I circle past Tim, then see people scurrying, the car inching its way up several steps. "This is bad, Rachael!" I shout, then move us away from the sound.

Rachael turns, draws a gun from nowhere, and screams, "Everyone down on the floor!" Tim jumps as she lunges at him, pushing—no, slamming—him to the floor. "Car bomb, get down!"

Patrons freeze with hands up, like it's a robbery, despite her instructions. The family scoops their kids and vanishes through the back door.

"What the hell did you do that for?" cries Tim, facedown, retrieving his tortoiseshell spectacles.

"Everybody stay the fuck down and cover your heads!" she shouts, then turns and crouches at the front entrance, left foot in front. Just like at the pistol range.

She yells to whoever's outside, "Get your hands up where I can see them!" No response. "Dude, get 'em up or I'm smokin' you!" she bellows, voice cracking. The car engine dies, then we hear another language. Monotonic, guttural, barely without pauses as it crescendos.

Rachael again. "Drop it. Drop it, motherfucker. Now!"

The eerie chant ends, and I peek through the triangle of my folded elbows. I see the car half on the steps, bistro tables splintered, and the driver's hideous, want-it-now grin through the windshield. I cower, almost in fetal position, expecting my end is near.

Then, just like on the mountain, there's a volley—one, two, three, then four shots, deafening without ear protection—then I cringe expecting more, but there are none.

Rachael is a statue, staring at whomever or whatever she shot, then drops, covering Tim with her body, wrapping her own head in her arms. She's breathless as she shouts to her phone.

"Vee Bid! Repeat! Vehicle-borne IED, did not function, one driver occupant, tapped four head shots, device status unknown." A pause. "Affirmative. Had a switch in his hand, but doubt it was a dead-man or we'd be down hard. Don't know about a time fuse or remote backup."

I slowly raise my head off the floor. Rachael glances at me with a furious wave for me to stay down.

"Roger that. Clearing the premises via back door. Standing by for a sweep and bomb squad. Repeat likely a Vee Bid, so please send the best you got."

I hear sirens as she slowly stands, surveying Tim, me, and the staff cowering behind the counter.

"I'm sorry, sir, uh . . . Tim, was it? Are you okay, sir?" as she helps him to his feet.

"Yes, Tim it is." He laughs, kneeling while adjusting his glasses and sweater. "But the next time you do that, young lady, you better buy me lunch first."

She smiles at him, then out comes the badge. "Okay, FBI. There may be a car bomb out front, so stay cool and follow me to the back and wait there until I tell you to come out." There's frantic Spanish spoken by the crowd assembling at the kitchen door.

Rachael hugs the wall, slowly moving to the back door. A few seconds later she shouts, "Vince, help Tim and the others down to the alley, and wait there for the cops and paramedics!"

I nod to my friend, Tim, the cooks, servers, and bussers, all of whom stare at me in silence. None need help exiting. Even Tim bobs down two steps at a time.

Rachael inches back to the front door, looks outside, then descends the stairs, pistol in that chest-hugging ready position.

"FBI, listen up! This may be a car bomb, so get away and stay away!" she yells at bystanders, her voice cracking again. There's screaming, running.

I inch to the front—curious, but checking on Rachael—she being my only link to survival. I see traffic slowing and her doing her best to halt it far away from the restaurant. A weathered green Nissan sits with all four wheels on the sidewalk, having just bulldozed now-shattered tables and chairs into the entry steps. A solitary white running shoe peeks out from under the car. There's a ragged ten-inch hole in the sun-glistened windshield, behind which sits the driver, nearly headless, an arm out the window dangling a brown and white doorbell switch through splayed fingers.

"Rachael, shouldn't you be back as well?" I fret.

"Just get everyone the fuck out, now," she snaps. "I'll be there when I'm there. I can't leave until this scene is secure. You'll be okay. Carolyn's on her way, and she'll beat the cops to the alley. If any other car comes down the alley, holler to me, then lay face-down and don't fuckin' move till I tell you to."

As soon as I get to the alley, I see Carolyn's car speeding toward us.

"Get in!" she shouts through the window, and I motion for Tim to go first. "No, just you, Vince. The cops and med buses will take care of the rest."

My hands flap apologies to Tim, whose arched-eyebrow expression gets more perplexed.

He gives me an understanding wave-off, enlightened gentleman that he is, and cautions, "Vince, are you sure you know what you're doing getting in that car with her?"

I was asking myself the exact same thing.

# FIFTY-FOUR

"WHAT THE HELL JUST HAPPENED?" I ask.

"Rachael said that someone tailed you guys to the restaurant and tried to detonate a bomb—"

"A goddamn bomb vest? Like we're in fucking Kabul not Santa Barbara, Cal—"

Her phone rings; I zip it.

"Talbot . . . you're kidding," she says, mouthing, *Oh my God.* "Wait, say again." There's a grimace. "Unbelievable. Can they tell if it's got taggants?" She looks at me, biting her lip, slowly shaking her head. "How much? Holy moley. Okay, Rach, call me when you can. And you know you can come up here with us if you want. Just let me know. Okay, babe. Thank you—really."

"Tell me if you can . . . I don't really care at this point." I'm jacked up and pissed off.

"It wasn't a bomb vest. The entire ass-end of that car was packed with ANFO and, from how it struggled to get over the curb and steps, Rachael suspected a vehicle-borne improvised explosive device. If that had functioned, you, Rachael, the building, plus the ones on both sides of you would be dust."

"Where are you—" I stop myself as we rocket onto the 101. "Where are we going?" I haven't had dry mouth like this since I took my board exams twenty years ago. Like then, I want to run away. Fast.

"Outta town. Over the mountain," she says, taking the airport exit and getting waved through the general aviation gate.

We park close to a Jet Ranger helo, and Carolyn gives the car keys to the guard after pulling a duffel bag from the back seat. In two minutes, we're turning and burning over the Santa Ynez mountains into Happy Canyon.

"Front lawn is okay, all the wires are underground," Carolyn intercoms the pilot. He circles once around a hundred acres of vineyard surrounding a taupe adobe ranch house, a stable, and a few other small buildings, then gently sets it down with a gentle bounce.

We exit, and I duck instinctively even though the blades are way above me. The helo lifts off, and then Carolyn, in tears, squeezes the hell out of me. I nuzzle her neck and say, "I'm scared, Slim."

She whispers, "I'm happy for the near miss."

"You're happy?" I laugh. "That was my most exciting food run of all time."

I do a three-sixty, gazing at the house and grounds and, as she's about to speak, I raise a palm. "I know, been in the family a long time."

It's, of course, another paradise on par with her home—and why would I expect anything less? Every room has chili-colored Saltillo tile floors, vaulted wood-beamed ceilings, and stonework that could have been hewn from native stone by the early Chumash. There's mahogany-colored leather and vivid orientals that look like they came from a university club.

Once the wow wears off, I notice that she's got an indigo chambray shirtdress and sandals, and I'm here with nothing but the purple polo shirt and jeans I'm wearing. "I can go into Santa Ynez and get some clothes tomorrow, but if you have a washer and dryer, I'd rather not."

"I went to your place and got some stuff for you—"

"How did you get in?" I interrupt. Here's the eyes-wide look saying, *Did you just really ask me that?* as she continues.

"—then locked up. I grabbed a few books for you that were at your bedside, also. We may be here for a while."

"Thanks." Carolyn's skill set comforts, but how the hell did she let her partner and me almost get vaporized? "How do they know—"

"I don't know how they're tracking us, but we have everyone working that, Vince. We're tearing your car apart, too."

I nod, but hope they don't have any clue on our helo ride.

"Listen, I'm going into town for some groceries. This is a working ranch, and my ranch hands—all longtime good guys—are finishing in the vineyard, so don't freak out when you see them coming back to the barn. I promise you this place is secure." She reaches into the duffel bag. "Here's your loaded Glock 42 that you left out on the nightstand, like a chooch, may I add—in case you need it." She racks it. "It's ready to go, so don't play with it."

She squeezes my hands; sorrow squeezes my heart. I don't want to be alone.

"Vince, it'll still be light out. I'll text you when I'm driving in."

I nod with a bit of a frown.

"Okay, Cowboy. Just don't accidentally shoot me when I get back. Oh, and, after today's drama, I need you to fuck the living hell out of me before sundown."

I walk her to the garage where she cranks up a black Range Rover. As she backs out, the window drops. "Vince, sit in the front room. You can see everything from there. And maybe go over the flip charts in the bag so we can brainstorm when I get back."

"No problem, Slim." I hear, no, I feel the angst of hunted prey bleeding through my words, but hell, I refuse to give in.

///////////

Rather than skitter inside like a scared rabbit, with the sun still riding high, a breeze carrying the balm of vines and cilantro, the songbirds give me pause—a Proustian moment?—I sit myself on the porch like I did during summers of my youth.

I hear the ranch hands singing, laughing, living. Living what they know is a great life, working for Carolyn's family, and now for her. What do they think of her? Approachable, generous, understanding, warm, I'd bet.

And what do I think of her? Brilliant, beautiful, a true soul mate. Yet wounded, traumatized. Crazy? Yeah, I'd say you'd have to include that word to describe this woman who can even think about getting nailed after a day like today. Perhaps sex is her drug for whatever godforsaken shit may have given her PTSD. Maybe that's what happens when your CIA friends, our military, towns of innocents get slaughtered by sneering little terrorist assholes.

Someone tried to kill me today. The rules have changed. So, PTSD be damned—I loved seeing that weasel's head split in two by Rachael's swift talent. And, truth be told, it sent a twinge through me that got me hard. Who wouldn't be fucking crazy?

# FIFTY-FIVE

AS THE BEAUTIFUL AFTERNOON IS slipping away, I'm distracted by a sound like the slap of a yardstick on a blackboard followed by laughing from one of the ranch hands. I turn to see him, proud and squat in his sombrero, holding at arm's length a four-foot rattlesnake—dead, not stunned, I hope—on display for his coworkers. He tosses it onto the back of a flatbed truck, then smiles in my direction. I give him two thumbs-up and head for the house, wary of every blade of grass in front of me.

I grab a Coke and my pistol before laying the charts on the carpet in the front room. Carolyn's right—I can see the entire ranch, its foothills and orderly grapevines weaving into the afternoon shadows.

I study the bullet points on each sheet, including Carolyn's scratchy emphatics, and try to recall the conversations. Except for Reza and the Stingers, we never considered any of them related. They're just dumps of random crime data.

It's a huge pile of nothing, a patient with some nonspecific complaint like "not feeling herself," the exam and labs all normal. Nothing. But your gut says something's up.

I settle onto the ottoman, fingering the Glock's blunt angles as I look around the room. On a mahogany leather-topped partners desk is a stack of bright green Post-it Notes. They're the same color I use when teaching my favorite class, Problem-Based Learning. Med students use them to mind-map—fluff talk for brainstorm—key findings of a patient's mystery disease. Then they go nuts on the possibilities and what they want to know next. I grab a handful, a Sharpie, and start papering the window.

Reza, likely Jackie's limping visitor, whose presence here scares the crap out of the JTTF, gets his Post-it at center stage. They seem to think he's here as the guy with the cash for upgraded Stinger software. But why would he risk coming to America when he could do laundered bank wire or Bitcoin from the safety of Iran?

Jackie and Brent—my vibe says they're Reza's tools—get both names on one Post-it that I overlap with Reza's and Salaam's.

Stingers, the high-tech beasts that introduced me to Carolyn. I push that sky-high. It's something that could cripple air transport, the economy, not for five days or so like after 9/11, but indefinitely, the randomness they could provide. And it'll be the puzzle of the decade to figure out how many are out there, who has them, where they are, and where they'll be tomorrow.

ANFO. Low-tech and deadly. Today it could have taken out a hundred people and half the block. After hearing Carolyn expound, it's portable, and somehow they got a carload of it with no hint of its diversion on ATF records. Troubling. It goes below Reza and the Carters.

I step back. There isn't much there besides Stingers and, as Carolyn pointed out, with Jackie and her husband under high surveillance and JTTF hunting Reza, things should be under control.

I walk the room, circling the flip charts on the floor, begging for something to connect, when I see one of Carolyn's ranch hands in a dump truck shuttling an enclosed trailer out to one of the vineyards. That reminds me—truck thefts. I slap a note next to ANFO.

The remaining leads aren't sexy, but in mind-mapping everything's sexy no matter how boneheaded it seems. I post the uptick in assault rifle and ammo sales. Then two with question marks: the intruder's phone data and any new DNA hits that come in.

I'm still nowhere, so a little lubrication may be in order.

///////////

I pull a Sanford Pinot Noir hidden in the wine cooler. The delicious vintage rockets to my head, taking me straight to Janelle's today, when hell opened. Then on to Carolyn with her crazy, beautiful head. Then to a mirror reflecting how I built a wall around my heart, renamed loneliness, and let it—no, that's a lie—I stuffed it into all work, no play. Self-medicating with booze and artificial intimacies, I'm half a person.

Back on the porch, I watch a dipping sun play the hills and shadows. A warm breeze gathers swaths of crops into blue-green waves lapping at the mountains. Nature can't show me the way, and Carolyn can't bring back my lost years, but she sure as hell awakens my soul and opens my eyes.

After another sip, I hear a vehicle's crunch on gravel heading my way, and it's not Carolyn's Rover.

It's a vehicle on a field road behind a knoll of olive trees. Leading a swirl of dust, I see the ranch hands' truck pulling a trailer like the ones Rachael said are being stolen. As they reach the barn, the driver—same guy who whacked the rattler—honks and waves.

Through the pinot's cherry-colored legs coating my glass, I see the door of the van burst open and a small army of ranch hands come hopping down the ramp, shielding their eyes from the setting sun. Some have hoes, pick-axes, or shovels slung infantry-style over their shoulders; others have tool belts sagging with pruning shears, machetes, or small handsaws. The last few carry large orange water jugs over to a well pump to refill them.

I finish the last of the wine and watch as they exchange good-natured poundings and back slaps. In an instant they're in the barn, the truck buttoned up and parked.

I study the window plastered with Post-its, then back to the truck sitting there radiating enough heat to make the air shimmer. *What if ranch hands were a small army? And rakes and shovels were AR-15s and Kalashnikovs?*

There's the rumble of a vehicle again. It's Carolyn. I run to my notes inside, not giving a damn if I step on a snake or not.

# FIFTY-SIX

CAROLYN GLIDES IN ON A smile with a shopping bag. I jump up to help.

"Was that you who left me a present draped over the fence out there?"

I'm lost.

"The reptile?" she asks.

"Oh, yeah. One of your guys—"

"That would be Pedro—"

"—smacks it with a stick, then immediately picks it up."

She doesn't stop unloading the groceries. "He learned that from his grandmother. Lived on the ranches in Mexico. She used to grab them and snap their heads off, but he was too afraid, so she taught him the exact spot behind the head to whack them." She expects amusement but sees me biting my lips. "Hey, you're not freaked out by rattlers, are you? They don't attack unless you do something stupid. We need them out in the fields for rodent control and . . ." She trails off. "What's wrong, babe?"

*Babe?*

"Vince, what's up?"

I lead her to the front room where the setting sun is giving each note its own little halo.

"Jeez, I gotta get these windows done soon," she says. "Okay, so, Post-its. What have you been up to?" She bounces foot to foot, like she has to urinate.

"I took the main points from our charts, then put each one where I thought it belonged in the hierarchy of everything we know."

She scans the window, silent with an occasional nod. "Okay, you've got it all, but it's meaningless. I can't connect anything here, can you?" she asks, smug and arrogant. It pisses me off.

"Yes," I say, locking my eyes onto hers. "You're fucking CIA, I get it, but you're not the only one with permission to think." Round two.

Her upper body resets with a quiver. "Okay, what do you see here," she says with a Vanna White spin, lifting a mocking hand to the window. She pauses for max mockery. "What am I missing?"

"I'll tell you what you're miss—"

"No," she interrupts, a finger wagging so fast it's practically invisible.

My head slumps, then I approach, maybe a little too close.

"Carolyn, just goddamn listen. Look at the groupings of what we know," I say, pointing with the Sharpie.

She de-escalates and collapses onto the ottoman, breaths exiting a loosely clenched fist in front of her mouth.

I start at the top. "Okay, we know about Stingers, right?" No response expected nor given, just a hint of an eye-roll. "Salaam is connected to that through his history with Jackie and Brent—but now Reza's here, so something's up, correct?"

She's silent, faint signs of brow movement. I proceed.

"So that leaves all of this . . . intel." I resist doing air quotes. "All of this intel floating off to the side here." I tap twice on each, as I speak them: "ANFO, truck thefts, assault rifle and ammo sales."

Carolyn, fangs and claws retracted, takes her eyes off the tapping marker and turns to me, forgiving. "Vince, this intel comes in all the time. This is nothing new—"

"No!" I shout. She jumps, arms folded on her body like a strait-jacket. "No, Carolyn, this is not noise. This is a busted trend, a steady increase in all these signals!" I shout, tapping them hard. "Don't you see what's coming together?"

She's eyes-wide; her face laughs at me. "I don't know? You tell me, Doctor, what?" Her head continues its bobble.

Lamaze breathing time again, Vince. Then, calm but firm, I say, "This isn't a game. I'm on your side. Put it in context. These are the fucking pieces to put together a small army—guns, ammo, explosives, and transporters to move them to targets."

"Yes, onesie-twosie lone-wolf attacks on soft targets. Who cares?" she blurts, arms moving. Her eyes say, *You fucking idiot.*

"You know what I think, Slim? I think you actually believe Potter's bullshit plan today. 'Watchful waiting.'" Now the air quotes and an aggressive lean into her space. "In medicine, that's what we say when we don't have a goddamn clue what's going on. So, we can safely move our pack of students and residents out of the room to the next patient where we can maybe provide some healing. Watchful waiting is our code for 'no fucking clue.' Your watchful waiting is code for head in the sand. It's terrorist roulette."

I pace in front of the window. I can feel her studying the notes.

I ask, "Why are all these things trending up now?"

She shrugs, no smugness now, and lies back on the ottoman, elbows on the couch with a long leg bouncing. "I haven't a clue, you tell me," she demands, kicking off her shoes.

I've learned this is her signal to approach for sex, but ignore the green light and continue. "If your data tells you these trends are increasing"—her torso ascends with a breath; I halt her with a raised finger—"even if they're increasing very slowly, it's a signal you have to explain, Carolyn." I pause and wait for pushback, but all I see is pursed lips and more foot bouncing. She gives me a stageworthy bow to continue.

"Today, sitting outside, enjoying some of your Sanford—"

"I noticed that and—"

"—which I'll replace as soon as possible—I watched your ranch hands coming back from the fields. They pull up in front of the barn, truck doors opened, trailer gate drops, and all the guys were out in three seconds. And it could have been forty guys in a trailer that size."

She sits up, attentive, arms folded.

"Carolyn, a truck that size could have breached any bullshit barrier of a . . . a church, synagogue, college, medical center, stadium, shopping mall, you name it. But that's too easy. That should have happened by now, and we've seen the one-offs that you alluded to. The lone-wolf nut jobs."

"So what are you thinking?" she asks, blowing a poof to get hair off her eyes. And still rolling that goddamned ankle.

"This is an arms buildup." I let it ring. "There's news every day of southern border Afghani bad guys on the got-away list. Nothing's keeping ISIS-K head-choppers from entering. And Canada, the Pacific coastline, forget it—it's wide open to anyone with some hiking boots or a throwaway boat."

She shakes her head. "I don't know, Vince. It's just . . ."

"Just what? Say it. It's too easy. You're fuckin-A right it's too easy. Everything they need for an attack is right here"—I'm sweating big time now—"just like 9/11. The crappy screening, easy cash from ATMs, weapons . . . and most of all, big-ass targets. Our families, our schools, our hospitals, our way of life. Our freedom. Stingers are the diversion to multiple soft-target attacks."

"Vince!" She stands, waving down my pacing rant. "Vince, I get it. Calm down. Please." Finally, I know she sees the lucidity of what I'm laying out, then asks, "So a truck full of fanatics isn't going to do any damage to any of our institutions, but hundreds of them will?"

I look to the floor, then the hills, now barely green undulations licking the mountains. For some reason—9/11 talk maybe—chokes me, reminds me of Helen. Exhausted, I collapse to my knees, laying my head on Carolyn's lap.

She coaxes me up and onto her blue shirtdress, its belt hanging loose. I tug on it like it's attached to a Titanic lifeboat.

"When I watched Rachael and the car bomber today, I thought I'd never see you again, Slim."

I feel her body tighten and fingernails digging, branding me. Eventually, I ask, "So where were we?"

"You were about to tell me how we're going to save the world."

# FIFTY-SEVEN

WE SOMEHOW MAKE IT TO the bedroom and sleep the sleep of the dead when, a little after five a.m., the last thing we want barges in from Carolyn's phone: the weighty ringtone of Rachael Woods.

"Whatcha got, Rach?" Carolyn asks, still in fetal position, spooned up tight on me. Her gravelly voice betrays the strain, the booze, the lost sleep, the demands on her since we first met. Then her iPad dings, and I hand it and some pillows to her as she sits up. Her hair's an irreverent mess. I'm afraid to look in a mirror.

Lips cover her teeth a moment before she speaks. "Uh, I'm just getting it now." She squints, moving closer to the screen. "Holy moley. What the hell?" The scrolling picks up.

"Okay, Rachael, we're getting up and we'll be on our way in thirty." She points to me, then jabs toward the shower. "I'll text you."

I head for the bathroom, asking, "What?"

"She got a call from LA District FBI with what they got from Douche Bag's cell phone. It was on fire with calls to and from Reza. They intercepted over twenty new calls from Salaam to Jackie—three to Brent. Shit, there were almost a hundred calls yesterday. Why the fuck did FBI sit on this shit?" She's furiously typing an email, then stops. "They told her your car bomb had a bag of cesium-137 that would have contaminated Montecito for months."

"You guys—9/11 all over again. Why no cross-communication?" I ask. "Wait. Jackie and Brent are both in on it?"

"Rachael thinks something's going to happen with or without the assistance of Jackie and Brent. She wants to go to the Carters' this afternoon under pretext of following up on a government contract that Brent's company has with Defense."

I get it. Her job is difficult, but let me be generous and say at least half of this could have been predicted. It's Pearl Harbor when the military felt it coming but waited for orders from on high rather than using common sense. Watchful waiting again. No wonder she's wound up tighter than a ten-dollar watch.

Carolyn flips the iPad, jumps off the bed, and stiffens in a way I've come to know means she wants a drink. She looks at the ceiling, shaking her head, and barks, "Shower. Go! Please."

I consider pointing out, *It's noon somewhere*, but don't. We're each showered and collecting ourselves in the foyer just before six.

"You don't have to go with me. Do you want to stay here? With the rattlesnakes and ranch hands?" she jokes, knowing my answer.

"Drive or helo?"

"FBI picked up a car following us to the airport, but they have no clue where we are since we didn't file a flight plan. We have a little time, so I say we drive. Or, more precisely, you drive."

I nod, comprehending that's so she can literally ride shotgun in case any of Reza's goons are on to us. At this point, I'm too excited to be excited about being a target. Hey, been there.

We grab our clothes, a god-awful heavy duffel bag of assorted ammo, three extra handguns, and a shotgun—de rigueur for a relaxing drive down the mountain into Santa Barbara.

I push the Glock into my concealed-carry holster. I admit, it feels good there. She sees my smile.

"Do not ever hesitate to use that if you need to, Vince."

"Like we say in the OR, 'Sometimes right, sometimes wrong, but never in doubt,' so no hesitation from me."

There's a furrowed brow, then a nod. "Put this on," she says, handing me one of the fleece vests she pulls from the hall closet. Its weight is stunning. It swings like a wrecking ball as I wrestle it on.

"It's Kevlar, so you gotta deal with the weight and crappy styling. Wait, there's extra twelve-gauge double-oh bucks in the pockets." She puts them in the duffel. It doesn't help.

"Well, it fits. Sort of." The hall mirror disagrees. But when I focus on Carolyn's reflection, the last bit of fear evaporates. "Let's hit it."

She fist-bumps and says, "Okay, we'll take San Marcos Pass to save time. You good with that?"

"Yeah, we're just in time for a little daylight on the way down."

Cal-154 is a two-lane former stagecoach trail that winds over the Los Padres Forest to Los Olivos and beyond. Every year or so it manages to send a carload of wine tasters careening off, precipitating them into a canyon. I've made this drive many times—even post-winery tour—and know the danger spots.

But the thought of trying to outrun Reza's monkeys in the early dawn is a thrill I'd like to avoid.

# FIFTY-EIGHT

**I SLIDE ONTO A DESERTED** 154 just as some feeble light begins its dance on the mountaintops. Perfect timing. Except for the gas gauge. Forty miles range, not counting me driving like a lead-footed teenager.

"Slim, should we fill up before we get to Rachael?"

"Goddamn, motherfuck," she says, syllables synced with fists onto dashboard. "I wanted to do that last night." Her face tells of exhaustion catching up. Me? I've been avoiding mirrors.

"We can make town, but then we're five miles to bingo."

"Let's do it now, but don't turn around. There's a station on Painted Cave that's open early for the ranchers."

We turn off at the crest of a hill, and still no one in sight, coming or going. The pumps are in front of the two white clapboard barns of the farm supply store. A green awning leads to a small grocery store. But all I see is diesel.

"Gas is on the other side of the diesel pumps," she says, "so swing around and leave it running. I'll fill it, but go in and ask Norberto to turn on the gasoline pumps. If he's not there, the switch is just inside the door."

I take two steps and she shouts, "Coffee's free, so get one to share. Leave a good tip."

*Aye, aye, Cap'n.* A hand on my Glock, I give the door a shove. Bells jingle, followed by the punch of strong coffee. Norberto waves from the back of the store. He's tall enough to stock shelves without a ladder. He tells me to flip the pump switch by the door.

"So, you with Miss Carolyn?"

"Yep. I'm Vince."

He smiles and does some fairly deep bows. "I'm Norbo. Help yourself to coffee. Next to the ice chest."

I pour a *grande* but feel like pulling a couple longnecks out of that glass-topped vintage Coca-Cola ice chest. I lay a ten on the counter. "Thanks, my friend."

Replaying the hand-on-Glock, door-shove maneuver, the outside air's still crisp and moist, but our coffee will help. As best I can tell with the Rover's blacked-out windows, Carolyn's not sitting shotgun yet, so either Norbo's in-line gas filter's clogged or her Rover was thirstier than I thought. I walk around the Rover's back to see if she needs any help. She sure as hell does.

A man in black cargo pants and balaclava strangleholds Carolyn from behind, left hand grasping her shoulder, right hand flashing a knife to the neck. "What the fuck," I say, then drop the coffee with a plop and steam cloud. I'm not sure where to point it, but the pistol's out.

"If he wanted me dead, I'd be dead. He wants something, Vince." She talks like she's teaching a self-defense course, but her face shows more disappointment than anger. Yeah, I get it.

"Here." I lower the gun an inch, raise my free hand in the manner of surrender. "You've got me. Let her go, then I'll put down the gun."

He nods. "That's good, people. Give me the man."

"That's what you want, right, Cowboy?" she asks, her arms now in a slow dangle, rag doll style. "He's going to put the gun down very slowly—right, Vince?—then Cowboy lets me go."

How the hell's that going to work? He'll slash her, then come at me. I hesitate, wishing I trusted my aim. I don't, so I lower the gun to the oil-stained concrete, but ready to jump for it.

"You're happy now, right, Cowboy?" she asks, her eyes going wide, talking to me.

As his mouth opens, Carolyn's right shoulder pops up as both her hands pull down on Cowboy's forearm, letting her snake her head out from under his knife. She grips the knife with him, then her hands rhythmically guide his arm in quick plunges of the blade into his chest. It's slow motion. I'm frozen.

"Any day now, Vince!" she shouts.

I drop for the Glock, he drops the knife, and hobbles off for the road, I follow, but after a step, I'm tugged back by my coat sleeve.

"That's survivable trauma," I say, getting a quizzical shake of her head, then a violent one of my arm.

"What are you, Florence Fuckin' Nightingale?"

She yanks the car's door and pulls out a matte black shotgun. Well, sort of—it's about two feet long with just a stubby birds-head pistol grip. There's a booming flash, and pieces of Cowboy's jacket, hoodie, and possibly a few internal organs leap out in front of him. Now he's the rag doll, as what's left of him crumples into the gravel.

"Jesus, Slim."

"There. Is that better trauma for ya?"

# FIFTY-NINE

**WE BURN OUT OF NORBO'S,** still no cars in sight.

"Where the hell did he come from?" I ask.

Carolyn, hyperventilating, does a rapid head shake.

"Next time, take the goddamn shot—I can take care of myself."

"Obviously. But all I had was about four inches of his head showing behind yours." I glare at her. "You'd be dead now."

She lets out a long, loud, screaming sigh. "I know. You played it right, Vince. Thank you."

Right after we turn onto the highway, Carolyn points to a sedan way off on the shoulder, driver's door open, a lifeless body hanging out of it, one hand lying on the pavement.

"That's where he came from," she says. "They must have followed us, lights off from the ranch, then Cowboy decided not to split the reward on your ass. This is gettin' gnarly, so run anything and everything in front of us."

"No argument here." I step it up, winding in and out of the rock cuts. She calls someone, letting them know there's a cleanup needed on aisle three at Norbo's.

"So what was it that you used to turn him into a piñata?"

She gives me that mischievous smile. "Boom stick. I never drive without one."

///////////

It's early, so we're off the mountain and into Santa Barbara before the morning rush, just as Rachael calls.

"We're here and you're on speakerphone, Rachael," answers Carolyn. She gives me the finger to lips, then mouths the word "later." Omertà on our piñata adventure.

"Hey, Vince. Can you guys talk?" All business, tense as hell.

"Of course, what's new?"

"What's new is," she fills her lungs, "we asked SB County to keep an eye on the Carters' place for us, and they just called with news of a dark SUV in their driveway that wasn't there an hour ago. Rental, Nevada plates, nothing yet on who rented it."

"You want to move things up or just"—Carolyn looks at me—"watch and wait?"

I close my eyes, head tilted heavenward, and she knows the fuck why.

She continues, "Rachael, it might be a family visit, but who cares—"

"No, that's why I called. I want to move now. If it's family, we fall back and surveil, but if not, we're already an hour late. I let my backups know that you guys are joining me."

We agree; Carolyn confirms the address and puts it in the Rover's GPS.

"We'll be there in seven minutes. You want me to walk to the door with you or lay back with Vince?"

"No, I don't need to posse-up under this pretext, so I'm good. I'm in a G11 that I'll park in front. See ya soon." The call ends.

"What's that?"

"Government car. Basic Chevy or Ford." Carolyn fidgets.

"So what if she calls you in, should I wait out front or leave?"

"If she needs me, things are not cool, so haul ass to my house until you hear from me or one of my crew—they'll use my name as proof they're legit. Got it?"

"Got it." *One of my crew equals she's toast.* "What if Jackie or Brent sees me?"

"These windows are blacked out, so don't fuckin' roll 'em down. They stop bullets, too." Naughty smile again.

"Appreciate it," I say, no reciprocating smile.

We enter the Carters' neighborhood on a high access road and see Rachael's white Taurus circle the block, then park in front of their mansion on El Encanto Lane. Two red brick pillars frame a sloping driveway, open gate. Rachael gets out; we lay back.

"I don't like that," Carolyn says. "See how that Tahoe's parked in the driveway? Diagonal. No car can get out of the garage."

Carolyn motions for me to drive on, closer to the front of the house. I move in behind the Taurus but let a hedgerow block the view of us from the Carters' house.

"We can barely see anything here, Carolyn. How the fuck are we supposed to back her up?"

"She's got her backup on the way. Stay cool, honey bunny."

Channeling *Pulp Fiction*? No better time to launch into a silent, *"The path of the righteous man is beset on all sides . . ."*

I see Rachael, badge displayed, peek through the door's glass side panel, then ring the doorbell. It seems like an hour until she slams the knocker, which we can hear from where we lurk. No answer as she waits, pistol now in hand.

"Fuck," Carolyn says under her breath. "Move to the house and let me out, Vince!"

I plow onto the lawn, then Carolyn bails, launching from the moving car and running toward the house. As she closes on Rachael without turning, she's frantically waving for me to get the hell out of here, but that ain't gonna happen.

Then I see it. The door of this stately residence in Montecito creeps open less than three inches.

# SIXTY

**SO FAR, I'M CONFUSED BY** Carolyn ejecting, then things get interesting as I watch her hug the house, slowly converging on Rachael at the door.

Rachael drops to one knee, leaning back trying to pull the door closed. It doesn't move. She stands for leverage, then there's a cloud of blue smoke and sparks followed by a deafening boom. It flattens Rachael against the entry alcove.

The door swings wide as she begins a slow slide to the ground, leaving the white wood behind her smeared with bright scarlet—arterial. Not good. On her way down, I hear two familiar cracks that I guarantee are from her 40-cal. My turn to eject from the car and run to her.

Carolyn gets to the doorway, then button-hooks around and into the house. I see her scan every corner of the room while holding her weapon up and close to her chest. I hear the sound of a gun sliding on a wood floor. She shouts, "Clear!"

Yeah, right. Like I'm fuckin' going in there.

I get to Rachael, sitting on the ground, legs splayed out, back to the wall. Aside from the entire upper left of her white shirt being red and her hyperventilating, she doesn't look that bad to me, well perfused and talking. But it's early.

"Tell Carolyn . . . Reza's the fucker . . . shot me."

"Okay, I'm going to lay you flat and see what we have here. Can you move your arm?" Her left arm is already turning that god-awful greenish-tan color of death.

She moves it. "Whatever. Are you a doctor?"

Carolyn, who just came back to the door, says, "It's Vince and Carolyn, kiddo. Stay with us. Keep talking."

"It was Reza, Carolyn—"

"You're right and he ain't going anywhere, Rach."

When I get her flat, I hear a faint buzz—one I've heard before when an artery's hissing blood. "Carolyn, we need a bus stat."

"On its way, Doc. Keep talking to me, Rachael!"

I tear at the entry hole in her blouse and find an open chunk of glistening yellow fat and bright red blood pooling between her neck and shoulder, as if something inside her exploded. The sound is a torn left subclavian artery, hissing a foot-high spray of her life onto the tan bricks.

"Jesus Christ, Vince. What can we do?" asks Carolyn.

I pull off my sweater, using it to sponge out the divot in Rachael's shoulder, but it refills in seconds. The wound makes more sense now. The bullet shattered her clavicle, driving a triangular splinter into the subclavian, the rest blowing back onto the inside of her blouse. The pressure I apply doesn't stop the leak—there's nothing firm to compress against. I try grasping it between my fingers, but it wiggles free. Even skinny people have enough fat to make a wound a greasy mess.

"Fuck! Stay with us, Rachael," I say, no answer expected, her face now pretty much a gray, shocky washout.

"Slim, do you have a shoelace?" I turn for a second; apologetic penny loafers stare up at me.

"What about those plastic handcuff thingies you guys use?"

"Zip ties. Check her pockets, Vince. She always has some." Carolyn helps me roll her to her good side, and there they are, peeking from her pocket.

"Carolyn, listen to me, okay? Just pay attention."

She nods but seems to be turning Rachael's color. I wring as much blood as possible from my sweater, ball it up in Carolyn's hand, and press it into the wound.

"Hold it there as tightly as you can. You're not gonna hurt anything, understand?"

"Yes." Rapid nods, but she looks away.

"You can't turn away! I need your help here," I snap. "Sorry, this part's important, and I'll tell you exactly what to do."

"I'm sorry, Vince, I'll stay with it."

I walk her through: Get the tie around the artery on the heart side of the leak. No digging, no sawing, no more damage. But given the alternative, get it done. Now.

"Okay, closer to the middle of her chest are important branches of this vessel that I need to stay away from. I'm going to have you use two fingers like a retractor to help me see where I am."

Rapid blinking, hands shaking, she finally says, "Okay, Vince."

Rachael's left arm is duskier each time I have the guts to check, but the good news is I hear sirens. I take two of Carolyn's fingers and hook them over the flap of the gaping entry wound, showing her how to retract while keeping her other hand applying pressure to our makeshift sponge. She watches me gently bend the end of the zip tie so it stays in a slight curve.

"When I tell you, just slowly roll the sweater toward the heart— away from the arm, so I can see where the tear is. Got it?"

"I do, Vince." She sniffs. "Is she going to die?"

"Not going to happen, Slim." I rehearse the anatomy—don't bag the vertebral artery and stroke her the fuck out. Don't drop a lung. "All right, very slowly roll it."

Carolyn is perfect. I see the rent in the artery, now flaccid due to nosediving blood pressure, encircle it with the zip tie, and cinch it down—slowly, not too tight!—just until the bleeding stops. I hold for a second, then let go.

Carolyn and I stare at it in silence, praying blood doesn't pool up again. It doesn't, and Rachael's color improves a little. Our gaze jumps to each other, then back to the wound, seeing the zip tie bob with each beat of Rachael's heart, but no more bleeding. We sink back on our heels. Carolyn's in a daze, but our eyes are glued to the hole in Rachael's chest. I glance in the direction of swarming first responders.

She rocks me in an embrace, beaming at the paramedics. "He's a surgeon."

"And she's a nurse with a gun, so don't piss her off."

# SIXTY-ONE

**"WHAT DO WE GOT, DOC?"** asks one of the paramedics as they swarm over Rachael, who's still breathing on her own and has a pulse. Barely. In seconds, oxygen's on her, two IVs are in, and she's on a cart.

"She took one at close range by someone at the door," I say.

The first responders startle and see Carolyn, badge on display, thumbing toward Reza. "He's 10-45, three more in the kitchen. I cleared the house but didn't do a bomb sweep. So no one goes inside until the bomb squad says okay."

"I got to her right after it happened, but she was fading." I motion to Carolyn, feeling dried blood crack on my fingers. "She and I tied off the proximal left subclavian."

"What's this cable tie?" one of them asks as they replace my sweater with a compression dressing.

"That's keeping her alive. It's around the pumper."

The disbelieving crew look at Carolyn and me as they roll Rachael away. "Great work, you two." One of them turns and tosses something that resembles a gooey football. "Oh, here's your sweater, Doc."

Finally, Carolyn and I—bloodied head to toe—can breathe, but I ask, "Should I go with her?"

"No, I need you to identify people. Will she make it?"

"Yes. Thanks for staying cool, Slim. I couldn't have done a thing for her without you."

"Well, thanks for teaching me." She looks for a blood-free spot on my face, air-kisses instead. "Let's get to work."

///////////

The bomb squad and FBI evidence team began sweeping the place while we were getting Rachael into the bus. The team lead pulls Carolyn aside, going over notes. Then Carolyn calls me to join. I'm introduced and given the okay to enter the scene escorted by her. I can't imagine what lies ahead.

She grabs nitrile gloves. "Follow me, Vince. Just to be safe."

We step through the doorway and she points to the floor.

"Reza. And his beloved Colt Cobra."

He's face up, an entry wound above his left eye and another dead center over the heart. I don't see a blood trail, so he probably died on his trip to the ground. Thanks, Rachael!

"Of course, he's running hollow-point cop killers in that Colt."

Of course. And I think: *Rachael's probably still in the OR.* Carolyn reaches for my hand before we get to the kitchen. Her grip is inescapable.

It's large with all the high-end gadgets and an octagonal table at the far end. At first, nothing strange, no sign of a struggle, until Carolyn motions to the table. I see Jackie's face. It's upside down.

"Jesus fucking God in heaven," I murmur.

Carolyn tugs my shirt. "Are you okay? Let's get closer."

The Carters are tied to chairs with yellow nylon rope.

"It's Jackie for sure." Almost decapitated.

Next to her is Brent. Throat cut, cleanly and surgically, not with furious vengeance, as I picture Jackie's was.

"That's him. That's Brent."

Carolyn nods and points to a bloody black combat knife that's buried an inch deep into the smooth surface of the wooden table. "This is signature Reza. Loves drama killings."

I see multiple shallow cuts on their forearms and thighs, less so for Brent. "Are those defensive wounds?"

Carolyn shakes her head. "See the regular spacing, same length and depth? Nothing random. He was working them." She's savoring the forensics, a touch of exhilaration on her face. "Real greaseball shit."

"Wait," I ask, "why both? Jackie was helping them, right?"

Carolyn lobs it back. "What do you see here?"

"Jackie got the worst of it."

She nods. "Why?"

"No clue. Brent had the Stinger upgrades . . ." It hits me. "She couldn't get Brent to hand them over, so Reza made Brent . . . watch her suffer . . . to get him to cough up?"

"Excellent, Doctor. No luck with blackmail maybe, but I'd guess Brent finally produced, then got iced."

She puts a hand on my shoulder. "Ready to keep going?" Like she's a frickin' realtor on a showing.

"Yeah," I say, shuddering.

We walk through one of the kitchen doors leading to a patio. Just three feet past the threshold lies a man, facedown.

"Decerebrate," I say.

"What's that?"

"Your brainstem is severed, no connection to your cerebrum. You're a reptile." The victim models it all. "Your shoulders, arms, and legs rotate inward, arms extend, you make fists, you clench your teeth. That's all I can remember. Hated neuroanatomy."

"Would this cause that?" She extends a leg, the sole of her suede Ferragamo lingering on the handle of a knife protruding from the base of the dude's skull like a joystick.

"Yep, that'll do it." I shake my head. "Immediate incapacitation, no flinching, no nothin'. It's over. What the hell's with these guys?"

"That's vintage motherfucking Reza all right. The bastard knows exactly where to plunge the knife to drop the guy instantly." She rolls him enough to show his face. "Seen him anywhere?" She gives me a five-second look, then lets him flop with a stiff bounce. "Didn't think so. I think I know where he came from."

She surveys the scene like it's a favorite movie. "Let's keep going. We're almost done."

It's grotesque. But it's infectious. I want more.

We walk the yard to a side door of the garage. When she opens it, I'm met with the unmistakable stench of dog crap. Inside the four-car garage are two elegant German shepherds, asphyxiated, hung with the same yellow rope the motherfucker used inside.

So far, I've been okay. Dead humans—no biggie. Seen it all. But this?

"Why? Why, Carolyn? Why not just lock them in the garage? Why the hell—"

Her hands chop. "Do you see what I mean, Vince? Do you see why I'm . . . why anyone would be crazy? Do you get it? Do you see why . . ." Her voice cracks.

I lunge at her, stroking her hair. "Carolyn, Carolyn! I got it. You're not crazy, you're angry and so am I. So let's do something about it, for God's sake. Reza being dead ain't the end of this. Let's close in on these bastards."

# SIXTY-TWO

CAROLYN LETS FBI KNOW WE'VE positively IDed Jackie and Brent and we'll be at her house until we can visit Rachael. The drive home is stunned silence.

We shower together. I wash her hair, seeing Rachael's now rust-colored blood circling the drain. As soon as we're dressed, Carolyn makes the call to FBI agents guarding the hospital's ICU, where Rachael should be recovering at this point.

"This is Talbot. Can you give me the latest on Rachael Woods, please?" she asks. Carolyn does a thumbs-up and winds up the call. She turns and says, "You were right, Doc. Not only is she going to make it but should be talking in about an hour. She'll still be junked up on pain meds, but they want me to go debrief her."

"She's as tough as I thought."

"You're as amazing as I thought, Doctor."

"Thank you, nurse."

I get a slap on the butt and an invitation to help her go through new intel Rachael's team found while all this unfolded. In the kitchen, she displays her iPad on the flat screen. She drops salads and Pinot Grigio in front of us.

I study what's displayed, and Carolyn explains something I don't recognize, a "dirt box." It's military slang for Digital Receiver Technology, Inc.—DRT—made back in the late nineties. It mimics a cell tower, so calls in the vicinity go through it and can be monitored, rerouted, blocked. It started out the size of a microwave oven, but now it's shrunk to the size of a mobile phone. Rachael used one to monitor the numbers from Carolyn's intruder's phone. The list included Jackie, Brent, Reza, and a few dozen others who had been given alphanumeric codes such as "UM-5," "UF-23." Unknowns, male or female based on voices. There were calls to Salaam's old phone that stopped after he supposedly went headless in Pittsburgh. Now we know he's UM-11, has a new burner phone, and talked over an hour with Jackie, then one minute with Brent yesterday.

"Can we get recordings of these calls?" I ask.

"Transcripts. Coming later today or tomorrow."

I point to the call length, saying, "Jackie wins the talk time sixty minutes to one over Brent. This could be pillow talk, but I'd say she and Salaam were working him."

"Blackmail." She nods. "That's where I'm going with this. Problem is, we haven't got any audio from the Carters' house or car that supports Jackie as a blackmailer."

"How'd you get in their house?"

"We didn't. It was passive surveillance."

"Passive?" I ask.

She puffs up her cheeks, deciding whether to go on. "Do you know how that electric guitar your mom gave you makes sound?"

"Well, the guitar strings vibrate over a magnet in the pickup, which creates a feeble electric current that gets amplified. Which moves another magnet in a speaker coil that creates sound when it moves."

"Very good, Doc," she says, nodding and gleaming like my old physics prof. She lifts an eyebrow and points to a Sonos speaker on the counter. "Now run that backward."

"Our voices make the speaker magnet vibrate, producing a feeble electric current that—no frickin' way."

"We detect, amplify, and turn into voices. NSA doesn't even need speakers; window glass vibrations are enough."

This spooks the hell out of me, forgive the pun, so I change subjects. "Was Brent high up enough, rich enough, secure enough to just say to them 'fuck you,' then go public?"

"Our intel says he loves money and would sell out to keep it. When Rachael saw the blizzard of calls Reza made to the Carters in the past twelve hours, she felt that she needed to get there fast to get them talking. Rachael"—just the name makes hands wipe tears before she can face me—"had no idea how deep the Carters are into this. Or, *were* into this."

You could mop the floor with her tone. She needs to back up, go big picture.

"Carolyn, she probably felt the car bomb, the calls, your intruder—all of what's been happening—were signs that things were about to unravel. My guess is Reza, or whoever pulls the strings on this, got spooked thinking Jackie squealed. So better move up the attack."

"But, Vince." She aborts, turns the heat down. "Vince, look at me. You're right, you really are. But we need to put these pieces in place before we escalate the livin' fuck out of this."

"Why are you so goddamn afraid of being wrong?"

Eyes wet, she reaches for my hands. "Because I've been wrong, Vince, and it cost lives. Friends shouldn't die for my mistakes."

"I get it. I've made mistakes that have cost lives too." That's a lie—close, but no dead patients yet. "But we do our best, knowing we can't always be perfect. And sometimes we screw up. We have to go back to the OR—"

"Or lose friends that counted on us? Has that ever happened to you? Has it?" she shouts, hair on fire.

"My patients are friends, not customers, and they put themselves in harm's way every day because they count on me doing things right. Not sitting back, doing nothing, afraid to make a goddamn, fucking decision." I spit the response, then let it sink in.

"You're right." She opens up, calmer. "So, how do these signs—signals as you say—point to anything other than more of the same lone-wolf, idiot stuff." For the first time, I realize she speaks and dines like a patrician: tines down, fork and knife flowing like ballerinas dancing with her words. I also see love and patriotism in her eyes. "I mean, I see the patterns, Vince, and . . . and it's brilliant, but I want to understand how it works."

"The patterns obviously show they're building a small stockpile of weapons, right?"

Her knife and fork say, *Yes, continue.*

I ask, "But where have all the lone-wolf attacks been?"

She shrugs, her silverware prompting again.

"They've been so-called soft targets, right?"

"Vince, so just because they have some AKs and some ANFO and some delivery trucks, you can't be thinking that they're going to try to hit hardened sites?" she asks, her laugh nearly silent.

"Not what I'm saying. They're going soft—real, real soft, if you will."

"What's softer than an outdoor concert or a shopping mall? Really—help me out here, Doc." She leans in.

"*Who*, Carolyn? It's all about who. *Who feels the pain this time?*"

"Vince," she pleads, "what the fuck could be worse than the pain of seeing friends and other concert-goers dying?"

I knock back a good draw of wine, letting it roll over my tongue while she stares blankly. "Wealthy parents burying children. Rich people, who for once can't buy their way out of hell, escaping to expensive distractions on sacks of money." I stare at the floor, then into Carolyn's watery eyes. "They always watch the poor sons of bitches in the big cities grieving while they escape to their clubs, their upscale restaurants, and plush watering holes, vacation homes, and—"

"Stop it, Vince. Stop!" she says, the creases of doubt in her forehead ironing out.

Carolyn looks down at her clasped hands, then at me. "Have you ever heard of a CCA? Do you know what a 'complex coordinated attack' is?"

I swallow hard.

# SIXTY-THREE

"VINCE, YOU'RE DESCRIBING A COMPLEX coordinated attack. That's what you think's heading our way."

"So what happens?"

Our eyes lock. She drops her head some, like I asked her about her first sexual experience or something. I can't tell if she's going to cry or laugh.

I take her hands and break the silence, fumbling a question, "I mean, is it just like . . . like a bunch of active shooters that get a call and start at the same time?"

She extricates her hands from my grasp only to swallow mine more firmly. "A CCA involves coordinated assaults against multiple targets—cultural, political, population centers. It hits groups of civilians, government or commercial centers, infrastructure, transportation systems. The attack groups are small—ten, twelve at the very most—and mobile, the best way to get around security measures. And it's usually not one group marauding around but several spread out. They're in communication with each other—that's the coordinated part—fed by a central source of information, usually coming from some fuckhead with police scanners or glued to cable news. Sometimes they're in black, balaclavas, body Kevlar and shit, playing army. Sometimes they just dress like regular guys and gals—"

I'm wound up and interrupt. "If there's just a few, they need to last, right? So they wear tactical gear and body armor? But if there's a crapload of them, who cares if a few drop, right?"

"Exactly. They use multiple levels of weaponry such as IEDs, vehicle-borne explosive devices, vehicles themselves, and of course direct and indirect firearms cover." Carolyn pauses, seeing me stunned, horrified. She sniffs, then goes on. "Multiple locations, multiple modes of attack. That's the complex part. It's a mass casualty event, but not one that conventional first responders can handle. It will overwhelm. It's designed to overwhelm, to demoralize, to crush spirit and will."

Here she's got herself stunned, more serious than I've ever seen. I avert my eyes, picturing what she's laid out. I open my mouth but can't find words, so she continues.

"There're going to be multiple active shooter attacks, preplanned and coordinated, that we'll only realize after it's over, just like Paris, just like Mumbai, just like the school in Beslan, Russia. Not until it's over will we have time to connect the dots—"

"Bullshit, Carolyn! We have to connect dots. Let's map out Rachael's phone data to see the locations where the calls went."

She huffs but makes the screen split, one side a US map, the other a table of intercept locations.

"Start with Reza," she barks, "and read the locations to me."

Chronologically, early calls go to southern California, then move quickly through Vegas, Chicago, Dallas, Minneapolis, Cleveland, Pittsburgh, ending up in cities up and down the coast. Providence, Boston, Miami, Palm Beach, and Sanibel, with New York City and Washington conspicuously absent. There are a lot of flyovers, as snobs say. I tell her nearly all calls were to cell phones—brief, fifteen seconds at most—with a few longer calls to banks or businesses. When I finish, I look at the map, then at Carolyn, who's pale. Very pale. I slump, defeated and hopeless in equal proportions.

"So is this the CCA?" I ask.

"This is the coordinated part." She goes into lecture mode. "Reza is messaging his soldiers—leading, coordinating—but the good news is if we rushed him, he might have to use new recruits instead of waiting for experienced guerrillas to cross the border. He may have all idiots. Clowns like the intruder at my place and the car bomber at Janelle's. And he may have to cut team sizes."

The what-ifs of our so-called idiot encounters flash by. The intruder idiot who almost killed Carolyn and the bomber idiot who almost pancaked a block of our village, nearly killing Rachael, me, and scores of others. I guess all things are relative to CIA.

"What if they're not idiots? Or, what if their jobs can be done by idiots, say, suicidal fanatics?"

She nods rapidly. "Yeah, this could be bad, very big and very bad."

"Okay, Slim. What do we do?"

"Don't you see, that's what's so fucking dangerous about a CCA." She stands, bending into my space. "Where do you start? Do we start with the Stinger threat and ground-stop air travel? National Guard perimeters around every major airport won't work. Do we try to surveil everyone who rented a truck in the past month? Do we interview everyone who purchased ammo, body armor, assault rifles? Do we bring the army into every major city? Do we . . ." her hand does an infinity roll, steely eyes on me like I'm a fool.

"Yes," I say, puffed up, then plead. "Don't we have to start somewhere?"

She continues excoriating me with her eyes.

"You're right, Carolyn." I realize the limited utility of the map.

"Let's use the best level of evidence—not to go clinical on you—and pick the effort most likely to take us to the leaders."

"That's the beauty of a CCA! Once launched"—she chops both hands—"no leaders needed. Teams communicate internally, just getting updates on target defenses, if any. CCAs work better if teams are left to themselves. Sound familiar?"

"Nine-eleven, of course." Then a bead of hope. "But Reza's dead, so maybe—"

"Vince, no way was he the only one in that fucking command chain. These mopes are all expendable, so no one person holds all the cards. The signal to go may have been Reza's call, but now that's moved up the chain to, I don't know, maybe someone else in the States or maybe someone in a fucking cave with a SAT phone. Who the hell knows. It's just too—"

"Wait!" I shout, mentally going down the hierarchy of evidence. "Okay, one person on a satellite phone can start connecting it all, but we know some of the dots, right? The phone numbers from Reza and others, right?"

"They'll be throwaways, burner phones, shuffled SIM cards bought with cash, replaced every few hours during critical times of an op."

I throw my head back at her bullcrap, glass-half-empty retorts, her excuses to sit back and play defense. It's the same twaddle her asshole boss has been beating into them.

I take a breath, then steeple my hands. "We know the locations of Reza's phone calls, which tells us maybe not who but probably where. Am I correct?"

She breathes to speak, shaking her head, but not as vigorously as before, saying nothing.

An opening, so I lunge for her hands. "The locations are a gift that we've been given. Maybe just a few numbers are still active and those dirt box things can find his people before anything goes down, if we're lucky. If not, then we move on to the next best level of evidence, and that would be . . . what?" I ask, trying to remember my notes stuck on the ranch's window.

She gazes up, also trying to remember, then bites a knuckle and says, "We can get the locations of the cell phones that he contacted, starting with major cities where the most damage could be done, then move out to the other locations to—"

I interrupt with a squeeze of her hands. "Agree, with one exception. If the minor locations have high-value soft targets like big schools, universities, where the human price is enormous, we should move them up the list."

Her eyes brighten. "Good idea. We have a criticality list, kind of a heat gauge of potential targets, but it's mostly asset driven. Business. Money. But this time we don't just count the zeros. We count bodies."

I shiver. She's awake. I massage her hands, wondering where the fuck Carolyn's energy has been since the intruder at her house tipped her back into the abyss.

"How much time do you think we have?" I ask.

No reply, just a slow head shake interrupted by Rachael's ringtone. Carolyn looks bewildered.

"Answer it!" I shout.

# SIXTY-FOUR

"RACHAEL?" CAROLYN'S HESITANT VOICE IS one you'd use when waking a child, a stroking hand on his or her back. She goes on speaker. We hear Rachael's voice far off, then fussing, some shuffling.

"This is Miss Wood's nurse. She wants to let you know you can visit with her now."

Carolyn jumps heavenward, then crumples onto her knees. I tell the nurse we're on our way.

So during another silent drive, I study Carolyn in black jeans, a pearl necklace swinging over a red silk tank top, and realize where I am. Carolyn's a brilliant professional, a little PTSD-fueled revenge crazy, which is good if you want someone's ass in a cold-blooded way, but strategically, it doesn't always work. Rachael's amazing, also a little revenge-crazy, but not yet seeing beyond the next crisis. I understand now why big things—government big—often don't work well, why there's dysfunction. There are too many chest beaters, no single mission. That brings me to me, still a basket case, all things considered. Then again, I just deal with life or death one person at a time. With myself as the boss.

Carolyn points to the visitors' lot—no security gates or ID card bullshit in or out—if we have to skedaddle. She says to park facing outward.

In the lobby, being a stranger lately, I'm hit by that hospital smell people despise. The volunteer at the visitors' desk smiles, her face saying, *I can't wait to tell everyone Doctor Vince has a lady friend.* I admit, after years of being the mysterious loner, it feels good to have a leggy blonde strutting next to me.

Carolyn flashes her badge and asks where we put people in Rachael's condition. Surgical Intensive Care Unit. Third floor.

The elevator doors open onto a new world—chaotic is understatement—that might be mistaken for the din and dazzle of Caesar's Palace, minus the cigs and alcohol and cheap cologne. Continual dings, dongs, buzzing alarms from every direction, slurping suction machines, x-ray units rolling by with the finesse of bulldozers, ventilator hoses being tended to. Lighting is, by design, restaurant soft (think Morton's) to delay burnout of the hero nurses who routinely raise the dead in this sacred place.

Carolyn focuses on two Santa Barbara cops and a suit looking exactly like all the fit, short-haired FBI men in movies.

"Can I help you?" the suit asks, stretching and strutting our way.

She pulls her badge, CIA this time. The cops shuffle away, smirking. J. Edgar does a badge-to-face and back, then nods.

"He's with me. He's also a physician here," she says.

I call the bout a TKO in favor of Carolyn. We go to 509, the big room directly behind the control desk. I don't tell Carolyn it's for patients expected to bleed out or arrest so the Code Blue circus train has room to maneuver all the crap they run in with when patients flatline.

I expect to see a half-dead rendition of Rachael—gray, festooned with chest tubes, central lines, and wire leads everywhere. I was right except for the half-dead, gray part, as I see when the curtains part. I let Carolyn enter and hear a hoarse shout from the head of the bed.

"Where the hell have you clowns been?" Rachael growls, spry as ever. She elevates the head of the bed, her right arm embracing Carolyn, then me. Very impressive this soon.

"Oh my God, Rach! I want to squeeze you but I'm afraid to!" We're all in tears.

"Help me sit up, but watch my left shoulder," she asks. A nurse hears us and comes to help. I see a compression dressing on her left shoulder the size of a calzone. No chest tubes draining into canisters.

Her nurse, a long-timer with a little too much makeup this late in the seven-to-three shift, turns to Rachael asking, "He's a doctor on staff here. May I tell him about your condition?"

"Yeah, he's a friend. You can tell it all." And she does.

The surgery took a little more than an hour. She needed a whopping five units of red blood cells. Most of her blood is now donors', the last burgundy bag still hanging. "It missed the apex of her lung, so no pneumo, no chest tubes. A vessel graft repair and cleanup of a few bone fragments." She turns to Rachael. "An FBI guy took the bullet and the glass from your other shoulder, so you have to ask him if you want it, honey."

Wait, glass? Carolyn, also perplexed, asks, "Where'd glass come from? I don't remember any shots through windows at the scene."

"And no blood on her right arm," I add.

The nurse flips through a clipboard. "Well, let's see. After they controlled the bleeding, they got portable films in the OR to rule out any other trauma and found it . . . cylindrical, about two by five millimeters. Like I said, given to FBI."

Rachael protests, "Nothing recent. Old farm accident?" She turns to me, like it's a question I can answer. I shrug and look at the nurse quizzically.

"That's all I have here, Doctor Vince. I'll find the FBI guy for you."

"Thanks very much . . ." I'm grateful, but fumble for her name.

"I'm Mary Ann, Doctor Vince. You can't expect to remember every nurse in the hospital."

"Well, I'll never, ever forget your name again, Mary Ann. And this is my friend," I say, not sure of Slim's cover-name-of-the-day.

"Carolyn. Nice to meet you and, as Vince said, we appreciate all that you do here." An impatience in words and handshake.

Rachael says, "Well, as long as we're having a love fest, I want to make one thing clear to you all. I'm blessed to have Carolyn and Vince as friends." She turns to Mary Ann. "And, ma'am, I wouldn't want to be anywhere else. This hospital is perfect."

With that, maybe it's the newness of the hospital smell, the sight of Rachael bandaged up, the stress, but something's not right.

# SIXTY-FIVE

**RACHAEL'S FACE TELEGRAPHS,** *I let us down, didn't I?* Carolyn's emotional quotient comes to the rescue.

"Vince wouldn't be here if it weren't for you," she says, stroking Rachael's hair. "You did the best anyone could do at the Carters'."

Rachael's chin sinks. "Yeah, right. All the intel's gone. I've left a goddamn trail of bodies all over town. It would have been great to turn all of them. Especially Reza."

Carolyn glances. We know she's right, but like I learned in residency, good judgment comes from experience, experience comes from bad judgment. *Move on, the clock's ticking.*

"Rachael, can you remember anything that happened when you got there? Was anything going on?" I ask, hoping retrograde amnesia hasn't blanked the last thirty-six hours of her life.

She takes a big breath and grimaces. "Crap, that shoulder hurts when I do that." Another breath, then she blurts, "Carolyn, I'm sorry! I thought he was going there to . . . to . . . to keep working with them, not to kill them. And now we have nothing to go with except more waiting—"

"Rach, you did the right thing," she says, giving me the look, minus eye-roll. I hope it's *get over it*, not *of course, Rach, you screwed the pooch*.

"Rachael, what do you remember when you got to the door?" I ask, distancing the name-blame-shame game that doctors play.

"Right, okay," she says.

Carolyn, restive and feeling the need to futz, hands her a tissue, which Rachael promptly balls up and tosses. I do a "take it easy" wave off and hold Rachael's clammy hands. "Okay, just tell us what you remember—and we realize it's fuzzy from anesthesia."

Her face freezes in concentration. We wait.

Carolyn cocks a hip to the side, fingers messing with her necklace. Like she's watching a zoo animal, waiting for it to do something entertaining.

Rachael holds up a finger.

"Here you go, kid," says Carolyn, guiding a straw to her mouth. Two long sips. "Why am I so dry?" she asks me.

"Atropine. Anesthesiologist's fault," I say.

"Okay, I can talk. I saw all the cell traffic coming from Reza and knew something was up. So I called you guys, but should have called for major backup, not just standby."

Rachael's eyes beg for affirmation. Carolyn, cool, says, "Of course . . ." I wait for an absolution, but none's offered.

"Reza answers the knock, hiding his right arm behind the door, so I drop and pull on the door for shielding, but before I can get it closed, I'm hit—at least I thought I was. It didn't hurt, not like it does now."

"Cortisol, endorphins," I say. "Great cocktail. Then what?"

"I light him up. I remember sliding down the wall, getting two off that I knew probably iced him. I sat there making sure he was down. Then I heard someone going out a back door and thought, Christ, why am I here alone? I'm thinking they're coming around the house . . . for . . . for me, game over, I'm dead meat. Then I saw you guys and took up the best defensive position I could. The rest is blackout."

"Wow," I say, seeing Carolyn, who's biting her lip.

"Yeah, I know, guys. Dumb. And I was never so fucking happy to see the face of that nurse as when I woke up in recovery. And she told me what you guys did for me." Now tissues.

Carolyn takes Rachael's hand and asks, "Did they tell you what we found?" I hold my breath, thinking *please don't mention the dogs*. She doesn't need to know that, ever.

"During debrief all they said was I got Reza but it was too late. The Carters were already dead. Obviously Reza did it before our shoot-out."

"Yeah," says Carolyn. "They also found one of Reza's crew stabbed just outside the kitchen door to the patio. Could that have been what you heard from the kitchen, Rachael?"

I shake my head, knowing a knife into the brainstem drops someone instantly. No running, no walking, no crawling. I zip it for now.

"No. It was deliberate. I mean, it was not struggling or thrashing. It was someone running, heavy footed." She looks between Carolyn and me, her dark eyebrows together.

"You know, I heard someone moving things—definitely not normal kitchen sounds. Someone was clattering something, not metal but maybe wood. Made me think wooden handles. I was waiting for a knife attack—but then I fogged out. Did they find anything like that on or near the victim that would have made sense with that noise?"

Carolyn appears puzzled and worried, and I feel the same. "No, nothing like that on the preliminary, but let me call the team. This is info they need to know. I'll be right back." She steps just through the curtains and makes the call.

I smile at Rachael after she shakes her head at me. "You're going to be good as new, kid," I say. "Why does Carolyn call you 'kid'?"

"I don't know. Don't make me laugh. Damn, it hurts. She thinks she's my mom sometimes."

"Yeah. She'd make a great mom." The words catch in my throat.

"I agree, Vince. Take care of her."

The curtains rustle and Carolyn reenters with a scrunched-up face, looking down at her phone.

"What's up?" I ask.

"Micius is up," she says, laying a gentle hand on Rachael's right shoulder.

Another strange thing to learn while hanging with FBI and CIA.

# SIXTY-SIX

**"WHO THE HELL IS MICIUS?"** I ask.

Carolyn looks at me, then Rachael. "The glass is a cylindrical tube with a nanochip."

This news triggers a cough from Rachael, who, bracing her shoulder, says, "What the fuck? Someone chipped me? Like a dog?"

"Wait," I ask. "You would remember that being done, right?"

"Never happened, guys," Rachael says, a glare drilling Carolyn.

Carolyn's on defense. "It's not our RFID chip. Way smaller. Less than a millimeter in diameter, could fit through a hypodermic needle like a flu shot or tetanus."

"I got the usual typhoid, rabies stuff the agency gives before Afghanistan, but that—"

"Get boosters over there?" Carolyn asks.

Rachael's head nosedives, nodding. "Yeah." An eye-blinking silence, all three of us seeming to process, then Rachael continues, "Well, aren't I just the all-around perfect teammate today?"

"Please, relax kid," Carolyn says, taking her hand. "Remember all those local med techs the navy rushed into J-Bad—and we trusted—to handle immunizations."

"Did you get boosters over there, Carolyn?" I ask, then add, "And if it's not radio frequency, then what is it?"

Carolyn shakes her head, saying, "Quantum entanglement. Einstein called it 'spooky action at a distance.' A laser simultaneously creates two photons that are forever linked. Put one in a glass cylinder"—and here she points to Rachael—"the other in a base station. Spin one, the other instantly responds oppositely."

Rachael's stunned. I'm almost there, but ask, "I've heard of this, and it's big-time science stuff. Taliban, ISIS, I mean, can they—"

"Micius was a fifth-century Chinese philosopher. They put up a satellite for quantum science in 2016 named after him."

*Great, now China's in on this.* I try to help. "At least we know how they were tracking us."

Rachael gives me a weak smile, then turns to Carolyn asking, "What other good news you got for us?"

"They found a Staples bag in the Carters' home office with empty cartons for eight-gig flash drives. Fifty drives in all. None turned up in the search of the house. They were plastic."

Rachael, nodding, says, "That fits the clattering sound."

Carolyn stares for a moment, then asks, "Vince, you don't remember hearing anyone come around from the back, correct?"

"Absolutely not." I push a thumb toward Rachael. "But you and I were kinda busy . . ."

Carolyn stays in the doorway, stroking her cheek. "This could be the Stinger flight control upgrades. It's about two gigs, unzipped, and can be added though a USB port on the launcher. And CEO Brent would have easy access to the files, bring home a memory stick. Then even goddamn Jackie could have gotten to them."

I ask, "But who cares? I mean, if they're going to be used close range, why do they need to be upgraded? They still work, right?"

Rachael sits up. "I was thinking the same thing."

"You're both right," Carolyn says, "but the old algorithm worked great if you're in the mountains of Afghanistan and there're one or two targets you're engaging. You pick one, fire, and forget. If you're near a busy airport with tons of infrared signals, your chance of target acquisition drops off big time. This fixes that."

"So the fifty flash drives means what?" I ask. I think I know the answer, but Rachael explains.

"It means that they have minimum fifty launcher teams poised around the country. They can't send these files over the web because they're tagged and NSA screens for them, so they have to get them out to the leaders of their Stinger squads."

"I don't know," I protest. "I still think the Stinger thing's a distraction. Then the real havoc starts. In wealthy areas, their schools, clubs, restaurants. The places where big-shits feel secure."

Rachael's face crinkles and she turns to Carolyn.

"I think he's right, Rachael. This one is going right to our heart. They already did their grandstanding, their monument-bashing on 9/11."

Rachael lifts her good arm. "Well, what the fuck are we gonna do? Let's get going!"

Carolyn starts a slow shake of her head.

I jump and shout at her, "No, it's not too late! We know what we have to do, Carolyn. Make some calls, do that JTTF shit you guys do. You guys are experts. You're perfect for—"

I stop, they stare. Now I'm the zoo animal.

Carolyn moves close to me. "Vince, what?"

"Before. When Rachael said to Mary Ann, 'This hospital is perfect.'"

"So?" asks Rachael.

"When you said that, for some reason it creeped me out. But I just remembered something. Jackie was adamant I tell Sal the exact same thing. 'This hospital is perfect.'"

Carolyn and Rachael freeze, staring at each other. Rachael murmurs, "Salaam must have had her scouting soft targets."

Carolyn moves to the bedside, her cell phone on speaker. "This is Talbot. I need command ops."

The phone crackles. "Stand by." In about five seconds, a military-sounding male voice, "Com ops."

"This is Carolyn Talbot. I need an emergency command center set up at my present location."

"Understood. What're your coordinates?"

"We're at Santa Barbara Community Hospital, Los Olivos and De La Vina, Santa Barbara, California."

"Wait, what? Do you really want the command center there?"

I retreat until I'm against the back wall of the room. Carolyn's blue eyes laser right through me.

"Sir, I think we're exactly where we need to be."

# SIXTY-SEVEN

**CAROLYN'S RIGHT BACK TO THE** day we met. Official. Professional. No-bullshit scary.

"I need a large interior room that has cell coverage. Big enough for five or six of us, maybe more. With a projector. Two of them would be great and reliable Wi-Fi."

"Alice Watson!" I blurt, like an autonomic reflex. Carolyn turns to me with moon eyes that say: *Who the fuck is that? Details, please.*

"The Alice R. Watson Conference Center," I start to explain. "It's in a separate wing where we do grand rounds. It's perfect. It's bigger than a conference room, sliding walls and everything, and it's packed with all of the electronics and audio-visuals you need. Completely refurbished, thanks to a large grant from one of Watson's kids." Without hesitating for Carolyn's answer I pick up the phone and ask for the nursing supervisor to call us. The operator does better and has the supervisor show up at the door. It's Stutz, official with clipboard in hand, moonlighting from the ER.

"What's up, Vince?"

"Stutz, this is my friend Carolyn, who's—"

Carolyn thrusts her badge. "Carolyn Talbot, and this patient is Rachael Woods, FBI and Homeland Security."

Stutz nods, stands at attention, bug-eyed but cool. "Whatever you need, uh, Miss Talbot, Vince, and Miss Woods. Is there something happening I should know about? I mean, should I call in extra staff? Is this because of the shootings today? Are we expecting—"

"Yes," Carolyn says. "Better safe than sorry."

Stutz puts pen to the clipboard. "Like trauma surgeons, blood bank, extra nursing staff—"

"Yes," I say, the others' eyes prompting me. "Think mass casualty event. Possibly. Nothing definite, but we need to be on alert. Anesthesia, transporters, ER staff, switchboard, security."

She jots down a few notes and turns on her heels for the curtain.

"Wait, Stutz!" I shout. "We need three or four large tables in the Watson Conference Center and a phone in every wall jack that's in there in case cell coverage gets spotty."

"Okay, Vince. I'll go down and get them on this right away."

Carolyn extends a hand to Stutz before she leaves us. "Thanks very much. I'm going to alert SWAT assets but not bring them here unless things happen. This is a real threat—not a drill. But like Vince said, it's not certain, so try not to scare the fucking crap out of everyone, okay? And media blackout, right? All questions come to me."

"Understood, Miss Talbot, understood."

Stutz has the calm eyes I've seen many nights in the ER, as she stared calamity in the face. I raise both hands. "And Stutz, I'm here. So when the administrators start flipping out, send them to me, okay?"

"Sure, Vince. Thanks."

Carolyn moves to the curtain and says, "I'm going out to the car and bring in my gear so we can go over that map of Reza's calls. When can we go to this conference center and set up?"

"The room's unlocked all the time. Let me go to the car and get the stuff, then meet me in the lobby and I'll take you there."

She's still staring blankly at me, a magician in a trance. "Vince, when we came in here I noted there are two driveway entrances to this hospital. Is that all there are?"

"Yes, correct. The main entrance and the service road to the ER. Why?"

"Can they ever be gated, just in case? Do they have strong gates?"

"No." I envision the soft-target scenario unfolding right below us. "I have a friend with teamster connections. He could get us some heavy trucks that could move in as barricades if—"

"Excellent. Have him bring enough so he can fully block any vehicle access, but tell him not to position them until we give the word, okay?"

"Will do," I say, hoping Henry Datillo is reachable.

I turn to Rachael, who's staring up at the empty blood bag and other IVs hanging.

"How much longer do I need this bullshit? I feel fine," she growls, twirling the IV tubing in her fingers.

"Don't pull that out," I say. "Just wait till I check with the intensivist. They can probably put in a hep lock—it's like a port to plug the IV back into if needed."

I hear someone just beyond the curtain. "Hello, it's Mary Ann again. Excuse me, Doctor Vince, I overheard you." She peers around the curtain, looks at Rachael. "Your blood count is almost normal, so we're gonna convert that IV to a—"

"Hep lock, yes!" Rachael blurts out.

"That's excellent, Mary Ann," I say. "I'll be right back for her."

Carolyn tells me what to bring from the car—our duffel, another one that feels like it's five-hundred pounds, and some satellite phones hidden under the rear seat. I grab it all, haul it to the main lobby where I offload one of the duffels to Carolyn, and we hustle to the Watson Center where we will set up camp.

It's a space the size of a small auditorium or mini-gym, where you sink into wine-colored carpet, and where walls of vertical rosewood slats draw your eyes to softly lit portraits of the hospital donors and benefactors with ridiculous money. But this is no gym. It smells of oiled wood and erudition yet exudes corporate excess and misspent tax exemption dollars that could have gone to more noble medical purposes. Whatever. It's got Alice Watson's name on it, so mission accomplished, I guess. I come here some evenings to relax, read, nod off for a few minutes. And now I fear what it's to become today.

We plop the duffels on conference tables with a couple of thuds. She doesn't have to ask how to access the AV equipment, not that I could help her, and in a few minutes the map of calls we studied is on the front screen. She has one stage monitor showing the hospital's security cams, another projecting cable TV—something I never knew possible, but good to know. Assuming we survive.

"Vince, could Rachael come down or is it too soon? Maybe in a wheelchair? At least let her know that some of the task force from LA District are on their way? I mean, only if it's safe for her to come down."

"Okay, can I come back here, or do you want me out of the way?"

She doesn't look up from her laptop. "Are you crazy? You stay right here with me. I need you." She laughs. "And you need me."

"I was just gonna say that. I'll be right back."

"Okay, have them lock all the doors to this room except the front. I'll put FBI out there to screen folks."

"Got it." I turn and jog to the exit while calling Datillo's cell.

"Vince!" Carolyn shouts as I push the door. "We're going to be okay."

"I know we are, Slim, I know." This time I really believe her.

# SIXTY-EIGHT

HENRY'S AT THE MEN'S GRILL at Santa Barbara Country Club, and somehow sober. I explain what's happened and what we need. He tells me he'll put two tri-axle dump trucks on standby at each entrance and keep his mouth shut. He asks if we should be worried. I end the call, pretending I don't hear that last part.

With a wheelchair, I push back the curtain to Rachael's room to find her unplugged, pacing, and pissed.

"Why do I need a goddamn wheelchair when everyone can see I'm able to walk normally?" Her good arm is palm up.

"Uh, because you just had surgery and the hospital doesn't want you to sue them when you fall and crack your fucking head open. So you just have to play the game with me, okay? I can't pull rank. Not on this one." She turns away, huffing, shaking her head. "Hey, Rachael, I'm on your side, remember?"

She drops her head. "I know, I know, I know. It's not you or your hospital," she says, a face of tears and remorse—not what I'd expect from this fearsome woman. "I just screwed up royally today, Vince. I want to go back and do it all over."

"And what would that be?" I'm in her face, nearly shouting.

"Maybe fifteen minutes earlier and you would have saved Jackie and her husband? I don't think so, because then you would have had two, maybe three dudes coming at us. And they still would have finished off the Carters. What would you do differently? Not shot Reza in the head? Then you and he both would've been dead at the front door. Go to the Carters' with the cavalry, so they'd all clam up and we could deal with their lawyers for six months? What would you change?"

She squinches, hiding a faint smile, looking better after my rant. "Aren't you little Mister Counselor today?"

"Well, I'm sorry, Rachael, I mean . . ." It's not my nature to lose it. "Listen, we're all tired, and you've been, been frickin' shot, in and out of surgery for Chrissake. So let's calm down and go help Carolyn before these clowns blow anything up, okay?" She accepts my help to the wheelchair, and we head to the elevator.

Stutz introduces me to an agent posted at the center's door. I show ID, she knows Rachael, and we're in. Carolyn wields a blue laser dot, explaining the map to another FBI-type, this time a guy with a friendly smile in business casual except for a big-ass pistol in a shoulder holster. I immediately like the guy and I'm not sure why. He gives a gentle fist bump to Rachael, then scans me as Carolyn does the introduction.

"Vince, this is Spence, Spencer Gillette from FBI. You spoke to him the night you called FBI."

I reach for his hand. "Thanks for taking my call that night, Agent Gillette."

"Call me Spence, and thank you for calling us, Doctor. We all appreciate your vigilance, and we know it took some courage to do what you did."

My eyes jump to Carolyn. "You're blushing, Vince, but he's right."

"Well, thank you, Spence. I hope we've got time to figure this out. What is it, "see something, say something"? I just wanted to say something and get the heck out of the way."

"Ha! What happened with that?" Spence asks.

My eyes find Carolyn's.

Our gaze breaks when the agent outside the conference center door bangs it open. We all jump as she shouts, "The team just called. They're almost here. They said to turn on cable news immediately!"

# SIXTY-NINE

**WHILE THE CREW'S GETTING CABLE** TV on the big screen, Agent Gillette freezes in front of a thrumming printer as it spits out a page.

"Dang," he says, holding the printout up for Carolyn and me. "And I've got the recording on my phone."

It's a transcript of an Air Traffic Control recording at LAX that FAA just sent to him. We circle around, listening and reading along.

> ATC: United 1093 heavy, contact approach 124.9.
>
> UA 1093: Going to 24.9, United 1093 heavy, good day, sir.
>
> UA 1093: So Cal approach, United 1093 heavy at FUELR.
>
> ATC: United 1093 heavy, descend and maintain 3000.
>
> UA 1093: Okay, down to 3, United 1093 heavy.
>
> ATC: United 1093 heavy, fly heading 280 and join the localizer runway 25 left.
>
> UA 1093: 280 on the heading and join, United 1093 heavy.
>
> ATC: United 1093 heavy, maintain speed 180 knots or greater to LIMMA.
>
> UA 1093: We'll do 180 to LIMMA, United 1093 heavy.

ATC: United 1093 heavy, cleared ILS approach runway 25 left, contact LA tower 133.9 at LIMMA.

UA 1093: Going to tower, 133.9 at LIMMA, United 1093 heavy. Thanks for your help, ma'am.

UA 1093: Tower, United 1093 heavy just outside LIMMA.

ATC: United 1093 heavy, tower. You're following an American 737 who's tracking about 165 knots across the ground, so reduce speed to 160 now if you can, sir.

UA 1093: Back to . . .

ATC: United 1093 heavy, acknowledge reduce speed to one-six-zero.

UA 1093: Yeah, tower, this is United 1093 heavy. That 737 we're trailing . . . ah, we just saw a smoke trail come up from the ground just off to the north, and now their starboard engine is torching. We'd like to go around.

ATC: 1093 heavy, say again?

UA 1093: We're going . . . [unintelligible]

ATC: United 1093 heavy, LA tower, say again?

ATC: United 1093 heavy, do you read LA tower?

ATC: United 1093 heavy, LA tower.

ATC: United 1093 heavy, how do you read?

# SEVENTY

THE CENTER-STAGE SCREEN OF THE Watson Center awakens blue, then blinks to a cable newswoman in front of a video that appears to be streaming from a news helicopter. The screen banner sickens me: "LAX CLOSED. ALL INBOUND FLIGHTS DIVERTED." This alternates with "TWO AIRLINERS SHOT DOWN, POSSIBLY MORE."

The news helo video scans a circle over water beyond Marina Del Rey to an image of a large airliner, nose down, bobbing in the Pacific. The airport's in the background where yellow fire trucks are spewing white foam onto smoking wreckage on a runway. Lines of ambulances converge ant-like from every direction. In another few seconds the sound comes up with a female's voice. And it's not what we want to hear.

"At this point, it's just what we're getting from the ground control radio and police scanners. Thanks, Brad. For viewers just joining us, tragedy in Los Angeles at LAX. Two commercial flights are down in the vicinity of the airport. At first thought to be a midair collision, eyewitness reports appear to indicate that both planes may have been struck by missiles before they crashed and . . ."

Carolyn mutes the sound, pounding a fist on the table. "Cocksuckers! How did they get those flash drives down there so quickly?"

Then she goes blank, silent, looking . . . I'd say defeated, demoralized. She's someone watching failure occur right before her eyes. I raise my palms to her. "Okay, Slim, that's just LA—ninety miles from here. The others may be on their way to other target airports, and that gives us some time, right?"

Gillette nods. I suspect he senses Carolyn's exhaustion and rush to disengage. He directs, saying, "Check the map of call destinations and see how fast FedEx, UPS, pony express, anybody who could get an envelope or small package to any of them. Forget bulk shipments. They probably split them up into onesie-twosies to make them tough to track."

Carolyn puts the map up on a side screen, points, and throws out a rueful question. "Here it is. We're only as good as our next save. Where do you want to begin?"

I tilt my head to get her to chill before asking, "Okay, how would they try to get the memory sticks down to LAX? Were they driven, airline, private plane, Amtrak?"

Rachael, who's ditched her wheelchair, wobbles to the table. "The time from when they left the Carters' kitchen until the attack was what"—she checks the TV—"six, maybe seven hours?"

"Any of the above except rail could have made it," says Gillette. "Even a decent pleasure boat. Rachael, if you're up to it, check the harbor patrol to see what left the docks. And maybe Amtrak, too."

"I'll get all the SBA-LAX departures, passenger manifests from airlines, and private plane flight plans from flight service," Carolyn says.

I flinch when there's a commotion at the door as a dozen or so LA District CTTF members come piling into the room like wound-up school kids at recess. With them are a couple of naval aviators from Point Mugu Naval Air Station in flight suits and headsets. Today, instead of scrambling their F-18s, they're pushing a noisy metal cart stacked with comm gear ahead of them. Carolyn turns, holds both hands high, and addresses the entourage.

"Before you ask, we're here because we learned of a credible threat against this hospital from the Carter woman when she was a patient. We've got a defensive perimeter going up, and Agent Gillette here will assign who'll go outside to manage that and who will stay in here on close monitoring. If there're more attacks in town, we'll have access to first responder and survivor accounts that may put us out ahead some. If needed," she turns to Rachael and me, "our team will have immediate medical assistance." She scans head-to-head, looking for questions. Or fear.

Spence Gillette turns to the agents, shouting, "Everyone outside, and coordinate with law enforcement on the perimeter—everyone except the communication team! I want you to set up right here." Most of the assembled group race outside while two agents peel off with the navy guys and head to a table, as Spence turns his attention to them and continues. "Get up on national comm lines pronto. Let them know what we have, and let us know what they have! Have they hit anywhere else?"

One of the aviators, now sitting behind a bank of equipment, says, "No, sir, nothing yet. We blocked two denial-of-service attacks earlier."

As Spence busies himself with the aviators, one of the agents at the comms table calls me over. She's fiftyish, in khakis, green polo short and a blue nylon jacket with foot-high yellow "FBI" on the back, and by no means unattractive, just like in all the movies. And honestly, I'm in awe. But for the big yellow letters, she's an everyday soccer mom buying groceries and piling them into an SUV full of kids. The male agent sitting next to her is equally anonymous in appearance, an unre-markable guy with three folds of fat on the back of his neck who looks like he's twelve. Yet that same blue jacket ominously distinguishes him as well. The things you don't know about your neighbors. I bring Stutz with me to their table.

"Thanks, Doc. And nurse . . . ?" asks the soccer mom.

"Stutz. Please drop the nurse crap," she says with a rare laugh.

"Okay, Stutz it is. I'm Intelligence Special Agent Natalie Lopez, and this is Special Agent Robert Lyons, but let's just stick to first names cuz we don't have a lot of time to waste. We would like to know about vehicular access to this hospital."

Stutz and I repeat what I told Carolyn earlier, that there are really only two general public entrances, the ER and the main entrance lobby. And even as we're explaining this I'm thinking, *God, there are a bunch of service and emergency entrances all around the back of this place. Some for meat wagons and service vehicles, some for people. They're supposed to be locked at all times, but . . .* I try to shake the thought, then let them know, as if to make it all better, that I've sent for several heavy-duty construction vehicles that can block both, if needed.

Robert asks me, "Any predictability to your ER traffic?" His associates nod, as in, *good question!*

Stutz and I chuckle as she lets the Nevada in her explain, "Honey, the only thing predictable is when you're short staffed, you know you're gonna be busy as hell. Other than that, ain't nothin' predictable about any damn ER I been in."

I do a hold-on finger at them so I can answer a call from Henry. "My teamster friend says ten dump trucks are outside waiting for instructions. He had them loaded with construction debris for more mass."

"Excellent idea. Tell him thanks," says Natalie.

I move back to the front of the conference center, where Carolyn and her crew are gathered at the main table in front of all the monitors.

"What do you think, Slim?" I ask.

"Gillette thinks the Stingers at LAX didn't have upgrades or those planes would have come down like confetti rather than landing hard. The warheads probably detonated too far away rather than shooting right up the ass of the exhaust plume. There're survivors, no numbers yet."

"So, maybe that's promising. The flash drives might still be around here?" I question.

"Yeah, but we're under attack, Vince. A lot can happen."

"Like what?"

"All your CCA stuff. An attack on, say, a school, a café, a—"

I stop her. "We just stay ahead of this. Let's go back to work."

She nods and turns back to her crew. I hear the FBI comm crew calling to Stutz and me again.

"One more thing!" Robert shouts across the room. "Which road leads to your cancer center? I just sent an ambulance to the ER."

We freeze. The room goes silent. Stutz leans back, looking over a lifted shoulder. "What the hell are you talking about?" she says. "There's no cancer center here; it's ten miles away in Goleta."

"Talbot!" shrieks Natalie, eyes wide.

"Now what?" Carolyn hisses while she walks to us with Spence as the room around us returns to noisy chaos like the floor of a stock exchange.

Natalie says to her partner, "Tell them, Robert." A scolding tone, as if Robert really is twelve years old.

Newborn pearls of sweat cover all space between his nose and upper lip. "Before we set up a vehicle checkpoint perimeter, an ambulance came in the main entrance asking for the cancer center. We didn't know, so we said follow the signs to the ER, but . . . I guess there's no cancer center here." Despite dry mouth, he adds, "It was negative for radiation." Like that makes everything good again.

Carolyn, hands on hips, moves in, stealing his oxygen. "Okay, before VCPs went up, and what was the branding on this ambulance, agent?"

"Ma'am, it . . . it . . . it was white with a magnetic sign on the side."

"What, like a fuckin' pizza truck? Did it have EMS markings, a goddamn roof light, any orange? Paramedics inside? A patient maybe?"

Robert vibrates.

I lay a firm touch to Carolyn's arm. "I'll check the ER, guys—"

"Stay here, Vince. Robert can check on it."

*Sorry, Slim.* I sprint for the ER. *Not even you can stop me.*

# SEVENTY-ONE

I'VE RUN THIS HALLWAY JUGGERNAUT on many Code Blue sprints to ER to help save a life. This time I move like I'm helping save more than one life, more than one Helen, like I'm trying to save a community. I wonder what it feels like to get shot. Patients say they don't feel anything until minutes later. What about having a limb blasted off? Fuck it—I don't care. Actually I do, but I can't worry about that now.

As I approach the ER door, I see it. Riding low, one guy behind the wheel. Definitely no ambulance. No pizza delivery, either. And it's coming our way.

Everyone at the ER nurses' station jumps and turns when I crash onto the panic bars of the door and stop.

"Okay, get everyone away from these doors stat. As far as possible. There's a car bomb outside, so let's move!"

The ER doc shouts, "Code Black stat!"—bomb-threat protocol. Then that's the end of shouting as everyone clicks through their memory items starting with a rush to patients. Cubicle curtains are flung back as we fly through disconnecting, unplugging everything—anything essential has battery backup.

I help as much as I can, mostly herding families out of the ER and as deep into the hallways as possible, assuring them that their loved ones will be right behind us on their gurneys and wheelchairs.

"Vince."

I turn and see Jane coming at me, rolling an empty wheelchair to pluck a patient from peril. I want to say, *Are you crazy? Turn around!*

"Just be quick, Jane. We'll be all right." I'm sure my eyes shout fear.

After depositing my group of family and ambulatory patients in the core stairwells, I turn back for stragglers. Jane and a few patients disappear into a stairwell, but behind them Carolyn is running at me.

"Turn around. ER's empty," she pants. "You got everyone out."

I tow her by the hand. "The stairwells and earthquake shelters are full. Let's go to the front of the hospital."

We ram through an emergency exit door, red warning lights and loud sirens going off, and burst onto the dewy grass of the front lawn. I relax, but Carolyn tows me this time. She climbs onto one of the lawn's park benches, scanning.

"We have to be able to see if another van comes in this way or that idiot circles back here," she says. "Damn, if Rachael was healthy she probably could have gotten an angle on him to take a shot. She's fuckin' crazy enough to walk up to his window and—"

Carolyn freezes when there's a flash of impossible brightness, a second sun rising behind the hospital. Then we hear—no, feel—a throb that whomps our chests, followed by a hideous rumble from the opposite side of the building. Before we can comprehend, the windows are a shower of glass hailstones rattling onto the circular drive. Silence. A moment later, terra-cotta roof tiles slide just before the building's east-wing facade tips and falls away, leaving a dollhouse view of patients and beds and equipment on all three floors. Nurses pull back from precipices. Something, no, *someone* falls from the third floor.

"Under the bench," she says, pulling me. "Put your arms over your head!"

As soon as we hunker, pieces of metal and stucco start raining down around us, some clattering on the bench's slats. I sneak a peek and get a head smack.

"Stay the fuck down. This'll take a while," she says, shivering and panting. "Jesus, that was huge."

More debris, smaller, falls like snowflakes. We hear a slap and get misted by a moist spray. We uncover our eyes and, about a yard in front, sitting like a decent serving of soft tofu, is half of a human brain. An ear flutters down not far from it.

"Car bomb," Carolyn says, jabbing with an elbow. "A vest blows outward and up, so the fucker's head comes off the neck clean and bounces down perfectly intact."

She's going technical, like me in a surgical calamity. Focuses, buys time, relieves stress. Hides trepidation. For sure she's rehearsed this in the Middle East.

"Good to know," I say. "Can we get the hell out of here and check on our people?" Survivors begin to trickle out, dazed and disoriented.

She kneels, surveying the lawn while a blue miasma curls over the roof of the building. There's the distinct smell of bleach.

"That's C4. This is probably just round one."

Far across the lawn, Rachael waves through the main lobby's shattered door frames, her bandage showing new blood. "Run!" she shouts.

We hightail it toward her, sidestepping a human foot, sitting upright, toes in the damp grass.

I pull us to a stop, short of the front door, Rachael beckoning.

"What?" asks Carolyn.

"I have to check. Check on patients."

She points now, jabbing her words. "You *are* Florence. Fucking. Nightingale. Aren't you? Are you insane? Do you understand this whole goddamn place could pancake any second?"

"I gotta do it, Slim."

"You *don't* have to do it. Bomb people will be here to clear the place. How do you know there's not another device in there?"

"Yeah," I jab now. "I don't know that. But what if someone's in there, trapped, and I don't go in to find them and save their ass? How'd you like to live with that the rest of your life, fucking Miss Know-It-All? I'd rather be Florence Nightingale than a goddamn fucking know-it-all!"

She jackknifes, hands covering, then sweeping back from her face. "I knew this was—I knew you were crazy. Just like me. Go ahead."

"I have to go—"

"Go! Fucking go! Nice knowing you."

I climb the hill of crumbled facade, stepping into gray powder billowing from the exit we just used to save ourselves.

"Vince!" Carolyn calls.

I turn to her from the doorway.

"She's not in there, Vince."

# SEVENTY-TWO

**EMERGENCY LIGHTING'S ON, BUT IFFY.** There's a crescendo of a dull hum before the harsh bluish light cuts out for a second. A clunk, then it's on, making the ghoulish swirling dust cloud look afire. The grit hits me in the face but only goes to my waist, so I bend low. My familiar place could pass for new construction—small piles of rubble, walls of exposed metal ribs, wires, and ducts dangling from an open ceiling—and smells hideous, a noxious mix of concrete, burning insulation, sewage. It's either mouth breathe or sniff the sickening mix. I pick up a towel, snap it in the air to roust off the dust, and hold it to my mouth and nose.

I rush past empty rooms, seeing crushed chairs and bloodied beds. I'm slipping on crimson footprints. I want them to lead to people who survived, escaped.

I breathe through the towel, hoping to filter dust and the taint of bleach from the C4 explosive. Check my phone. No signal but its flashlight works.

"Anybody here?" I shout as I run. It's quiet—quiet as hell.

At the One-South corner, where this hall turns toward the ER entrance, I expect to see some daylight—windows, a blasted out wall?—but it's a cold, black cavern, the flickering lights dangling from blown-out fixtures. I inch along, phone high, my hand on the wall's glassy tile—more comfort than guidance—every passing grout seam a marathon run.

I stumble on some ceiling tiles and stop. I now see what blocks the light. There's a clog of steel and concrete not twenty feet from me. I also realize the bloody footprints I track are heading toward this dense pile, not away.

Dazed and breathless, I check my phone—sweet baby Jesus, one glowing bar of hope! I tap to call Carolyn, but it goes right to voice mail.

"Slim, I'm in the One-South hallway but it's blocked. Repeat, One-South hallway where—"

I hear three dull beeps. Jesus has left the building.

"Fucking hospital dead zones!" I shout to the phone. The cavern responds with an echo that shivers me to the bone.

I lay the phone down and claw at rubble with bare hands, trying to clear a passage. I uncover a loose length of metal electrical conduit—steel, thank God—the size of a baseball bat, touching it with the back of a finger, just in case it's hot. I survive. I use it to climb, then pry and leverage cement blocks, drywall, and sheaves of metal studs out of the way until there's a square opening at the top the size of first base. Still dark, though.

I climb to it and scream, "Hey! Anybody there?" Nothing.

From the top of the heap, I use the conduit to leverage my weight against a metal rafter, shoving enough tangled crap out of the way so it's big enough for me to slide through.

I poke, prod the opening, testing yet hoping the jagged mouth collapses and becomes my excuse to turn back. But the gaping jaws hold.

I lead with the flashlight, scraping the hell out of my stomach when I elbow halfway over the summit. No bodies. But it's a sloping obstacle course of shredded ventilation ducts and chunks of concrete all the way to the stairwells where people sheltered. There's also the hiss and splatter of leaking pipes.

With the phone in my mouth, I ease one leg over, then the other. A few well-planned but abrading slides get me halfway down. I stand on the springy mass, my conduit a walking stick. I test my next step—the footing is solid—but the instant it lands, a groaning, spewing avalanche drives me to the floor. There's a muffled crunch—my bones?

I'm up to my ass in metal studs and loose tile. It's heavy, but all my parts seem to be attached, the bones work, and I squirm free. That was close. Time to regroup.

I turn back toward safety, but I've lost it. As dust clears, I see the avalanche was not just the settling mess that used to be our One-South admin offices wing, but the crush of Two-South down upon it.

Disoriented, I stop at the first room, scanning my light on a well-kept space. Against the far wall is an immaculate bookshelf, a bottle of hand lotion, a healthy plant, its leaves covered with dust, and framed pictures on top. Between it and me, there's a crappy institutional desk and chair, squashed squarely to within two feet of the floor by a concrete beam weighing a million tons. Between beam and desk, an arm outstretched with a feminine hand welcomes, says, "Sit down. Make yourself at home." I see wrinkles, prominent veins, a ring. My mother's age spots. I touch it. Ice cold, no pulse. I kneel to see if it's detached; a survivor close by?

No dice. It's owner's head of reddish-brown dyed hair is down on her desk, a bucketful of life oozed out by the beam's weight. I can't turn away. *Do I know this person?*

At the next office, my light tells me I've been here, hung out, though I can't say when or with whom.

"Hello. Anyone here?" Not even an echo this time.

I cross the open doorway, stepping over thick binders that splay from a huge, overturned file cabinet resting on the same collapsed beam. There's a desk, an empty chair. I turn to leave when my light catches a binder's label: "Medical Staff Bylaws." Of course—General Counsel's office—I've been here and it wasn't always fun. Except for gossiping with a young lawyer.

"Hey, you in here?" *Ellie was it?* She's always in here, at her desk. "Ellie, answer me." All I hear are busted pipes dripping in the hall, an occasional spark from a dangling short-circuiting light fixture.

When I lean over her desk, there's an iPod earbud cable leading to her office's back wall. I can't make it there without sliding the file cabinet from where it caught the edge of the beam. I give the beast a careful shove, pausing, expecting a major collapse. Another. And the cabinet slams down in a vortex of dust. When it clears, there's a narrow tunnel through to the wall. On all fours, I fumble with the light, then jolt back from what I didn't expect.

Ellie sits—on the floor, back to the wall, earbuds sizzling with Adele's voice. Her deep, vacant stare asks me why.

# SEVENTY-THREE

I SCRAMBLE UNDER THE BEAM to her. Every few seconds, more debris is crashing randomly, groaning of skewed support walls in the distance, an occasional electrical pop, gritty powder trickling down.

"Okay, hang in there. I'm getting you out," I repeat on my crawl. I reach her—skin damp and cold, probably just shock—take hold of her ankles and pull with care, supporting her as best I can so as not to worsen any trauma.

Once she's out, I move light onto her face. Bruised raccoon eyes stare without life. No carotid pulse, no breathing. A path of drying blood exits one ear while her nose spills a rivulet of spinal fluid. There's a slanted black bruise from temple to forehead where something massive—the beam itself?—toppled and, from what I see, cracked the base of her skull.

"Ellie!" I cry out, shaking my head, knowing she's gone. "Ellie, it's Vince!"

Panting, I move to the acrid stench in the hall, but it turns me back.

"I've gotta keep looking, Ellie. Survivors. You get that, right? Are we good?" Louder, "I'm sorry I survived. But I know you understand. Thanks for that. It means everything to me."

I'm out-of-body now, watching myself talking with, petitioning for the okay from a goddamn corpse. Yet, I'm also overpowered with . . . with ecstasy, a strange, restful peace and joy that I don't want to end. I'm surrounded by an all-encompassing light of luminous shades. *Is this The Tunnel? Am I dying?* Without warning, my lips tingle and I'm in a vertiginous fall to the floor.

*////////*

Without a clue as to how long I've been down, I awaken to a sequence of cracks, like snapping ribs of celery, from above. I listen, thinking it's first responders, survivors, someone coming my way. But it's not. I check my phone, needing to see something from Carolyn. Nothing. As I stand, thin columns of gray dust drop, and more ceiling in the hall crashes down in a writhing tangle of acoustic tile and metal framework, forcing me deeper into Ellie's office. It tells me I've got to get the hell out. After a last look at her.

The path that got me here—the avalanche route—is now packed with new debris. The only way out is to move down the windowless hall toward the ER. Toward Ground Zero.

My first few steps, soft underfoot, have me picturing my fatal drop to the basement. I test with my metal conduit. It seems solid, so I pick up the pace. When my phone dings a low-battery alert, I kill the flashlight, using light from the screen.

Ten yards later, I need the flashlight to help figure out why I just slammed into a mountain of twisted hospital beds. I scan top to bottom and see some beds aren't empty either.

No one moves when I shout and poke. I climb a few crushed beds and see a leg move. I prod it. Again it moves, but so does the whole pile. I jump back, realizing the leg, unattached, had been a wedge between two sections of drywall that, now free, chase me face-first to the ground.

The clattering stops, leaving me surrounded by leaking pipes, unbreathable air. I'm pinned. I'm the victim now.

A deep breath, some coughing up of what feels like sand, a glance toward Ellie's office, then a decision: *No fucking way am I dying in here.*

I scan in front of me through sweat-stung eyes, needing options. Pulling close a cracked concrete block, I do the best one-arm push-up I can do under the circumstances, then jam the block just under the drywall along my side before my arm gives. Another push-up, now with the conduit in hand, using it to push the block farther back. With each awkward push a sliver of space opens up, and the weight of the wall eases, giving me some hope. I begin hammering the block—gently, don't break it into useless gravel!—with the end of the pipe. Each blow drives it farther under the debris, leveraging it higher, while also gashing a trench into the side I'm on. I reach another block and gouge it against my other side. Finally, I can elbow-crawl to where I can get back on my feet, standing in the dim mist. Ding. Battery, ten percent. Still no signal.

I'm at the foot of the hideous Everest of hospital and body parts that nearly crushed me. Somewhere beyond is the open gash the fucker's bomb sliced into the ER. And freedom. I hope it's that and not another mountain.

The slide left a gradual incline of beds, furniture, and red med carts. One area has small intestine draped like sausage loops in a butcher's window. That's when I first notice the smell of blood and wonder why I didn't notice it sooner. But I've got to focus. From my vantage point, it looks like there's some space over the top of the pile between the rubble and concrete block. It's my best shot.

I start a slow climb, avoiding oily entrails and any foothold that's not solid. A few things give. I crouch and panic, hearing more electrical pops. I hold a moment, then keep going. I hear and see the pops growing louder where I started my climb. The valve of an oxygen tank that slid must have cracked, blowing an electrical short into a sparkling arc more blinding than a welder's torch.

I'm about halfway up and out of time. I can't tell if there's light flickering through the gap on the heap's summit or if those are reflections of the oxygen-fed flames growing behind me. I flash back to the ER, recalling firemen bringing in charred bodies popped open like hot dogs.

"Hey! I'm here. On the other side. Anybody there?" I stop breathing, listening. Distant sirens at least, so I go on.

I fly to the top on all fours like a crazy man, shove my forearm through, flailing, trying to feel something, anything. Nothing but bed linens and the heat at my back from the fire that's now got molten metal dripping from a stack of metal trusses. I grab another towel to breathe through.

More prying, more flailing, more nothing. Exhausted, I keep stabbing at the edges, realizing I'm creating a chimney for the fire that's now incinerating the debris that forms the unstable base of where I stand. I take the bat-like conduit and swing for the fence. But on the fourth or fifth slam, I slip back to within a yard of the flames.

Drained, I summon everything I've got, dig back up to the summit. I decide this is it; this is how it goes. I'll try to chip my way out. If I fail, I'll type my last text to Carolyn. I'll tell her I realize now how dearly I want my life back—my new life with her, the life I just discarded when I barreled like a jackass into a bomb site. Then I'll toss the phone through to the other side, hoping it will be found. I'll slide down, say a prayer, then put both fists around a live wire.

But first, I'll do this one for her with the ferocity she'd unleash on our attackers.

I gulp air before it's all smoke, wind up, and give it my best. The blow zings through to my marrow, but a hopeful chunk of concrete gives way. My next swing's even better. I turn to the flames, shielding my face as I shove an arm through to my shoulder.

Slower flailing this time, and again nothing. Then, as I start to pull back, something. Soft, warm, alive. Alive with three quick squeezes.

# SEVENTY-FOUR

**HOLDING TIGHT, I PEER THROUGH** the open crease and I'm face-to-face with an angel whose eyes say, *I'm sorry*. Mine say it back.

"Move away from the opening, sir," someone behind her shouts, tossing a rope, "and hang on."

A generator purrs, hydraulics, then the grind of a chainsaw's diamond-tipped blade, spewing milky cooling water—which looks good enough to drink for some reason—as it shaves concrete from the top of the puny opening that's my only portal to life on this earth. In several passes, the hole is big enough for a firefighter to pull me onto the aerial platform of a rescue truck and into Carolyn's steady arms.

"I thought you were gone forever, Vince. Are you okay?" she asks with a smile full of tears, releasing her embrace just enough to look over me and my tatters.

"Yes, no, maybe." My head bobbles.

"Let's get off so they can shore up this void and search for people," she says, motioning toward the truck's ladder. It is only then that I realize I've somehow climbed the debris pile to a point somewhere between the second and third floors.

On the ground, with arms around her, I shudder when I see what's left of what had been the south wing of our hospital. Half of floors two and three have collapsed, as I'd guessed when I felt something go, like the aftershock of an earthquake. What remains of each is a cantilevered, pathetic lean-to, hanging precariously from the remaining internal wall. I can't believe I survived, and more astounding are these fearless men and women who are climbing back in to save others.

Carolyn asks, "Tough to look at, right?"

I turn, seeing her fixated on it, wondering how many times she's stood before ruins entombing friends. "Yeah. This was my second home—maybe my first. These people were family."

"Vince, there're survivors. You got a lot of people out of there."

"*We* got a lot of people out of there. Thank you."

"And the entire north wing is untouched. It'll get inspected and be back up in—"

"Slim. The survivors are all that matter. Once, when I was upset over a fender bender with my first car, my dad sat me down and said, 'Vince, remember this: don't ever fall in love with something that can't love you back.'"

She presses me harder.

"And you were right," I say. "She *wasn't* in there."

Carolyn's head tilts; eyebrows converge.

"Helen. But I settled up with her ghost."

///////////

We walk the perimeter road to the north wing, stopping for me to ditch my filthy clothes for a pair of scrubs and resuscitate my phone battery. We hustle back to Watson, where emergency lighting adds new dimensions to the hospital's usual shadowless personality.

Drawn weapons and open ammo cases are everywhere. I'm relieved Stutz and Robert are okay. Rachael looks good as well, except for a blood splotch the size of Texas on her bandage.

"What the hell? How are you?" I ask.

"I jumped when the bomb detonated and jiggled the drain in my shoulder. I'm okay." Attempting to lift it, she winces, her speech becomes strained. "SWAT's on the way. What happened on your end, Carolyn?"

"The van was an IED," she says, "obviously." She glances in the vicinity of Robert's shoes. "Tell them, Vince."

"When I got to the ER, I knew it didn't look like an ambulance. It was riding pretty low." I give Robert a shrug. He scans our glum faces. "It was hard to see, but looked like one guy in it. We hustled everyone away from the door and out of the ER. Then . . ."

"Nice work," says a gentler Carolyn, then asks, "what's left of the ER?"

Stutz, still hyperventilating, says, "It's gone. Nasty dust everywhere. Windows busted, ambulance bay doors all pushed in. The car port came down, so there's no way in or out." She avoids a cry with a loud sniffle. "Upstairs lost most of the facade. Beds are there, IVs dangling, but patients are missing. Dead maybe."

"Did you see any assailants moving in after the blast?" asks an agent.

"It was a dust storm," Robert says, "so we checked on the people inside, then ran back here through the hallway. Paging and two-way radios are out, but the hardwired PA's working, so I called a hard lockdown, shelter in place. The radiation med guys say it wasn't dirty, but we'll verify."

Crap, I didn't even think dirty bomb. Carolyn's glare confirms the enormity of my reckless adventure.

Robert continues, "This wing and the outpatient clinic are intact."

Stutz turns to me. "Vince, there's a group of middle school kids over in outpatient that came in for ECG sports screening. They're okay—their parents know that. Some carpool moms are lined up in the parking lot waiting for them, calling 'em. I told the techs and kids to lock down and don't open for nobody except an all-clear or police, but should I talk to the parents?"

Spence shakes his head. "No. No one leaves until SWAT sets up and sweeps. I'll take an agent with me and talk to the parents."

"I'll go with you," I say. "They'll feel better seeing a doctor's ID along with your badge."

Carolyn nods. "Just a quick pass. Tell them the kids are okay, and get your butts back here A-SAP. No details to anyone."

I start to walk with Spence but get a text. "Jesus Christ."

"What?" Carolyn and Spence ask and circle me.

"Henry. My friend . . ." I freeze.

Carolyn grabs my phone, reading aloud.

> Shooters at country club. SWAT on way.
> Pray, Vinnie!

She wipes her brow with the crook of her arm. "Spence, what's the bandwidth on SWAT in Santa Barbara?"

"One major, two minor engagements. Eighteen headcount. But Ventura is on the way to help."

"No, they're not!" shouts an agent, ripping off her headset.

"What?" Spence shouts.

"They're not. There're at least five people with body armor and AKs that have the 101 blocked where it goes to two lanes. Ventura Tactical says forty-five minutes minimum to engage 'em. They're trying to get the air unit to move some assets up here, but one of their

Hueys took rounds and bugged out. Active hydraulic leak. They launched their OH-58 helo as backup observation, SAR if needed, but no weapons on it."

"What the hell? Can't police overcome that?" asks Spence.

"I guess two units were hit with RPGs as soon as they arrived on scene."

He turns an ear, as if he's misheard. "Come again?"

"Yes, sir. Rocket-propelled grenades."

"The parents outside are gonna panic, Spence," I say. "I better talk to them."

Spence lays an arm-block on me. "Someone get a national media update, please," he says. "Let's hit it, Doc."

# SEVENTY-FIVE

**SPENCE AND I DOUBLE-TIME IT** across the conference center's luxuriant front lawn (it could host several field hockey games at once) separating the hospital's adobe facade from the main road. It's littered with paper shards and other light debris, some of it fluttering in a gentle breeze. The moms, most in designer jeans and silk T-shirts, driving SUVs and luxury cars, had somehow beaten the order to blockade the entrances. They're now trapped in the semicircular driveway that loops toward the main door, hemmed in by the cops' two black and whites and Henry's almost military-looking column of oversized trucks out by the road. They cluster in small groups by their vehicles. It could be paralytic fear or denial, but they actually seem pretty calm.

As Spence and I approach the first group, a redhead, a bit too stocky for her sun dress, leans on a pearly white Escalade—Texas plates—and speaks for her pack of friends.

"Hi, I'm Chrissy." Her voice cracks. "What the hell happened?"

We introduce ourselves; I defer to FBI. "Chrissy, all the kids are unharmed, but we've had an incident—"

"Ya think? That almost knocked us over. Was that a gas explosion?"

"We're investigating as quickly as possible, and once we're sure it's safe, we'll escort the children out to you."

"What kind of incident?" another mom asks, pissed and anxious.

"That's all we can say now. It's under investigation by FBI and the police here at the hospital. More SWAT assets are on the way, so don't let that alarm you when they show up. Doc and I here will be out as soon as we learn more, but I emphasize, the kids are all safe and unhurt."

The women widen their circle around us, understanding what Spence told them. I shout to the other parents as they approach, "Your children are unhurt and safe! We'll be back when we have a timeline on getting them—"

Chrissy flips hair out of her view, pointing. "What's this wang-doo-dle think he's doin'?"

We turn to the road and see a landscaper's truck and trailer driving in the wrong lane and weaving recklessly, like the trailer and cab might jackknife at any moment.

"Jesus, this is a hospital. Slow the fuck down!" another woman shouts. "What the . . ."

The truck jumps from the road, flattening the hospital's flimsy black metal fence, and careens across the hospital's lawn. Black exhaust billows as it accelerates, nothing between it and the main door.

Spence gets on his radio, shouts into it frantically, "Possible vehicle-borne IED inbound, main entrance! Repeat, IED main entrance! Talbot, keep everyone in the conference center and take cover! Repeat, take immediate cover!"

"Oh my God!" shouts Chrissy. "This is the real shit." Her friends scatter in all directions, but she lunges for her Escalade's door handle, jumps in, and fires it up.

Spence shouts for her to stay put, but she floors it, jumping the curb onto the lawn, spraying mud and grass through the air in a wide arc as the car fishtails, then begins gaining traction and speed. I'm thinking she's hightailing it to the road; I'm dumbfounded when the Escalade, instead, barrels toward the hospital building, on a collision course to beat the truck to the front door!

At the last instant, Chrissy bails, purse absurdly in hand, rolling across the turf just before the truck T-bones her SUV, wedging it sideways into the front doors like a battering ram, and now blocking the entrance. She avoids the jackknifing trailer with a dive to the pavement. I'm in disbelief—this can't be happening—yet waiting, cowering, cringing, for the inevitable blast. It doesn't come. Parents panic and scream into cell phones. Some start to run to the hospital but realize the only entrance in front of them is completely blocked; a few jump in cars, madly trying to flee.

Spence and I stumble toward Chrissy, but before we get there, the truck's black-clad driver bats at the airbag, then stumbles out, brandishing an AK-47. I freeze, waiting to feel what Rachael felt, but I'm ignored. He circles around to Chrissy, lying flat on her back, a streak of blood glistening from a cut above her left eye. He stands over her, grinning, raising the weapon toward her head.

"You big hero, lady, huh?"

"Fuckin-A, buzzard bait," she growls as a gleaming, nickel-plated pistol slides through the side pocket of her purse. She does a full mag dump into his chest while her friends yell her name in unison, like a chorus of avenging angels.

Spence radios the team, telling them what just happened—and that we still might have a timed IED sitting directly in front of the main entrance. There are no words spoken as we race to Chrissy and the wreckage, knowing we might be running to our deaths.

There's no stopping Chrissy's friends as they, too, converge on her, one woman in capri pants going so far as to kick the rifle away from the stricken driver. "Just to be sure," she says. We're all standing there, surrounding Chrissy on the ground—one of those moments where time seems to stop for a couple of nanoseconds, as if waiting for reality to catch up with it. I look at Spence. The shock registering on his face probably mirrors my own.

"What the hell's going on here?" I demand to know.

And smiling like the Cheshire Cat, the woman in the capri pants looks at Chrissy and purrs, "Girl, you crazy Texan, you. Thank God you dragged us to that concealed-carry course."

"Oh shit!" Spence groans. "Okay, seriously, who's carryin'?" he asks. Three of the four raise designer purses. "All right, ladies, no one pulls unless I say so—we've got friendlies trying to move out here to deal with this situation and SWAT on the way. Got it?"

They nod, sort of. I'm thinking that this particular scenario probably wasn't covered in that concealed-carry course. And I'm thinking, get back to business.

I kneel, compressing Chrissy's wound with a tissue while chaos continues amid the distant wail of sirens. I help her up and we hurry away from the Escalade's smoking carcass, following Spence and the others to take cover behind the line of cars.

A lanky brunette next to Chrissy shouts, "Shit, there's more!" as the trailer's tailgate slams to the ground.

Four—more maybe?—AK-toting men in black emerge, dazed and probably disorganized after Chrissy's stunt, but wildly shooting everywhere. The brunette spirals, blood spilling from a grazed elbow as we crouch behind an SUV.

Spence radios the crew inside, letting them know there are shooters at the entrance, along with three crazed mothers with semi-auto pistols. I ask about Carolyn and the others while putting a tight wrap on the brunette's elbow with her scarf.

"They're all okay. Kids are fine," he says, watching me work.

"SWAT team's done mopping up at the country club, so they'll be here soon."

I picture Henry and how terrified he must be, yet how measured his simple text was. Like our dinner prepared him for this hell.

"Carolyn thinks it might not be an IED, just a load of attackers."

"I agree." It fits with her rendition of a CCA.

"She said you left your pistol inside."

I shake my head. "Agree with that too. I'm fuckin' *stunad*."

"Here," says the brunette, her leg shoving a pink purse. "Sig P365 ready to go. Ten in the mag plus one."

I tie a knot in the scarf and stare. "Thanks, I owe you."

"We're even. Now just save our kids and everyone else inside."

"This can't be real! What's happening?" one of them shrieks, hysterically covering her face with her hands. "Chrissy, you killed one of them, and you can bet the ranch they're coming for us now."

"Wrong," says Spence. "Listen. Calm down and listen. If it was us, they'd have engaged us." The sobbing and heavy breathing slows as he raises a finger, eyeballing us. There's another volley of shots into the hospital's door followed by sounds of kicks, cracking wood, and metal being bent away from the entrance. "They want what's inside, ladies."

# SEVENTY-SIX

**I LOOK TO SPENCE GILLETTE** for our next move, while picturing Carolyn, Rachael, the students, patients, the staff . . .

The moms are quiet for a moment, then one shouts, "Let's raise some hell! The bastards want our kids." In an instant, the women's guns are out and racked.

Spence cautiously rises, looking through the tailgate's window, then drops. "We can do this! I only see four, no body armor. The shitheads are all clustered by the door, and it's starting to give. Let's just stay low and move up, two on each side of the car in front of us. When we get to the hood, we open up." He points to his gun sight. "Remember, stay cool—no spray and pray. Aim first, then shoot."

Chrissy, up on the good elbow, says, "God bless the FBI. I'll back you guys up as best I can." She loads a new magazine into her pistol.

"Thanks, ma'am," he says. "Vince," and here he pauses, reads me for fear as my heart skips beats, stutters, "you stay here with her, ready to give cover fire if we retreat."

"You got it," I say, hearing my fear.

They move after some hesitation, but stick to their plan to go six feet forward. Spence fires first, four shots, and the two closest drop.

The others turn, surprised to see us on offense, and start moving backward in a black blur. The women unload a volley, and the two other attackers fall. One stays down, inert, the other one stumbles to his feet without his weapon, running from us, his hands covering his head.

I keep him in my sights, then Spence turns to me, screaming.

"The truck's blocking me. If you have a shot, take it, Vince!"

"He's mine!" I open on him. First shot puffs up concrete a foot ahead of him, second shot fluffs his pant leg. He drops to one knee but immediately bounces up and keeps going, hopping now. I squeeze off one more that chunks off a corner of the building just as he pivots around it and disappears.

"Fuck. There's a service door there!" I yell to Spence. "Goddamn it!" I curse my poor aim.

Spence comes over to settle me down, then gets on the radio. "Talbot, three of four down, one without an AK, probably hit, we're chasing him, but he might be armed and possibly inside."

Spence looks at me. "Relax, Doc, you hit him. Let's go find him, but stay behind me, okay."

I give the nod of a bases-loaded strike-out man. "Spence, the corner he took is a blind alley between hospital wings. There're two no-entry emergency exits; one service door leads to outpatient."

Spence furrows his brow. "Damn."

"Yeah. Where the kids are. If he gets in, he'll be in a narrow hallway that leads to a mini-clinic, exam rooms, and utility closets."

"Can he open it?"

As I start to answer, he alerts Carolyn to this possibility. A volley of expletives emanates from his earphone.

"No handle on the outside. Sometimes they prop it open for ventilation. Also, if it's not latched all the way, you can pull on the bottom and open it."

"Follow me, Doc." We take a step; he turns. "You've got eight rounds left by my count."

He radios Carolyn and the crew our plan. She says they'll move to outpatient, check and guard the emergency exits. When we get to the corner where my missed shot left a crater, he stops.

"Stay back." He takes a small metal mirror from his pocket, using it to see the alley. "It's clear, but be ready for him to pop out."

We hug the alley's right side, like Carolyn did at the Carters'. Reza's stunt comes to mind for me. We hear a brief, rusty scrape. Spence raises a hand and we stop and crouch, me behind him. The exit door on the right moves an inch, then stops.

He centers his aim; I check behind us. Clear. Then the door opens farther, pushed by a knee in black jeans.

"I know that knee," I whisper.

He keeps his gun on the door and whispers into the radio. "Talbot, confirm position, east wing exit door."

I hear the voice—thank God it's Carolyn. We move to the door as it swings wide where she and two agents stand.

Carolyn fist-bumps me hard. "Thanks for taking care of him, Gillette. He's got a gift for sniffing out trouble."

When our eyes meet, I want to jump on her like it's my last squeeze of a human on this planet, but don't. Professionalism, rage, fight, flight—today the whole choir sings in my head.

"He did well, Talbot," says Spence.

"Of course he did." She laughs. "I taught him everything he knows."

# SEVENTY-SEVEN

**WE SPRINT TO THE CONFERENCE** center table with the closed-circuit screen montage.

"What do we got?" asks Spence. Another day at the office.

"Nothing, sir," says an agent, eyes on her screen. "Since you called in the runner, we've had CCTV on no-delay and haven't seen entry or exit from that alley except for you guys."

"What the hell?" Spence says, turning to me.

"The two emergency exits and the service door to the outpatient clinic are the only ways to go once you're in that alley. Except up."

Carolyn studies the CCTV feeds, then scans around the table. "So what the fuck? He's Spider-Man? Fuckin' Spider-Man with a nine in his ass?"

She makes her point. I know I hit him, and so does Spence.

Natalie says, "I checked. Those exit doors were locked and latched. If he got in through the outpatient clinic service door, where could he go from there?"

"Nowhere," I say. "It's a hallway lined with supply carts that ends at the door to outpatient."

"Is there a camera on that hall?" she asks.

We're all blank. The agents scroll channels, shaking their heads.

"Stutz would know," I say. "Stutz!"

"Where is she? And where's Rachael?" asks Carolyn.

Dead silence.

Robert, now looking aged beyond twelve years, says, "After the shooting stopped out front, the three of us checked the lobby. Then Stutz and Woods went to calm down the kids in outpatient."

Spence moves behind the monitor crew. "Rewind the first-floor channels, see what we got."

Robert's right. We view Rachael and Stutz moving down the hall to outpatient clinic. At the clinic, we see Stutz apparently yelling, knocking, and showing her ID under the door.

On split-screen, the camera inside outpatient shows the barricaded door but none of the students.

"Where the hell are the kids and the tech?" I ask.

Finally, we see some of them come to the door, move chairs, helping Rachael and Stutz enter the room. As we're watching the feed, suddenly a radio crackles.

"Listen up! SWAT is arriving at the ER side now," says Spence. "Twenty-plus injured are coming in behind them."

Both hands push my hair back. No way can we handle a mass casualty event on top of this. "Okay, well, SWAT will secure the place so we can try to run a trauma center again."

Carolyn's barely perceptible smile calls bullshit on me.

Spence points to his agents. "You, you, and you load up and come with me. We're going into the alley and breach that door to outpatient. He's got to be in there. Talbot, keep the comms coming on what you're seeing in there."

"Will do," she says. "Do you want to wait for SWAT backup?"

"We're out of time, Talbot."

The three agents saddle up and follow Spence Gillette. One

of them holds a pry bar, another a brick of gray plastic explosive wrapped in det cord.

The cams are calm, then Carolyn leans into a screen.

"What the hell are they doing?" she asks, pointing. We watch Nurse Stutz herding the students into the service hallway.

I walk to the monitor and say, "Well, usually that's a safe exit to the lawn, but . . . they don't know we lost an attacker."

Carolyn grabs her cell phone and calls. Our hearts tumble when Rachael's phone rings on the table behind us.

# SEVENTY-EIGHT

**CAROLYN PULLS ME ON A** run to outpatient, an arm out to freeze me as she checks each hallway we run past. At the clinic's door we shout and knock without a response. I give it my hardest shove, but as thrifty as hospital construction material is, it goes nowhere. Carolyn and I then try together. Nothing doing.

"Can't you shoot the lock open?" I ask.

"That only works on television." She turns, saying, "Wait, we passed a TV cart back there, right?"

I sprint and return with it. The wide hall gives us good runway as we slam into the door, cracking the wood by the lock. After one more, we're in and see Rachael, back to the students as she herds the last of them into the dim service hallway. Her weapon is trained on us, like she didn't expect friendlies crashing her party.

"Thank God it's you! Stutz says this leads outside to an alley where we can make it to the front lawn."

Carolyn raises both arms. "Time out. Four attackers: three down, one wounded—dropped his AK—but possibly armed. He's loose, and the last we saw, he was in that frickin' alley."

"Did you hear anyone open that service door?" I ask.

Rachael has an uncertain squint. "The hall's been dark the whole time, but we mostly covered the door you guys just breached. Stutz and I also cleared the exam rooms."

She walks us to the calm crowd of students, all in shorts, T-shirts, and flip-flops. Their curious eyes lack fear—I guess that's what active-shooter drills do to kids—but their silent faces scream. No doubt they trust us, but these young lives have been immunized by repeat doses of televised school violence.

Rachael yells for Stutz, whose answer echoes.

"Yeah, we're good. Just waiting for you so we can move out."

Carolyn and I weave among the kids to assess our exit. Our goal is a door at the end of the dingy green hall. There are linen carts with yellow patient gowns on the left, a stack of folding chairs on the right, but good running room smack-dab down the middle.

Carolyn shouts, "Everybody listen up! FBI agents are moving to the door, so until I make contact and tell them it's us exiting and not bad guys, just stay cool, okay?" I'm thinking, ridiculously at this moment, that she'd make a good soccer coach.

Rachael continues. "When we leave, we're going out with hands up. Don't take anything with you. I need a verbal yes, everyone."

Jesus, a flight attendant doing an exit row briefing. Stutz gives a thumbs-up at the front of the pack.

Carolyn sighs. "Rach, I can't get comms to Gillette in this hall, so I'm moving into the clinic. I'll be right back."

"Got it," says Rachael. "So guys, hang on until she gives us the okay. Remember, hands up, leave everything behind, right?"

I see more nods as Rachael passes by me to check on Carolyn.

At the pack's front, Stutz yells, "We're cool, Doc! Just say when."

Before she finishes speaking, not twenty feet behind her a linen cart jiggles, then a thick figure in black rolls out from its bottom shelf and stands. No rifle, no pistol, his face expressionless. The crowd's near silence turns absolute, allowing us to hear his unhurried and calm footsteps. At this point, hell, he's a scared-shitless employee from central supply who hid out after the blast, right? He brushes himself off and I relax. But why is he here?

Stutz, in nurse mode, says, "You look like you're hurt."

I hear Carolyn's distant, "What the fuck . . . ?"

Ten feet from us, he stops to scan us left to right, his face carved marble. Then, like it was an apple, he lifts a grenade from his jacket's breast pocket. The crowd's frenzied wave propagates as he looks at it as if reading directions, pulls the pin, and arcs it into the middle of our small crowd of students. He watches until it hits the floor, then runs for the door—the very door that was to be our exit route.

"Why you goddamn bag of crap!" Stutz screams. "These are children!" I spread my arms, ramrodding the group back into the clinic with Stutz tugging at the stragglers.

Lightning fast and weaving against the stampede, Carolyn goes to ground as if recovering a fumble. She comes up with the hissing device and line-drives it perfectly so it rattles around in the corner between the exit door and Mister Bag-of-Crap. "You dropped something, motherfucker," she says over her shoulder, pushing the last of us into the clinic.

A flash comes from the hall. Then a blast-wave blows me and a dozen kids in front of me off our feet hard to the floor. I cover, waiting to see what chunks—human or otherwise—will follow. I feel reverberations jiggling bodies all around, under, and on top of me. Then, it's over.

For the second time today, I confirm all my pieces are attached, then roll off a person who then sits up and smiles at me. As my flash-blindness fades, I see the echo tech and she's okay. Over an increasing ear buzz, I hear a voice—male, I think. I match the voice with Spencer Gillette, who enters behind three SWAT guys. And standing over me is Carolyn, offering a soft hand.

"I think we're all okay, Vince. Everyone's okay."

"Where's Stutz?" I ask.

"She's fine." She points by the door Stutz had just shoved us through.

Stutz laughs and hobbles to show the pocket of her scrub pants where the force of the blast shattered one of her beloved red ballpoints. "Well, at least it just looks like blood, right?"

"Yeah," I laugh. "You stayed cool, Stutz."

Carolyn sidles up to her and says, "He's right. Where the hell did you learn to stay cool like that?"

Stutz's gaze drops to the floor. "That came from one of my boys. He was in Iraq."

Carolyn and I sink, expecting heartbreak.

"Told me he made it back 'cause he stayed cool," says Stutz, giving Carolyn a wide smile, then asks, "what the hell, Supergirl? Tossin' a live grenade! Where in the name of God did *that* come from?"

Carolyn's chagrined, goes technical. "You've got four to five seconds on a good fuse. And if it's a short fuse, it ain't your problem. It's a problem for the asshole throwing it. Speaking of . . ." Carolyn turns to Spence and the SWAT team. "What's with the dude who tried to kill us?"

Spence looks at the SWAT commander. "Sergeant?"

"Well, ma'am, depends which half of him you're asking about."

# SEVENTY-NINE

NURSES TREAT A FEW STUDENTS for minor scrapes, ruptured ear drums, their unscathed classmates refusing to leave without them. Then SWAT escorts the group outside to subdued applause of jittery, joyful parents.

The clinic now belongs to the evidence team. In the middle of the room, Carolyn and I stand alone. She hesitates as she faces the entry to the shrapnel-pockmarked service hall, where shafts of sunlight coming through the blown-out door make the settling dust sparkle. She walks to the attacker who's not strictly cut in two, but say, butterflied at the waist. The air near the body's an effluvium of explosive residue—trust me on this one, sampled it twice today—pulverized plaster and the smell of raw liver. Human and raw.

Carolyn stops short, staring down at him. She turns to me, trembling, as if needing permission to approach. Eventually, she stoops to take a picture of his face.

She nods, murmuring, "He's one of Reza's goons," then sleepwalks outside, halting. I follow. As she stares into the blue, I first see anger, then she silently shakes her head with eyes closed.

Our eyes meet, I break down, our arms entwine. When I can speak, I step back an inch.

"Do you think it's over?"

The tip of her shoe traces a slow figure eight into the dust. She opens her mouth, but tears force a turn away. Once more, this time with an apologetic smile, she says, "No way to know for sure." Her mouth sinks at the corners. "But I think so. There would've been a second wave of attackers by now."

"Good news is nice once in a—" I stop, look at the blasted-out door, then shudder. "Wait. How did . . . ?"

"Whiskey Tango Foxtrot," says Carolyn, lit up.

Her eyes say she knows the answer.

# EIGHTY

**CAROLYN CLOSES ON ME, NODDING.**

"No limp on the grenade dude," I say.

"No blood on either leg," she says.

"And runnin' like a fuckin' Super Bowl wide receiver."

"Yeah, not wounded, Vince."

"It was crazy out there when that trailer opened."

"War fog," Carolyn says. "That's okay. The grenade dude probably slipped in during initial contact. Smart move for him."

"Where's the guy I shot?"

"Dead, bled out. Or playing dead somewhere close to this service hallway."

Her tears are vanquished, replaced with the eager eyes and flushed cheeks I saw that crazy night in her garage.

"Let Spence know, right?"

Her index finger launches. "Let's think for a sec."

*Think about what? We need the cavalry. Does she want the thrill of this hunt for herself? Okay, today this is her hospital, her war zone gig, so I'm in.*

I point to the blown door and say, "He had to come in through this service hall, and that means he either got past Rachael and Stutz—highly unlikely—or he got into the clinic before Rachael secured it."

"What's in the clinic?" Fingers massage her temples.

"The reception area where we huddled after the grenade, and behind that, about five exam rooms that Stutz and Rachael cleared and hopefully locked."

"What's in the exam rooms?"

"A dropdown desk, exam table, sink, cabinet. Typical doctor crap."

"Shape?"

"Square, no closets."

"Keys?"

"Keyless. Code's 6162."

She pulls her hair into a black velvet scrunchie that somehow time-traveled up from the eighties. "Call Spence, then stay an arm's length behind me while I unlock them."

I toy with saying, "Roger that," but just nod, make the call, pull my borrowed Sig, and follow her to the clinic's first door.

Thank God the electronic locks are functional. And loud as hell, so we're not surprising anyone. I expect a rain of lead through the door after she enters the code, both of us well off to the side. She motions for me to move farther away as the door swings with a Hitchcock-ish squeak. She uses a mirror like Spence did, then flies, gun first, across the doorway. Empty.

Second door, same thing, squeakier but quicker. She's on a roll.

Approaching door number three, I tap her shoulder and point to the latch side of the doorframe. There's a maroon stain brushed on at about knee level. I get a thumbs-up and we bypass it, moving to the fourth room, clearing it.

She whispers, "If we need to cover, we've got open rooms on both sides of us. Just don't fuckin' shoot me by accident."

I pause. "Roger that." Hey, I've got chest pain, so I'm saying whatever the hell I want.

She puts me on the safe side of the door—against room two's wall—so no hellfire can come at me from whoever's holed up behind door number three. She opens it, uses the mirror, then shakes her head, a smiling lottery winner. And I smell blood.

I tip my head back; she tosses the mirror to me. The exam table is a mountain of torn clothing, tape, gauze bandages. She gestures to the near corner of the room, then I see him. Short, stocky. A human fire plug.

She waves me closer but short of entering. She peeks in, her weapon's laser sight locked on his forehead.

"Let me see your hands, asshole. It's over."

Slumped in the corner, his skin color's matching the clinic's ugly beige tiles. One leg's wrapped with a mile of gauze. One hand's empty, the other comes up quivering, holding out a grenade. Same tattoo as Douche Bag, by the way.

Carolyn eases around the corner enough to see him yet still able to get outta Dodge, if needed.

He keeps waving it, an offering in her direction. I can't tell if he's shocky and out of it or having language issues. Carolyn's laser jumps from his head to his free hand, and with a thundercrack half of it's gone, a bloody mess that flies against the wall. He yelps, seeing what's left of his hand with a sick smile, good hand brandishing the grenade.

"Oh, damn, you should've pulled the pin. Now what are you gonna do, Einstein?" She inches closer to him. "Are you sittin' on one with a pulled pin? Are you fucking with me? Joshing? Yanking my chain? What's so goddamn funny?"

Carolyn heel-stomps his leg wound, making him roll enough to make sure he's not sitting on a death trap.

"Slim!" I yell.

She slaps back a wave, then snatches the grenade from his hand, shoving it into his face.

"Pull it with your teeth, tough guy. Come on, do it!" Her volume drops as she rolls it over his forehead, using it to give his head a few nice, resonant knocks against the wall. "Just you and me. Let's go together. Then I'll be one of your virgins, how's that sound?" New tone now, Carolyn points to the counter, asking me, "What's that?"

"Cordless hair trimmer to shave op sites before surgery."

"Nice!" She flips it on, off, on again, laughing.

I turn to distant footsteps and, thank God, it's Spence in the back of the service hall. "Slim, the crew's almost here."

When I turn back, she's got him sporting quite a nice Mohawk. And it's all on her iPhone.

"Crap, we're just getting started." She stands, hands me the grenade, then turns to the attacker. "Well, here's a little of what it would feel like."

I can't look away when she taps the barrel of the gun against the side of his hairless temple. I wait for flying pieces of skull in a pink haze of cerebrospinal fluid. But she slides it down low on his cheek, and another forty-cal blast finally wipes that sick smile off his face.

# EIGHTY-ONE

CAROLYN TURNS. AND HERE, AS she and I share giggles in this ungodliest of situations, in the aftermath of mayhem, it strikes me, rather ominously, just who I seem to have become. And as Spence and the cavalry swoop in, I make a mental note to think about that, sometime, later on, after the dust has settled, literally.

"Exam rooms are clear!" Carolyn shouts, pointing. "This clown needs a new hand and a dentist."

He's head down, burbling his own blood with each breath. At least he's breathing.

I pass the grenade to a SWAT officer before Spence walks us to the exit.

"What happened, Talbot?" Spence asks.

"What happened, or how am I going to write my report?"

He looks at me. I'm primed with a shrug and a story. "I was fogged up the whole time, standing outside the room." Technically true.

Spencer Gillette's eyes ping-pong between Carolyn's and mine before they validate, a subtle smile he puts on just for us. "Nice work, you two."

"Thanks, Spence," says Carolyn, looking at me. "Let's get some air, Doc."

"Talbot!" Spence shouts. We turn. "Talbot, the good doctor there has a thing for this. Find out if he would ever care to ditch his day job and join JTTF."

We smile at him, and just like that she and I are off to the front lawn, standing by the bench we hid under during the bomb blast. A spiderweb I hadn't noticed then is now a diamond-sparkled billboard for foolhardy insects. We stare at the south wing, a jagged pile that clatters and settles still. Small plumes of smoke rise from a few areas scattered over the remains. I picture electrical shorts seething and frizzling deep inside.

"Carolyn, I'm sorry I went back in there and—"

"I would have done exactly the same thing." She puts an arm around my waist.

"Something pulled me, made me do it."

"I get it, Vince. Don't try to understand shit like that. We don't have to. I get it."

We're still for what feels like an hour.

"What happened today?" I ask.

"War."

"Are we alive?"

A pause, no turn of her head. "A-ffirmative."

"I died in there. Hallucinating or something, when I was trapped. I was outside looking in. At everything."

I see Carolyn's nod in the corner of my eye. "It happens, Doc."

"How did you do it? I mean, living this all the time over there. How did you survive?"

"Oh," she bleats, "so you think I survived, huh?"

"Yes, I do."

"It gets easier. You 'embrace the suck,' as we say."

When I thought I couldn't ever again, I laugh.

"You like that one?" she says, grinning like that day in my office. The day I was hooked forever.

"I have to remember that. I'll use it on med students and whining attending physicians."

Another pause, then a turn to me. "How did *you* survive today, Vince? I feel awful I didn't follow you in. I should have been there with you."

"Carolyn, you *were* there with me."

# EIGHTY-TWO

**I PUT AN ARM AROUND** Carolyn's shoulder and proceed to weave the two of us through the chaotic labyrinth of military and SWAT people, debris, and discarded equipment at the hospital's front entrance.

"How's the rest of America doing?" I ask.

She flips through texts. "It's still sketchy, but in Cali, LAPD stopped five vans of attackers. Bel Air, Beverly Hills, Marina del Rey, Venice, Brentwood. Two carloads of terrorists had already kicked into restaurants and lit 'em up—multiple confirmed civilian casualties and wounded. No counts yet. All attackers fought to the end; a couple of 'em lit themselves up rather than be taken."

"Any clues on their battle plan?" I ask.

"No IEDs except here, some malfunctioning AK-47s. Like they weren't ready." She shrugs, keeps reading. "Orange County sheriff and CHP chased three suspicious vans, but the bad guys abandoned them after fanning out into Santa Ana."

"Maybe just street gang crews?"

She stares her phone down with a face of fury. "They had AKs, suicide vests, Disneyland maps in each van. Sound like a street gang?"

"Jesus." I pick up the pace. "Let's get back to Watson Center."

After the bomb did a facelift on the ER entrance, the front lobby became our triage unit, minus the dumbass piano. The first person I see, moving patient to patient, is Jane Clark. Serious, confident as hell.

"Doctor Clark!" I shout. "You holding up?"

She walks over, a clipboard in fan mode, and shrugs. "Since they called us in, I haven't had time to think about it. The attackers out front were easy. They all bled out before the bomb dogs cleared them." A satisfied smile grows on her. "We're doing okay, though."

"Jane, this is my friend Carolyn."

Jane's mouth drops, head tilting back, but she doesn't speak.

"Carolyn Talbot, Jane. Nice to meet you"—Carolyn sounding all official again as she extends a hand—"and thanks for all you do."

Jane ditches the gloves, then a smile straight from her heart tells me she gets the "friend" part. She points to the CIA badge. "Carolyn, I don't want to know what you do, but this could have been so much worse, so you're the one who deserves a big thank you right now."

I motion to the clipboard. "Do you have any info on a Henry Datillo? Friend of mine."

"Uh, one of the golfers, right?" she asks, going down her list.

Carolyn's hand tightens on my arm.

"He's out of surgery. Abdominal GSW, through and through, right lower quadrant. He'll be okay. It was way lateral, and I triaged him upstairs with stable vitals."

"Oh, man, if your scrubs weren't so damn bloody, we'd give you hugs."

"What else happened at the club?" I ask.

"The sheriff's department was totally on top of that. Both wounded officers got triaged as threes. One deputy took a round in the thigh, missed the femoral artery. Another had chest pain after getting hit in his vest but no ECG changes. Three other golfers had minor injuries from running for cover in the woods, but none of them got hit. We're observing them for a while. The deputies got to them before they made it to the clubhouse dining room and the pool."

"Attackers?" asks Carolyn.

Jane slaloms a finger down the clipboard. "Eight DOAs . . . uh, survivors, one shot twice in the abdomen, then surgery, now in SICU, four with limb wounds we just wrapped and sent to the FBI lock-up."

Lock-up. Yeah, right. Carolyn smiles at me.

"Thanks, Jane," I say. "We'll be in the Watson Center, but text me if you guys need help out here." Jane gives Carolyn and me a good gaze. She gets it.

At the stairwell, I stop. "Slim, come with me." Up one floor, we enter the recovery room, and there's Henry. Right where Jackie was.

His nurse—Camilla again—says, "Henry, try to wake up a little. You have visitors."

I lay a hand on his shoulder. "Henry."

He lifts his head a few inches, and his eyes stop on Carolyn. "Vinny. Vinny, I'm dead, right?"

"No, dumbass, you're out of surgery. You're going to make it," I say.

His head thuds back to the pillow, then he slurs, "Then why is there an angel here? Maybe an FBI angel, Vinny?"

Camilla laughs. "He's still waking up, Doctor Vince."

"Yeah, that, and he's a born flirt," I say, seeing Henry's faint smile.

I lead Carolyn on a weave through a bustle of patient carts and cops on our way to the conference center.

"Wait," I stop, turning to her. "Should I feel worse about this?"

Head tilted, she studies me. "Have you ever lost a patient?"

"Of course. I mean, no fault of my own. You do your best and—"

"You move on, right?"

I nod.

"Nurses, doctors, first responders, CIA officers—long list. The great ones excel because we switch off emotionally when we need to. We go from intelligent, sensitive souls to on-demand, detached psychopaths. It's perfect for people like you and me."

Wait, was that a compliment? A cleansing breath, then I nod again.

////////////

I expect the Watson Center to be a fucking blame-storming circus, but I forgot: these are professionals, not physicians. It buzzes with SWAT and military. Rachael sits as a nurse replaces her bandage. There's a national map up on the big screen. Spence paces, headset on.

"What a day, huh?" he asks.

"What a week," Carolyn responds. "What's the news from LAX?"

He moves his pointer over the map. "We found launch tubes in pickup trucks on side streets, but no one around saw anything, so they say. We're working a perimeter."

Grim news comes from one of the Point Mugu Naval Aviators, who steps up. "Ma'am, the first plane that took a Stinger landed hard on Two-Five Left, collapsed gear, fire, but they kept it on the runway before it broke up. Aircraft and fire rescue was ready. They blew the chutes, and everyone who could move got out, even a few with serious injuries. So far, fifty-seven casualties. The plane in trail got hit, taking out the number two engine. They tried to go around but must have had debris in number one, lost thrust, and ditched in the Pacific just off the end of the runway."

We hold our breath.

"They're still running the passenger manifest, but it looks like everyone got out—a miracle, but not on the Hudson this time."

Spence turns to Rachael and says, "Tell 'em what you got."

"Based on performance, those Stingers weren't upgraded."

"Agree," says Carolyn, exaggerating a nod. "What about the flash drives?"

Rachael is sullen, and not from the nurse jigging around with her wound. "A G-550 filed an IFR flight plan from Santa Barbara to LAX. The time frame fits for whoever left the Carters' with the flash drives to make it on board."

"Okay, but SBA is Gulfstream City. What's the big?"

"They amended the destination en route to Vegas. But McCarren approach control said they never checked in after the LA center handoff. Went NORDO, killed the transponder. No reports of a crash anywhere after they went below radar."

"Goddamn son of a bitch," Carolyn says, dropping a few f-bombs under her breath as she pounds a table.

"Other airports?" I ask.

Spence says, "Once we saw the tactics at LAX, FAA issued a ground stop and we alerted law enforcement to check for similars."

An agent reads from her iPad. "They found a pickup with four empty missile tubes—no launcher—in a rail yard in Bensenville right next to O'Hare. No hostiles. Same thing at Pittsburgh International on Moon Clinton Road. Palm Beach International, twenty-four-foot cruiser anchored on Pine Lake, no launcher but an empty launch tube carrier, no one aboard. Still searching."

I ask her, "Was it bad weather that stopped them?"

"Sir, it was clear and a million everywhere. Just like 9/11."

Carolyn studies the map, then Spence, then me. "So, somehow their timing fails and they abort. Why didn't all teams engage at zero hour?"

"No air traffic?" I venture.

"No, it was rush hour everywhere," says Spence.

Carolyn's eyes stay with me. "I think we rushed their op before default backup assets were in place. And Reza was in command. And their timekeeper."

# EIGHTY-THREE

**I HELP JANE TRIAGE THE** last patients, make sure the OR doesn't need me to scrub in to assist, then head back to Watson to check on Carolyn. She knows I want to stay—or at the very least, that I'm willing to stay, to carry on—but convinces me the ops people have things under control and we need a break. I'm in.

It was close to the action, but Carolyn's black Rover only shows a powdering of the day's dust. No busted glass or dings. No human remains on it, either.

"I haven't seen soot like this since J-bad," Carolyn says. This observation relaxes her—peace I've not seen in a while. "The only things missing are some HESCO barriers, and we may need those here soon." She's contemplative, the CIA Carolyn, fortified by the unpredictable, the near-death shockers. I wonder how long until this stokes her curdled revenge.

"HESCO?"

"A wire mesh basket. Cloth lined. You fill it with sand, rocks, maybe what's left of your blown-up building. Goes up fast, stops bullets and bad guys."

I swipe the side window, play dumb. "Bomb dust, right?"

She looks at my finger, nods, saying, "You never know what's in that dust. It takes at least three shampoo-rinse-repeats to get the crap out of your hair."

"Really?"

"Plus, it gets into everything. Screws up the electronics, the A/C. This car's toast."

"I'm sorry."

"Vince." She holds my eyes, enjoying a moment's tension. A smile grows from her lips to her eyes. "Vince, never fall in love with anything that can't love you back."

"Well said, Slim."

Over the top of the steering wheel she crosses the fingers of her left hand as she turns the key in the ignition with her right. Thankfully the Rover fires up and we're on our way.

Carolyn adjusts the mirror, saying, "I still can't get why the other Stinger teams didn't engage and try to lock up other aircraft. They were in place, they had weapons, they probably had pinpointed a 'zero hour,' but for some reason they broke off. Does that make sense to you?"

I fixate on the blurry mess of my hospital we're viewing through the windshield. "I'm not downplaying the terror at LAX, but those were duds, for lack of a better word. Maybe that was their test of Stingers without the upgrade?" I ask.

"You mean tactical tests? Then those teams would give a 'go, no-go' to the others based on the outcome at LAX?"

"Something like that."

"Yeah, but why tip their hand? Maybe whoever left the Carters' house with the flash drives called it off? Brent may have told them how important the upgrades were. Maybe the LA crew didn't get the message." She shrugs, then smacks my leg. "I don't know, Doc. That's our next puzzle."

She takes Coast Village Road, slowing to a crawl in front of the yellow police tape ringing the café where Rachael and I almost bought it, where we would have become bomb dust that might have fallen that afternoon. My eyes go damp.

She takes my hand while drawing a sigh and putting the scene behind us.

I ask, "Did their assault teams fight the good fight when SWAT found them?"

"They fought to the death but could have been better trained. We've found Blackwater-type training camps for jihadists getting cash from sympathizers. But the trainees run around with air-soft BB guns. It's not real prep."

I'm recalling playing cops and robbers as a kid, then she goes on.

"These guys were zealots, thugs, thinking this was just another attack on defenseless victims. And, just like you predicted, they went after the movers and shakers, captains and kings in places where they were most vulnerable. They were ready to die, but we caught them early. They would have been more savage had they already engaged some soft targets, the schools, clubs, restaurants. The taste of blood changes everything."

"So no elite fighters?"

"Hell, no." She shakes her head, eyes fixed on the road.

Still, I ponder the limitations. "If they had waited for well-trained zealots, we would have had a real fight on our hands, wouldn't we?" The realization is sobering.

"Oh, we would've prevailed, but with way more casualties." Her knuckles blanch on the wheel. "That's one thing we learned today. These guys had dogma, but probably less than twelve months of training. Next time it won't be rump, barely trained bands. And that brings more blood to both sides."

# EIGHTY-FOUR

**WE MAKE IT FROM OUR** showers to the patio just as the clouds mimic the creamy, red-tipped yellow Rio Samba roses that surround us. A salt breeze tugs a hint of eucalyptus along as it climbs ravines that rise into the foothills. Carolyn, in seersucker shorts and royal blue tank top, sits, combing fingers through her damp hair. The dipping sun slants onto her arms, scintillating tiny golden hairs.

Life around the fire pit is not the same as before the attacks, when we were safe, smug. The wine still works magic, though I don't need it to remind me to thank God for my connection with the woman sitting here. A woman who makes it all worth fighting for.

When we sat in this house trying to identify Reza's unabashed shuffling in pursuit of vengeance against America, we sat in denial. His scheme was laid at our feet as one more potential failure to grasp the passion of those who hate our freedom. But also, it was a gift to America. One that we didn't ignore. We're awake now.

"Slim," I break the silence. "Thank you."

"What?" she asks, behind an uncertain smile. "You got us ahead of this."

"You believed me. I mean, how'd you know that I wasn't just another whacko, paranoid about terrorists?"

"I just did." A shrug. "Experience maybe? Intuition . . . Hard to put a finger on it."

"So now what?"

She sips, ponders. "First, we have to find the Stingers, not to mention a G-550 with a bag of flash drives. That should lead us to some more bad guys."

"Then what?"

"Then we figure out who the leaders are—Salaam isn't alone."

I shake my head, asking, "If he got on that plane with the flash drives, why didn't he deliver them to the teams at LAX?"

"Great question." She smiles, and coy would be an understatement. "We're dealing with heartless crusaders who are dealing with ruthless arms dealers who are dealing with greedy traitors. And the homegrown elements they could recruit. Anything goes."

"You think they'll strike again soon?"

She stares over my head, thinks. "No way. Something spooked them into aborting a nationwide CCA. And we've got to figure out what it was before they fix it."

"Who's taking over for Reza now?"

"If I knew, he or she would be in rendition."

Restless, I move to her terraced gardens that drop away into the twilight. Carolyn follows, facing me as I lean on a railing.

"What?" she whispers. "Don't leave, Vince. Let's go inside—"

I gently lay a finger to her mouth. Those goddamn eyes. She strolls into my soul with perception, with compassion I saw the instant we met. "Did you ever lie on your back on a night like this with a zillion stars? Just lie there, staring up at them, wondering?"

"Yes." She comes closer. "We're insignificant, this is—"

"Everything."

We lock hands, gazing at a southern sky that gathers deeper indigo by the second. The sun dips, stars greet us, and I feel their energy playing out through our fingertips. I pull her closer, burying my face into her neck, gathering a handful of her moist hair, inhaling. I don't want to leave this spot on the earth. Ever. And I'll defend this woman to the death.

"I love you, Vince," she breathes.

"I love you, Carolyn. But what kind of world—"

This time, it's her silencing finger.

"Let's continue the philosophy while I cook dinner for us."

In the kitchen. Me on the sit-and-observe side, her on the business side. There's a bottle of rosé from the cooler; Diana Krall pumps from Sonos. I reach into the bag of books she stole from my bedroom and hold up Yeats.

"So you like poetry?" she asks, an eyebrow up.

"Yeah, and so do you, I'd bet."

"College English lit courses killed it for me. Yeats, T. S. Eliot, Larkin, Shakespeare. Never enough time to let them soak in, you know?"

I nod. "Absolutely. But you get a second chance, a third, fourth—as many as you want—with poets." I hand it over. "It's funny that you picked out this book among all the others. Right after we met, I actually went out and got this for you. I wrote something inside."

She drops her tools. "Vince. My God, what a sweetheart! Thank you." She crosses over the island for a hug, reading aloud: "Dear Carolyn, This collection will become your friend, if it isn't already. Read 'When You Are Old.' You'll want someone in your life reading that to you straight from his heart. Love, Vince." She's a speechless CIA chick. Not what I expected.

"Do you know the poem?" I ask. She shakes her head. "All I remember is the middle stanza, but it's the best thing ever."

Carolyn squints. I close the book and recite as best I can: "How many loved your moments of glad grace, and loved your beauty with love false and true. But one man loved the pilgrim soul in you, and loved the sorrows of your changing face."

I offer a sleeve as we both erupt in laughter with damp eyes.

"Okay, Slim. How can I help?" I scan the kitchen, the center island strewn with cooking tools, bowls and pans, and recipe ingredients.

"Just sit, sip wine, and be with me. And don't make me choke up anymore," she commands.

I watch her move like, well, like a chef. She does mise en place, then gets a carbon-steel skillet smoking hot while working peppery escarole and dandelion greens onto oval plates. Olive oil, then plump white sea scallops into the copper skillet. In a few minutes, candles are lit and we're face-to-face, savoring. I raise a frosty pink glass; she beats me to the toast.

"*Saluti a te*," she says, grinning and wide-eyed, as if caught stealing. Which she just did.

"Hey, my line, but it's better coming from you, Slim."

"Did I pronounce it correctly?" She does her right-of-center pucker.

"Langley's proud. But let's make it *saluti a noi*—cheers to us." We clink and sip.

She practices. "*Saluti a noi*. I like that better."

"*Perfetto, bellissima*. Now, where were we?"

"Life," she says, then cocks her head.

"Life. Fate. As in, now that we found each other, what kind of world are we in after this week? It's clear to me even the inner circle has no idea what could happen next."

"What do you mean?"

"All the spies and satellites and intel," I say, "put you in a dream that you're in control. But it's illusion. It's way more complex."

"You're right." A gentle evening breeze rattles the wooden blinds. She lays a hand on mine. "Do you think you can recover?"

"I'm a doctor." I pause, because I mean this. "I'll do what I have to do for patients—and for you. More than I'd do for myself. It's Hippocratic bull, but medicine's a calling. And now you've balanced it."

She tightens her grip. I look at her hand, then eyes.

"How about you, Slim? Can you recover?"

Her lips roll over her teeth for a moment.

"Hell, yes. I'm a warrior, and I'll do what I have to do to win any battle for you and our country. Nation, agency, mission before self. That's Langley's bull. Now I have even more reason to be in the fight."

We're silent, deep into each other's thoughts.

"You're a male version of me, Vince."

She's right, and my face shows it. "Well, we both like sex."

"Seriously. You love being a hero at work, just like I do—and we're both great at it. I guarantee, Vince, there's more of this to come." Her look is scary serious. "We're a good team. I can be so much better with you."

*Right again. So can I.*

She adds, "Life's not life until you're sharing it." She gives my hand our three-squeeze code, which I return.

A final ribbon of sunset yields to night, dissolving the horizon, fusing earth and sky into one. We stare into the void over the vicious innocence of the Pacific, like we're facing eternity. We look at each other and, as if on cue, shiver. Today was savagely violent, but Carolyn and I helped contain it. This could have taken many more lives and changed countless others.

*We now have cred.* That means she and I stay in the fight, starting by telling bureaucrats to stuff it if they try covering up things like missing antiaircraft missiles.

We also pick up our hearts at lost and found and get ready for whatever this grim new world throws our way. Trust me. I'm a doctor.

# ACKNOWLEDGMENTS

**THERE ARE MANY PEOPLE WITH** immense patience who have helped make this book a reality. First, though, I should state that any references to so-called classified information and methods of intelligence and tradecraft beyond what is publicly accessible are products of my imagination. I guess that means that I own all errors, but if pressed, I'll plead innocent, citing literary license and dramatic liberty.

I'll start by thanking Erin Young, who reviewed early drafts and encouraged me to keep writing, followed by Edmund Pickett, who encouraged me to sit down, be quiet, and keep rewriting. Their expert advice and trusted guidance helped get the work to a respectable form. I cannot overstate my gratitude for my editorial team at Greenleaf: Erin Brown, Art Lizza, Simha Stubblefield, and Pam Nordberg, who have been marvelous at showing me the way toward clarity, precision, and enhancing whatever is good about the book. I would also like to thank Brian Welch and his team for keeping the project moving and Neil Gonzales for bringing its design to life.

To my wife and family, who have endured the highs and lows and offered to be early-stage readers, thank you.

# ABOUT THE AUTHOR

**JOSEPH PURPURA**, MD, is an obstetrician-gynecologist, patient safety expert, and award-winning faculty member at Northwestern University's Feinberg School of Medicine. He lives in Santa Barbara, CA. This is his first novel.